The Reawakening of Edgar Porlock

By the same author

The Exile of Nicholas Misterton

The Reawakening of Edgar Porlock

Vance Wood

With best wishes.

Vance Wood

03 December 2015

CONJUROR

First published in the UK 2015 by Vance Wood
www.vancewoodnovelist.co.uk

ISBN 978-0-992-96132-9

Copyright © Vance Wood 2015

The right of Vance Wood to be identified as the
author of this work has been asserted by him in accordance
with the Copyright, Designs and Patents Act 1988.

All rights reserved. No part of this publication may be reproduced,
stored in or introduced into a retrieval system, or transmitted, in any form,
or by any means (electronic, mechanical, photocopying, recording or otherwise)
without the prior written permission of the publisher. Any person who
does any unauthorized act in relation to this publication may be
liable to criminal prosecution and civil claims for damages.

This novel is entirely a work of fiction. The names, characters,
with the exception of a few historical figures, and incidents portrayed in it
are the work of the author's imagination.

1 3 5 7 9 8 6 4 2

Typeset by Ellipsis Digital Limited, Glasgow
Jacket design by Ian Cardwell
Printed and bound in Great Britain by Clays Ltd, St Ives plc

This book is sold subject to the condition that it shall not, by way
of trade or otherwise, be lent, re-sold, hired out, or otherwise circulated
without the publisher's prior consent in any form of binding or cover other than
that in which it is published and without a similar condition including
this condition being imposed on the subsequent purchaser.

For all those I love.

I would like to thank Debi and Ian at Ellipsis and Rebecca at Clays for their support in the production of this book, and I am eternally grateful to those who inspired me, in different ways, to write the story.

Chapter One

She wiped her brow on her sleeve, and tucked her stray blond hair, hanging like a piece of straw, behind her ear. With a staff outstretched in her right hand, and her left completing a crucifix, she shooed the cows across the lane, from one field to another, where the grass was longer, greener. She clicked her tongue, made other strange noises to encourage them to make haste. This was the moment she hated, when one or more might escape. Then she would incur the wrath of Master Symondsbury, now that Billy Eype had pushed his luck too far and had been dismissed.

"Bloody cows!" she cursed. "Big red buggers, the lot of 'em. Too many for a poor maid to handle."

She had named each one, milked them considerably, knowing which ones were stubborn and reluctant to start, which squirted as soon as her fingers rippled down the teat. They swayed and barged her in the barn, stamped their feet in a huff if her hands were too cold. But now she was on her own. The others – Elsie, 'Tilda, and Ada – had gone the same way as Billy Eype, for not pulling their weight, and though she was glad they had, because they kept things from her, laughed at her for not understanding their rude jokes about men, she had grown so lonely that she had taken to talking to the cows. "Lonely as a wind-bent tree atop a high hill," she had once described herself.

When they were all in the new field, she roped the gate shut, and breathed a sigh of relief.

"Big, red cows!" she called. "Don't get the better of me, you don't. No cow get the better of Winifred Drimpton!"

She triumphantly waved her staff at them, and danced a little jig to mark their compliance. Her cheeks were poppies, and she sang:

"A maid is not for milking
when the sun has slipped away;
there be youths out there a-trying
to lead a maid astray."

She sighed, then screamed when she heard rustling in the grass. Snake! was her first thought; adders' nest, most likely.

"'Twas well sung, that verse, and I must apologise for stopping you singing the second, though you would have found me out, soon enough, in this hedge-bottom, what with me about to sneeze, my nose a-tickling so."

The man, who had been woken by the cows and Winifred's singing, stood up and brushed himself down. What was left of the moonball he had eaten was in his bag.

"Oh, sir, you nearly stopped my heart when you spoke, and me a-dancing and making a fool of myself with a bunch of rubies. I hope you didn't hear me a-cursing, as 'taint befitting a woman, even a common milkmaid, to use bad words in public, sir."

The man smiled, then sneezed. Out came his handkerchief, which he applied after he had turned his head.

"Forgive me. The pollen, I think," he explained. "Summer's lingering."

"'Taint finished growing, the grass, which be why I bringed these cows here from the upper meadow."

"And they are all *your* responsibility?"

She nodded, sensing his sympathy. There was something in his appearance that reassured her she was in no danger. Though there was stubble on his face, his clothes looked of good quality. Around his neck he wore a red cravat, which drew her eyes to his face. And she could hear some of her own language in his, as his notes traced mounds and vales.

"Now Elsie, 'Tilda, and Ada be sacked, cows be down to me, take it or leave it, and though, some days, my poor body begs me to leave it, I can't, me being on my own."

The man shook his head.

"Your master is too harsh."

"'Taint all his fault. Master Eype and the others were sent a-packing, leaving just me. They did bad things."

In appreciation of his support, she bobbed, almost curtseyed, and the man laughed.

"You don't need to do that."

"It's just you been kind. 'Tis instinct in me."

"Who is your master?"

"Master Symondsbury, up at the manor."

"And I've been sleeping in his field?"

Winifred nodded, suppressed a giggle.

"Yes, sir, and you been nearly trampled to death by his cows!"

He laughed, ran his hand through his brown hair flecked grey at the temples. She tried to guess his age. Older than her, definitely. An itinerant man, but not poor; someone passing by, with good manners and eyes of lapis lazuli.

"Forgive me, Winifred, but I have not yet introduced myself."

"How you know I be Winifred? And why do you always ask for forgiveness when you aint done anything wrong?"

"I heard you calling after the cows, and *forgive me* is just an expression, signifying nothing at all bar a way into explaining things."

Winifred screwed up her freckled nose, rested her plump chin on the end of her staff, as if inspecting him.

"Men don't talk such wisdom like that, these parts. You a Dorset man?"

He looked over his shoulder. His horse, munching grass, was still tethered to a tree. She could see the stranger shaping his reply, and wondered why he was weighing up his answer, as if the truth might incriminate or endanger him.

"Somerset."

"Not Dorset but almost its twin."

She saw the grey, heard it snort impatiently, suspected the man would soon be on his way, and was intrigued by him. "Don't go yet," she wanted to say. "Stay for a few more words, till the light deserts us, when I must return to the farm, where ghosts rattle tools and murmur in the night, and I must hide under that single blanket, which once kept a horse warm. I be lonely."

"Almost. Not an identical twin but close."

He looked at his horse again, prepared himself to say goodbye, but did not want her to think him rude.

"Where you going?"

He smiled, blinked slowly, remembered what he had to do, why he had slipped, as full of regrets as a bulging sack of windfall apples, out of Somerset, and galloped into the beguiling lanes of Dorset.

"To a place. Am I near Bridport?"

Winifred shrugged.

"Heard of it but never been. Beaminster girl, all my life, till I comes a-asking at the manor, when my parents went, that cold winter, when everything woke up white, and 'twas like we were deaf, 'twas so silent. Father went as quick as a swift, and mother started hacking so bad she stained her white pillow with red berries of blood."

He did not want to leave her with all those cows. She was as lonely as him, but could not escape, bound by milking times and what he guessed to be an unfeeling master. The light was skinny. Shadows would soon slip over the hills and into the fields, and stretch.

"Forgive me, but I must go."

"There you go again!" she laughed.

He broke away, strode to his horse. She watched his unhurried walk, and he felt her eyes on him. Do not look at me like that, he begged. Do not make this journey harder than it is already.

He mounted his horse, and returned to the gate through which she had guided her cows. In the time it took, his kindness filled her with hope that she could have civil contact with people again, that there might be a new life awaiting her, maybe at Bridport. Men, chances, like him did not find their way very often into those parts, where women on their own withered, flowering only once, in their youth.

She moved to lift the rope from the gatepost, and impulsively seized her moment.

"Sir, I want to ask you something, a favour, which I hope you will not find bad in a maid who would not hurt a tick on a sheep."

He smiled down on her, noticed, now he was relaxed, her body's fullness.

"Then ask."

"Will you take me with you, sir? Let me ride on your horse, so I don't have to go back to the barn and sleep with the chickens a-clucking and a-crowing? Oh, please say you will, as leaving me here will add up to sending me to my maker, this winter, which, if it be a mirror to the one which snatched my mother and father, will make me a stone statue in a graveyard."

She took a step sideways, to block his way. He looked beyond her, his eyes not daring to see her mask of passion. How easy it would be, he knew, to reach down and haul her up behind him, let her wrap tightly her plump arms around him! His eyes closed as he contemplated the warmth of her body next to his, her cheek against his back as she clung on.

"No," he said, shaking his head. "It cannot be like that. Your life will change for the better. We do not know each other. I am your father's age, and these grey hairs and crows' feet are signs of that. Winifred, let me pass, please. 'Tis the right thing to do."

She took a step backwards, lifted the rope, and opened the gate.

"You're a kind and good and true man, sir, and I be ashamed I ranted and raved to go with you. But you cannot know what 'tis like to be a solitary milkmaid. I open this gate, and you be free, but 'tis the door of a gaol to me, every day of my life, which be more like a death."

"Come now, Winifred," he said authoritatively, "enough of this gloom, for your life will soon rise. You are young, and should sing youth's song, not the dirges of middle and old age. There will be time enough for that, one day. You have an honest mien, one a young man will see and admire so much that he will ask to look at your heart, too, and will find 'tis as open as your face. Now, see what you have done: made me sound all flattery when all I wanted to do was raise your spirits."

"Go now, sir, for I know 'tis true what I say, though your words will keep me warm for many a night to come in the cold, ghastly barn all draped with spiders' webs."

He passed through the gate.

"Don't be late back, Winifred. The cows will still be there, in the morning."

"Sir," she called after him.

He turned his head, and said, "Will you not let me go?"

"You never said what name they call you."

He hesitated before saying, "Edgar."

"Edgar? 'Tis a name I've heard not, not even in the Bible, which be full of strange callings."

"'Twas the name given to me, and which will be nailed in my coffin with me."

"And you have a bigger name?"

"Porlock. I be Edgar Isambard Porlock."

"Three names? Two be heavy enough!"

Hearing her laugh, at last, he heeled his horse into a canter, and smiled when he heard her sing the second verse of her song:

"And a man will kiss a maid
when the moon's too shy to shine,
then leave her all a-wondering
if he'll ever say, 'Be mine.'"

He made his way towards the coast, using the incandescent pillow of hills on which the sun lay down to pick his way south. If I can do anything to help Winifred, one day, I will, he promised, but his thoughts were interrupted by the thunder of a galloping horse approaching, and the cry of a woman spurring it on to a faster pace. The lane was narrow, not wide enough for two horses to pass each other without danger.

"Whoa!" shouted Edgar, turning his grey's nose into the brambly hedgerow.

The approaching horse soon appeared, and its rider pulled on the reins, so that the horse had to slow down. It reared in fright, and only the skill and strength of the rider prevented an accident. The bay twisted left and right, danced in shock, and was gradually soothed by sweet words.

When it was fully under control, Edgar said, "You came upon me so quickly. I called as soon as I heard you. These lanes are narrow."

"It is not my habit to ride so recklessly. I wanted to arrive at the stables before someone else."

The young woman was breathing quickly from her exertions. Her red hair rippled loosely onto her shoulders, bouncing when she moved her head. Edgar put her in her early twenties, knew her to be an able horsewoman, saw the way she had stayed in her saddle: knees gripping the flanks as tightly as a farrier a horse's leg as he pares its hoof; leaning towards the neck so closely she could kiss it; and gripping the reins so tightly it whitened the knuckles of her freckled hands. Her eyes were bright emeralds, her lids fluttering in embarrassment at the stranger she had endangered.

"You are racing someone?"

He smiled, and she reciprocated.

"Yes, though I fear he will catch me any moment, and the day will be lost."

Edgar's smile faded.

"Then let me not detain you. No harm has been done."

Do not look at me with those eyes, he thought. Let them gaze upon a younger man.

"Do you know where you are?" she asked, coming closer.

"Dorset."

She laughed easily, locking her eyes on his. She sees my admiration for her beauty. In all of Dorset, I find myself where I must not tarry, lest I make a fool of myself.

"You are on Symondsbury land."

"I was nearly killed by a marauding herd of Symondsbury cattle, not an hour ago! Red brutes, they were. Ripped me untimely from my sweet slumbers in the ditch."

Again, she laughed, her voice like wind chimes.

"You were in a ditch? Yet you do not have the air of a tramper. Your clothes are well made. Your face is not ravaged by want of food or shelter."

"May a man not lay his head in an English field and sleep when he needs?"

"You answer me with a question of your own. Word games, sir. Answer me plainly my next. What do you on Symondsbury land?"

Edgar could see she was intrigued by his reluctance to reveal his purpose. You are so close our horses nearly touch, and yet you must come further, know more, ensnare me, which is the way with women.

"I will say only if you tell me with whom and whither you race."

"I will never tell that to man with no name!" she cried.

"Nor I to a woman."

"Then we are at a pretty standstill."

"Indeed, we are."

The impasse lasted only briefly, as into the lane surged a third horse, ridden wildly by a young man, who interposed himself between Edgar and the woman. When he was near enough, the man knocked Edgar off, dismounted, and bawled:

"Now, you blackguard! Come, and I shall break every bone in your worthless body. To halt a woman in a country lane, no doubt to rob her, is a cowardly deed, and you will be punished for it by me, and then by the magistrate. I shall see to it that you swing by your scrawny neck. There will be no mercy."

Edgar looked up at his assailant, who was younger but not bigger than him.

"Geoffrey, no! You are gravely mistaken," pleaded the woman. "This man is no common highwayman but one whose quick thinking averted a collision between my horse and his, on this very spot."

She crouched to Edgar, who was dazed. Down his chin trickled blood from his bottom lip. She took his hand to help him up. There was no time to resist her offer of assistance, and her hair dangled in his face, tickling his cheek.

The man she called Geoffrey fidgeted nervously, reddened at his hasty, erroneous assumption that Edgar had waylaid her.

"I had expected a warm welcome from Dorset, but not as warm as this!" joked Edgar, who rose to his feet with his hand still gripped by the woman's.

"You are a hothead and a fool, Geoffrey, and nothing short of an apology to this stranger will suffice."

Edgar saw that her castigation was far more painful to Geoffrey than any blow he himself could deliver, though he did not risk the triumphant smile he was tempted to wear.

Geoffrey stared icily at her continued contact with the stranger, and returned to his saddle.

"I shall see you back at the stables, and will consider myself the victor of today's race."

He dug his heels angrily into his horse's gleaming flanks, whooped, and disappeared from view.

"Are you recovered?" the woman asked. "Your lip is cut."

"I shall live."

She released his hand.

"I must apologise. He - "

"Meant well. Remember: I, too, was once a young man."

"And not too long ago?"

She was back to her teasing; they had returned to where they had left off before Geoffrey's arrival.

"You were just a babe in your mother's arms when I was your age."

"How do you know that? You cannot know my age."

Edgar smiled; he had hoped to find a bed for the night. Some friendly cottage, an inn in a village or town, but the light was now grey.

"I must make my way," Edgar said nonchalantly. "'Tis late, and a ditch, I can assure you, is not a comfortable bed."

"Whither go you?"

"On a journey."

"How romantic! But whither? I am intrigued."

"I must find a place to sleep. I am not familiar with these paths."

"I know just the place. My father will repay your quick thinking with a room. You are not too proud to accept our hospitality?"

"But we do not know each other."

He was tempted by her offer, but the prospect of another encounter with Geoffrey deterred him from rushing towards acceptance.

"Why, this is even better, more romantic than any book I've read."

"My name is Edgar Porlock."

She shook the hand he offered.

"And I am Cressida Symondsbury. You see, Mr. Porlock, your journey has brought you into the heart of our estate, and I have taken you prisoner!"

"And my would-be assassin?"

"Geoffrey Burton-Bradstock."

"Then no brother of yours."

"No, Mr. Porlock. He is my fiancé, and we are to be married in Whitchurch within the next twelve months."

Edgar mounted his horse, and looked down at her. She knew what he was thinking: that Geoffrey Burton-Bradstock was not worthy of her.

"Would you be so good as to point me in the direction of Bridport?"

"I see you think that I should not marry him. You are kind to spare my feelings, but I would rather you be honest with me."

"'Tis nothing to do with me, but may I ask you a favour?"

"You may ask but 'tis no guarantee that I shall oblige."

He put his hand into his pocket, and took out a few coins.

"There used to be a girl, these parts, a milkmaid: Winifred Drimpton. She work for you?"

"Yes, up at the farm. A quaint, jumpy girl. Survived my father's recent cull up there."

"Please to pass these on? A cousin of mine."

"A favourite, judging by this sum."

"My mother's niece. Is this the right road to Bridport?"

"Stay on this, and you will drop onto it. I shall tell my father you have spurned his hospitality. There is something that fits not: you are a stranger to these parts, yet you have a cousin nearby."

"Tell Yeoman 'tis nothing personal."

And with that, he took his leave.

She called after him, "How do you know my father is called Yeoman?"

11

But he did not reply, only said to his horse, "Come, Wellesley, and down to Bridport. You've had your dinner, and now 'tis time for mine."

The streets of Bridport were almost empty. He turned into the coaching inn, and was met by an ostler, who shuffled towards him wearily, as if Wellesley were one horse too many, that night. In the air: wood smoke, the smell of meat and vegetables. Across the yard scurried a rat, which burrowed into the straw. A faint whiff of stale sweat and cider introduced the ostler, who scratched his flanks, and yawned, as if he had just woken from a deep sleep.

"You a place for Wellesley?" asked Edgar. "He'll need a good feed and watering, the miles he's done today."

The ostler stared into the middle distance, as if trying to remember where he had heard the name Wellesley before.

"'Tis a name to bear, that. Full of importance, which cost a shilling, his supper thrown in."

"And there is a room and a plate of food for me, too?"

The ostler farted ostentatiously, scaring the rat out of the straw, and pointed to a door.

The landlord, a man barely cleaner than the ostler, yelled irritably to his wife, who waddled in from the kitchen, sweating like a basting goose.

"Good evening, madam. Is there a plate of whatever smells so delicious for a weary and hungry traveller?"

The landlady was weeping; she had been peeling onions.

"There *will* be, come the next chime of the town clock. Always cook by the bells, me. Meat always tender when stewed by the bells' peal."

"Then I would like a room for tonight, and a generous helping of your intended repast. I shall wait for the bell to summon me. I'll take a stroll to ease the aches and pains of being in the saddle so long."

In the fireplace, two oak logs were just catching, sending sweet smoke up the chimney, in which two hams were curing. Candles were already lit, and two regular patrons were manufacturing a fug below the yellow ceiling, and commenting on the weather. There had been, of late, a nip in the air, sharp enough to provoke a search, observed the taller of the two bald men, for his bed socks, which did not usually reappear till late November.

A perfectly satisfactory hostelry, decided Edgar. Infinitely preferable to a ditch. And time yet to do what he intended. The ostler lent him a lantern, and Edgar looked up and down the main street. Bucky Doo was empty bar the cakes of excrement deposited by the herd of cows driven up it, that afternoon. In curtainless rooms, oil lamps were like saints' auras in church windows, and were splashing ghastly light onto faces.

"You were a fool, and still are, your hopes will o' the wisps, but 'tis a fresh start, and wrongs must be righted, apologies made, for me to reawaken, so start now," he muttered.

The house was smaller than he remembered it, twenty years earlier. He knocked, and the door opened. There stood Emma, as he had hoped, with her candle held aloft, as if she were toasting the return of someone long awaited.

"Emma?" he asked. "Are you Emma Broadoak?"

In the lantern light, she squinted, then recognised him. He had kept his word, at last.

"Alfred? After all these years? You back?"

Like the house, she appeared smaller, had pinned her hair into a loose bun, and not left it lapping her shoulders, as she used to. The intervening years had changed her, but he could not see clearly how. She was still Emma: shrunken, yet more round, somehow, and, in faint light, plumper in the chin, with dimmer eyes which stared unblinkingly.

"'Tas been too long, Emma, and I have come to say sorry."

"Sorry? Whatever for? Come in."

She stepped aside, and he hesitated. Her parents? Her father had been suspicious, had thought Edgar too ambitious to make a Briddy girl happy. Amos, was he called? Or was it Henry? And her mother: Hettie, easy-going, had liked him, had seen his potential as a good husband for Emma.

He stepped into the front room: a bare table – in the middle a cruet set - and two chairs; a dead fire-grate; a sideboard on which sat an urn; on the wooden mantelpiece, a clock whose ticking had become her companion.

"Your parents?"

She caressed the urn, and shook her head.

"Both together, where I can keep an eye on them."

Her voice was flat, and did not match her intended humour. Her speech had once shone as if polished, but was now dull, neglected.

The walls were cracked, the spaces cramped. There was a smell of damp and tripe and onions, which made Edgar heave. This was not how he remembered things. What had he done, coming back, but destroy what they had? He had meant well. She deserved the apology.

"I left you, and I said we would be married when I returned before the hoar came."

"And so we were, Alfred. And 'twas a great feast, as I remember. Look, here be our family portrait, and this be my ring." She held up her hand. "But where's yours?"

She went to the sideboard, and took out a framed painting.

"Emma, I . . ."

"There we be. That be our sweet Charity, and that be little Arthur. See, Alfred. All together. Remember when we chose their names?"

He looked at the stick figures a child might have drawn.

"Who are these?" he stuttered. "I don't understand."

"Why, that be our family, Alfred! Our lovely family. Don't tell me you forgotten 'em!"

Edgar, now frightened, turned and quickly left.

"What have I done?" he cried. "Oh, what have I done?"

Emma sat down in the weak light, and said, "Gone again so soon, Alfred? And me about to put your supper out on a plate. You still like a bit of mackerel? You be back for it tomorrow?"

Chapter Two

"Why, you aint touched a thing! Tatties too hard? Shouldn't be. Meat and veg all been a-stewing for the best part of three tollings, and the town clock never spoilt a meal yet. Nobody never left nothing on one of my plates, not even a puddle of gravy. Why, I even lick my own plate afore 'tis washed! My gravy be like nectar."

Edgar had been robbed of his appetite and colour. In the corner, he sat, almost shivering, listening to the landlady's haranguing. He was hungry, and his meeting with Emma had not gone to plan. Prepared for changes in her physical appearance – he himself, he knew, had grown stouter, greyer – he had been shocked to see her haunted eyes bulging in the candlelight, and to discover she had deceived herself by imagining that they had been married, after all, and even had children. He felt responsible for the madness that had gripped her. If only I had written, told the truth, that I had changed my mind, then she could have started again, fallen in love with another Bridport man, had a proper life, instead of loyally awaiting my return.

"I'm sorry. I've had a bit of a shock, that's all. Nothing to do with your excellent cooking," he explained.

"Shock? You seen a ghost? 'Taint surprising. Briddy be full of 'em. Boney's French army, they say, come back to haunt the soldiers who killed them in battle. Why, my husband won't go near Bucky Doo, of a night. He hears and sees 'em. Not many got the gift. Sees 'em all a-skirmishing under the clock, their swords a-glinting in the moonlight. 'Won't this town ever be at rest?' he says. 'Don't 'ee put customers off coming here be all your talk of Boney's revenge, as 'twill be the end of us,' I say. 'Don't 'ee believe it,' he argues. 'A ghost or two will pack 'em up to the rafters!'"

"A ghost and yet not a ghost, if you see what I mean."

"No, I don't rightly. A ghost be a ghost, which be dead if I aint mistaken, and a person be a person, who be alive. Leastways, that be how I see it."

Edgar felt defeated by her irresistible logic, and offered to try again the meal eyed jealously by others in the room.

"I'll try to do it justice," he promised.

"Just eat it, be all I asking, and 'twill do wonders to banish your shock, which seems to be a hill shaped by God himself and not a mole, judging by your white face."

"I came to see someone, and they had altered, that's all. Time changes us."

The landlady folded her arms, and leaned slightly backwards, as if about to pass judgement, as she was in the habit of doing in her own establishment. The few other customers were watching the stranger, and eavesdropping.

"Then that person be like the devil, or maybe at death's door, for only something terrible could paint your face as 'tis now."

Wait there all you like, but it's no business of yours; no one must know my purpose here.

"Please, let me try again, and then I shall retire for a good night's rest."

"Every last morsel and drop of gravy!" she commanded. "Don't want my reputation a-spoiling on account of your shock."

Gradually, his appetite returned, and he ate his supper. The others watched him, and he felt their staring; they missed not a mouthful. When he had finished, he wiped the gravy from his lips with his napkin, and rose.

"You from these parts?" asked the man nearest, at the next table.
"No. Devon."
"Sound more Somerset than Devon, though voices get all mixed up like one of the landlady's stews."

Edgar felt flustered. All he wanted was to return to his room, not face all these questions. And yet it was inevitable, he knew, that it would not be easy, this return of his.

"If you'll excuse me."

Edgar dug into his pocket, and pulled out a coin or two, which he put under his plate.

"You fresh, these parts?" repeated the second man.

Edgar did not know how to look at him; the questioner's eyes stared in different directions.

"From tolerable far: Devon way."

"Then you must have a particular reason for being here, though you looks at home, as if you been here before."

The landlady wobbled over to the empty plate, and her red cheeks plumped up at the sight of it.

"That's what I expect to see: not a tattie, neither a turnip left. Now, you come again, and you can try a little chicken leg or two. Plucks 'em myself till they looks like my legs." She lifted the plate, and saw the coins.

"A token of my appreciation," explained Edgar.

"Why, thank 'ee, Mr. . . . "

"Porlock. Edgar Porlock."

"Not many of that name round here," she remarked, "though 'taint a sin to own it. There be worse."

When the landlady had gone, the man nearest said, "Porlock, eh? Now let me think. Years ago, 'twas, I knew a man looked like you, though he answered to a different name. Good family."

His friend then remarked, "Lots of good families in Briddy."

"If you'll excuse me, gentlemen. Goodnight," said Edgar.

"Goodnight – *Alfred*," replied the first.

Without turning, Edgar halted, then resumed his exit.

Up in his room, he was troubled. How the deuce does he know my name? I'm sure I said it was Edgar. Or have I imagined it, my mind all flung about like straw in the wind? Twice he contemplated returning to the men, and asking the one who had used his name how he knew him, but realised that he would have to explain events that had been buried in the crypt of his past.

In bed, he heard the faint murmuring of male conversation spiked by the shrill laughter of women. One woman struck up a song, and the men joined in the chorus. It was a jolly ditty, accompanied by a fiddle, just the sort he would have liked to sing himself, had he not felt so miserable.

There was, of course, the matter of what he should do next about Emma. How could he possibly begin to do the other important things until he had made his peace with her? That task now seemed impossible, in the light of her behaviour, earlier. Perhaps, she would be different, the next day, or maybe he had damaged her irreparably, scarred her with his disappearance, driven her to madness.

It seemed important now that he should find out, by whatever means necessary, what had happened in her life. She had lost both parents; that, he knew already. But surely she had done something with those intervening years, apart from sit in her house and wait for her intended to return and make her a bride!

As she could not say herself if she were really suffering a permanent delusion, others must tell him. That was what he should do: speak to others, make enquiries, but wisely, stopping short of arousing suspicion. That decision made, he fell into a dreamless, uninterrupted sleep, from which no one could drag him.

The next morning, he rose early. The landlady was waiting for him, at the foot of the stairs. Wafting both her hands, and holding her nose up to appreciate the wonderful aromas drifting from the kitchen, she said, "Now aint that just 'eavenly? Fried eggs a-spitting and a-nestling up to some devilled kidneys and slices of bacon. You want some of that for breakfast? My husband can't get up a-doing beout all that. Fridays, I throw in a few tatties if he's been a good boy and done all his cleaning and bottles."

Edgar hesitated, not wishing to bump into anyone from the night before. The food smelt enticing, and he knew he needed nourishment, so that he might think clearly, and sustain his investigation to its conclusion.

"Thank you. Your husband is, indeed, a very lucky man."

"Then you run along to your own table, and the victuals won't be long. When you hears the chimes, then you knows your plate won't be tarrying."

He sat in his seat from the night before. He saw yet the bald men, his inquisitors, one of whom had called him Alfred, though the chairs were now empty. His skin prickled. What cannot the imagination do when the mind or conscience is troubled! he mused. The old boys are not there, yet I see them still, their thin, cracked lips sucking on their pipes pulsing smoke, one man's eye wobbling in all directions, as if wanting to inspect all corners of the room, to pre-empt any move anyone might make against him.

Seconds after the town clock clanged, Edgar's breakfast appeared, and so tasty was it that he left extra coins under the plate, eliciting a cry, from the landlady, which was a mixture of joy at his generosity, and mock-admonition for deeming her so wonderful a cook.

"Really, sir, 'tis more than enough!" she said, dropping quickly the coins into her fat-spattered apron pocket.

"I'm sure it is not. And here is money I hope enough to cover Wellesley's fees, and my room."

Again, she pocketed more than he owed, and concluded the conversation, as she had her husband's breakfast to do, with, "And you ever be round Briddy again, then you and your horse will be as welcome as a good harvest supper, which be as tasty as anything can be."

In the inn yard, the ostler yawned, scratched his infested armpits, accepted the coin Edgar gave him, and returned to the lodge, without a word. Wellesley was all tacked up, and pleased to be free of a stable with more rats than horses.

The day was cool, the sky cerulean, the light clean. Leaves were beginning to curl and crackle. Out in Bucky Doo, a rickety cart was making its bumpy way towards the harbour. A woman, sleeves rolled up, was washing her windows, and a young boy was wandering aimlessly, till he spotted her.

"Clean 'em for a penny, Mrs.?" he begged.

"Clean 'em myself for nothing. You from round here?"

The boy, hands, face, and knees unwashed for days, looked all around him, and shrugged.

"Where is this?"

"Bucky Doo. You know Bucky Doo?"

He shook his head, and carried on walking, till he turned, and shouted, "You got any bread to eat? Any water?"

The woman went inside to fetch an apple, but when she returned, he had gone, with her bucket.

Emma's house was five doors away, and Edgar walked towards the woman, leaving Wellesley tethered to a post near the clock. She sensed someone approaching, and glanced at Edgar.

"Excuse me, please, but I wonder whether you can help me."

His voice was different, confident, not the sort she heard often. She would give directions. Anything else, particularly what men want for a penny or two, she did not, as she already had a bit put by, where her thieving, lazy husband could not get at it.

"Just going in."

Seeing an opportunity about to disappear, Edgar stated his request.

"Do you know a neighbour of yours by the name of Emma Broadoak? I believe she lives alone, a few doors down."

"And what if I do? 'Tis early morning, and I be vexed to be asked questions by a man who don't offer his name or purpose."

Again, she made to enter her house, but stopped when Edgar took out a coin, and pleaded.

"Please, it's important. I knew her, years ago, and simply enquire after her."

The woman looked at the coin. There was little she knew about her, and what she did know was common knowledge. No harm in saying what anyone else would. Why should he give the money to someone else? So she took the coin, which would help to keep them alive, buy a bit of meat, milk, fat for the pan.

"What I know is what folk say, which be only a spickle, but 'tis damning enough to make 'ee cross over the road if she be coming in your direction. She always wears a red scarf round her neck, and though 'tis ragged as the King's colours which were paraded up here after we scuttled Boney, she won't throw it away. I understand that, in her day, she was as pretty as Marshwood Vale in summer, but that she got married, had two children - though nobody ever seed 'em - and then something happened that sent her mad."

The red scarf he had bought her for her birthday! It had to be. Yet two children? The child-like portrait she had shown him, the night before: Charity and Arthur. Desperate to know more, he fumbled in his pocket and took out another coin.

"Please tell me. Did *you* ever see those children, or her husband? What happened to drive her insane?"

He thrust the coin towards her, his earnestness scaring her.

"You may offer me a treasure chest of dubloons, but I swear I've told all I know. She comes and goes, head down, a-scurrying like a field mouse, as if she must get back home as quick as possible."

"And has she any friends? Any at all?"

"None that I know of."

"And church? Does she go?"

"No idea. All these questions!"

Just then, an upstairs window opened, and a wild-haired, unkempt man, wearing a ripped vest, stuck his head out of the window, and called, "Who the buggery be that you a-chattering to, this early? Woke me up, you have."

Edgar looked up.

"I'm sorry. Your wife was just giving me directions, for which I have amply - "

"Grateful!" interrupted the woman. "For which you be eternally grateful."

Her raised eyebrows – her back was turned to her gap-toothed husband – signified that Edgar should refrain from referring to the coin he had given her, and he bade her goodbye, concluding his enquiry in a low voice: "And if you ever find out more, and you ever see me, please to stop and tell me, for 'tis a matter of grave importance."

When the husband had retracted his offensive head, Edgar passed the coin into her hand, and no more words were necessary.

He returned to Wellesley, undecided about what to do next, feeling compelled to go again to Emma to see if she was still as he had witnessed. Was her account of the intervening years unreliable, in the light of her neighbour's information? It was important not to exacerbate her condition; she had suffered enough, at his hands.

Then he had an idea: he would visit the vicar. If she had been married, there would be a record of it in the parish register. His heart quickened at the prospect of finally knowing the truth. And there would be a record of baptisms, too. If she had had two children, then she would certainly have had them christened; she had been a devout church-goer when he had courted her.

Luckily, the church door was open. The verger was busy, removing dying flowers that had once lit up every gloomy corner the stained glass windows could not paint, and the vicar had entered to pray, as was his wont, at that hour.

The verger pressed a forefinger to his lips to prevent Edgar from speaking, and pointed to the kneeling vicar. Edgar sat in a pew at the back, and was suddenly imbued with a sense of well-being and peace, and he watched the light filter through the darker air, and illuminate the stone pillars. It had been many years since he had last been in a house of God, and he had forgotten the silence, the feeling of security no other edifice can inspire.

Eventually, the vicar ended his prayers and walked back down the aisle towards him. Edgar stood, indicating a wish to speak to him. The vicar was not the one he remembered when he was last in Bridport. That had been a man who had eaten and drunk more than was good for him, but who, nevertheless, had exhorted his parishioners to be abstemious, as Man lives not by bread alone. The vicar now before Edgar was tall, with a face like a pumpkin, and a nose as purple as a plum.

"Good morning, sir. Come to pray? We are glad to see you. Each day, I open the church at this time to allow my flock to worship, but, alas, it seems that once, sometimes twice, on a Sunday suffices. Ah well!"

"And I, too, must disappoint you, for, though I once attended Sunday Service here, twenty years ago, my business here is more prosaic. I am afraid God and I had an altercation, and my heart is yet too dry to seek forgiveness for abandoning him."

"Your honesty becomes you, Mr. - "

"Porlock. Edgar Porlock."

"Still, you are welcome back. The Lord is eternally forgiving, is he not, Mr. Overmoigne?"

"That he be, vicar, that he be, though it don't do to go pushing his patience, as 'tas been known for him to - "

"Yes, yes, Mr. Overmoigne. God is omnipotent, as we know. But tell me, then, Mr. Porlock, your reason, prosaic or otherwise, for coming here."

"I wish to examine the church's record of marriage and baptism to satisfy my personal curiosity over a little matter."

The vicar took some time to assess the request, not absolutely convinced of its integrity. Eventually, he agreed to open up the vicarage and make available the books. Some of the handwriting had faded, though the names were still legible. Carefully, Edgar ran his finger down each page of the two tomes. Occasionally, he rubbed his eyes, paused a moment to rest, and then continued his search for the name of Emma Broadoak. By the time he reached the last page, he was relieved to find her name not there, and, therefore, had no need of the baptismal records.

The relief he felt was, he acknowledged, a selfish one, as he was glad, in a perverse way, that she had stayed loyal, even though her fidelity had been injurious to her.

"Thank you for your help," said Edgar.

"I hope you have found what you were looking for."

"Yes, I have, and my efforts have been rewarded with some small consolation. Good day."

"Good day, and you are most welcome here, any time."

The vicar turned to the verger, and excused himself.

"I shall do my parish rounds now, Mr. Overmoigne, and return to the vicarage by lunchtime. Charming fellow, that Mr. Porlock, just the sort we could do with in the congregation."

With that, he left to visit the sick and needy in Bridport. His first port-of-call was the workhouse, in which he led prayers, and after a few words with Matron, he visited in town people whose names had been passed to him as requiring spiritual help. He had still the compassion to visit, at grave risk to himself, those with consumption, and was able to speak loudly enough to those who could not hear well. Yet his last visit played on his mind, some time before he actually paid it.

When he arrived, he knocked, and Emma opened the door. Unusually, there was a hint of a smile, the muscles in her face fighting the misery which had moulded it.

"Come in, vicar," she invited. "You see, I expect a guest."

"It is a bad time to call?" he asked, his heart lifting slightly at the prospect of avoiding what was usually a disturbing occasion.

He sniffed the air. Soup, if he was not mistaken. And her dress was different, though the red scarf, threadbare and faded, was draped, as ever, round her neck. She had washed her hair, and had tidily gathered it into a bun, which was kept in place by a comb. Yet her manner was markedly different. She was uplifted, charged with more energy, welcoming. Holding the door for him, she directed him to the table she had set with a tablecloth, two bowls, and cutlery.

In a fleeting moment, the vicar imagined that one of the places was meant for him.

"Please to sit, vicar," Emma said.

"It's kind of you, Emma, but - "

Her laugh cut him off. Such a joyful sound he had never heard from her. Why, had God answered his prayer, and healed her?

"Don't 'ee fret, vicar, as 'tis not for you that I've dressed the table, but for my husband, who came back yesterday to see me. Soup a-simmering on the fire for him, see. All manner of things in it: vegetables, bit of lamb. His favourite."

He looked at her. In her face there was not a trace of madness. She looked genuinely happy.

"I have never seen your husband before, Emma. Please tell me about him, if you like."

"Well, his name be Alfred Morcombelake, and he's as handsome as any of the apostles, though not Judas, who betrayed Jesus. More like Peter, the Rock, or be that Andrew? No, he be the fisherman, or some such trade. He wears good clothes, and his hair be frosted at the temples. And he speaks like a wise one, like you, vicar. He came to see me yesterday, and caught me unawares. But the main thing about him is his blue eyes. They be the colour of West Bay when the sun warms it. Or just like bluebells in a wood."

The vicar suddenly frowned at the mention of the eyes. Only an hour or two earlier, he had looked into eyes so blue that he had briefly envied them their intensity.

"And does your husband wear a red cravat, and a blue waistcoat?" She nodded and grinned. "And does he have brown hair, apart from grey here?" He touched his temples, and Emma nodded more excitedly. "And you're sure his name is Alfred?"

"Yes! Yes!" she cried ecstatically. "Alfred."

"Then I will leave you to await his arrival."

As he made his way back to the vicarage, he began to think that he had already met him, that Alfred Morcombelake was, in fact, Edgar Porlock.

"A curious case," he muttered. "A most curious case."

Meanwhile, Emma stirred the soup gently, humming to herself. Then she went to the sideboard, took out a mirror, and looked at herself.

"Alfred liked his soup, as I remember, though not Jethro. No, Jethro always eats like I be trying to poison him."

Chapter Three

I must rent a house of my own for a short while. There's privacy there, no interrogators. He decided that another night at the inn might lead to further questions, or an increase in his weight, due to the landlady's generous portions. When he asked passers-by in the street if they knew of a room to rent, they shook their heads. Then a man pondered a little more on Edgar's question, and stroked his beard, which clung for dear life to his neck but shunned his chin and cheeks.

"Let's see. Was a house, down the hill, a-going. Belong to a man who makes rope. Kind soul, by all accounts. Fair to his workers, but cold as winter when anyone cross him. Not sure if it still a-begging. Lives up the shoulder of the town, somewhere shy, as most folk with money round here do, case anyone a mind to steal it. If the house be a-tekken, then knock on my door yonder, and a bed be yours for a couple of nights."

"Thank you. 'Tis kind."

"You look a man who be a-holding on to something he been let slipping. You beout work, you best be off to the hiring fair at Dorchester, tomorrow, where you can put a roof over your head on a farm, though mind where you takes up, as some don't pay more than a turnip, and ties you in for a whole year. You make your mark on some's promising word, and you end up nailed in a box."

Edgar shook the man's hand. The rope-maker's house sounded

tempting, but would, no doubt, cost more than a room. He had money, but had worked too hard to earn it to waste it.

"I will take up your offer, if I still may."

"I works down the harbour at West Bay, where I keeps my boat to catch a few fish."

"Then I'll pay you, in advance, and you can tell me all about the hiring fair: what I must do and say if I choose to work. I cannot be idle."

The man shook his head when he saw the coins in Edgar's palm.

"Later. 'Tis Bridport market today, and I'll bring the morning's fish to sell in Bucky Doo, God a-willing. Come see me then, and we might go home to a fillet or two of fried mackerel, though the biggest I keeps back for Miss. Symondsbury, when she deign to come. Too much to say for herself but pays well, so that don't matter."

Edgar wondered whether Cressida had handed over the money to Winifred Drimpton, or had temporarily replaced Billy Eype and his ne'er-do-well entourage.

The man touched his hat, and set off to the harbour.

Edgar found Wellesley a field and a stream. A kingfisher flashed, plummeted, and plucked a fish. From the fallen tree on which he was lying, Edgar could see the moon hiding in the pale blue, eavesdropping.

"Today is the market, and tomorrow is Dorchester, Wellesley, so rest those haunches now, as tomorrow they take me to a better future. Never used a pitchfork, but got two strong arms. Turn my hand to most things, I reckon. When the time comes, I'll even take up my profession again, when I've forgiven it for humiliating me. I must take time to mend myself, and heal those whom I have hurt."

He slept well, and the sun had banished the moon. Thirsty, he cupped clear water from the stream into his mouth, and onto his face.

The market hummed. A man was holding up four rabbits, two

in each hand, by their legs. They had convulsed in a futile struggle to escape the nets, that very morning.

"Smell them," he invited the woman to whom Edgar had spoken about Emma. "Skin 'em, fry 'em, stew 'em, eat 'em. Your husband'll love you for a few tatties and a side of rabbit. Goes well with a smearing of mashed horseradish and wild garlic. They say it does wonders for a man."

"It'll take more than a rabbit to do anything for him!" she scoffed. "He's useless."

The man sidled up to her, and said confidentially, "Then what say you cook me one of these, and let me show you what they can do for me."

The woman glared disdainfully at him.

"A man who catches rabbits be worthless. No future in rabbits."

She flounced off, and the man called, "I can show you a good time, Lady Tongue-lash. My hands work wonders on you!"

"Not with rabbits' blood on, they won't."

Edgar caught her eye as she moved away. She nodded, and the man saw her acknowledgement, felt second best.

"You her husband? Like one of these for your dinner?"

"No to both. Tonight be mackerel."

"Don't no bugger like rabbit no more? Fit for a king's table, these."

Edgar looked for the fisherman, shaking his head at a boy who asked for a penny to clean his shoes, and smiling at a girl who offered a posy to him. Sheep and goats were bleating and depositing excrement all over the road; cows lurched from side to side, guided by rope through rings in their noses; and women proferred baskets of eggs. And nowhere could he spot Emma, though the very heart of the market was outside her house.

The fisherman had laid his mackerel out in neat rows on the back of his cart, their heads all pointing the same way, their bodies parallel. A few flies and wasps were investigating them, and the man wafted lazily at them with his hat.

"A good haul?" asked Edgar.

"I'd say so, though they baint shifting very quick, and Miss. Symondsbury not been today. Folk all a-tarrying till I knocks down my prices. Crafty lot, Briddy women."

Then some regulars came, and he offered three for the price of two, wanting to keep his customers sweet.

"Wouldn't you be better on the other side of the road, market days? That be where the throng go."

The man shook his head vigorously.

"I never walks on that side of the road, market days. Till the day I die, I shall never tread there; not even my shadow will touch it, though the telling of the reason be saved for another day. See him yonder? The one with the fat belly?" Edgar nodded. "Market days, that be his spot, so I never walks there. You come back here, next banging of the clock bell, and we'll go home to the frying pan."

"'Tis certain, but we know not each other's name. I am Edgar Porlock."

The man looked him up and down, as if the name were a new coat. It sat well on him, on the whole, yet a little loosely round the shoulders, and its cut, thought the man, was a little too stylish.

"And I be Leonard Shaftesbury."

They shook hands, and Edgar went to check on Wellesley, who was content to wait by the clock. The man had said he had a small yard, though Wellesley would be more comfortable by the stream, where he could drink if he wished, but Edgar feared he would be stolen, so chose the yard.

Later, Leonard pushed his cart, which transported a few fish for dinner, accompanied by his guest. The house was thin, as if it had squeezed between two other, bigger houses, to escape a downpour. The curtains were closed, and Edgar stood still while Leonard lit the lamp. There were few comforts: a table, a chair, some boxes, and the fireplace. The air, trapped all day, was salty, musty, fishy.

"Sit you down," invited Leonard, indicating the chair, "and I'll fire up the grate. Will you manage two?"

The mackerel were a good size, and Edgar was hungry.

"'Tis kind."

The wood snapped and crackled as the kindling caught, and Leonard melted some bacon fat, which had set in the pan. Soon the fish were splashing in it.

"Fingers only, in this house. Fish flake when they've cooled a bit."

They sat in silence, watching the pan, listening to the spitting fat. Edgar noticed a net, a crab pot. The lamp's wick was almost out, and the flame guttered and expired.

"And the man with the paunch?" asked Edgar, in the firelight.

"I stays well away from that side of the road when he sells. If I didn't, I'd stab him with my gutting knife, cut out his heart, and feed it to the gulls, who would probably leave it alone, as it be bad meat. A gun be too quick, too easy, though I have one, and would use it if I had to. Though 'tis three harvests since he wronged me, 'tis not forgotten, and the memory of it lingers in my nose like a rotting seal left days on the beach."

Edgar knew from Leonard's snarl that it was too evil an act to tell, and did not press him further.

Leonard stared unblinkingly into the flames as he savaged his fish, and Edgar fell silent, till he had wiped his lips on his sleeve, and said, "A feast, Leonard. A veritable feast."

"Kept me alive, these years, mackerel. 'Tis a good looking fish, full of flavour and goodness. You'll take a drop?" he asked, fetching a bottle of French brandy from a shelf. "The ones the Revenue miss are always the best."

Leonard grinned; his anger had subsided.

"Let me swear to secrecy first!" laughed Edgar.

"And now I must be out for an hour."

"If you will show me to my room, I shall retire. I will be off early, in the morning, to the hiring fair, and Wellesley must get me there.

I'll pay you now, for if I be hired, our paths may never cross again."

Leonard shook his head.

"I shall accept what is due and no more, though we shall meet again, 'tis certain. These fish, this fire, are now part of your life. You may forget them betimes, then, one day, this brandy's smell will sweeten your nose again."

"Go you to The Red Heifer? I found it passing comfortable."

Leonard ignored the question.

"This be the only key. Go you abroad tonight?"

"I am too tired, and will leave only to look on Wellesley."

"Then I shall be off. Your room be upstairs on the right, and be no bigger than a coffin, but the bed be passing soft. There be no pot there, so use the field, where the straw be yet dry and don't cut your arse, but mind you don't leave the house for long. There be trampers about, nights."

When Leonard had gone, Edgar went to his room. The floorboards creaked, and the door did not fit properly. Inside was the promised bed, nothing else. Do not be ungrateful, he told himself. Leonard has been kind: fed and housed me, told me about the hiring fair. This now is the life I will lead: asking for nothing, in the knowledge that I shall certainly receive little.

On the bed, he fell to thinking about Emma. Does she work? How does she pay her rent? I would like to improve her material circumstances, even if she does not understand why I did not keep my promise to return.

There were times, since he had last seen her, when he thought he might have imagined what she had said, how she had acted. Perhaps, he had exaggerated her invention of a family, had not listened properly. Did she not deserve another chance, a full explanation, even if she had been robbed of her comprehension?

He rose, stole another glass of the brandy, and went into the street. The key, he thought. I cannot lock the door. For a moment or two, he hesitated. The street was deserted. Back inside the house, he drew back the heavy curtains, so that the fire could be seen from outside. Folk'll think the house occupied, he reasoned, and won't attempt to enter. Besides, I have no choice. My business is urgent, and I am fuelled by brandy, am powerless.

He walked back to Bucky Doo. There were a few reminders of the market: apple cores, discarded bottles, too much animal excrement. The only person he saw was on crutches. As he neared him, Edgar said, "Good evening, sir." He looked down at the man's wooden stump. The man turned, his left eye socket hollow as an owl's nest in a tree.

"Look on me as others do, sir, and I'll not blame 'ee. 'Tis my lot, and 'tis to be hoped that you baint too shocked. Boney's men a-snatched my eye and leg, and, though they can't have known it, at the time, my fiancée, too. We were to be married when I returned. That's what I promised her. 'Off to war,' I said, 'and when I returns, we'll a-wed in church, and sit out in the garden for the rest of our lives, you a-shelling oysters, and me a-smoking a pipe.' And she replies, ''Twill keep me going while you does for Boney.' But 'tis passing strange, as she says I baint me any more, not the man she promised to marry, and that she a-waiting for him to return. And I knows then that she gone mad. Nothing I could do. Her mind gone off like rancid butter."

Edgar gulped.

"I have some sympathy, sir. Tell me, did your fiancée improve, or is her condition permanent?"

"She's not like that any more, sir."

Edgar took hope from this. Then maybe Emma might improve, too, even recover completely.

"Then I am heartily cheered."

"'Tis nothing to cheer."

"And why not?"

"Well, she be dead and buried, sir, long since. Some say she was a-done for by a broken heart, but 'twas Boney did for her, him and his French army."

The man's voice had become tremulous. Edgar took out a coin, but the man fell back against a wall, and waved his crutch at him.

"Money can't buy me anything of worth, sir. 'Twon't buy me an eye, or a leg, or a sweetheart!"

Edgar nodded, and passed him, less confident now.

Emma's window was faintly lit. *She is in, so my chance has come again.* He edged slowly towards the house, and looked in obliquely, so that he would not be seen. There was movement. Emma was in her nightgown, hair down, so that her face was obscured. Then, he thought he saw someone else, a man, his back to the window. Emma stretched out her hand, and the other put coins into it. She smiled, and dropped them in a tin. Edgar saw her clasp the man's hand with both of hers, and held it till Edgar could bear it no longer.

"It cannot be!" he muttered. "Not Emma. And yet this explains much: how she pays her rent, buys clothes, and feeds herself. I cannot bear this."

Overcome by jealousy and anger, he reached for the door handle, but held back, wanting to look again at them, in case his eyes had deceived him. Emma and her visitor continued to talk, facing each other. The man was looking intently at her, and she nodded to him. *She has taken money from him. Perhaps, he abuses her, takes advantage of her weak mind, her madness.* And maybe, Edgar thinks, there are other men who come, as this man does, to quell their urges. Edgar himself knew what it was like to fight them, till you must give in, against your better judgement. It is one thing to know you must remove yourself from the temptation, but another to do so.

His torment was interrupted by the man with one leg, who had caught him up. Edgar turned his back on him. *Emma must not* hear voices outside, or his presence would be discovered. That danger disappeared, slowly; no amount of wishing could hasten the veteran's passage.

Edgar resumed his vigil, at the window. They seemed closer to each other now, as if edging towards an embrace. Breath held, Edgar watched. With her hair down, Emma seemed younger, more attractive than the time before.

I know I have no right to be here, no claim on her, but she has the right to know what took me away from her, and I shall not be deterred.

Then, as if she had spotted him peeping at her, she went to the window. Her nightgown did not hide the outline of her breasts and hips. She closed the curtains. He did not think he had been seen, but he debated what to do next. He could retire to some other place in Bucky Doo, to spy on the door, and return when the man had left, satisfied, though there was no telling how long that might be. He did not want Leonard to return home and discover that it had been left unattended. Leonard had been generous. There was now, however, a risk to Edgar's personal safety if he entered, unannounced, Emma's house.

He made up his mind. The hand hovering over the door handle tightened. When the handle could turn no further, he thought what he might say, do. The man had not yet had what Edgar supposed he had paid for. He might have a knife, could be a cutthroat. Geoffrey Burton-Bradstock's attack would seem insignificant compared with the disarming of a frustrated, knife-wielding assailant.

Gently, he pushed against the door, but it would not budge. He peeped through the keyhole, but the key was not there. Locked or not? he wondered.

The door, after he had applied force with his left shoulder, gave way, and Edgar fell into the room. Emma screamed, saw him over her visitor's right shoulder.

Edgar's mouth was open, but no words came.

"Alfred? 'Tis 'ee? If 'ee'd said 'ee was calling, I'd have a bite on the table. Soup, such like. That still your favourite?"

Her visitor turned and said to the intruder, "You no right a-bursting in here like you was the sea crashing over the harbour walls. This here be a private house."

"'Tis only Alfred, my husband, come back home. Comes and goes like the wind. Blows in, blows out. Likes soup."

"Alfred? You say your name be Alfred?"

Emma answered for him.

"Yes. He be my very own, and it be my fault for not introducing you proper. This here be Alfred Morcombelake."

Edgar's spirits sank, and he averted his eyes from the man's, embarrassed.

Leonard sneered.

"Really? Then this be a pretty mess, this."

"I can explain," said Edgar.

"I hopes you can."

"And this be Jethro, Jethro Sherborne, who don't like my soup. Now we all acquainted, there be no misunderstanding."

"Jethro? Not Leonard?"

Leonard made to leave, but turned and said, "I find my house ransacked, you won't be going to no hiring fair!"

"Jethro, where you a-going? Alfred, make him stay. Only been here two minutes."

But Edgar, too, beat a hasty retreat and ran after Leonard.

"Who are you?" Edgar asked, out of breath.

"I tell you who, but then no more questions."

"All right. Then tell."

"I be Jethro Sherborne, Emma's brother-in-law."

Chapter Four

Blossom frothed all pink and cream on the trees, and the grass in the field was too long for the maypole dancing. Farmer Canonicorum stroked his brambly beard, and shook his head.

"'Less we round up an army of men with sickles, there bon't be a May Day dance, which means there bon't be much of a corn yield in summer, as 'tis that which be important as rain and cow muck for the growing. There been a plaiting of ribbons round a pole in this field since the Armada tried its Spanish arm, and was scuppered by Sir Francis Drake, who was a-playing with his balls, so to speak, on the Hoe. 'Tas been my family's job to make sure the pole be raised, that there be victuals a-plenty, and that the grass be short enough for our young and older girls to bob and weave. And as they be coming at each other from different directions, a tuft too long bill bring a tumbling and shame on me."

The listeners agreed but knew it meant back-breaking work.

"You speak wisely, Frederick, but there be time and muscle enough to make this field smooth as a pebble on the beach. But be there chosen a May queen yet? 'Tas been a problem in years gone by, when there been argumenting amongst the girls and their mothers, though 'tis thought that, this year, it bill be the red-haired beauty, who has stolen the heart of young Master Yeoman Symondsbury. The rumour be that before the hoar nips, he will take her for his bride, and make her mistress of Symondsbury Manor," said John Fleet.

"An' if she be May queen, then 'tis certain there bill be a child within a year of their marrying, as she be a comely lass, and turns the eye, even from a distance," added Christopher Denhay.

"The usual method be they pick straws from a sheaf, and the largest wins, though even that has brought disputes when the straws have been evenly matched. 'Tis my opinion that it ought to be the red-haired girl who live, they say, at the top of the town, for never in my memory has there been a red-haired girl the queen, and 'tis known that red be the colour of the locks of our ancient ancestors, these parts, and down through Devon, to the toe of Cornwall. But let us to the grass, for beout a flat field, the colour of the queen's hair be as important as a mayfly."

They came from all over Bridport, this regiment, their scythes sharp and slung over shoulders like rifles, and they moved in a line, a safe distance from each other, swinging their tool in a smooth arc, horizontally to the ground. Behind them followed the women with their gap-toothed rakes, and soon the long grass was gathered into flat nests, ready to be lifted into carts and taken to the barn for winter feed.

When the field was shaven, the labourers mopped their brows and drank cider, in great gulps.

"'Tis a good job you done," praised Frederick, "and tomorrow we raise the pole and ribbons."

A big cheer rose from the crowd when the two wobbling carts arrived, and the men and women dispersed, happy in the knowledge that the dance would now make the soil fertile.

The next day, a group of young men carried the pole to the field. One of them, a youth with bright blue eyes, led the way, the pole resting on his right shoulder.

"Follow my footsteps, men, and we shall deliver it safely. Anyone takes his own pace puts it at risk," said Alfred.

The others looked down at their feet, and adjusted their stride and timing, and soon they arrived where Frederick was waiting, hands on hips, in a supervisory pose.

"Just you lay it down there, boys, ready for the women folk to hang up the ribbons, on the day itself. Though the skies are full of swallows and swifts, we might get a downpour 'twixt now and then," he instructed.

"And 'tis certain that the rumour be true the queen be Clementine Purbeck?" asked Alfred.

Frederick nodded.

"And 'twas her straw the longest?" asked another.

Frederick shook his head.

"She been a-chosen by last year's queen, and 'twill be the preferred way from now on."

"And what if a queen got her favourite? 'Taint fair," protested Alfred. "There be a girl drawn short straws, these last three years. 'I be cursed in this,' she says, 'and soon I be too old.' 'Tis a shame."

Frederick moved closer to Alfred, and rested his hand on his shoulder.

"And we know Emma Broadoak be your meaning, and that she be one you takes a special interest in, so fairness be about as flimsy as a spider's web. 'Twill break, sooner or later, as will custom and practice. 'Twon't harm us none. There always been squabbling. Let it rest, Alfred."

Alfred's cheeks were ripe plums; the others, too, had understood Frederick's allusions to his feelings for Emma.

"There be others put out, too," Alfred informed him, anxious to deflect the attention away from himself.

Frederick grabbed at an annoying fly, and missed.

"Emma been a dancer three harvests, and others not yet had a go. No, I reckons Clementine Purbeck will make as good a queen as any. So, everyone, enough of this grumbling, and back to the barn where the long tables be waiting to be cleaned and brought down."

Frederick made towards the farm. The others looked at Alfred to see if he had accepted defeat, and he followed him, knowing that, once Frederick had made up his mind, there was no changing it.

On the first day of May, the sun had licked the grass dry by mid-day. Early, coloured ribbons had been fixed to the pole, and the pole itself had been erected. Frederick had fussed over its uprightness, reckoned he had the truest eye in Dorset.

"The tiddiest bit to the right. No, you gone too far now. 'Tas to be perfect upright, as we don't want it a-falling on anyone's head. Now, again. Easy, boys, easy. Stop! Now you hold it steady, while the earth gets squashed. Said, last year, we'd get a frame to put it in, but we forgets, over time, so we must do it as normal. There, boys, fill the hole, and march on it as if you were the King's own regiment!"

When it was up, and the ribbons were lazily fluttering in the light breeze, they all stood and admired it.

"And yellow is for the sun," began Frederick.

"And green is for the shoots," continued Alfred.

"And blue is for the water," added Christopher.

"And red is for the earth," finished John.

The dancing was due to start at two o'clock, so there was time to set out the food and drink on the trestle tables. The dancers had practised their steps in Bucky Doo, had gone to put on their dresses, and to have flowers woven into their long hair. The band consisted of five fiddlers, and a drummer who kept them in the proper rhythm, and after that morning's rehearsal, they took a drop of special ''lixir', as the lead fiddler, Stephen Lulworth, called it.

"'Twill make our elbows supple, as the bowing be long and up and down all through the tunes, and we must make sure we don't get carried away and let the dancers rush us, as that leads to sore joints, which, at our age, we don't want," he said, passing on the bottle. "'Tis a Dorset tradition, and we must guards it, and practise it, or it bill disappear, and we be left with a barren life."

"'Tis certain," agreed Timothy Durdle, "and I for one won't be guilty of letting our ways and manners be gone. No, sir. Here, 'tis my turn, and, as my elbow be a-playing up lately, I shall take a stronger swig, so that my fingers don't lock, and wander onto the wrong notes."

Soon, the fiddlers had the supplest elbows in Dorset, and they meandered to the field, where the crowd had thickened. Up in the farmyard, the two carts had been festooned with flowers, and the two groups of dancers, younger and older, were sitting on straw bales from the barn. The girls brushed and tidied each other's hair, and kissed. Each would receive a small gift, at the end of the day, and they chattered excitedly about what it might be. A little distance from the carts was a magnificent chestnut horse, decorated with polished leathers, brass bells and chains, and plumes, and on it nervously sat Clementine Purbeck, the May queen. The other girls eyed her enviously, in some cases, even spitefully. Emma Broadoak, who had now come to terms with the likelihood of never being queen, sighed. There was no doubting Clementine's beauty. Her red hair had been gathered up expertly, revealing her long, white neck.

Clementine's and Emma's apprehension was due to not only the occasion, but the fact that there was someone in the crowd they wanted to impress. Yeoman Symondsbury and Alfred Morcombelake awaited their entrance equally nervously, and when they set eyes on, from afar, the young women they loved, they were rapt, felt that all around them were watching for a sign of their admiration.

The fiddlers tuned up again, and the carts rocked into the field to loud cheering. All eyes turned to the dancers. Soon, the crowd hushed, and the girls, including the queen, grasped their ribbon. Somehow, Emma located Alfred: near the front but not too advanced. And Yeoman was in a similar position opposite him. Clementine saw Yeoman, and blushed.

The first notes were played, and the younger girls skipped and strode in a theatrical manner, weaving and ducking in and out of the advancing older girls.

Alfred never took his eyes off Emma, who glanced at him and smiled, each time she passed him. However, it ill becomes a queen to be too obvious in her recognition of an admirer, and Yeoman had to be satisfied with a coy nod of Clementine's head at the end of the first dance.

The girls sought their families, and Alfred knew he must intercept Emma before she met hers.

"Emma."

He took her wrist lightly, and she looked about her, fearful of being seen by her parents.

"Alfred, we be in the public gaze, and, though you have expressed love for me privately, this is not the place to secure my affection by embarrassing me."

He let go, hurt that she should not yet publicly acknowledge her true feelings.

"Then meet me behind those trees next to the harbour road. Do not deny me the chance to say what I have to say, for if I do not express it on this day when you are my May queen, then the words will never be heard but buried in the catacombs of despair."

"You be too earnest in your pursuit of me, Alfred, but I will go by the gate, and you must find a way at the bottom of the field, for to go together would incite my parents."

"Then be as nimble in keeping our tryst as you were in the dance, for my words are so perfectly assembled that a delay in their expression might mix them up again."

Emma skipped towards the gate, as if practising for the next dance, to avoid attention. There were still a few minutes to go, time to hear his special message. Her heart continued to pound, and not just because of her exertions. She waited what seemed an eternity, was sure her parents would be looking for her. Then her wait ended when Alfred appeared, scratched on his hands and face.

"I fell into the hawthorn after climbing a tree and jumping into the lane, but I misjudged my effort," he explained. "'Twas a sweet pain to bring me here."

Instinctively, she reached for him to examine his wounds.

"Poor Alfred! You risked life and limb for me?"

As her hand touched his face, he closed his eyes, felt the balm of her fingertips.

"I would die for you," he gasped.

"Oh, Alfred, please don't do that, not when we are —"

Emma stopped, and Alfred opened his eyes.

"In love? Is that what you were about to say?"

She lowered her hands.

"Yes, dear. I love you more than I can say."

"And, Emma, I love you, too. Your voice I hear in every gust of wind. It keeps me awake at night. 'Tis a siren, and today I nearly asked the others to lash me to the maypole, as Ulysses asked his men."

Emma screwed up her face.

"To a maypole? 'Tis a name I know not, Ulysses."

"'Tis a myth which, one day, I will tell, but let me to what I have to say. Emma, I am a young man, but 'tis eternity without you, so I ask you to consider the power you have to save or destroy me, and to consent to marry me as soon as I can earn enough to keep us as man and wife."

"Such power is a great responsibility, and I must think."

"Think? Then think quickly, as each second of your thinking is a torture."

"I *am* thinking, though I be best known for my thinking at a moderate, not quick, pace."

"You tease me, maypole beauty, and 'tis passing cruel. I beg you, answer me."

"Then my answer, darling Alfred, is yes, though no more talk of

44

lashing to poles and people with funny names, or I'll think I'm marrying a strange fellow."

Alfred bent down on one knee, and said, taking her hand, "I will marry you when we have some money."

"And how will you earn money?"

"I have a profession in mind, but that is for another day. Today, you are my May queen, and I am your loyal subject."

She took his hand and pulled him up.

"Hold now, Alfred, that tongue of yours, and say not too much, as to overuse it to polish your promise makes the promise glitter too much to be sincere."

The flowers in her hair seemed to glow faintly, as if they possessed their own natural light. They were like precious stones in a crown. She was truly his queen. He leaned forward and kissed her lips. Her fingers intertwined clumsily with his, and she closed her eyes.

Their silence was then broken by the fiddlers tuning up again, ready for the next dance.

"I wonder what mother and father will say," she said.

"I must come and ask your father's permission for your hand."

"May I introduce him to the idea first? Prepare him?"

"You doubt he will be pleased?"

The flavour of the kiss had all but gone. She wrestled with the truth, and acknowledged it.

"'Tis true he knows about us. Bridport has eyes and ears in every window, every alleyway. Each doorstep whispers, so that if something be done, it be known within the hour. Father knows more about us than we think. He has spoken to me, and, to be plain, he thinks you are too clever by far, that we are not well suited. Your words be the potion of a conjuror, he once said. But I must go; the dancing is about to begin."

She reached up, kissed him on the cheek, and was gone, leaving him devastated that her father had yet to be won.

Back at the maypole, he joined his friends, who passed him a pot of cider.

"Drink, Alfred. 'Twill wash your face of its sourness, for you look as if you've a mouthful of gooseberries," advised Timothy Durdle.

The others laughed, and Alfred drank his pot in one go.

"'Tis well done, and another will put ripe strawberries there instead."

Alfred drank again, and his friends cheered, unfortunately attracting the attention of nearby spectators. There was Emma's father, to whom Alfred mockingly raised his pot.

Soon, the dancing began, and Clementine Purbeck followed Emma. It was natural, therefore, to make comparisons. Some said that Clementine moved more elegantly, that she had the neck and grace of a swan; others that Emma, though plainer, had more vitality, that her hair, not the burnished copper of her pursuer in the dance, had the natural thickness, lustre, and movement of the archetypal Dorset girl.

Alfred's eyes strayed from one to the other, and the strength of the cider excited his imagination, so that he began to wonder how Clementine's lips might feel and move. Yet when the reel revealed his love's face again, he felt ashamed that he had let her down already. And she herself was displeased when his friends were patting him on the shoulder, and digging him in the ribs, as if he had told them what had passed between him and her, earlier, before he had spoken to her father.

Between the dances, Emma stayed with her friends, but kept a furtive eye on her husband-to-be. When they said who had caught their eye, Emma remained silent, as did Clementine, whom the girls treated with a mixture of aloofness and curiosity. She was one of them, yet not, and so Emma felt an affinity with her. On the left hand, she wore a ring, given to her by Yeoman Symondsbury. All the girls looked at it, envying her.

"Be you married?" asked Emma of Clementine, when they were close enough to talk.

"No, but 'tis a sign of our engagement."

"And when will you be wed?"

"Before the hoar clings to branches, and the robins sit like giant berries in the hawthorn."

"'Tis romantic, that," sighed Emma.

"And do you have a man to love?"

Emma was now taken aback by the suddenness of the question, which asked her to do what she thought Alfred had done: shared their intention to marry before her father's consent had been obtained. Yet Clementine was in the same position, young and in love, and would surely not tell anyone else.

"There be no ring yet, but I been engaged, this very day, not an hour since, though Alfred not spoke to my father yet, as is the custom. 'Tis a small matter, and one which will be attended to as soon as possible."

Clementine leaned over and kissed her.

"The man who weds you will be a lucky one, for you are so beautiful that you should wear my crown. Here, have it. I am ugly compared with you."

Clementine took off her crown, and attempted to place it on Emma's head.

"No, 'tis wrong to wear it when *you* be May queen!" protested Emma.

"'Twill not harm you to try it, just for a second. I know I was chosen, and that others resent me, so this is my gesture to show that, in my heart, I am a Dorset girl, like them."

She raised it above the hands that had initially refused it, and placed it on Emma's head. The others saw the new queen, and gathered round, asking if they could try it, too. Clementine allowed them to, and received hugs and kisses for her generosity.

"And is your lover here?" she asked.

"Yes. That be him there, walking to the table."

Emma nodded instead of pointing, so that others would not notice.

"He is handsome."

"His eyes are of the most perfect blue, as if part of the sky. 'Tis like God's light shines through them."

Frederick called the dancers to order, and the crown was restored to its rightful head.

At the end of the dance, Clementine searched for Yeoman, but he had gone to water her horse. She looked behind the tents erected in case of bad weather, and she heard voices. The couple seemed to be having an altercation, the woman clearly angry and gaining the upper hand.

"And why is it I aint seen you for days? Took your kisses and ran, you did, so's I don't know where I stand."

"'Taint what you think, Flora. A man can't be dancing to a woman's tune, all the time."

"You still love me?"

"You know I do," gave in the man.

"Then kiss me now, here, like you did before, or I shall never let you touch me again. Never!"

Clementine cupped her mouth to suppress a giggle.

She's got him, well and true, and knows how to rope him in, she said to herself. Quickly withdrawing while they were kissing, Clementine pressed herself between two tents, so that she was out of sight but could listen.

Soon, she heard the woman say, "And so I'll meet you in Bucky Doo tonight? And you are truly sorry now?"

"Yes," said her lover, unconvincingly.

After a few seconds, the man passed the gap in which Clementine was hiding. Striding away quickly to escape the girl, he showed enough of himself for Clementine to recognise him as the man who had, that afternoon, made Emma Broadoak one of the happiest women in Dorset.

"Well, well!" said Clementine. " Seems this poor girl deserves better than that, and that Emma be deceived on this the day of her engagement. If that be the way of men, I must watch Yeoman closely, and kiss him well enough and often, so that he don't stray. But 'tis too late for Emma, and 'tis a shame, as he done it once, and, most probably, will do it again."

Chapter Five

After Jethro had finished explaining the reason for passing money to Emma, Edgar hung his head. His presumption that she had been paid for an act of immorality had been shamefully erroneous.

"Then no apology of mine will appease you. I had thought the worst of you both, and I ask your forgiveness, which I hope you will grant when I have told you my reason for returning, after all these years."

"Then take a straight road there, as I be not inclined to listen for long. Whatever your story, I won't turn you out tonight, but, at first light, you must leave for Dorchester. I be a man of my word, which be as strong as oak."

So Edgar began his tale: how he had not kept his promise to Emma, and had returned to unburden himself, so that he might start the next stage of his life looking the world in the eye. He was, however, careful not to divulge what had happened to him during his absence, it being a private matter.

Back home again, Jethro poured them both a brandy.

"To better times," proposed Edgar.

Jethro raised his glass, and Edgar nudged it with his.

"For us all."

What Jethro had told him about Emma did not keep him awake but occupied his thoughts on the journey to Dorchester. It was at first suspicion of dawn that he awoke and mounted Wellesley.

Fortunately, the moon was bright, though not full, and the road eastwards, a silver ribbon, was visible.

Near Dorchester, he met others: carts of twitching hens, men, some solitary, others in groups, lines of cows, their tails flicking from side to side. All were drawn to the town, from which drifted the solemn chimes of mid-day.

Wellesley was tired, and a man reached into his bag, and fed him a carrot.

"Thank 'ee, kind sir. Wellesley be fond of carrots. Dorchester feels like the other side of the world from Bridport, so I expect he's hungry."

"Bridport?"

"Come for the hiring fair, get fixed up. Don't like idle hands."

"Me, neither."

"Want a ride? Worth a carrot."

"'Tis kind."

The man smiled, so Edgar reached down and pulled him up. Though uncomfortable, the man was glad to cling to him, to arrive before others. The fair was due to begin, and the hiring started on time.

"What you looking for?" asked Edgar.

"Farm work. Sacked from my last job. And you?"

"Turn my hand to whatever be going. Can't be fussy."

Wellesley followed the crowd, which thickened as they approached the market facing Maumbury Rings.

"Thank 'ee," said the passenger.

"'Tis nothing," shrugged Edgar, and Billy Eype walked away, whistling merrily.

The other men were wearing the apparel of their trade: smocks for shepherds, leg leathers for farriers, an ear of corn in the hat for day labourers. Many knew each other. Some had come from afar, and wore all too familiar signs of distress: ragged clothes, dirty, gaunt faces. And women, too, were there, in impromptu groups, headscarves tidily keeping their hair out of their faces, and dresses fraying at the edges where they had trailed on the ground. Many had been sent by elderly parents, whose limbs had become as crooked and knobbly as bare branches. All had to earn money to fix the hole in the roof, to pay rent, and to put an end to desperate foraging in the woods, for a time, by buying a chicken or two, so that they might enjoy a few eggs before necking and eating them.

Edgar was conspicuous in his finer clothes. Only his face stubble and weary look of a hungry and thirsty traveller defined him as one of the others.

Farm managers mingled, some avoiding eye contact with labourers they had previously mistreated, others looking for men with hands scarred with scythe-inflicted nicks, muscles like skeins of rope, and a steady hand. Edgar watched them concentrating, saw the disappointment on the faces of those who had been refused.

Edgar turned to his neighbour, and asked, "And what be they doing?"

The man replied, "Put out your hands like this," and showed him what to do.

Edgar copied, and the man decided, after a few seconds' close examination, that Edgar would find work.

"Perfect. 'Tis certain that not a drop has passed your lips in a long time, for 'tis the shaking hand that gives it away. A farmer don't want drunken workers, as they cost him money, see. They sleep too long, and tire quickly."

"I see."

The man concluded with, "Tatties and turnips and corncobs all need lifting and a-scalping, and a man who shivers like he just back from a blizzard works too slow for his master's pockets."

Edgar tried to catch the eye of the important people. Mingling, he saw relief on the faces of those taken on, but he himself had no token of his skills on his clothes, so had to approach the hirers.

"And what use be you to me?" asked one. "Ever followed a

plough and a horse? Rolled red earth into perfect pipes?" Edgar shook his head. "Used a long knife to top and tail turnips?" Again, he indicated no. "Well, you baint a milkmaid, not with those smooth hands, so there's no point in me setting you on, on account of you not used to doing hard work."

"Don't mean I can't do it, though. Strong for my age."

The hirer looked him up and down, and Edgar's clothes put him off.

"You from round these parts?"

"Bridport. Came, this morning, on my horse."

Wellesley was tied to a fence.

"Got a horse, eh?"

"Wellesley," said Edgar, indicating him.

"A fine name."

The man stroked Wellesley's nose, ran his expert hands down his flanks.

"A horse like this costs. Something don't fit with you. Don't know what it is."

"Watch."

He turned his back to the adjacent cart, and gripped it. Pushing up from the knees, he raised the cart and held it. His face reddened, and the hirer was impressed.

"You'll do yourself a mischief. Put it down."

Slowly, Edgar lowered it, looked for approval, but none was forthcoming.

"Use anyone like me?"

"Yes, but why you here? You look to have money. Only hunger keeps a man working."

Edgar turned away. It was no use with this man, who could sniff out the compliant ones.

Then he saw people jostling each other, and went to see what was happening. A man was saying, "'Tis a farm manager I'm looking for, someone who knows how to plough, sow seed, and harvest.

Need milkmaids who have a gentle song or two for the cows so's they fill the pails. Anyone here think they can do that?"

One of the women cried, "My hands be the most coaxing in Dorset, and I sings. Not better than a nightingale, nor even a blackbird, but more like a thrush, or a sparrow. Something like that. Leastways, a little fellow with a beak and two wings."

"Then let's hear 'ee," urged the man.

The girl cleared her throat, and struck a pose that made the others titter in expectation of a performance.

"Oh, the snow it brings such sorrow
 when the pond begins to set,
and the icy winds that follow
rut the ground that was once wet."

She looked at her audience, who applauded her.

"'Tis a pretty voice, though not a bird's, and one which I as well as the cows do like," said the hirer's wife.

"But tell me, girl, as 'tis equally important. Do you know right from wrong?" asked the hirer.

"I knows right from left!" she laughed.

"But if a man said to you, 'Take this wine, girl, as 'twill warm you in the chill,' what say you?"

The girl put her forefinger to her chin in mock-consideration.

"Why, sir, I would say, 'No thank 'ee, as though the good Lord turned water into wine, he drank not a drop himself, and I follow the Lord's example!'"

Everyone laughed.

"Then come to my farm, as it has neither wine nor stronger."

The crowd grew, and Edgar, too, approached but kept his hat pulled over his eyes, so that his face was mostly hidden, and he was looking downwards, listening. Edgar was then distracted by a man who was smiling and looking attentive, who moved his hand slowly towards the hirer's frock coat pocket. It had happened to Edgar, in Wells, in a crowded street, when his pocket had been emptied, a long time ago. A woman had engaged him in discussion, wanted directions to the cathedral, while her friend had used the press of the throng to disguise the theft.

Now, in Dorchester, Edgar waited till the wallet emerged from the hirer's pocket, then seized the pickpocket's wrist with his right hand.

"Thief!" he yelled.

The wallet fell to the ground, and the man tried to run away, but Edgar grabbed him round his neck with his other arm, and wrestled him to the cobbles.

The victim, startled, felt his empty pocket, and realised that the wallet on the floor was his.

"I never felt him, the scoundrel. Why, he's no more than a common thief. Send to the gaol!"

In the scuffle, Edgar had lost his hat, and the woman looked down at his blue eyes and white flecks in his hair. Yeoman squinted in vague recognition of his saviour, under whose weight the thief had given up his struggle.

Soon, the thief was taken away, and Edgar was able to dust himself down. Yeoman waited with his wife, who told the would-be labourers to return later, and the crowd began to disperse, disappointed that the hiring for the Symondsbury estate had not been concluded.

"Sir, I'm most grateful to you for your vigilance," said Yeoman. "I felt not a thing."

"Your mind was on the hiring. 'Tis their trick: to occupy you, and strike, and if you are not occupied, they find a bigger distraction. I learned the hard way in Wells."

"The wallet was my father's, a family heirloom, made in a London tannery, and sewn by a skilled seamstress. Your swift action has kept it in the family. Here, take this. It is little enough, I know, but I'd thought not to bring much, knowing 'tis hard won but easily lost."

Edgar politely refused it.

"The reward most fitting is knowing that I have helped someone I have not seen or heard for years. And you, whom I assume be Clementine, Yeoman's wife, once ruled Farmer Canonicorum's field as the May queen, near Bridport Harbour."

Clementine's eyes widened at the recollection of the occasion.

"You were there, that year? You were one of my subjects?"

"Yes, indeed, and a loyal one. I helped Frederick and the others erect the pole. You arrived on horseback, if I am not mistaken."

"Why, so you did, dearest," confirmed Yeoman. "And you, sir, were there? Fancy! And I was your fiancé, at that time, Clementine. Both of us were younger. But look at us now. I am older and bear the scars of the years, but my wife is frozen in time, and remains forever my queen. Eternally youthful, is she not, sir? Let not our separation inhibit you . . . "

"Porlock. Edgar Porlock."

For a moment or two, Yeoman studied him. Those eyes. There had been someone like that, he recalled, but the name was lost. Not Porlock, though, he was certain.

"And now I am most fortunate, Edgar, in having a daughter whom Nature has made an exact copy of her mother."

"'Tis well said if 'tis so."

Two swans. Then you are a lucky man, indeed, Yeoman, he mused.

"And that day," remembered Clementine, "was the day I realised that being May queen can be a lonely experience. The other girls were most envious. And you, sir. Did you have a sweetheart ever be the May queen? A dancer, maybe?"

Edgar blushed.

"Yes, and on that day, you let her wear your crown, so today I repay your generosity with the capture of the thief."

"Then 'tis well said and done, indeed," said Yeoman.

"And did your sweetheart become your wife?" pressed Clementine, delighted that Edgar had reawakened memories of that day.

"Alas, no."

"My dear, do not ask such questions. 'Tis passing prying of 'ee," Yeoman chided. "So tell me, sir. Are you here to hire labourers?"

"No. I've been living in Somerset, since those days, and now must earn a living here in Dorset."

"An educated man like you – for you impress me as such – a labourer? Why, there be work a-plenty with us, if you so wish, though your garb and manner betoken a different life to labouring. Books, Edgar? Has your head been in books, these past years?"

"Now it be my turn, Yeoman, to stop these personal questions. 'Tis passing vexing, I'm sure," objected Clementine.

"And you be right. But will you come work for me, Edgar? I'm looking for a farm manager. I had to sack the last one – a lazy, immoral fellow by the name of Eype – and a few milkmaids for following his example."

His connection with Yeoman, through Emma, that May Day, all those years ago, made him feel disposed to accept the offer, but working for Yeoman would bind him to the past, when he wanted to wake up from it. Yeoman saw the hesitation, had yet to mark the saving of his wallet with a gesture of gratitude.

"I fear you would be disappointed in me. You need more than a strong pair of arms. I know not the exact hour of the seasons, when to plough and plant. Never touched a cow's udder, nor slit a pig's throat, and 'tis in my nature to *eat* eggs rather than collect them."

Yeoman laughed.

"My guess be that you could learn all these things as quickly as the wind howls in from the west. Come sup with us tonight, and see the estate in the morning, and then make up your own mind. 'Twas lack of sound judgement that Billy Eype had the job, and I won't make the same mistake twice. These new milkmaids will go in the cart which follows us. My wife collects a dress here, and then we will return to the manor. Follow us, do, and we will feed you well, and rake over the embers of our youth, till a scene or two glows. What say you? Come, I'll not take no for an answer."

"Nor I. 'Tis often said a man can never refuse a request from a May queen," added Clementine.

It had been a long time since anyone had shown him such kindness, and somehow the prospect of going back to that May Day with his hosts might remind him of a time when he was happy as well as fickle.

"Then I shall follow on Wellesley, if he has the legs. 'Tis kind."

"Meet us here in an hour. The journey is long. Refresh your horse well, and yourself modestly, as our table groans with the weight of viands and apple tarts."

Clementine showed the newly appointed milkmaids to their cart before collecting the dress she had ordered, and Edgar went to The King's Arms. He was tired and hungry, needed nourishment for the journey back, despite the promise of a feast on their arrival.

He ordered chops and cider, which raised his spirits, but when he felt for his money bag, it was missing. He explained that, in catching a thief, he himself had let down his guard and fallen victim to a similar rogue. The landlord said, "'Twas ever thus, and will remain so while there be those who have plenty, and those who have nothing. But 'twon't make me a rich man giving away free meals."

"I will pay you twice what I owe you, 'tis certain, the next time I be in Dorchester, and Edgar Isambard Porlock be a man of his word."

"Then you be one of an ever dwindling number, these parts. Yours be a name I shan't forget come heat or hoar, and 'tis better to pay your dues than be shot in your bed, a-snoring!"

On the way to Symondsbury Manor, the milkmaids cast him a glance or two, and giggled. At first, they annoyed him, then pleased him with their light conversation.

"Why, sir, will you join us in our song?" asked Violet.

"If it be a sweet one which don't climb in notes too much, and if 'tis an acquaintance and no stranger."

So Violet began, and the others joined in. Even Clementine, in her coach, sang, though Yeoman slept through it all.

"When hedgerows bare their branches brown,
all lovers' lips grow cold,
and fickle hearts behind a frown
make young hopes swiftly old."

The melancholy mood of the song unsettled Edgar, so he asked for a more jolly air.

Rose replied, "'Tis naught but the truth which we should sing, and not remain silent."

"Well said," added Violet. "Another verse, then a lighter ditty, girls."

"The stars all crackle in the sky,
and upwards lovers look,
and make a vow an infant lie,
then, trembling, kisses took."

The promised lighter mood followed, much to Edgar's relief, and soon they arrived at the manor.

"There be a bite to eat in the kitchen," Clementine told the new milkmaids. "In the morning, you will milk the cows at sunrise. We have only one maid, at the moment, and that is Winifred Drimpton, who has managed the herd. She will show you round the farmyard."

"And be the man with blue eyes the manager?" asked Violet.

"That be no concern of yours," admonished Clementine. "Now, follow me."

In the hall, Edgar marvelled at the portraits on the walls, and a big fire roared and spat.

"My ancestors, all dead," said Yeoman, noticing his interest. "Ah, Cressida! Come nearer. Let me introduce you to our guest and long-lost friend."

She had heard of their arrival, and come to greet them. Her green eyes were full of frenzied flames, and she smiled at him.

"Guests and friends are always welcome, as are wayfarers who do a good turn," she said, offering her hand.

"Edgar Porlock."

"And I am Cressida Symondsbury."

Edgar was embarrassed that he was colluding with her in her pretence that they had not been hitherto acquainted.

"Edgar knew your mother, years ago," said Yeoman.

"Did he, indeed! Then the world is full of surprises!"

She was enjoying keeping their previous meeting a secret, and now she understood why he had refused to go with her and stay the night as a gesture of her gratitude for his averting the collision of their horses.

"Take him to the south room, Cressida, and pour him a drink. I shall be there soon," said Yeoman.

When Yeoman was out of earshot, Edgar asked, "And did you give the money to Cousin Winifred?"

Cressida raised a hand to her mouth; she had forgotten.

"No, I'm sorry. Let me do it now. 'Tis forgetfulness, and not spitefulness. There is yet light, and she should be back from the fields. I will put right what I have done wrong as soon as possible."

She fetched money and led him to the farm, a walk of some five minutes. Edgar heard the cows, then smelt them.

"Your horse is kept here?" asked Edgar. "That speedy stallion?"

"No, the stables are at the back of the house. See, though, how the farm is ravaged. The plough is rusted, and there is no midden stacked to spread; 'tis everywhere the cows leave it. Foxes drag off the chickens at will, and 'tis father, not a gamekeeper, who shoots the pheasants for the table. The farm is a mess."

Edgar risked a question.

"And your fiancé is still angry with you?"

"He is always angry with someone or thing. But let me see if she is back. Winifred!" She opened the barn door. "Winifred, be you there? Your cousin is come, and I have brought you money he passed to me, a few days ago, but which I forgot to give you. So 'tis here, in my hand."

There was no reply. Under the roof, an owl flapped and screeched.

"You come to her often?" asked Edgar.

After a pause, Cressida said, "No. I help mother in the house where there is much to do."

"Then 'tis a passing lonely life she leads with no one to talk to."

"'Tis certain."

They stepped further into the barn. Signs of her existence were few: a small leather case, a cup, a plate, a cracked hand mirror, a half-spent candle. A gust of wind intruded from behind, and Cressida thought she saw something move in the corner. The light was weak, so she edged nearer, and screamed. Edgar, too, saw the terrible sight.

"'Tis Winifred!" he cried.

On the floor, the chair on which she had stood had been knocked over. Winifred's chin was on her chest, like a sleeping pigeon.

Edgar felt her hand, which was cold, and when he let go, it made her swing slightly, like a tired pendulum.

"We must get her down, though cutting the rope be pointless. She be gone."

Cressida turned and buried her face in Edgar's chest.

It is my fault, he cried within. If I had taken her with me, she would not be dangling at the end of a rope. She begged me, in her time of need, and 'tis another woman I have let down.

He felt Cressida clutch at him, so she could not turn and see Winifred again. Her breath was a hot spot on his chest as she sobbed.

And this is what happens when we do not get involved, he told himself. Coins are useless to a woman whose real need is friendship.

Chapter Six

Bartholomew checked the length of the coffin he had just finished. There had been a request to make it a lot bigger than Obediah, the deceased, to accommodate a few personal possessions he did not wish to leave behind, on account of their sentimental value. His tankard, which he always took to The Red Heifer, would go in his hand, even if his fingers had to be broken – because of rigor mortis – and bent round the handle. His pipe, which had stained his white beard ginger, would slip between his stretched, leathery lips. And his dog, used to retrieving birds shot by Obediah, had died on the same day, and would be squeezed between his legs, Nimrod's chin resting, as was his wont, on his thigh.

"'Tis all for today," said Bartholomew to his apprentice, Ned, who scratched his head.

"'Taint tolled the hour yet."

"'Tis certain, but there been enough sawing and a-banging for today, so off you go. I need to lock up and see to other things."

Ned needed no more encouragement to go, whipped off his apron, donned his cap, and left, calling, "Thank 'ee, master. 'Tis passing kind."

Bartholomew smiled.

"Coffins been in my family for years, and 'taint the gloom folk believe. Somebody got to make 'em, and nobody nails in a corpse better than me. 'Tis said that no body-snatcher, who gets paid a pretty penny by folk wanting to carve 'em up in the name of science, has yet prised open one of my lids, and that be a fact, and a cause of pride."

He went home, washed, and put on clean clothes. After he had combed sawdust from his hair, which hung as a fringe on the back instead of the front of his head, he slid on his wig, and examined himself in the mirror. His frock coat would not fasten, despite his strenuous efforts, and his collar was too tight, but he was not dismayed.

"Brother Jethro may be thinner and more handsome, but has nothing else to recommend him, whereas, though I be portly, got from my father, I have a job paying well enough, and which be always there, as long as the Lord decree that Man has but a short while to live. I have half of my hair, a few of my teeth, and a disposition kindly enough to win a maiden, I hope. Mr. Broadoak said six, so I'd best be off. 'Twould look bad to be late."

Emma was sitting nervously. Her engagement to Alfred was still a secret, and her mother noticed that she had shown no sign of delight when her father had told her that Bartholomew had sought permission to ask for her hand.

"I hardly know him," she had almost whispered, alarmed.

"There be plenty of time to get to know him. He has a house, a job, and is well thought of," had pointed out her father. "'Tis a man well set up."

Now he looked to his wife, who suspected the reason for Emma's lukewarm response, for support.

"There be nothing at fault with your words, but 'twill be Emma's decision to accept him or not."

Emma smiled weakly.

"Well, she must know that I have given my consent for him to ask, and he will be accorded the respect he deserve."

"He be a birthday or two older than me, and 'tis likely we won't get on, in time," pointed out Emma.

A knock at the door prevented her from revealing the name of her true love.

"On time!" declared her father, as the clock on the sideboard chimed. "A man who sticks to his word is a reliable one, and will make a good husband."

Emma glanced at her mother, who whispered, when her husband was greeting Bartholomew, "Don't worry. 'Twill come to a squall, that's all. Be polite. Make your words pretty enough, but not beautiful. Answer his questions by promising them careful consideration. Acknowledge his merits without building false hopes. Who is it, Emma? Tell me now."

"'Tis Alfred Morcombelake, mother, and we are engaged!"

Her mother smiled and squeezed her daughter's hand.

"He's a handsome one, though beout prospects, as I see it, if it be the one I'm thinking of. But quiet now, and remember my instructions."

Bartholomew ducked as he entered, and seemed to fill half the room. In his hand was his hat, the removal of which had slightly disturbed his wig, a sight nearly causing the women to burst out laughing.

"It be Bartholomew, come to talk with you, Emma."

"Ladies," said Bartholomew, inclining his head slightly, as if greeting a customer come to order one of his finest oak coffins, rather than addressing a prospective wife and mother-in-law.

So forward did he lean respectfully that the wig almost slid off his shining pate, and he instinctively grabbed it. Emma giggled, and her father glared. Her mother bit her tongue to inflict pain, a trick taught her by her own mother, who was lying comfortably in one of Bartholomew's father's coffins.

"Unfortunate," acknowledged Bartholomew. "Unfortunate, indeed. I hope you'll forgive this little accident, as 'taint usually in my character to lose my wig so carelessly, and I hope 'twon't sway you against me, Miss. Broadoak, as I be here, with your father's permission, as is the custom, to speak to you about a most solemn matter."

Bartholomew glanced at Mr. and Mrs. Broadoak, was hoping that they would quit the room to afford the necessary privacy, but they stayed. Mr. Broadoak particularly seemed determined that Emma should not bring shame on the family.

Emma looked at her mother, whose eyebrows moved almost imperceptibly as a sign to allow Bartholomew his moment.

"Miss. Broadoak, words baint me as much as a hammer or saw, but when I've finished, I hopes my request be as perfect as any of my coffins. And I stand here, all of a tremble, and I've never before said what I intend to say, so you'll forgive me if my words aint as exact fitting as my coffin lids. My life be genuine enough though beout a wife to make it a perfect one, and 'tis time for me to have a wife, if she'll have me."

Emma could not bring herself to look upon her suitor during his speech, though all present interpreted her bowed head as modesty rather than opposition.

"As 'twas once the time for me to ask *you*, dear," put in Mr. Broadoak to his wife.

"Indeed, Mr. Broadoak, as if you hadn't, I wouldn't be standing here this very minute!" pointed out Bartholomew. His attempted humour was not understood immediately, so he continued, undeterred. "But forgive my digression, as 'twill only take me to Lyme to get me to Charmouth, so to speak. So I comes to my point, Miss. Broadoak – Emma, if I may make so bold – which be to ask you if you will be my wife, and come and live with me in my house, and let me care for you, as a devoted husband. You'll want for nothing, I promise, and though I make coffins, my house will be a joyful one, without any token of my profession hanging over your head."

When he had finished, he looked at Mr. Broadoak, as if to ask, "What happens now?" but Emma had been planning her response while she had been listening. She was, towards the end of his peroration, touched by his sincerity, and compared it with Alfred's passionate, almost wild, proposal. At least, Bartholomew had come to the house, was well enough off to care for her. There Alfred was sadly lacking. But Emma did not love Bartholomew, and did love Alfred. How to manage this awkward moment?

"Bartholomew, I am grateful to you for coming, and a-proposing to me in such an open way. But I hardly know you, and 'twouldn't be right to say yes or no today, as I must think, for my heart and mind are of equal weight."

Her father frowned; he wanted the matter deciding, there and then. Her mother, however, thought her response just right, positive enough to buy time to think and talk about life with Alfred, but equivocal enough to rule out total agreement to marriage.

Just as Mr. Broadoak was about to put more pressure on Emma to accept, Bartholomew said, "And I have come prepared to give you all the time in the world to consider. What is a few more days, weeks, even, when a lifetime of happiness is at stake?"

Mr. Broadoak was glad that Bartholomew's generosity did not stretch to months, and now faced the task of keeping him in the house, so that Emma became more used to him.

"Will you stay and take a bite? We've a bit of rabbit stew prepared, as you can, no doubt, smell," he offered.

Emma looked at her mother, alarmed that Bartholomew might interpret that as an opportunity to reduce from weeks to days the time she had to consider, but need not have feared, as he put up his hand, and said, "No, though 'tis passing kind of 'ee. I've said what I've come to say. Miss. Emma knows how I feel, and I shall do nothing more to sway her, except to say that I hope that, in time, we can grow old together, and remain in love."

So saying, he ducked, without losing his wig, and left.

Mrs. Broadoak dabbed her eyes. Emma, too, had not expected his considerate refusal to stay, and his sincere expression of commitment and love.

"Now look what you've done!" scolded her father. "The man deserved better. And now he a-gone all churned up like butter."

"He spoke well, father, and I shall weigh his words properly, though 'tis true I baint in love with him, and feel that he is nearer your age than mine. You press me too hard, and I must be honest and say that I cannot see myself marrying a coffin-maker."

"But 'tis a job as good as a rope-maker's, which keeps you in your finery, and puts rabbit on the table!"

"Now don't raise your voice, dear, as 'twill more than likely bring on one of your fainting fits. 'Tis best the girl be honest. 'Taint you got to live with him," advised his wife.

"Now all that you've done," he continued, but in a calmer voice, though still far from agreeable, "is make me look a fool."

Oh, Alfred! Emma cried within. 'Twould matter not a spickle if you made coffins, or buried them in the ground. And if only you could support us, and would come to my parents, as this decent man has done, then I would not feel so unhappy.

"Fool?" came in his wife. "Fool? Why does she make you a fool when you do that yourself, with your ranting and bullying? She herself would be a fool if she accepted Bartholomew."

"And why be that? She bill not get a better offer, though she be as pretty as a snowdrop."

His wife's mouth shaped to say, "No!" when she saw Emma stand to tell the truth, but she was too late.

"I'd be a fool, 'tis certain, and I'd break the heart of my true love, who has already asked me to marry him, and 'twould shatter my heart to see him, having already accepted his proposal."

"What? You're pledged to another?" gasped her father.

"'Tis certain."

"And who be this man?"

"'Tis Alfred Morcombelake, and a better husband I cannot take, for he loves me as one only loves once in a lifetime. There. Now you know, and 'tis done. What else could I say to Bartholomew?"

"Say? *Say?* And will you tell Bartholomew in the time he allows you, or now? I will not let you make a fool of him."

With that, he left, leaving Emma to fall, sobbing, into the outstretched arms of her mother, who rocked her, and kissed comfortingly the top of her head.

"And why didn't you tell us?"

"It happened on May Day."

"But you've only just told me."

Emma sighed. If only Alfred were here, she wished, to take me away so that my father could not condemn me so.

"And what will father do now?"

"Go make his apologies to Bartholomew, who deserves the truth, now 'tas shed its skin and become the butterfly it should be."

"Poor Bartholomew! I think now I should have told him my answer proper, but father stood over me like Pilsdon Pen, and I thought if 'twas in the balance, the mist would lift, in time."

"I think you'd better bring your fiancé here, once your father be calm again. We a wedding to sort, so best meet the groom!"

But her mother's attempts to make her feel better did not succeed. Emma had to see Alfred; the next day was too far away.

It was early evening, and her mother's advice to return quickly as it was nearly dark made sense. Emma knew where he lived, and made her way towards his house. A man stopped and stared at her, and she refused to make eye contact. She felt him watching her as she passed him.

"Why in such a hurry?" he slurred, but she did not look back.

She had never been to Alfred's house, or seen his parents, but he had once shown her where he lived. They had always met out of the public gaze, though he had let his friends know she was his sweetheart, in case anyone tried to steal her from him. It was there, his house, on the left, down a dark alley, hiding from Bucky Doo, as if it should not be there.

There was little light in the alley, and she was afraid of turning her ankle on the cobblestones. She felt the wall with her left hand, to steady herself, as a man who is returning home from the inn. A rat ran past her, scaring her with a squeal. And he lives here, my husband-to-be? Such a man lives here in this darkness?

She knocked: two raps of her knuckles. The door rattled. She listened for movement inside, but heard none, though she sensed someone behind it, waiting, perhaps fearful of a visitor at that time of night.

Her knocking had hurt her knuckles, so she called, "I've come to see Alfred Morcombelake, if he be here. 'Tis Emma Broadoak come to see him. Tell him it be important."

A key turned, and she stepped back. The door opened a couple of inches, and weak lamplight slipped through the gap.

"Who be it?" called a man from the back of the room.

"What 'ee want?" asked the man who had unlocked the door, which opened enough to reveal three men sitting round a table, on which were cups and a vial of dark liquid.

Emma could smell a foul odour: stale sweat, alcohol, burning coals, and something pungent, which made her take a step backwards. She looked beyond the man at the door to the others slouching in their chairs, their eyes smudged, lidless, as if about to fall out of their sockets, down their cheeks, and onto the floor.

"I've come to see Alfred Morcombelake, who lives here," Emma said.

The person at the door, a gaunt man with dark eyes and a black mouth, shook his head, maintaining his lifeless stare at her.

"There be no man or woman of that name here," he said.

The others swayed in their seats, finding it difficult to remain upright.

"Yes, 'tis here he lives with his parents. He told me, pointed to this house, said he lived here," she insisted.

"Then you best come in and wait for him," invited the man.

He cackled at her, and she stepped backwards, frightened.

"She coming in?" called one of his cronies. "Let her come in, and she can sit on my knee!"

"No, mine!" said another.

"Mine!" argued the third.

The three got up to join the party, but Emma ran away, somehow floated over the cobbles and back home. Out of breath, she stopped. There was no sign of the grotesque group, and she knew she had to compose herself lest she scare her mother. She wondered whether she had mistaken the house. No, she was sure it was the one Alfred had shown her, but she had never seen him enter or leave.

She had arranged to meet him by the church on the road to Bridport Harbour, the next day. Then she would tell him about Bartholomew's proposal, challenge him about the weird men down the alley, and he would explain things to her complete satisfaction, would find work, marry her, make her happy again.

Yet, the next day, she was unhappy. Her father had caught up with Bartholomew, and told him the truth.

"Say something, then, even if it is to abuse me!" had said Mr. Broadoak.

"I am a coffin-maker, a truthful, honest worker, and what I said stands. Let her take her time, for I promised her weeks, not days, but weeks may stretch to months, for I keep my promises. 'Tis a blow you deal me, but making coffins helps me to prepare for bad news. Every time the doorbell rings at my workshop, it be to tell me someone else has died. Emma hasn't died, so I goes on. That's what I does, go on, which be my way, till a son of mine builds me my own box," Bartholomew had replied, continuing on his way.

Emma went up to her room. Half-expecting her father to come and protest again, she locked the door. She replayed in her mind Alfred leaping into the lane and scratching himself, his demonstrative proposal, and his promise to find work to keep them, but that pleasure was diluted by her puzzlement at him not living where he said.

She stepped inside the graveyard, at the agreed hour, not wishing to attract attention. She read some of the headstones, the loving tributes chiselled on them. Who will write such words for me? she wondered.

Alfred arrived, approached her warily. Not daring to imagine that matters could be worse, she threw herself into his arms, which encircled her loosely. When it came, his kiss was void of its customary ardour, and his eyes did not close, as they normally did.

"Is something the matter?" she asked. "Do you have something important to say, as well as me?"

"I do, but there is nothing for you to worry about."

"Then why is your face a mask? 'Tis not yours as I know it."

"If 'tis a mask, I will change it, I swear. Now, come, tell me the news which robs you of your halo."

Emma shook her head.

"Play not with your poet's words, which fall upon deaf ears today. I be no more saint than you be sinner."

"I be no sinner, though you be nearer to God than me. Now, what is it that troubles you?"

"I have received a proposal of marriage from a good man." Alfred let her go, took a step backwards, and his brow furrowed. "My father brought him, and I, of course, refused him, being engaged to you, but when I came to your house to tell you, to be comforted by you, I found foul, old, leering men hunched over a table, drinking a strange potion."

"Tell me they touched you, and I will kill each one with my bare hands!"

"Oh, Alfred! Why were *they* there and not you? Did I mistake the house? You do live down that alley you showed me, don't you?"

He shook his head.

"I have lied to you, dearest, but hear me out. I showed you that house when you and I were not promised to each other, and did not know that we would, one day, be pledged. 'Tis a grave matter, to take home a fiancée," he explained.

"And that be all? No other reason?" she probed.

"'Twas the action of a youth, and not the man I will become when I have told you of my decision."

"And that be what carved your mask of white stone so?"

"'Tis certain."

"Then end this suffering, and tell, for I am innocent in all this."

"Dearest, I said I would find a profession, and I have."

Her face lit up, but his did not.

"Then, excellent news, Alfred!"

"'Tis passing excellent, though hear me more. I have the chance to study, and become learned, and then I will return, and we will be married."

"Return? You're going away?"

"I am going to Wells to learn Greek and Latin, and then we can live comfortably. I can build a school here. I have heard of towns and cities where poor children can learn to read and write."

"But may I come with you? I am frightened we will grow apart."

"No," he declared. "I am doing this for us, and I will save the money I earn when I give tuition. Besides, we are not married, and would not get lodgings. I am no farmer, no rope-maker, like your father, but I am drawn to words, know their letters, and want to give them to others."

"Then you have my blessing. When will you go?"

"Early, tomorrow."

She recognised guilt in his eyes. It was all so sudden, his plan, only days after their engagement. There was not even time for him to meet her parents.

"So soon."

"The coach for Wells leaves The Red Heifer at eight. Let this be our parting, not full of sorrow but hope."

"But how long will you be gone?"

"I know not, but I will write often. Till we see each other again, remember me by this kiss."

And then he was gone.

Chapter Seven

Edgar was conscious of Winifred swaying ever so slightly, as if she had been nudged by a zephyr, in front of him, and when he tried to ease Cressida away from him, so that he could release Winifred, she gripped him more tightly, horrified that she had found a suicide in the barn.

"I must get her down," he said firmly, prising Cressida off. "She can't stay there. Will you run like a deer and fetch your father? Warn him well, as 'tis a sorry sight to see a young maid on the end of a rope."

Cressida inched to the light, careful not to turn and face Winifred.

"I will, though I fear we must all look into our hearts honestly when we try to fathom the reason for this."

Edgar put the chair back into position. How he wished that he could reverse time so that she could be revived! She could remove the noose that had bitten into her broken neck, and step down from the chair on which she had tied the slip-knot. Then she could resume her milking, albeit in solitude.

He stepped up, and the chair wobbled, forcing him to grab her arms to steady himself, just as Cressida had clung to him. Winifred's hands were cold. He put his cheek to her lips, as if permitting her one final, passionless kiss, to detect any faint breathing, but there was none. The knot was tight and could not be loosened until he had lifted and rested her across his left shoulder, leaving his right hand free to tug.

"Come down now, girl, and let me lay you on your straw mattress. 'Tis no place up here, a-dangling from a beam, no matter how much you too far gone."

Down he stepped, and carefully put her on the straw. If I cover her, will she warm up, find a spark to bring herself back to life? No matter how much he tried, he could find no suitable pose for her to soften the agony of death set in her face and limbs.

"Winifred, girl, how could I have known how desperate you were in that field? How could I have explained my refusal to take you? They would have been meagre words. And now I must walk around the rest of my days with the image of you suffering before my eyes. And yet others left you here alone too long, with only the tantrums of cows to occupy you. Why, 'twas passing cruel to have sent away Billy Eype and his hoydens and not replaced them before now. And so others, too, must share my guilt," he opined.

While he waited, he reflected upon the contrast between the warmth of Cressida's body against him, and Winifred's hardening coldness, and on how quickly our heat disappears. New milkmaids were waiting to work, but now they had to begin with the shadow of death lurking in the barn.

His reverie was disturbed by the rattling of a cart's wheels, and the snorting of a horse whipped into a hurry. Yeoman was the first to appear, then Cressida. Clementine had stayed to delay the new milkmaids, to find a reason for Winifred's disappearance.

"Well, 'taint what should happen to a maid, 'tis certain," began Yeoman.

Cressida hung back, fearful of looking upon Winifred's death mask.

"Too young to go, too lonely to stay," said Edgar.

"Lonely?" echoed Yeoman.

"Yes, lonely, father. She been up here all on her own too long.

Too many cows to milk and manage. Up in the cold dawn without a human word for her to listen to."

"'Twas Billy Eype's fault. I spent all my time sorting out his little games. But this? She didn't have to do this, did she, for want of a bit of company?"

"She is Mr. Porlock's cousin," Cressida informed him.

"Then I be truly sorry. 'Taint the way things should be, 'tis certain. And though sadness sits on your shoulders like a heavy cloak, you must help me carry her onto the cart. I will take her to the church, where she can rest, till a coffin can be made to fit her."

Edgar was quickly onto his feet; he would carry her, gently, as if she really were his cousin. Cressida stood back to allow him room out of the barn, and he laid Winifred carefully on the cart.

"I will remove her possessions," Cressida told her father.

"'Tis a good thing. We don't want the new girls all afraid afore they even touched an udder."

Hastily, the few signs that Winifred had lived there were removed, and Edgar untied the knot that had squeezed her neck. 'Tis all it takes, he reflected. 'Tis a slender thread of breath we live by, barely as wide as a spider's yarn.

This erasure of all signs of Winifred's existence they worked at together, for the sake of the new milkmaids. Cressida stayed close to Edgar, avoiding dark corners, as she sensed the deed hanging in the barn like a stubborn November mist lingering in the vale.

"And what shall we do with this?" asked Cressida, holding up a rag doll, which was under Winifred's blanket.

This was Winifred's home-made companion: untidy stitching, sparse sheep's wool for hair.

"Put it in her case. 'Twas her only friend, most like, a-waiting her return, each day," Edgar speculated.

Again, tears welled in Cressida's eyes.

"Oh, 'tis too much to bear!" she cried, instinctively going to Edgar for comfort.

He held her close, absorbing the shock of her convulsive sobbing. With his right hand, he stroked the back of her head.

"'Taint you or me gone, so we must temper our grief to deal with the living as well as the dead," he advised.

She tried to control her shuddering by slipping her hands inside his coat; not ready yet to face him, she was reassured by his warmth, his heartbeat in her ear on his chest. His lips were resting on her hair, not quite kissing it. This should not be, he told himself, yet 'tis natural. Then she looked up at him, seemed to wait an eternity for him to wipe her lips glistening with her tears.

"Geoffrey," he reminded her. "Today been more than a step to the hoar a-coming. Sometimes a death does strange things to a body."

Edgar looked at the gaping doorway, and thought: if he walked in now, he would fall upon me with his sword, yet my lips would utter no regret, no apology, for what is Providence.

"There can be no wedding, and, though I have known it for some time, today has made me admit it to someone else. He bursts with his own exploits, boasts about his skill as a horseman and hunter. He can be kind yet behave like a warrior from the Middle Ages. My mother and father say it will pass, that he will mature like a wheel of blue vinney, but he has doused my heart with his lack of tenderness."

"You are upset at Winifred's death. 'Tis true that, like many others who live these parts, she felt at the mercy of her solitude and poverty, but we are all alone, to a lesser or greater degree. Do not let her passing make you act in haste."

"You are wise, and your words are bluebells in a dark, overgrown wood. Will you stay and manage the farm for my father? You must not leave me," she implored.

"I am no farmer, yet I lack work."

"My father and mother knew you, years ago, and there is some memory between you which breeds affection, but you are different from them. You will stay and be my protector?"

"I will," he pledged.

She closed her eyes, and kissed him lightly on his motionless lips.

"You should not have done that," he whispered.

"'Tis natural. Wash your lips in the stream if you are poisoned."

Edgar looked beyond her, and she saw that he had noticed someone there, so she, too, looked over her shoulder, as an owl does.

"You betray me in the barn still reeking of suicide?" said Geoffrey, quietly. "This be a tableau that has destroyed my sleep for some time."

"I have not betrayed you, Geoffrey, for I have never loved you but merely thought I did. You have more than adequate affection for yourself."

Cressida stood by Edgar's side, and Geoffrey understood completely.

"I had come to offer you help," he said, "but I see you have more than enough. And you, sir, I believe are the man I thrashed within an inch of his life, in the lane. I should have finished you off, but it would have merely postponed this day. Look carefully to her, sir, for she has betrayed me, and will, 'ere she meets you at the altar, dally with another. 'Tis her nature. She dances pretty enough, matches your steps well, but when the reel flings you apart, she smiles and flutters at her admirers. Look carefully to her, sir, and take it not amiss when I say that, though your magpie's plumage intrigues her now, she will flit to another branch when your feathers are *all* snowy. And you, Cressida, must explain yourself to your parents, for I shall never set foot on Symondsbury soil again, and would ask you to stay away from Burton-Bradstock land."

With that, he turned, mounted his horse, and, without his customary whoop, rode away.

Cressida looked up into Edgar's eyes.

"'Tis a day I shall never forget," she said.

"'Tis certain."

"Come, let us finish our task. The milkmaids must sleep here tonight."

They finished gathering Winifred's belongings, and hid them under straw in a corner too dismal to be of interest or use to the new girls. The last item was the rope, which he took into the wood and threw away, leaving it like a long dead snake in the grass.

Back at the manor, the maids had been told by Clementine that Winifred had left of her own accord. It seemed a plausible explanation.

Yeoman summoned the vicar, from Bridport. The vicar, in turn, sent a note to Bartholomew, who had in stock a coffin he had fashioned for a man who had been, he had been assured, breathing his laboured last. The man clinging so desperately to life had made such a rapid recovery that he was soon able to sit upright, following a rushed prayer by the vicar, who had not wished to protract his visit and himself catch the disease which had carried off so many other parishioners. So it was that the coffin arrived at Symondsbury church with indecent haste, and that Winifred was put inside it. The lid was not nailed down but rested on top, in case anyone wanted to pay their last respects.

"There is one matter," the vicar told Yeoman, "and I have no room to accommodate an alternative point of view."

"Speak it, then. If it is the Lord's wish, then fear not the utterance of it. 'Tas been a long and trying day, and my hunger bites me like a mastiff."

"The girl has no relatives?"

"She be Beaminster, and came to us all alone. No one been to see her, save her cousin, who's not seen her for years. Never mentioned her family."

"Then I must tell you that I cannot give her a Christian burial, on account of she took her own life, which God had given her. Never seen her a-bowed in a pew. Seemed she was in a hurry to go."

"Good worker, though. Held the cows together in high water or drought. One by one, she milked them, and her pails made cream, butter, and cheese for Briddy. I'll not see her buried outside the church boundary," insisted Yeoman.

"I would be replaced by the bishop if he discovered I had allowed her to rest in consecrated ground."

"Then we'll not tell a soul, and this shall buy your ignorance of how she died."

Yeoman counted out money into the vicar's hand, and the weight of it suppressed his sense of ecclesiastical obligation.

"Yet we all know that God forgives sinners," said the vicar, "so I shall instruct the grave-digger to prepare a modest plot under the yew tree in the far corner. 'Twill not attract attention. I assume there will be no headstone."

Yeoman shook his head.

"No. No headstone. The words on it would strike at my family, and I'll not have that. You must deal with it. Bury her as soon as possible, though common decency allows her a night in the chapel."

The vicar nodded. A quick calculation revealed that, by the time he had paid Bartholomew and the grave-digger, there would be enough left to have a new hat and cloak made in Dorchester.

Yeoman spoke privately to Clementine, who had paved the way for the maids' smooth transfer into the barn. They were all experienced, and would need no call to warn them of the time for the first milking of the next day.

"And there is one thing, Yeoman. I told Geoffrey where Cressida was, but he did not return with her. I asked her whither he had fled, and she said back to where he belongs. She had been crying, I could see. I told her that he was invited to join us for dinner, but she sneered, and said, 'he will never eat with us again.'"

This was too much for Yeoman.

"How dare she treat him like that! His family are of good stock and worthy neighbours. Their land kisses ours four miles hence, a snugness which breeds cordiality between his parents and us. Yet we are ready to sup, and 'twould spoil the life of the table for our guest. In the morning, we shall speak privately with her, and she will explain herself."

The meal began solemnly, as if Winifred's ghost occupied a place at the table. Yeoman spoke of his plans for the renaissance of the farm, and hinted at the acts of immorality that had devastated his workforce. Cressida ate slowly, speaking only to respond to others, and never beginning a new topic. Edgar thought it wise not to refer to the May Day dance again, lest they thought he was using it to secure their favour, and confined his utterances to Cressida to matters relating to the history of the manor, and to her horse.

"You may retire to your room," Yeoman told her, when the last crumbs of cake had gone. "In the morning, your mother and I will speak with you in the library, at nine."

Cressida said nothing, a quick, uneasy glance at Edgar her only acknowledgement of what had passed between them.

"And will you give serious consideration to my offer? My need to revive the farm is urgent, and though you lack practical experience, you, I know, possess moral integrity and an appetite for work. I have friends, merchants, farmers, who will teach you. Our meeting in Dorchester, after all these years, will be of mutual benefit. And let not this girl's death delay your decision. A cousin she may be, but there must undoubtedly have been reasons unrelated to her work which drove her to take her own life."

"I thank you for inviting me here and being most generous in your hospitality. We share happy memories from our youth, and my intervention in Dorchester was fortuitously what brought us together again. I shall sleep on your offer. It is true that I was looking for work, but I am less convinced than you that I would make a good farmer. I do not wish to raise false hopes in you."

Clementine smiled weakly, stifled a yawn, and rose.

"The day has been arduous, and I long for sleep to erase the sadness surrounding the young maid's death. I shall retire now.

Yeoman, show our guest to his room, and send up a maid to feed the fire with a faggot or two. The night is chilly."

She departed, leaving Yeoman to do as asked.

Edgar lay down on his bed. The wine had made him drowsy, but he could not fall asleep, not while he could still feel Cressida's tears on his lips, and her hair on his cheeks. He had not intended to comfort her with such empathy, but she had clung to him tightly. Only a real physical effort would have deterred her.

The fire was dozing, and the oil lamp's flame had shrunk. He draped his coat across a chair, and took off his boots. How his feet ached! On his table was a Bible and two other books. He flicked through one: poems, the author unknown to him. The other, a history of the manor, including a plan of the rooms. I am too tired to read, which be a sign of my age and not the themes, he lamented.

Then came a knock at the door. What if it be Cressida? She should not come to my room, not make assumptions about me in her state of release from her engagement.

"Who is it?" he called.

"'Tis only I come to fatten the fire. If the wind blows in the night, you will feel draughts as raw as any outside. There be a faggot or two in my basket, and they will stay awake till you end your sleep, in the morning."

This was the girl Clementine told her husband to send.

"Come in," called Edgar.

There was no reply, and no immediate entrance, but hesitation. Outside, an owl screeched. Edgar felt conscious of his bare feet, and slipped his shoes on again.

The woman entered, glanced at him, and made straight to the hearth, where she knelt, back to him, and looked at the fire, assessing where the first of the two faggots might best be placed. The second fitted more snugly, and the fire crackled as if annoyed that it should be disturbed so late at night.

Edgar looked for money. His bag had been stolen, but he found her a coin in his pocket.

"I have nothing much to give for your troubles," he said.

She stopped on her way out.

"Troubles, sir?" she asked, turning to him.

"The fire. We should not take each other for granted."

"The fire be no trouble, sir. For a moment, I thought you were talking about the other troubles."

Confused, Edgar lowered his arm.

"I know not of your troubles, nor wish to pry."

"No, sir, 'tis certain you don't, which be the way with men."

Her tone had hardened, become tempered with bitterness, which Edgar felt was connected with him.

"Not all men are the same. I am Edgar Porlock. What is your name? Put whatever offence I've given you in the light so I may apologise."

"That is exactly why I say what I say, for you baint Edgar Porlock at all but Alfred Morcombelake."

"And how do you know that?" he gasped.

"Because I am Flora, the girl you used, years ago, and I shall never forget you or your name."

Edgar examined her face, and there were still lines to it and the rest of her recognisable as ones that had once attracted him.

"But we were young. The young slip in and out of love as easily as a hand into a glove."

Flora shook her head.

"And 'tis true that you slipped in and out of me, and that I never seen you again till tonight, when I sees you a-passing through the hall."

"Let us be friends, Flora. I am a different person. Things change."

"Yes, they do, Alfred, and my life changed after I been your glove, and 'tis time you heard what slipping in and out can do to a maid."

Chapter Eight

The story he told his mother and father was the one to which Emma, too, had listened. He deliberately kept quiet his engagement to her, and his parents were pleased that he had set his sights on studying, so that he might return to Bridport, one day, a man so learned that the town's children would be able to go to school, and have the scales of ignorance peeled from their eyes.

His mother, who had taught him to read and write, was especially proud, though devastated that his chair at the table would be empty. His father took it badly, too, wanted to encourage him, and knew that the day he would leave was approaching, as his own had done, years earlier. He also felt prematurely the space Alfred would leave in his life, heard the silence under the beams, suspected the change it would bring in his relationship with his wife.

"Look after yourself, son," said his father, hugging him.

When Alfred withdrew, he saw his father's pain.

"Mother," said Alfred, inviting her into his arms.

"You got everything? Don't want to get to Wells beout your pen and ink," she sniffed.

Then he went with a wave, a smile, and his bag, to catch the coach.

The next day, a knock came on the Morcombelakes' door.

"That Alfred back already?" feebly quipped Stephen.

"Doubt it. A son don't knock on his own door 'less he worried he done wrong, and even if he back because his mind swivelled, 'taint a reason to knock."

But it was not Alfred. A conversation ensued on the doorstep. Stephen could hear voices, but Hannah had pulled the door almost shut, so that he could not hear what was being said. The young woman spoke earnestly, and when Hannah told her that Alfred no longer lived there but had gone to Wells, the girl pleaded, "Then, pray, let me have his address so that I can write to him."

"That be a spickle difficult," said Hannah, "as we ourselves don't yet know it."

This was too much for the girl, who burst into tears, and left, promising, "Then I shall come a-calling soon enough, and 'tis to be hoped he's written to 'ee by then!"

Hannah returned indoors. What the girl had said, Hannah decided to keep to herself, for the moment. Though the girl had seemed sincere enough, Hannah knew the wiles some women would use to catch their man.

"And who be that who knocks so early?" asked Stephen.

"A woman come a-selling her little posies. Gypsy girl, I reckons, who be passing through. Pulls a face when I says I aint got money to spend on what I can pick myself in the fields."

Stephen fastened his boots. And there was me a-hoping Alfred a-changed his mind, and come home to be a rope-maker like me, he wished. Plenty of work, too: navy, fishing boats, farmers. Hangman use it, so they say. Symondsbury estate take miles of it!

Meanwhile, Alfred was walking down a steep hill towards the sea. The sun and a few clouds had dappled the water with green, blue, and black patches. He quickened his step. This was a new place for him, strange yet feeling familiar. The cobbles were encrusted with dried mud and straw. He had left the inn, halfway up the street, after a breakfast of bacon and hard bread. Full of hope, he had stepped out into the light. Now he had to find work, a roof over his head. The money he had would not last for ever.

He knew no one. Weymouth had been his first choice, but Frederick had once said that there were too many cutthroats and smugglers there.

"You'd know who they were, lad, by their appearance. Eyes a-skitting about as if all of an itch, looking for the Revenue. Legs as bowed as a chicken's wishbone, from catching their balance when the ship been lurching this way and that in a swell," he had warned.

So though some big ships sailed from Weymouth, mainly to ports along the coast, and a few to France, now that secret trading had been re-established, Alfred had chosen Lyme Regis as his temporary refuge. It was not Wells, as he had told Emma and his parents. That had been to lay a false scent so that mistakes he had made in Bridport could not follow him like hounds a fox.

Lyme Regis was the port from which he intended to sail, work his passage to a new life. Along the seafront strolled a few women on the arms of their husbands. A few hundred yards away was the Cobb, against which fishing boats fidgeted to the pulse of the wind. He was prepared to wait for a good berth, hoped that one would present itself sooner rather than later.

Gulls fussed around the fishing boats. On the quayside, lobster pots were studded with barnacles. In Alfred's nostrils and mouth was the salty air. He watched men going to and fro across a plank to the *Lyonesse*. Preparations to sail were under way, and Alfred saw that each man knew his job, worked tirelessly.

"I'm looking for the Captain," Alfred said to a hand, who had just turned a barrel of rum on its side, and was at pains to roll it up the slope to the ship.

"And there he be," pointed out the man. "You looking for work, you come just right, as we be short, as some baint returning, on account, most probly, of them all a-cosy with their women-folk. But 'tis for the best, as a sailor who got only a woman's slippery silk purse on his mind be bad for the crew, as he day-dreams of firing his matchlock inside her, morn to night."

"May I come aboard?"

"If you want the skipper to put a bullet between your eyes, you may. Wait here. I'll stack the last barrel, and then I'll have a word with him."

The Captain looked down at Alfred, consulted his pocket watch, and said something to his hand, before beckoning Alfred to come up.

"You looking for work?" the Captain asked.

"Yes, sir."

"What a-been your last ship?"

"The *Lovely Emma*."

The Captain narrowed his eyes, and sniffed suspiciously.

"'Taint a ship I've come across." Alfred shrugged. The Captain picked up the end of a rope, and said, "Now tie me a reef knot."

Alfred did not know where to start. His father had shown him, many times, how to tie several knots, but he had not been interested, and had soon forgotten them.

"I'm afraid, sir, you've caught me out, so I'll tell it plain. I've never been to sea, but want to work. Will you take me with you? I'm strong and learn quickly."

The Captain sighed, having heard this a thousand times.

"Grip my hand as hard as you can." Alfred did so, and the Captain cried, "Hold! Don't crush my fingers!"

"I'm sorry."

The Captain wriggled them; there was a cracking of joints, but he declared his bones unbroken.

"Now climb up that there rope ladder to the top, and come down to me as quickly as you can."

Alfred attacked the ladder, and when he got to the top, he felt the wind jostling him. Looking down, he realised how high he was. The mast creaked and swayed as the boat moved, and Alfred tried to imagine the feeling of being up there when the sea was heavy.

Down he came, placing his feet carefully in the rungs. The Captain looked at his watch, and nodded.

"Not bad. You a name?"

"Alfred Morcombelake."

"Well, Alfred Morcombelake, I'll be honest. Some of my regulars gone soft. That's what a woman does to you, lad: makes you go all flabby. And a man at sea could go mad thinking about what a-waiting him at home. You married?" Alfred shook his head. "Then 'tis well, as you be one of my men now, for the moment, and we set sail for Porlock within the hour. Take my hand on it, only not so hard, this time!"

"Is Porlock far across the sea?"

The Captain laughed.

"'Tis round the end of England, on the coast of Somerset. 'Taint as exotic as some places, but 'tis passing pretty, though, like most things worth anything, there be plenty of work to do afore we gets there. There be rocks to miss, and strong currents we must ride, or the *Lyonesse* will be shattered into splinters, and we'll be supper for the fishies!"

The colour drained from Alfred's face. It was the expression the Captain had seen many times. It was best to let the new man know the worst now. Weak legs and a weaker stomach were of no use to a crew in a storm.

"And the wages, sir?" asked Alfred, timidly.

The Captain guffawed, and cried, "Wages? 'Ee'll be paid according to your use. Go find a man called Chard. 'E be a bull: wide, muscular shoulders from lifting cargo, and legs like tree stumps. Mind you don't upset him, though. 'E can be a nasty bugger when riled. He'll show you your bunk, tell you your watch. And make sure you're on time. 'E been known to rip a man's shirt off his back, and flog him for being late."

Chard found Alfred before Alfred found him. Other sailors

moved mechanically, scurrying all over the ship like worker ants. The sooner they set sail, the sooner they would arrive at their destination, and be paid. Chard's manner was not as Alfred had expected; not morose but animated, interested.

"You the new hand?" he asked, quietly.

"Yes, sir. The Captain asked me to report to a man called Chard."

"That be me. You ever sailed before, son?"

The term of affection surprised Alfred, but Chard's physique was as the Captain had described it. Though not tall, Chard's muscles were twice the thickness of an ordinary man's.

"First time, sir."

Chard eyed him from top to toe, as if assessing his suitability for sailing, his worth as a man. It was not a hostile scrutiny but one that led to further questions.

"A man can go to sea to work and earn money, or he can be running away from something, anything from the hangman's noose or loneliness. Why be you a-joining the *Lyonesse*, which be mostly full of homeless wanderers, men who forgotten their roots?"

Alfred flinched just enough to let him know. He shuffled, hung his head slightly, could not think quickly enough to deceive this man in whom the Captain put so much trust.

"No work at Bridport save the land, which be so still that I think I've died when I'm on it. Just the rope factory otherwise, where my father works. 'Taint the whole world, Briddy," explained Alfred. "Just a spickle."

Chard smiled and said, "'Tis what most say, though all tell me the truth by the time we pull into port again. Now let me show you your hammock. Today you'll fetch and carry, do odd jobs. The night watch needs a sharp eye, and you be new to this, so sleep tonight. You'll get your chance soon enough to stay awake on deck, and hear the ropes and timbers creak so much you'll think they can stretch no more but snap and shatter."

The sleeping quarters were cramped and lit by an oil lantern swinging from a beam, casting swooping shadows, even at that time of day.

"There," pointed Chard. "That be yours."

Alfred dropped his bag underneath his hammock, and joined his shipmates, loading boxes and barrels.

The men toiled, speaking only when necessary, and soon there was nothing else to do but wind down and assemble on deck, ready for departure. A few people had gathered to watch the *Lyonesse* go, her sails now flapping excitedly, noisily straining to resist the strengthening wind.

The Captain appeared on deck, and all eyes turned to him. Chard took up his customary position behind him, arms folded like a reef knot.

"In a moment, I shall ask Chard to raise the anchor and untie the moorings. You all know your jobs. The weather be kind as a mother, at the moment, but she can summon up a temper, and give us a tongue-lashing at any time, so be prepared. No a-tampering with the cargo. Anyone found doing so will be tied up for the rest of the voyage and taken to the nearest gaol after pulling in. Now, fellows, this ship baint called the *Lyonesse* for nothing. *Lyonesse* a-been once a kingdom of Cornwall, so 'tis said, and 'tis now asleep at the bottom of the sea. Now I don't know about you, but I be a superstitious bugger and believe that this ship will, one day, return to its namesake, but not under *my* watch. I repeat: not under *my* watch. You all know what I mean by that: you jump when I or Chard says. Chard, take over, and let's put to sea."

Some of the men had heard the Captain's stirring speeches before, but still let rise a cheer that could be heard in town. Alfred, too, found his voice, and, within minutes, all thoughts of the wounds he had inflicted in Bridport had vanished.

"Morcombelake," called Chard. "The Captain wants his cabin all clean and ship-shape, and when 'ee done that, 'ee can do mine, which be less grand but still needing a wipe and a brush."

"Yes, sir."

"Chard be what they all call me."

"Yes, Chard. Sir – I mean, Chard – will I learn how to navigate, see the charts we follow? I would be interested to see them, so that, one day, I might be a skipper."

Chard frowned.

"No, Morcombelake. Not this trip. You only been on the ship two minutes! Tell me how many times you sat up there?"

Chard pointed to the crow's nest, near the top of the mast.

"Why, never!"

"Precisely. So you've never looked out for danger: storms, whales, other vessels. It takes time to learn, build up confidence and experience. Too much ambition be just as dangerous to a man as too little. Now, follow my orders, and start on the Captain's cabin."

Chard pointed out the two cabins, and the cupboard where the cleaning materials were stored.

Alfred entered the Captain's room after knocking three times and getting no answer. There was the mahogany writing desk, on which the ship's log was open. On a second table was a navigational chart, a scroll unfurled and kept flat by a tankard at one end and a book at the other. An open oak chest was in the corner, and in it were clothes, ready to be taken out and worn. On the wall was a wooden cross, no great feat of carpentry but two pieces of roughly hewn wood nailed together, almost certainly the work of the Captain himself. The window, not quite the width of the ship, looked onto the vast expanse of sea and the ship's wake.

Firstly, Alfred cleaned the windows, paying particular attention to the corners, where moisture had made a paste with grime. Then he swept the floor, on which a carpet was laid in the middle, to add a bit of warmth and colour. Slowly, he moved towards the desk. Try as he might, he could not keep his eyes from the Captain's log. The handwriting was neat and legible. I imagine the ship's owners require it so, to keep an eye on their investment, thought Alfred.

He noted that, though the Captain had complained that several hands had failed to return to the ship, he was pleased to have recruited a number of 'decent enough men, including one Alfred Morcombelake, a young man with bright blue eyes and an air of a good upbringing about him.' Alfred smiled, surprised and pleased to have made such a good impression.

He had become quickly used to the erratic pitching of the ship. Only the lurching which came when a strong cross-current was met troubled him, when it seemed to slow down the ship and resist the course on which the Captain had set her. Alfred's gait resembled the stagger of a drunkard, and now, in the Captain's cabin, he chose to sit down and flick through the pages to previous voyages, to peruse the stories recorded. He found the names of men who had fallen overboard and from the rigging, and one who had even died from a pistol shot.

Then he began to read the most compelling narrative of all. The ship had been bound for Brittany, and a disease had broken out, taking the lives of several poor souls. The Captain had anchored a mile off shore, and a boat had rowed out to meet them. The French had refused to offer medical assistance and leave to land and fill the hold with brandy and wine. The Captain had begged them to help, but they had refused, fearful that the disease would spread. The names of the dead had been recorded carefully, and the dates on which their bodies were buried at sea noted. Alfred read those names several times, and looked up at the wooden cross. There, last of all, the Captain had made special mention of his own son, who had selflessly tended to the sick, before himself giving in to the disease.

It was then that the door opened, and the Captain entered. Startled, Alfred jumped out of the seat, and said, "I'm sorry, Captain, but I couldn't resist reading about that voyage when all those poor men were lost to sickness. It must have been a terrible time for you."

The Captain bowed his head, as if the memory had returned all too quickly, and had dampened his anger at Alfred.

"And is this the way you clean my room?" he croaked.

"I'm sorry. I truly am. But I was interested to know what a Captain writes."

"No doubt you were, but you had no right to pry. That log is between me and the owners."

"Yes, Captain."

"And I suppose you read what I wrote about you."

"Yes, Captain."

The Captain took his chair, and invited Alfred to pull up another, an act of unexpected conciliation.

"Somerset be a day or two away yet. What will you do when we arrive?"

"Come back with you, I hope, Captain."

The Captain shook his head, and said, "No, Alfred, it cannot be. I will not bring you back. You are meant for better things, as was my son. These other men, they were all born to this, but you, no. And you are on this ship to escape something, I suspect, and that is the wrong reason for being here. You have an enquiring mind, untypical of the common sailor. Put it to better use, as my son should have done."

Alfred dropped his head, and yielded.

"'Tis true, though my shame prevents me from telling you why. I wish for a new life, and this seemed as good a start as any. I must lose my name, and be lost to Bridport for ever. 'Tis the only way."

The Captain smiled.

"Then let your name be Porlock, the place where we next drop anchor."

"'Tis passing clever, though I must lose Alfred, too."

The Captain rose and paced up and down his cabin. Twice he glanced up at the wooden cross, seeming to wrestle with an idea, closed his logbook, and went to his window.

"The corners are clean," he remarked, running his fingers over the tar seals.

"Thank 'ee."

It was Alfred's turn to smile.

"Edgar Isambard," the skipper said, at last. "Edgar Isambard Porlock."

"Thank 'ee for christening me anew."

Two days later, when Alfred had said goodbye to the Captain and Chard, and had disembarked with more money than was his due, the niggling suspicion that he had heard his first two names somewhere before grew. Yes, he remembered, at last. They were in the logbook, and belonged to one of the dead men. Slowly, he realised whom he had become. Why, he has named me after his own son, who, through me, lives again! I shall take care of that name for I believe that Edgar Isambard must have been a good man, just like his father.

Chapter Nine

Flora did not raise her voice when she told her story. Not wishing to draw attention to her presence in the room, she spoke quickly the words she had rehearsed many times in the intervening years. The temptation to convey the different emotions she had suffered – loss, unrequited love, anger, and humiliation – she resisted. He was a guest, and she would not risk jeopardising her position there. The facts would speak for themselves in due course.

As she spoke, there were questions Edgar wished to ask, but she did not allow him the chance to get close to her. He had forfeited the right to know her full history; there were other people who had to give their permission, too, to reveal everything.

He trembled, had not expected all this. Winifred had left his life, after a brief inclusion, and Flora had returned to it, within hours of each other. And in the morning, he must commit to managing the farm and seeing Flora often, or leaving again. It was an agonising choice, and he covered his face with both hands, in shame.

"So I am a father," he whispered.

All these years, I could have loved my child, looked at its smiling eyes, felt its tiny fingers inquisitively touch my face, and now I cannot, for it is an adult, and Flora will not tell me his or her name. And it will despise me, he lamented, for abandoning it, and will not accept my ignorance of its existence as a reason for my disappearance. There is now a hole in me where it could have, *should* have, lived; I am an empty well.

"I must go, or I will be missed in the kitchen. You have done more than enough to damage my reputation for one lifetime," she said, with a chilling note of finality.

"Stay a moment longer, and tell me we will speak again. There are things I must know so that I can say and do the right things. What you have told me changes everything."

"For you, perhaps, but not me. Your coming back is years too late. My heart no longer hears music in the blackbird's song, or sees beauty in the sunset over Pilsdon. My heart is a grate of cold ashes."

With that, she left.

He tried to think logically. There must have been conversations, undoubtedly, between Emma and Flora, after I had gone. Emma must have discovered the reason for my failure to write and return: that I had betrayed her with Flora. They must all have learned the truth. My parents, Emma, her parents, and, of course, Flora and her family. And my reputation is now a scarecrow. If Farmer Frederick Canonicorum still lives, he will not welcome me back, though he once took a special interest in me. All must now know about the child, and I am the last to.

In bed, the candle extinguished, he thought ahead to the morning, and the answer he must give Yeoman. To run away again would be an act of cowardice. I am no longer that callow youth, and I must face life as it is, or I can never be the person I wish to be, he told himself. I will stay. I came back, and I must do whatever is necessary, or my life will never be peaceful.

He half-expected Flora to appear when the first knocks came on the door. Instead, there stood Yeoman.

"I've brought you breakfast. 'Tis late, and the table be cleared. You must have been tired," he said.

Edgar rubbed his eyes, stifled a growing yawn.

"I have abused your hospitality. Forgive me. I will be quickly dressed."

"You have considered my offer? I need a man I can trust."

Trust: not so readily won but easily lost, thrown away, even, Edgar mused. But he had another reason for staying now, and said, "I'll learn. I know little of farming, but I will try my best. As soon as I've eaten my breakfast, I'll go to the farm, make an inventory of the tools and animals. I have worked with a pen, and can bring my bookishness wherever it may help. I will make charts, and mark on them tasks to be done, and when. The accommodation for the maids must be improved; we need workers who *want* to stay, not who *need* to stay. It will take time for me to learn the art of making cheese and butter."

"I can see that you have been awake, thinking how to organise. That is a good sign. Let me know what you need, and you will have it. And now I must leave you. My wife and I must speak with Cressida, and that cannot be postponed. I've asked Flora to look in on you; you are welcome to stay in the manor till you have made the farmhouse habitable again. I'm afraid that reprobate Eype let it run down."

Edgar ate quickly. Anxious to start work, he dressed in a hurry, close to the fire, which was breathing warmly. After he had swilled his face in the vanity stand, he made for the door, behind which was Flora, who had come to fetch the silver tray. He stepped back into the room, but Flora remained in the doorway, like a framed portrait, the light brightening one side of her face.

"Please come in. There is something I must say."

She stayed where she was.

"'Tis too late for words. They are as frost to the early blossom."

"I shall work on the farm. We may see each other, from time to time."

"I shall not look for you. If our paths cross, you will be invisible to me, but if I do chance to catch your eye, my regard shall pierce your conscience."

"Shun me as if I were a disease-ridden beggar, if you wish, but you and I are tied together in a knot only death can unpick, and I have returned to right my wrongs. Know that about me, if nothing else."

He stiffly gave her the tray, and brushed past her, leaving her wondering how she might cope with him returning to Dorset.

The cows had been driven into the fields, and the milkmaids were resting in the neglected farmhouse. Clementine had sent down bread, cheese, and apples for breakfast, which they had eaten with relish, and they had all screamed at the sight of so many spiders' webs sagging with dust.

"We all need to set to scrubbing after our food has settled a spickle, on account of all this grime and grubbiness," said Rowena, drawing a stick cow, with her fingertip, in the dust on the table.

Lucy began to draw a house, and said, "'Twill be a palace when 'tis cleaned, you watch."

Then Edgar entered, making them all jump.

"We be the new milkmaids," explained May, "and be a-sitting a while after our work and breakfast."

Edgar smiled to allay their fears, and said, "I'm your new Master, come to sort out a thing or two. Some of your faces be familiar from the cart-ride from Dorchester, though your names have slipped from my memory like a kingfisher into a stream."

The maids looked at each other, and sighed with relief.

"I thought 'twas a wild man!" exclaimed Rowena, tidying her blond hair, which seemed to float about her head like wispy clouds. "They sidle up from Briddy, betimes."

"'Tis in all of us to be wild when the occasion demands, but I baint wild by nature."

He meandered between the table, chairs, and maids, inspecting the kitchen.

"We be going to wash down," Violet informed him, to break the silence. "'Twon't stay a hovel."

"How many rooms be there?" Edgar asked.

"'Tis one long upstairs," answered Rose, "where we slept, last night."

"Then let us clean up together, and when 'tis done, we'll rest till the cows be brung for milking. This house be as dirty as the farmyard, and we aint pigs to wallow in the mud. Upstairs first, then down," decided Edgar.

"Sir," said Rowena. "Have you a name to add to Master?"

"'Tis Edgar Porlock which follows Master, though Master be what you call me."

"Yes, Master," said Lucy.

"I'll begin in the farmyard. This house will be all new by the end of the day. Buckets be in the barn. Water be in the pump."

When he was outside, May said, "Master be so masterful!" and the others laughed. Edgar heard them, stopped in his tracks, smiled, and went to begin his inventory of tools.

He knew that when frost and snow come, no plough or hoe can cut and bite into the soil. It would be four or five weeks before the hills became white. There was yet time to peel the earth and flip it into wet, glistening ringlets, on which birds would sit and dig. This would be a visible sign to Yeoman that Edgar worked hard, had made a start.

The cows were now cared for, but the day would come when he would need labourers to tend to the sheep and goats he would buy. There were many jobs: fences required mending, woodland thinning, and the barn clearing to store next year's crops. Three permanent men would be useful, all year round, he calculated. One for woodland, one for fields, and one for animals. He wondered how the Burton-Bradstocks managed. Then he remembered Cressida's broken engagement to Geoffrey, and thought relations between the two families would now be too wintry for him to learn from Yeoman's neighbour.

What wood he could not use he piled up and burnt. The black, wild smoke, flames and haze shivered, purred and snapped, and Edgar rested on a log. The plough needed a strong horse. Wellesley was not a plodder but had a good pace and stamina to take him across the land. Edgar would go to the stables behind the manor, and see if there was a heavy horse available. Then he would exercise Wellesley.

When he looked at his inventory, he realised he had not enough tools to do the jobs properly, so made a further list of requirements to present to Yeoman. Though inexperienced, he knew that good tools were important. Frederick, he recalled, lovingly cleaned his saw and axe after every use, and wrapped them in cloths to keep out moisture. Edgar would do the same, would sleep in the farmhouse and not the manor. The milkmaids must know that *he* was in charge and hard-working. His room would be in the attic. There were steps up to a small landing leading to the maids' dormitory. From there, he could access the attic with another ladder.

Mid-afternoon, the maids emerged to drive the cows from the field, into the milking parlour.

"'Tis milking time?" Edgar asked.

"'Tis certain," called Rowena. "Udders like swollen cloths of curds."

"Don't 'ee go all a-getting to be his favourite," admonished Lucy, "when 'tis likely he'll go for more of a lady than you."

"Well, he aint a-wed yet, and though he aint as lean as he once was, he still a man to love where there be more hills and vales than men," sighed Rowena.

"Love a man too much and he gets to expecting too much," warned May, the eldest, who had heard her own mother say that so many times that she assumed it was true.

"Don't care what any of you thinks, he be a plum I'd like to pluck and get my teeth into," persisted Rowena.

"Plums have hard stones that crack your teeth if you baint careful," pointed out Lucy.

Unaware that he was now the subject of their conversation, he shouted that he was going over to the manor. The maids waved, and Rowena let her look linger over her shoulder, so that he noticed her. Then she began to sing.

"Oh, the frost be coming winter
when the sun lies down so low,
and the days be coming shorter
though the moon still like to glow,
and though he said he loved me,
my doubt it will not go.
'Tis years since I last seen him,
and my heart be full of woe."

"'Tis too melancholy a song," complained Lucy, seeing Violet's tears.

"'Tis a melancholy but true!" sighed Rowena.

Edgar found Wellesley not in the stable, but Cressida was saddling a horse. That morning's meeting with her parents had left her in no doubt of their displeasure at her breaking her engagement to Geoffrey.

"Love be like a woman's beauty," she had explained to them. "'Taint ever the same when time makes its mark."

"Where be Wellesley?" Edgar asked, concerned.

"Gone exercising," Cressida replied.

"Then whoever saddled him is a worthy rider, for 'tas always been his habit to play up and refuse anyone but me."

Cressida laughed.

"Then you have met your match. Wellesley be under the spell of a conjuror, was still and obedient, as a horse should be when all trimmed up to ride."

"'Tis passing strange. How long he been gone?"

"He'll be back soon. Stay here. I'll hasten him. I know the path he's taken. 'Tis the way Guy takes all the horses. Wellesley be in safe hands. Come, Hermes!"

Cressida's heels dug into her horse's flanks, and she left the stables.

"I need a strong horse or two for the fields," he called, but she ignored him, and galloped away.

At the far end of the stables, the farrier was working. With his rasp, he was filing a horse's hoof. Edgar watched the man's precise, quick movements, envied him his skill, the trust the horse had in him to replace an iron shoe.

"Is all well?" came a voice from behind.

It was Clementine, in riding attire.

"I believe all is well," replied Edgar.

"Believe? Do you doubt it?"

"I await the return of my horse, who is being ridden. Do you come to ride?"

She gave an extravagant bow and invited him to see her garb, her gesture sweetened with a smile.

"Forgive me. We have all had a tiring day at the farm. I'll need a strong horse, perhaps two, to help me in the fields, which must be turned before they become rock. The weeds, tufts, offend me. I must sow soon afore 'tis too late. Did Eype have horses?"

He followed her past the horse boxes.

"There," she pointed. "A grey and a chestnut. They have missed a year's pulling, but will be strong enough. There be nothing like the clanging of their chains, and the creaking of leather straps. In summer, the farmers take their heavy horses to parade in Bridport. They be topped with bells, favours, and feathers. Their tails and manes be plaited, and they be laden with buckles and brass. 'Tis a sight to marvel at."

Edgar remembered seeing similar horses in Frederick's fields, and being in awe of their gentle power, their steady but purposeful pace as they were led in front of the crowd.

"And I may use them? With such creatures, we will make the ground submit to our will before even the sharpest blade is blunted on the granite ground."

"Be the plough worthy of them? 'Tas lain idle, a-rusting, betimes."

"'I'll make it so sharp 'twill cut through the soil as if it were water!" he promised.

Just then, Clementine saw Wellesley being led towards the stable. Edgar followed the line of her smile towards the open door.

"'Tis Guy and your horse returned."

Wellesley had been ridden hard, and was walking compliantly. Edgar felt his horse now belonged to Guy, who was whispering reassuringly, and praising him.

"You have a special power," opened Edgar. "Usually, Wellesley will ride only with me."

Guy glanced at Clementine.

"'Tis a strong horse, 'tis certain," he muttered.

"This be Edgar Porlock, our new farm manager. He will plough, shortly, with the grey and chestnut."

Edgar felt the young man's reserve: Guy's hand was no sooner in Edgar's than it left it.

"Will you take your horse, or will I groom him?" asked Guy.

"What say you, Wellesley?" said Edgar.

But Guy, wanting a straight answer, led him away, and Clementine shuffled awkwardly.

"He is young, headstrong, like my daughter."

"He says a mere spickle."

"'Tis certain he wastes no words."

"Has he worked for you long?"

"A year or two. He helped originally on the farm. It was he who told us about Billy Eype's laziness and bad ways. Said he could not stay there."

Wellesley was now out of sight.

The farrier closed his bag, and made towards them. His tools clanged to the rhythm of his stride. He put his bag on the floor, and wiped his hands on his apron. Edgar saw the black cracks in the farrier's skin, envied what they signified, the man's grin of satisfaction.

"'Tis done – till next time. Shall I come soon?" the farrier asked.

Clementine said, "Before you go, check the grey's and chestnut's shoes. The two be working . . . ?"

"Tomorrow, the day after," guessed Edgar.

The farrier touched his hat, and made towards the horses.

Edgar's thoughts returned to Guy and Wellesley.

"I'm happy for Wellesley to remain here today, but I shall need him to stay on the farm, with me. The fields tip out of sight, they are so vast."

"I understand. I shall have him brought to you, in the morning. And now I, too, must ride. Nymph is impatient."

"I shall sleep in the farmhouse from now on. You may use Flora elsewhere."

"If you are sure. 'Tis best to start as you mean to continue. Perhaps, you could do me a favour. I'll be gone an hour. Give your message, if you would, to Guy, who is her son, and will see her before me."

Clementine led Nymph into the dwindling light.

Edgar's heart quickened.

'Tis so? Are those eyes which freeze and burn me with a glance my own? He mirrors me, though the white streaks be yet too shy to show themselves on his brow. If he be my son, and he knows me not, 'tis slowly we all must go, and Flora be wiser than me in this matter, which now puts Emma in the shade, when all I wanted to do was enlighten her. Why, 'tis a joyful yet sorry day, this, when a father and son speak as strangers. Yet there is no changing of the past, and I must show myself worthier than I once was, and hope that 'tis enough for him to acknowledge me.

Chapter Ten

The quiet hours were comforting to Edgar. At night, when the men were asleep, after they had moaned that Chard had driven them too hard, and had smoked their pipes till they had felt at peace with the world again, the motion of the ship felt like a mother gently rocking her child, up and down. The rumble and hissing of the waves, as they were sliced by the keel, were a lullabye. Some men whispered, others fell out of their hammocks to pee in their pot, and Edgar slept, the sweet tobacco-smoke above them an invisible cloud.

The men spoke to him when necessary, their tone generally neutral. Chard gave him relatively simple tasks. It was always an experienced hand Chard sent up the mast to spot other ships or rocks, and some men noticed how Edgar was protected.

"You lead a charmed life," one muttered to him. "You doing something for him?"

"I follow my orders," Edgar replied. "Do whatever I'm asked."

"Seem your orders be as light as a gull. Let's see your hands," demanded the resentful man, grabbing one of Edgar's, and turning its palm upwards. "No rope burns or calluses. Smooth as a woman's silk purse. You his favourite, that be for sure."

Edgar said, "I follow my orders," and moved away, not wishing to argue. The man's grip had been tight, too threatening for that.

Then Chard appeared and said, "Captain want to see 'ee – now."

"Yes, Chard."

Edgar went down the stairs leading to the cabin, and heard Chard call, "Porlock not far now, so you listen to the skipper well, as 'tis a fool who don't."

Edgar looked up at him standing at the top of the stairs. The hand who had complained about Edgar's light workload had been right; Edgar had received a degree of leniency others had not, and now he must heed the Captain's words.

The Captain was bending over his chart, studying the *Lyonesse*'s progress.

"Come see this," he invited, not turning to look at Edgar. "This where we be now, and this be Porlock." Edgar watched the Captain's thumb and little finger span the gap. "A mere few inches be two hours. Then we drop anchor, and the men will unload the cargo."

"Yes, Captain. And will we stay long?"

The Captain paused and looked at him.

"'Tis there that you leave the ship." He went over to his drawer and took out a leather bag. "Inside be a letter of introduction. You read, I know." Edgar nodded. "No point me keeping it a secret. 'Twill direct you to a house. There be also your wages, which should last long enough to get you to where I suggest, after you leave the house."

"But, Captain - "

"No buts. Edgar be born again, and will do what he should have done afore he persuaded me to let him stay on board. Present yourself to Chard when we drop anchor. Goodbye, Edgar Isambard."

Edgar shook the Captain's hand, which squeezed, then let go.

"Goodbye and thank you."

When he had gone, Edgar did not hear the Captain mutter, "And so you *should* be grateful, for I have saved your life."

As planned, Chard put him aboard a small boat, and a hand rowed it to the shore. Edgar stepped onto the stones, the bag the Captain had given him round his neck, his own in his hand, and the sailor returned to the *Lyonesse*.

"Get 'ee gone afore we land our goods. You must not come with us, 'case the Revenue comes," had been Chard's final words.

Inside the bag was a sum of money he had not earned by his meagre efforts on board. The letter was sealed with wax, and Edgar decided he would find an inn, and there learn what the Captain had to say, and the whereabouts of the house to which he must go.

The rabbit stew and cider were tastier fare than the potato slop and granite biscuits served on the *Lyonesse*. The innkeeper was surprised to find he had a customer he did not recognise. Porlock was rarely a destination for a stranger.

"You from round these parts?" asked the bearded innkeeper.

"Dorset."

"Then it's a good job you aint a-jumped ship today, what with the Revenue a-sniffing round. They flush out smugglers like gundogs pheasants on the Quantocks, and they aint too shy to fire their guns *before* asking their quarry to give themselves up, so it's just as well you a God-fearing man, here on business."

Edgar took the man's words as the warning it was meant to be.

"I be a-visiting a friend of a friend, so to speak, who will put me up, a night or two."

His hand reached into the bag, and took out the letter the Captain had written. He waved it in the air as proof that he was in Porlock on legitimate business.

"Dorset be a long way to here for a man without a good reason to come. Don't get no strangers nor nothing turns up here," declared the innkeeper, taking the plate, and brushing with his hands the crumbs from the table, as if implying that it might be needed, shortly, for another customer.

"I be Edgar Isambard Porlock, the last of an ancient line of Porlocks from the village. Churchyard be crammed with us, going back two hundred years."

The innkeeper stopped what he was doing.

"Know not a soul by that name, these parts," he said.

"As I said, I be the last, though my mother and father be buried in Bridport, so 'tis likely you won't know them."

"You want more? Slice of apple cake left."

"'Tis kind but no. I'll just get my bearings, and then I'll be off."

He patted the letter, and the innkeeper made his way to the kitchen, jingling the coins he had received as payment.

As he read, Edgar was puzzled. Why was the Captain going to such lengths to help him? Yes, Edgar reminded him, in some small way, of his own son, but the style of the letter led him to believe that there was a bigger purpose to such a specific set of instructions.

Seek out the road to Nether Stowey, and you will find, as you are about to leave Porlock, a white cottage. You will recognise it by its new thatch. Tell the woman who opens the door to you that I, and I alone, sent you. Give her my name. Tell her that I be the Captain of the Lyonesse. You will be safe with her. Rest three nights, and say your name. Tell her I have sent you to Wells, and she will give you an address. Thither you will go, a new man, to learn. Ask nothing of the woman, though your mind be of an inquisitive nature. At Wells, your life will change and be fulfilled. Never return to Porlock, as to see you again will give me false hope.

Edgar wondered who the woman was, how she knew the Captain, whose generous help seemed to inspire him, fill him with hope that, despite his mistakes in Bridport, he could lead a fruitful life.

So he set off to find the white cottage at the end of the main road to Nether Stowey. There it was, its new thatch conspicuous among the others where the reeds were turning green or falling out.

When she opened the door, Edgar said, "The Captain of the *Lyonesse* sent me. I am Edgar Isambard Porlock, and I will go on to Wells after three nights. 'Tis passing strange, I know, but he said you would give me an address, where my future will be determined."

He offered her the letter, to prove his identity, but she waved it aside, and said, "There is no need. Come in. The Captain's words be genuine. I would recognise them anywhere. They are beacons in the darkness, and have lit the path for many poor, unfortunate souls."

The house was neat and tidy, had the air of being lived in by others, too.

"The Captain is a good man," he said, when the woman put before him bread and cheese. "He made time for me, and saw that I was ill suited to a life at sea."

She smiled, and asked, "Have you ever been to Wells?"

"Never, but I once had a thought to go and study there, and return to Bridport, and open a school."

"And why did you not?"

Even in the lamplight, she could see his cheeks redden with embarrassment that he had given false hope to Emma.

"'Tis a tale I'd rather not tell, as it be a convict's ball and chain to me."

"I do not pry. Sometimes the telling of a sin does not remove it but sets it against the big hills, sea, or sky. Then it shrinks before our eyes, till it become a spickle that we remove as we would a grain of dust blown in our eyes."

"'Tis certain, though I know you not well enough. It be more of a confession to God which be required, and 'twould take a century to shrink my sin to a mere spickle, but 'tis kind of you."

The woman rose and went to her writing desk. She wrote a name, and address in Wells, and held it up to the light to check that they were correct; no accident should interfere with the Captain's plan.

Edgar read what she had written, and, with the impatience of youth, said, "'Tis kind, and if it be all the same with you, I'll start early for Wells in the morning."

The woman shook her head, and reminded him, "The Captain said to rest for three nights."

"'Tis kind, but I'd rather go in the morning."

"There always be a reason with the Captain."

"And, pray, what be his reason for detaining me when he has advanced my cause?"

"'Tis that the coach does not come till Wednesday. Porlock be unsociable in its location. Even when rain comes, it rushes down the street so fast you'd think it hated being here. But 'tis a romantic place in fine weather. Then the sea be the colour of your eyes, and the warm breeze soothes your brow, whispers to you. And now you be named after this village."

"Ah! Then I must wait, as the Captain said. And, if you please, I shall make myself useful to you. I will be no burden, and shall pay my way. The Captain paid me handsomely."

"There is no need to pay me, though you may bend your back, and pull any weeds that remain in the garden."

"'Twill be done at first light, tomorrow."

"The garden be long and tangled, and 'tis likely to make your body ache!" she laughed.

He set about the task with enthusiasm, and found that continuous crouching glued his hips, so that he could not stand upright without a cry of pain or discomfort. From time to time, he rested, and breathed in the air, which seemed to revive him. The woman watched him from behind a curtain, and wiped tears from her eyes.

The coach would stop at the inn where he had eaten.

"Be on time," the woman warned, "as 'tis a sharp driver, who waits for nobody, be they only a step or two away."

Edgar picked up his belongings, and ensured the name and address were safely in his pocket.

"Goodbye and thank you," he said.

"Goodbye till we meet again."

On the coach, later, he wondered about what she had said, and in what circumstances their paths might again cross.

She waited on the doorstep while he walked away. There was a degree of reluctance to leave in his gait. He had, several times, been on the verge of asking her the question which could not now be restrained.

He quickly retraced his steps, and said, "I have eaten your food, and slept in your house on the word of a man who be still a stranger to me, yet I know not your name, or how you come to know him."

The woman smiled.

"Tarry 'ee no longer. The coach be always on time, remember. I be Demelza, wife of Captain Lydeard, mother of my dear son, Edgar Isambard, lost at sea and now returned, on his way to Wells to learn a different life."

Edgar, too, smiled.

"Then I shall not linger, and 'tis a privilege to start again as your honorary son."

"The coach!" she cried, pointing up the road.

He left, and she went indoors.

The journey took most of the day. Travelling companions came and went; some tucked themselves into a corner, and steadfastly stared at the passing landscape; others were too familiar, asked questions he preferred not to answer. When the coach changed horses, Edgar took some fresh air, and stretched his limbs. This travelling through strange places excited him. The road twisted and turned, always withholding the middle and far distance. It kept him alert, enhanced his desire to arrive at the address the Captain's wife had given him.

"You going far, sir?" asked a man who joined the coach at Taunton.

"Wells."

"Ah, Wells! Thither, too, I am bound. You reside there, sir?"

"No, though I expect to, once I have found a particular address whither I am advised to go."

The man held up his monocle, which he had withdrawn from his waistcoat pocket, to his eye, and examined Edgar more closely.

There was a look of puzzlement on the man's face, as if he did not quite understand Edgar's lack of circumspection in going to live in a place he had not certified as desirable.

"And who is it that so freely sends you to a town you know not? There is a friend of his at this address? You go there to pursue a particular profession?"

Edgar did not like the effect the monocle had on his interlocutor's eye. It doubled its size, making its scrutiny of Edgar seem more intense. The huge eye fixed him, exerted some sort of power over him.

"In time, yes, though which profession I know not. I had briefly an ambition to be a ship's Captain, and though 'tis a worthy and lucrative calling, the Captain, my advisor, has persuaded me that I am more suited to something less dangerous, having lost his son at sea."

"'Tis'? You won't go far in Wells, 'tis-ing. The key to Wells is not in 'tis but in taking long walks, going to church, every Sunday, at least, and to read, read, and read. Do you read, sir?"

"I do, sir, though not as much as I would like. Once I'm comfortable in my lodgings, I shall read as if my very life depended on it."

"That is what I like to hear, sir: that a man in the prime of his life intends to read till he is so full of great men's words and thoughts that he will regurgitate them, and pronounce himself an even greater writer and philosopher! There, sir. You have the hand of Josiah Watchet."

Josiah slid the monocle back into his pocket, and the eye returned to its usual size.

"Alfr - Edgar Porlock."

Josiah shook his hand so enthusiastically that the others looked on in alarm. Why, thought Edgar, if a declaration of my intent to read elicits this response, what might the actual act of doing so produce!

When the hand-shaking had stopped, there settled a silence. A woman had fallen asleep on her husband's shoulder, occasionally snorted, and muttered extracts from her dreams. Her husband glanced apologetically at his neighbours, and said, "The journey, you see. Too long, too exacting. Still, it must be done. Yes, I'm afraid it must be done, and the embarrassment of a wife having nightmares must be borne stoically."

"Think nothing of it, sir," reassured Watchet, "for it diverts us admirably on this journey, which nears its end. Wells is but five miles hence, according to the milestone we have just passed." And then, turning to Edgar, and adopting a more confidential tone, asked, "May I see the address you have been given? Perhaps, I can be of assistance in giving you directions."

Edgar was surprised by this request. In the Captain he trusted, and did not want to test his advice against that of a relative stranger. What if, for example, Josiah Watchet liked not the neighbourhood, said something derogatory of its character, thus undermining the Captain? Yet Josiah was from Wells, knew it well, and could save him time when they arrived. What to do?

Reluctantly, he retrieved the piece of paper, and told him the address. Without the aid of his monocle, Josiah's eye again doubled in size, and with just cause.

"Why, sir, the very street to which you are sent is but two away from mine! If it does not irk you, I will deliver you there myself, and show you where Mrs. Watchet and I live with my niece. This is a remarkable turn of events. Here we have sat, talking about all manner of things, and we are to live within shouting distance of each other, though I would discourage you from shouting, or even raising your voice a little, as the neighbourhood is full of well bred, genteel people immeasurably sensitive to any increase in noise. Well, sir, this is a jolly turn up for the books! One of the jolliest I have ever known! What say you, sir?"

After such joy at discovering their mutual contiguity, Edgar could say nothing but, "If it is no trouble to you, sir, I accept your kind offer."

"Chops, sir, and turnips piled up to the ceiling! That's the welcome guests get at our house, sir: chops and towering turnips!"

They shook hands again, Edgar's fears somewhat allayed by the promise of such a fine repast.

The coach stopped at Priory Road, and the passengers alighted. They had been sitting so long that they looked at each other in a dazed state. Even Josiah turned a full circle to get his bearings.

"Ah, yes. Follow me, sir. St John's Street is on the right, at the top. My humble abode is on St. Catherine's Street, which is left, then left again. You will recognise my house immediately. It is the one next to St. Cuthbert's church. I shake your hand, sir, and expect you within a week for chops and mountains of turnips. You are never far from a saint in Wells, sir. If you are not yet familiar with the scriptures, my advice is to become so, sir, as you will, one day, draw strength and inspiration from them. And now to Mrs. Watchet and my niece, who await me."

So saying, he touched his hat and left. Strange, light, airy, and full of saints. The Captain had truly sent him to a good place. And now he was within walking distance of someone who would direct him to a better life. He picked up his bags. At the top, on the right, he remembered.

Then he saw the newspaper, left on a seat, he imagined, by an absent-minded saint. He picked up that day's Bath Chronicle, and scanned the front page. One particular headline caught his attention. As he read the report underneath it, his mouth went dry, and his hands began to tremble. All the crew had died, it said, and the ship had slowly sunk. Within hours of his arrival at Porlock, Captain Lydeard had rejoined his son, and the ship, the *Lyonesse*, with Chard and the rest of the crew, had sunk to the mythical kingdom with the same name, as the Captain had predicted it would.

Chapter Eleven

Edgar fell backwards onto the seat where he had found the Bath *Chronicle*. A second and third reading of the report did not alter its message: the *Lyonesse* had sunk, and no man had been spared. Demelza's husband, Captain Lydeard, and his first mate, Chard, had insisted that he leave the ship at Porlock. It was almost, thought Edgar, as if the Captain had done so with the eerie prescience that, if he did not, his own son would not have a second chance. And Demelza, who had welcomed Edgar on the word of a man she trusted implicitly, was now a widow, soon to be draped in weeds again. She must know by now, guessed Edgar, and will be staring at an empty grate.

He read again the name of the person to whom he should apply for lodgings: Mr. Jolyon Dursley. Here was a comfort, a refuge. Must Edgar be the bearer of the sad news that Captain Lydeard had drowned? It would be a cruel first meeting. There was much to discover: the relationship between the Lydeards and Jolyon Dursley, and those qualities, personal or professional, deemed necessary to shape his future.

The house had a formal appearance, with golden tones mellowed by the passing of time. It declared that its owner was wealthy but not ostentatious, welcoming but cautious. Indeed, its lines and architectural details were the perfect balance between imagination and restraint.

The knocker was a pendulous saint, his eyes closed, and hands clasped in prayer. It was stiff, as if not used very often, and Edgar's knock was not the three raps he had intended, but disjointed creaking and a strike so weak he wondered whether his presence would be heard.

Above him, a face appeared at the window, then disappeared. Again, Edgar knocked, applying more force, and heard faint noises: an interior door opening, a shuffling to the exterior one.

The man who greeted him had straight, white hair down to his shoulders. His black cloak suggested he was on the point of leaving or just arriving home from an errand. From behind him drifted the smell of ink, leather, and books. The clock, hiding in the dark mouth of the hallway, chimed, delaying Edgar's explanation of why he was there.

At the mention of Captain and Demelza Lydeard, Jolyon – for that was the man – smiled.

"And you have come all the way from Porlock? Then I congratulate you on your endurance! You must be tired and hungry. I am about to prepare a meal, in which I hope you will join me."

The invitation was confirmed by the door being more widely opened, and Jolyon stepping aside.

"Thank you. The food Mrs. Lydeard gave me I ate at Taunton."

"Then something must be done. I have just returned from a visit to the cathedral, and I, too, now have an appetite. Come. I had a mind to resume my work, but it would be the height of bad manners to neglect you. I shall build a fire, which should live well into the night. You'll take a glass of wine?"

"'Tis – It's," he corrected himself, remembering Josiah's warning that it was an expression to be shunned in Wells, "a drink I know not, except that it makes men jolly, sing, even."

The old man laughed, whipped off his cloak, and led the way into a book-lined room, in which there was a desk. On it, several bottles of ink were waiting to be used. A man of learning, Edgar deduced.

"All these books!" cried Edgar.

"You like books?"

"Oh, indeed, yes, sir! They draw me, sir, till I can resist them no more, and I am stuck in them till I have devoured each and every word."

Edgar smelt the wine before he tasted it, its aroma overpowering that of the books and ink.

"Your health," proposed Jolyon.

"You will not take a glass yourself, sir?"

Jolyon shook his head, and pointed to an armchair, in which Edgar sat down. The leather creaked, reminding him of straining ropes on the ship, and was cold to the touch.

"Later. I must work, this evening, now my questions have been answered by the Bishop. And you are excused from calling me *sir*. I like not that appellation. Call me Jolyon."

Edgar recalled Josiah's frequent use of *sir*, which he had unwittingly acquired, and said, "I will, indeed. There was a fellow traveller who used the word as a sort of curious punctuation, and I seem to have been infected by his habit. He lives but two streets from here."

"And his name, Edgar? You remember it?"

"Yes. Watchet. Josiah Watchet."

Edgar thought Jolyon's face altered briefly enough to suggest that he was acquainted with Josiah.

"You know him?"

"*Of* him. Come!" he cried, anxious to change the subject. "I shall light a fire and prepare a meal. You'll take sliced mutton? There is plenty."

"I will."

Jolyon left the room quickly, keen to prepare answers to questions he knew would be asked.

Edgar went over to the shelves, read the spines of the books, and ran his fingertips over the polished leather and gold letters. Such beautiful objects! he marvelled. If I could possess this library, why, I would be the happiest man alive! And in all these must reside such knowledge and wisdom.

On the writing desk, a book was already open, and next to it lay a sheet of paper, on which were scribbled illegible notes. On one page of the book was writing illuminated with gold capital letters outlined in red; in the border relaxed Christ; and a flock of angels crowned with haloes, their skin so translucent you would think them really alive, gathered round his shoulders. The blue of Edgar's own eyes, brown, green, and celestial gold glowed. The bottles placed out of reach, so that no accidental spilling of ink was possible, were the key clue: Jolyon was the scribe, painter, even, of this manuscript. Again, Edgar looked at the unfinished writing, and tried to decipher it. He made out *The Kingdom of God*, guessed the book was to do with the cathedral whence Jolyon had recently come, after meeting with the Bishop.

He picked up one of the pens, felt its sharpness, then another, its cut flatter for broader strokes. Excited by his discovery, he looked carefully at the illuminated manuscript, and copied *Kingdom* in the air. Thrilled that he could do it exactly like Jolyon, he tried other words, with equal success. And there, he noticed, are the faint lines which guide the pen from side to side. In that room, so different from the sleeping quarters below the deck of the *Lyonesse*, or from his own room in Bridport, was a creation so wonderful and transforming that he was glad the Captain had sent him there.

Jolyon came and found him close to the desk, though Edgar had put down the pen.

"The mutton is carved," Jolyon said.

Edgar followed him into a room in which a dining table had been haphazardly set.

"You must forgive me. It is Georgina's day off, and you must not notice too much the hasty preparation of the table. You'll take more wine?" asked Jolyon, replenishing Edgar's glass, as if an affirmative answer were a mere formality.

Both men settled into a relentless rhythm of chewing. Jolyon sipped water, his expression betraying his desire to resurrect the theme of Edgar's purpose in coming.

"You have many good books, and I could not help but notice that you are a master scribe," Edgar said.

"It is my life's work. It pays me well, and nourishes the soul, which is equally important. The body needs mutton and wine, but the heart and soul need beauty, without which they wither and die. It quickens the pulse, sustains our hope that there is a purpose to this unfathomable life of ours. See beauty, and let it embrace you. Only then have you truly lived."

Edgar felt he now knew the reason why the Captain had sent him to Wells, and then he remembered that he had not yet acquainted Jolyon with the loss of the *Lyonesse*. Jolyon listened, bowed his head, as if he had dozed in his chair. Edgar remained respectfully silent while Jolyon dealt with the news.

"I shall work now, Edgar, on my manuscript. The Bishop has provided me with important information for the completion of the book, and I must have total silence. It is necessary so that I can work without error. It is slow work. You will understand, I am sure," he said, at length, his exit ponderous, his head bowed once more. Before he left the room, he added, "We will speak more of the Captain, at a later date. My grief, for such I feel, prevents me from further discussion, at the moment."

Edgar slept soundly, through even the bells summoning Wells to morning prayer. Jolyon had left out on the table bread and cheese, and a note informing him that he did not wish to be disturbed, and that Georgina resumed her duties, that day. The key next to the note was an invitation to go out without fear of being unable to get back in.

Edgar gasped when he saw the cathedral. As he walked across the green, he shrank as it grew, till he stood in front of it, in awe of its size. The door was open, revealing candlelight. He peered inside, just as a woman and a child were leaving. The girl had almost white hair and a coat nearly touching the ground, giving the impression she was gliding. Her eyes were bright blue, like his own. He stepped backwards to allow the woman and child to pass, and saw how like the angels in Jolyon's book the child was. He remembered: *It quickens the pulse, sustains our hope.*

"Thank you," said the woman, leading the child past him.

He smiled, now torn between entering the church and watching the angel. Has God done this? he wondered.

"Have you said your prayers?" he asked.

The woman frowned, but the child answered, "I have."

"Come, Zillah. We must make haste. Your uncle will wonder if we have delivered his message to the Bishop. Then there are other things I must do. You must practise your reading and writing."

"Yes, though my legs cannot go as fast as yours!" Zillah protested.

"One day, this child will grow wings, and then you will know what it's like to keep up with a faster one," he muttered, when they were out of earshot. "'Tis a name to match her beauty, and though my words be awkward and troublesome betimes, they are also my crutches when I hap to stumble."

Soon the woman and child were out of sight, and Edgar resumed his visit to the cathedral. Which one of these men in holy attire be the Bishop? he wondered. They pray together, separate men speaking the same words, each man blending with the others, so that the whole be one voice.

As he looked up, he saw the patience of stonemasons, the signs of great men's ideas and imagination, and he wished to create something just as beautiful. But what? Perhaps, the answer was with Jolyon.

From there, he walked around the town, noted the inns. Outside one was a fiddler, but his instrument had not been tuned, and the notes insulted the ear.

"Here, friend, lend me your fiddle," said Edgar.

The fiddler did so, and said, "My hat is empty. 'Twould be full of silver in Glastonbury and Bath, but Wells be full of meanness."

"Your complaint has no weight, for the strings be the problem. Your pegs need adjusting. Let me do it."

Edgar, who had been taught how to play by Frederick, tuned the fiddle, and sang. The ditty was commonly heard, in Dorset, during harvest-time.

> "Oh, the stooks be tied,
> and the fields be bare,
> and the scythes be blunt
> but the maidens fair.
>
> Oh, the leaves be crisp,
> in the field a hare,
> and the days be short
> but the maidens fair.
>
> Oh, the frost be thick
> round the fox's lair,
> and naught warms me
> but the maidens fair."

Three more verses followed, and a small crowd formed, some of whom tossed a coin into the other man's hat.

"Bravo!" he cried. "'Tis a song to cheer us all and fill my belly, by the looks of it. My name is Alain de Bretagne, and if you be in The Snorting Pig ere the landlord turns us out, you shall have your share of the day's spoils."

"You are French?"

"Somerset, though my mother married a French sailor captured in Devon but pardoned as he was about to be hanged."

"Then you owe your very existence to a sworn enemy of England?" laughed Edgar.

"'Tis only countries and Kings be enemies and not the common folk, though they curse enough. My father was like the rest of his kind: a good man in the wrong place. But remember: The Snorting Pig!"

The man pocketed the money Edgar had earned, and moved to another location.

As Edgar wandered through the streets of Wells, his thoughts returned to Jolyon and his manuscript. I could start by copying something simple, perhaps my name, and embellish it, he planned. My first name be modest, but Isambard begs a colourful flourish. I am young, and maybe, under Jolyon's tutelage, can become as good as him, and earn a living. For a fleeting moment, he thought of Emma, of his lapsed intention to return, and was saddened by the impossibility of keeping his promise. Through the pen, I will pursue beauty, create manuscripts that will please the heart as well as the eye. I will ask Jolyon, when he rests from his work, to teach me, and then I must practise till I am his equal. He will be my master, and I his apprentice. This was Edgar's ambition to share with Jolyon, that night.

When he felt he had a good knowledge of the pattern of Wells' streets, he sought the house of Josiah Watchet. Next to the church, Josiah had said it was. Edgar decided to pay a brief visit, to say he was settled in his new abode, and was determined to follow in Jolyon's footsteps. The chops and mounds of turnips would wait for another occasion. He would introduce himself to Mrs. Watchet and, of course, their niece. To spend a few minutes with Josiah would be pleasant. There was still much to learn about Wells, and Josiah seemed helpful.

The house was less obtrusive than Jolyon's, and seemed to hide behind the church, separating itself from the street by a path and wooden fence. Its fringe hung shyly over its windows, as if the façade were afraid to make eye contact with the world. The house did not at all have the spirit of its owner.

The woman who opened the door was wearing a white apron, and, without her coat, hat and gloves, bore little resemblance to she who had passed him in the entrance to the cathedral.

"Forgive me, but I am looking for Mr. Josiah Watchet, who kindly invited me to share chops and turnips, though I call not for them, on this occasion, but to pay my compliments to him, and to thank him for directing me to my lodgings. I am Edgar Isambard Porlock, please to inform him."

The woman, however, recognised him as the man who had assumed the responsibility, which belonged solely to herself and Josiah, she had felt, to check that Zillah had said her prayers. And now she must allow him inside, as good manners dictate. This was not the first time a stranger had turned up at the door, following Josiah's invitation, and she was used to it.

"Then please to step inside while I fetch him," she replied, not exactly grudgingly, but without warmth.

She went to Josiah's study, and Edgar stood awkwardly. When Josiah appeared, he inserted his monocle into his eye socket, and examined his visitor. Edgar noticed immediately the collar denoting his office; Josiah had given no sign of his calling on the journey.

"Edgar Isambard Porlock," Edgar said, offering his hand. "We met on yesterday's coach. You invited me to call upon you, though I come not to eat your chops and turnips but to say that I am well provided for in my lodgings."

"Ah, yes! You've come, sir, and I am glad. The Bishop is playing silly games with me, sir. Silly games of the silliest type, I might add. But your visit is welcome as it drags me from my study, where my niece, Zillah, refuses to learn to write. I keep her at it, sir, from morn to night, but still the pen quivers and leaves but a spider's trail on the paper. And it is not good enough, sir; not by a long way!"

"There is still time to learn," observed Edgar.

"You believe me not, sir? Then come and be appalled by her efforts!"

When he saw it was the girl with translucent skin, blue eyes, and white hair, Edgar felt a frisson of surprise unsettle him. She should be illuminated in a manuscript, he thought. And how, he wondered, had she come to live there?

Zillah looked at him, and covered the paper with her left hand, anxious that her writing should not be subjected to public scrutiny.

"Uncle!" she cried. "I cannot do it at all! Please don't show your friend."

Edgar said, "It's all right. I come not to laugh but to help, if I can."

"Help?" interjected Josiah. "You succeed where I fail? That is most unlikely, sir."

"Will you do what I do?" Edgar asked Zillah, holding up his finger. Zillah imitated him. "Now, watch." And he wrote *Zillah* in the air. She watched the letters form in her imagination, and they hung there, as if burnt into it by a hot poker. "What word do I write?"

"Z-i-l-l-a-h. Zillah!"

"Now you."

Then it was Zillah's turn to write invisibly in the air, and her eyes widened with excitement at this unusual lesson. The letters flowed from her fingertips till her name was perfectly formed.

"I have done it!"

"There! You can write. Now, Zillah, pick up your pen, and write. Never look back."

Zillah wrote her name without hesitation or shaking. Such a smile Josiah had never seen before.

"Why, sir, not since Lazarus was told to pick up his bed and walk has there been such . . . "

But he had no words for what he had just seen, and neither had Edgar.

Chapter Twelve

The hoar nipped sooner than expected, covering the ground completely. Footprints of foxes, squirrels, and birds were looping chains. It was a month after Winifred's burial. There had been only Yeoman, Clementine, Edgar, and Cressida there. The vicar winced when two men from Bridport bumped the coffin into the roughly hewn hole. Solemn words were rushed, and Cressida took Edgar's arm for comfort. Yeoman led his wife away, now that what he saw as his responsibility was over, but the other two lingered, watching the gravediggers shovel back the soil. Cressida and Edgar stood, mesmerised by their rhythm: scoop, then toss, three times, followed by a brief rest.

"And 'tis wrong not to mark this spot with a tablet and words," said Cressida. "We all get a few letters, pauper or not. Beout 'em, we vanish, in time, as if all we been were thistle fluff blown in the wind."

"And it was your father's wish?"

"Yes. Says there must not be a stain on any Symondsbury."

"But her name, village of birth. Just a spickle on her, to mark her out. 'Twouldn't harm or cost. Why, look at all the marble your ancestors got!" protested Edgar.

She still held his arm. Her squeeze told him she knew what he meant, that she was sympathetic.

"Big busts and slabs of it. She be your cousin but only our milkmaid be the way father see it."

Is it meanness as well as shame? he wondered.

"'Twould have been better to have buried her in Beaminster, her home."

Cressida withdrew her arm. His insinuation that Winifred's burial on Symondsbury land was a second wrong stung her.

"Then you should have said. 'Tis too late now. I must go. The red soil has blood in it, and 'tis all of us who spilt it."

She left Edgar knowing Wellesley could have carried Winifred, too. That is all it would have taken: a ride to Bridport, where they could have parted. Now Winifred was in a hole of inconceivable blackness.

It was when the water froze that Edgar hastened his preparations to withstand the first assault of winter. Too late to build a wall of dry wood in the barn, he did what he could, relentlessly hacking trees into faggots that would fit snugly on the firedogs, in the hope that they would last till the end of what he prayed would be just a short, cold snap. His body burned, and sweat ran into his eyes, so aggressively did he chop, and when he stopped, he became aware of his clothes sticking to his skin.

Nothing happened on the land. Animals stretched their legs, and ate armfuls of hay, which had been drying in the barn, and giving off a sweet scent, but even that ceased when the snow came. It was felt before seen. Maids shivered as they made their way to milking, all glad when they were able to lean against cows, and steal their warmth. The cows, even the reluctant ones, welcomed this human contact.

The sky darkened and became silent. Flakes fell skittishly, and settled. The milkmaids huddled close to the fire like witches around a cauldron, till Edgar said, "Sit back and let the heat breathe into all corners," and they did, though grudgingly, as their clothes were damp. Their spirits were low, they started to cough, their noses ran, and they would have taken to their beds early were it not for the fire. "Set for a day or two," judged Edgar, "and, except the milking and keeping things tidy, there's not much we can do. 'Tis a Dorset winter, and the way to get through it is to think of the time it will end, leaving us with spring's shoots and warmer days. And let us be patient with each other, for thrown together like this needs good listeners more than sharp tongues."

They knew what he meant, and were glad of his wisdom, the way he cared about their souls as well as their physical comfort, so that when they became ill, they drew upon his reassurance that they would recover. The worst was braving the cold to totter towards the trees to relieve themselves, scratchy straw in their hand. The cold was one thing; the stares of others, when you left the fireside, another. Only the call of nature and milking took them outside.

Yet it was Edgar who, thrown into empty hours, felt the frustration of lack of activity the most. The girls always found they could move their tongues, if not their legs, but Edgar felt keenly the boredom. Cressida did not visit him, and he longed again for his pens and ink, which called to him like sirens. Occasionally, Emma slipped into his thoughts, until he remembered Guy, who would, he hoped, not ride Wellesley on the ice. Guy: his son? And Flora, his son's mother. Both stayed away.

Mealtimes broke the monotony, when all the anticipation of nourishment and a sense of togetherness reached a crescendo. They took it in turns to prepare soup. There was always pork. How the splashing and bubbling of fat on the hearth sharpened their appetite! Soon, they all helped each other, as if merely watching the preparation might exclude them from the eating.

He did his best to join in their conversations, but inevitably the women wanted to know all about him. It was hard to be their master at the same table, and their questions gathered pace, one after another, till there came a time when he knew what they were doing: vying for his affection by showing the most interest in him.

Day after day, it was the same, with now one girl stealing private time with him, now another, till he felt temptation again. Was this what Billy Eype had known? This imbalance between men and women? If so, then the curse must always be on such circumstances, when the master must be strong or weak. How proud he was of Guy that he had removed himself from all that! And if Guy were wise enough, so young, then so must he be – somehow. The farmhouse and yard were improving, and he knew what he must do with the land.

Wellesley's welfare was the pretext for his visit to the stables. There would be general enquiries, and then, rather than a direct path to Flora, he would take a circuitous one, and if Guy was as intelligent as suspected, then he would understand, step by step, where the stroll was leading.

Thankfully, Wellesley was in his box. Guy glanced at Edgar shaking off snow, and resumed his polishing of the saddle. Edgar knew Guy had seen him. This was Guy's domain. He is here because I have filled the space left by Billy Eype; Guy might have run the farm, in time, put right what was wrong. Flames of resentment flicker when he sees me. But does he know? Or is it his nature to be as prickly as thistles? All these thoughts heightened Edgar's tension as he strode towards him.

"You see your face in it?" began Edgar.

Guy recognised the attempted humour, and found it hard to be unfriendly.

"'Tis certain. A job I must do when the snow confines us."

"I see you share my fear that the ice be too treacherous to run a horse."

"I have walked them only. A man or woman would be a fool to risk a gallop."

"The delights of the fireside are preferable, 'tis certain."

"Then your purpose here be important."

"Wellesley. He fares well?"

Guy led his visitor to Wellesley's box. Wellesley had been groomed, looked his best: flanks shining, mane brushed, eyes alert, tail trimmed. Slowly, Edgar ran his hand across the horse's shoulder. Wellesley offered his nose, had not forgotten his master. Edgar murmured. Guy had done a good job.

"You have a way with him." Guy stayed silent. Edgar watched him proudly assess Wellesley's condition. "You prefer the stables to the farmyard?"

Guy picked up a pitchfork, and fluffed up the straw. Labour would trim his answers.

"'Tis all the same: work."

"So the farm calls you not? I am no farmer. Do you resent me? Say. You could have my job, make more of it. Yeoman, you see. I knew him, years ago. And Clementine. But I am no farmer."

Guy stopped.

"What are you, then?"

"In the past, a different man. You could run the farm better than me. I am not suited to it, though I try."

"So why do you stay?"

"'Tis true I know few, these parts."

Edgar moved to the other side of Wellesley, so that he could not be seen. There he could say things. Guy's eyes could not make his words crumble there.

"And shoes. I will pay the farrier. Will you let me know how much?"

"I will."

After feeding Wellesley the carrot he had brought, Edgar tiptoed towards asking, "So Flora be your mother?"

"'Tis certain."

There was more than a horse between them: a cliff top of uncertainty, of ignorance of each other. Guy was intrigued; Edgar was no Billy Eype. Flora had mentioned that there was a new farmer. "Best be wary of him," she had cautioned. "You know what happened to Billy. Just watch your step with him. His tongue is sweet." But Edgar was making time for him, taking an interest. Yeoman

130

could offer only instructions, interference. There had been times when he had turned up for no real reason, as only a master who has too little to do.

The mane was as groomed as Wellesley's tail. His saddle was almost a mirror. There was nothing else for Guy to do in the box. Wellesley was another man's horse, and it was time to leave them alone. There was something, though, in Edgar's mention of Flora that suggested the conversation was leading somewhere unexpected.

"I knew your mother a long time ago," Edgar blurted out.

He had struggled to find these words, but, in the end, they emerged as a halfway house. There was no response, so he came out of hiding, and repeated himself.

"'Tis passing strange, and yet not," replied Guy, revealing no thoughts or feelings.

"Bridport."

Guy smiled unexpectedly.

"I remember it not too well as a child. Rarely go."

"And your mother has told you nothing about your time there?" Guy shook his head. "And your father?"

Guy frowned.

"I know not my father, though 'tis no matter for you."

Guy's tone had sharpened, was warning Edgar not to stray too close.

"Look at me. Whom do you see?"

"A man who presumes a familiarity yet to be earned."

"You are right, but there is always a time to mend a wrong, and now 'tis my time to do so."

Guy half-turned to leave; there was an insinuation in the stranger's words that disquieted him.

"I will go. I will not listen further."

"Stay!" insisted Edgar. "And listen to what I have to say as 'twill change our lives for ever. Tell me: you know not who I am? Your mother has not forewarned you? Your prickliness suggests so. Speak. Has she told you?"

Guy's face went blank.

"She said to be guarded in my dealings with you. There is something belonging to the past you would have me know?"

Edgar drew a deep breath, trembled.

"Yes," he said. "I am your father."

Aghast, Guy looked at him, found no words, and left quickly. There were things he had to say to his mother: questions to ask, statements to make. What could he do until she confirmed or denied it?

Edgar thought his telling of it would bring relief, but it did not. He had taken a step, but reconciliation seemed a distant destination, at that moment.

There was comfort in Wellesley, a smell so familiar that Edgar put his head against him to inhale it. The air was cold in the stables, so Edgar took a blanket, and threw it over Wellesley's back.

"There, boy. Stay warm, for there is almost too much cold for us to bear, and I would hate to lose *you*, too."

Edgar returned to the farm. The maids all looked at him as they had done the first time they had met: strangely, as if they saw in his face a grave matter.

"You be all right, master?" asked Rowena. "You look as if you seed a ghost."

Lucy nudged her. Memories of Winifred's death had not yet faded. Superstitions were strong in those parts, and Rowena put her hand to her open mouth when she realised what she had said.

Edgar saw again Winifred hanging from a beam in the barn, and closed his eyes to shut her out. This reawakening was fitful, full of tortures and fences as sharp and painful as the hedge into which he had fallen on that fateful May Day.

"I shall be well soon. 'Tis a seasonal malady which will go. Come, let us be more cheerful, and talk no more of ghosts. The dead are dead, and we are living."

"But, sir, they say - "

But it was now Lucy's turn to cup Rowena's mouth.

"Enough! Master is unwell. Come, master, and sit be us by the fire. 'Tis a bright one, as you can feel, and 'twill raise your spirits, as 'tas done ours."

So he sat among them, and they looked after him: fetched him a morsel or two to eat, rubbed his dry hands to warm them. So hard it was to stop the tears at their love for him, and when they saw them, they each hugged him and kissed his head.

"Come," said Rowena, removing his sodden boots. "And now your feet."

"The hot aches!" he warned.

So Rowena started with her hands, held his icy feet, and he closed his eyes. Around his shoulders they placed a blanket, as he had done to Wellesley in the stables. The maids knelt around him, peered up into his face to see if he was recovering, and stayed quiet. This peace they were sharing endured. Without their master, they were nothing.

That night, snow fell so deeply that Edgar had to squeeze out of the door, and shovel enough away so that they could leave to relieve themselves. It had stopped, though, the snowing, and crunched when they trod on it. Up to the knees it came, making them lift their legs high to make progress. They laughed at the difficulty of it, and did their business quickly, to limit their discomfort.

Now the fire was fed continuously, but no one from the manor visited them, checked they had enough food. Then a knock came on the door. Only her eyes were visible, and scarves swathed her head. When he saw her, Edgar guessed her to be a desperate day-labourer risking life and limb to ask for work. She said, "We must talk – alone," and Edgar glanced over his shoulder, and said, "The barn. I'll get my coat." The woman did not wait for him but staggered across the farmyard.

She pulled the scarves down from her mouth, so that her words would not be muffled, misunderstood.

"Guy has told me you have spoken to him."

"I thought I would not, but there should be no empty spaces into which niggling doubt can creep."

Exasperated, Flora clenched her fists, tried to control her mounting anger.

"You disappear for years and think you have the right to return and disturb our lives? Why, you are more arrogant than I thought! And now he is angry with me."

"There should be no more untruths," stated Edgar.

He had once felt passion for Flora, had pursued her after she had looked at him and smiled, so that he knew she liked him. In his weakness, he had been unable to resist her. He had given her flowers: buttercups, daisies, wild flowers of lilac, pink and blue. All had been left on her doorstep, and when her mother had asked her the name of her admirer, she had said, "I know not. 'Tis a pity he did not leave them in the ground, where they belong," but she had secretly believed in her power, and had encouraged him in little ways, so that he had been unable to stop thinking about kissing her. And after the first kiss, she had imagined it meant he loved her, but it had not. It was Emma he loved.

"But why did you not speak to me before him? Your coming here, however much a puppet of Providence you be, has disturbed us all. There can be no more warm summers as we have known them. You will be a cloud which forever slips over the sun."

"You exaggerate, Flora. I be no more a cloud than you. Your hatred of me should have waned by now. I am no farmer, but, in time, Guy, who has shown some aptitude for the land, can again resume his duties, which were scythed prematurely by Billy Eype.

Guy may resent me now, but working together may show him that my character is not what it was. I am no Billy Eype."

"'Tis certain, I grant you, though you pronounce that there should be no more untruths. What be the truth, as you see it? Imagine it to be a clear night in August, when the eye can spy the sea from Pilsdon Pen. What then be the truth, Alfred?"

"I be Edgar now, and the truth is that Guy is my one and only son, whom I forsook through natural ignorance. That be the truth."

She shook her head, slowly, emphatically, tightening her lips.

"That be a tale from an old man's hearth. You can change your name but not the truth."

"But you told me, when you came into my bedroom, that you had conceived my child, that you would have told me about it had I not left Bridport. 'Twas afterwards you found out that I was betrothed to Emma."

"That be the unrobed truth, but I did not say that Guy was *your* son. My mother took our daughter from me, in shame, and where that child lives now is a secret buried in a dead woman's grave in Bridport. 'Twas to stop the gossip, the crossing of the street, the disapproving look of the church-goers. I was just a girl, but it was all my fault, and none of yours."

Edgar buried his head in his hands.

"No!" he groaned. "It cannot be. A daughter, you say? And she is alive? Tell me it is so!"

His hands gripped too tightly her arms, and she wrenched them away.

"Never touch me again! I tell you, she is lost to both of us, outcast, as are all those born out of wedlock."

"But Guy. He is your son? How old is he?"

"Summers enough to ask questions."

"Then . . ."

"Let your mind turn as a windmill yet you shall never know his history."

"His father? You chastise me, yet, two years later, you have another man's son?"

"'Tis certain, though you shall never know the man's name, even till the stars are snuffed. And there are no sermons I shall take from you on my conduct, which be, God knows, as clean as the driven snow. You are not Guy's father, and 'tis all."

She left, scarves up, ending their exchange.

Guy had not reacted angrily when Edgar had claimed to be his father. A daughter. Guy was no longer his son, but someone knew where his daughter was.

Edgar sighed. My journey, which I thought would be soon over, is only just beginning, but whither I must go I know not. I may as well consult the weathervane, which flies whichever way the wind spins it.

Chapter Thirteen

The grave expression on Jolyon's face worried Edgar. The summons to the room in which they had first met was delivered solemnly, adding to Edgar's anxiety. His fingers, in whose prints coloured inks had mixed to give them a strange hue, were evidence of the years he had spent learning and practising Jolyon's art. Various pens had formed ridges and depressions, which were now permanent.

"Please sit, Edgar. There is a matter of importance on which I must speak," began Jolyon.

"Your tone suggests so. I fear a wrong of mine is the nub of it. Speak if it is so, and I will mend it."

Jolyon shook his head, waved his hand, dismissing Edgar's speculation, as if brushing away an irritating fly.

"Think not so, Edgar, as my theme has a happier note, but is like a good story told around the hearth: there must be much pain and suffering before there can be a happy ending."

"I am pleased to hear it, though I still fear the telling of it."

Jolyon gathered his thoughts by adopting a relaxed but upright posture, his palms placed flatly on the arms of the chair, his gaze turned towards Edgar.

"Some years ago, you were sent here by two people I love dearly. One perished at sea, leaving a wife. I was, once upon a time, due to accommodate their son, in order that he might, as you, acquire the art of manuscript illumination, but, alas, he died of a disease which wiped out many other sailors. You came to me, having adopted that boy's name, because he himself, only happy with the crashing of waves in his ears, refused to come. Still, some of us are born to sail, and others to write. You have been spared." Jolyon waited for Edgar to acknowledge the accuracy of his summary of what had happened, and it came in the form of a slight nod. "And you have served an apprenticeship under me, and have rapidly become a master in your own right. There is nothing more I can teach you." He went to a drawer, and took out a scroll tied with a scarlet ribbon. "And so I release you from your studies, and give you this as confirmation that you are now a member of the Guild of Master Illuminators."

Edgar took it with trembling hand. "So it is over?"

"Yes, and you must now make your own way in the world. I have decided to retire and move to Porlock. This house is too big for me. Too many corners for dust to collect! And my work has been my only friend in Wells; there is no one, except you, with whom I could associate. The Bishop has been informed. He asked me, somewhat alarmed, who would maintain the illuminated history of the cathedral, and I took the liberty of recommending you. You are, of course, under no obligation to continue my work. By now, you will have discovered that such concentration and skill as are required cannot be nurtured by the promise of a handsome salary alone. I have *needed* to produce such beautiful writing for the nourishment of my soul, and you, too, have felt that compulsion. Though there is a little time to think about this, the Bishop will expect a decision in the not too distant future."

Light in hand, the scroll carried the heavy weight of the rest of his life. And Porlock, Jolyon's destination: never yet had he told Edgar how he knew the Captain and his wife.

"Porlock? But this house."

"I will sell it. You must find other lodgings."

Lodgings. The word somehow disappointed Edgar, who had

come to feel the house his own, and Jolyon a father-figure rather than a teacher. Years ago, fired with a youthful spirit of adventure, he had never worried about where the day might lead. Now, however, he felt anxious, having become inured to regular meals and a structure to his day dictated by his mentor.

"I shall miss this house," he said quietly. "It has become my home, but I am grateful for all that you have done for me. How soon will you go to Porlock?"

"Next Monday. My sister expects me. We shall have to get used to living with each other again, as we did when we were children. Neither of us is as young as we once were, but we will take care of each other, till we are called for by a higher authority."

"Sister?"

"Yes. My sister. Did I never tell you that the young man whose name my brother-in-law gave you is my nephew? Well, forgive my absentmindedness! You have been a more diligent student than he would have been. But that is in the past, which we can do nothing but accept."

Jolyon smiled weakly, patted Edgar on the shoulder, and shuffled out of the room, struggling to hold back the tears.

Edgar undid the ribbon, and read the certificate, which confirmed that he was a recognised Master Illuminator. Should he present himself to the Bishop, and continue Jolyon's life-long work? This was not an easy decision to make. Though Edgar wanted to write, he had hitherto been confined to copying existing manuscripts. "I make no apology for insisting on this. There will be a day when you can compose your own writing. Till then, you must ensure that no letter, except a capital one, strays a fraction of an inch onto any other. And you must sit them all on the line, so that they appear as choirboys in the cathedral. Your colours should never boast but suggest the theme and tone," Jolyon had instructed.

Inside me, Edgar said, there are things to tell, my own as well as other people's stories. Yet why cannot I do both the Bishop's bidding and my own? That is surely the next step after finding fresh lodgings.

So, after telling Jolyon of his wish to continue his work on the history of the cathedral, he went for a walk, and saw a different Wells: buildings had new sizes and shapes; the air tasted sweeter; and sounds were no longer muffled. His new awareness was exciting yet unnerving. Who had a room or house to let? Monday would soon come. A new owner might take pity on him, but he did not want to leave this to chance. What to do? Knock on doors? Perhaps, the Bishop could help, find him a room in the ecclesiastical courtyard.

Jolyon had paid Edgar for minor tasks, such as going to Bath to purchase inks, and Edgar had saved much of the money, but it was not enough to pay for several nights' stay at an inn, so on he went to the cathedral.

He was absorbed in his own thoughts, and did not see Josiah Watchet coming in his direction; neither was Josiah aware of the impending collision, so deeply was he in contemplation of his recent altercation with the Bishop. And so the two crashed into each other.

"Forgive me. I was preoccupied," apologised Edgar.

"The fault is mine, sir, or, more precisely, that of the Bishop, who has decided that my Sunday sermons need less dessication and more sprinkling with contemporary allusion. I would, sir, accommodate this wish were it his only complaint, but, alas, it is one in a catalogue where I am concerned."

It was during this rant that Edgar recognised Josiah, whom he had not visited since he partook of turnips and chops, a few days after he had found a way to help Josiah's niece, Zillah, to write. Despite that agreeable evening, during which there had been, as Josiah had predicted, innumerable chops and quagmires of buttered turnips, Edgar had failed to maintain contact. Even Mrs. Watchet's more charitable attitude towards him did not predispose him to further visits. This signal failure, however, did not prevent him from resurrecting their acquaintance when he said, "Whatever shortcomings the Bishop may believe you to have, they are infinitely smaller than the one of which I will be eternally ashamed. You do not recognise me as the man who accompanied you to Wells, and to whom you offered feasts beyond his wildest imaginings? I am that very one, but I have not returned to you since. I suggested an idea to help your niece improve her handwriting. You remember?"

Josiah tightly applied pressure to his monocle, producing a contortion which fixed his focus on Edgar, who seemed to wait ages before Josiah was able to confirm that he did remember him.

"Why, sir, I remember you well! Your appetite, I recall, was equal to the generosity of the portions. And my niece now writes well, though requires close supervision. She is of an age when young ladies become more preoccupied with the mirror than books. You would find her advanced beyond her years. And tell me, sir, what has kept you away from us? Neglect alone does not sit rightfully with your character as I know it. I suspect there is something weightier than indifference."

Still uncomfortable with his long absence from the Watchet household, yet proud of his achievements with a pen, Edgar said, "Under the tutelage of Jolyon, I have become a member of the Guild of Master Illuminators of Manuscripts. It has taken me these long years to complete my apprenticeship. Now that Jolyon is retiring, I shall, I expect, take over his work at the cathedral, though a more pressing matter is to find new lodgings. Jolyon is going to sell his house and return to Porlock, to live with his sister."

During this explanation, Josiah's face metamorphosed into various expressions: delight, surprise, and perturbation.

"This is, indeed, a momentous time for you. And you have a place in mind?"

"I was wondering if I could rent a room in the ecclesiastical quarter."

Josiah scoffed.

"Think not of that, sir. I rarely go there. It is the residence of pomposity, the font of the most obscene self-importance."

"But I have little time to look. Monday next, I must be out. Whatever the area's shortcomings, I must try there, knowing of no other place."

Josiah rubbed his nose, chin, and, finally, earlobe, before holding up his right forefinger in a gesture denoting revelation.

"Why, sir, you are spared that den of mediocrity, that home of false piety!"

"How am I?"

"How? *How*, sir? You say, '*How?*'"

"I do, sir, in the hope that you will enlighten me."

"You are spared by *me*! There is an empty room in our humble abode. You shall fill it well with all your books and inks and pens, and, as rent, you will act as tutor to my niece. She has missed your wizardry, sir, and your temperament will make her studies as palatable as Mrs. Watchet's chops and turnips with extra butter. What say you, sir? Will you still seek your ruin in the festering chambers of men who know not their commandments from their parables? Speak, sir!"

The monocle was again inserted into his eye's orbit, and gripped so tightly that it gave the impression that his eyeball was trying its best to pop out.

Given Josiah's unfavourable depiction of the ecclesiastical quarter, and the appeal of living free of rent, he found himself accepting the offer.

"Then come now, sir, and we shall let Mrs. Watchet know, so that she can buy more turnips. Splendid, sir! Welcome, sir! Oh, well done, indeed, sir!"

Put out that Josiah had invited someone they knew little to live under their roof, Mrs. Watchet gave a lukewarm greeting. Her restraint, however, was subjected to Edgar's quiet charm, and his joyous recollection of her culinary delights soon painted a smile on her face.

It was not until later in the day that he met Zillah again. She had grown tall and slim, and blushed when he shook her hand. Clearly no longer a child, she was conscious of her beauty, and Edgar was captivated by the translucence of her skin, and her straw-coloured hair, which she had swept up and held in place, at the back, with a comb fashioned by her uncle in the style of an ancient, Roman artefact he had found when walking past a barrow in Wiltshire. She is no longer an angel but a saint, thought Edgar. Her beauty is without equal. Why, if I could capture it in words, illuminate her portrait, then it would be eternal, not eroded by the years as a headstone the wind.

Zillah was mature enough to recognise the effect she had on him. Her eyes flickered tantalisingly, and he dared not look too long upon her.

"And your reading and writing: how go they?" he asked, deciding that it was better to initiate conversation with her.

Mrs. Watchet noticed the struggle within him. Josiah, jubilant that he had found a new friend who would not dismantle his sermons as the Bishop, spoke on a range of subjects – the French, the decline in attendance at church, the lack of education for the poor – and even invited Mrs. Watchet to confirm his opinion. She did, of course, but ventured her own, too, anxious to impress her new lodger, whose handsome appearance had prompted her to wear one of her best dresses, and to sweep up her hair in Zillah's style, so that he might think her younger than her years. But she was not as shy as Zillah, and held his eye directly, arching her eyebrows artfully as she listened to him, so that he could be in no doubt that she found his company refreshing.

"And Edgar, Zillah, will tutor you further to prepare you for when you become a teacher. You will, of course, call him Mr. Porlock, which is how pupils should address their teacher. One day, you will expect the same courtesy from your own class. She is, sir," said Josiah, turning to Edgar, "an able and willing learner, who will, in time, become one of the good teachers in a new school to be established by a benefactor, who insists on keeping his identity a secret. The Bishop has agreed, and, once a suitable building has been found, the funds will be released. Nothing, sir, would please me more than to see our dear Zillah passing on her knowledge to those in less fortunate circumstances."

Zillah's smile suggested that she shared this ambition.

"That was once a thought in my head," said Edgar. "I wanted to learn Greek and Latin, and to return to Bridport to set up a school. There are many who know not their letters and numbers, but I intend instead to satisfy my spiritual need to illuminate manuscripts. In fact, when I bumped into you, sir, I was on my way to confirm to the Bishop that I would like to continue my mentor's work when he retires and leaves, next Monday, to live with his sister in Porlock."

Zillah looked up at the mention of Edgar's idea of a school in Bridport, and said, with some urgency, "But it is not too late, sir. Is it not a more worthy calling to help the needy learn about the wider world? The Bishop can always find another scribe. In a school, you can create other worlds, whereas the copying of the Bishop's notes, albeit in a beautiful way, is repetitive and rather tedious, is it not?"

Josiah returned his monocle to its rightful place, and his magnified eye showed displeasure.

"Zillah, the work of the Bishop is God's work, too. You speak out of place. Mr. Porlock must not be challenged like this," he chided.

Mrs. Watchet said, "You are both right. Children are God's work, too. Let us put this behind us, and distract ourselves with the plum pudding, which steams unattended before us, and restore our conversation to lighter content."

Josiah humphed, but as Zillah and Edgar agreed, the subject was changed.

At the end of the meal, Josiah said to Edgar, "And now to your duties as resident tutor to Zillah. As she will provide a general education for her charges, I would be grateful if you could ensure she is proficient in numbers, Geography, History, reading and writing. A little Latin, too, works wonders, as you already know."

"I shall do my best, sir. Tomorrow, I must see the Bishop, and secure my employment as his scribe. If afternoons suit you, Zillah, then we can begin after my return."

"Thank you, *Mr.* Porlock. That would suit me well."

Her slight emphasis on *Mr.* was picked up by Edgar and Mrs. Watchet, and Edgar found this sense of humour welcome. Josiah, however, was unaware of it.

The next day, the Bishop shook Edgar's hand warmly.

"Jolyon speaks highly of you. Your work will be a major contribution to the archives of the cathedral. Your writing will be read in hundreds of years. How many of us can say that? Oh, my name will be there, but what will be my mark? Already I am the butt of tales whispered by scurrilous men huddling in candlelit cloisters. They plot against me, but that is reassuring. To bring about change for the better in this world is to necessarily court unpopularity. Take the school soon to open. I stand accused of patronising the poor. 'Spend the money on food and clothes. Knowledge nourishes only the mind and not the body,' they point out. But we shall never get this done again. Benefactors are as scarce as Papists, these parts."

Edgar's thoughts turned to more practical matters: his salary, and the notes from which he would work.

"I must eat, as must the poor," he said.

"We will meet once a week, at ten o'clock, on Mondays. I will provide you with a script, and you will continue to copy in Jolyon's style. You may wish, one day, to bring your own ideas to the illumination, but it would be odd if you adopted a different approach mid-tome. Better to change at the beginning of a new book. As for your salary, I will pay you half of what Jolyon received. There will be a period of two months' probation, during which I shall assess your work. If it is good, then I shall pay you the full amount. I trust that is satisfactory to you?"

As Edgar imagined it to be a fortune, he readily confirmed it was, and the Bishop ordered refreshments.

"A little wine is in order, I think: French. I hope French does not offend your sensibilities? Memories of the enmity which has divided our two great nations linger hereabouts."

"Not at all. The earliness of the hour and not the wine's provenance is a greater concern. I fear it might give me flights of fancy and an unsteady gait!"

"Think nothing of them, for we are all better for our strolls into the imagination. Shortly, I have, with a colleague, a discussion on a theological matter, and I anticipate it being of the heated kind. Is there any final question you would like to ask before I go?"

The Bishop raised his glass to Edgar's, and emptied it in one swallow. Edgar took a sip, and said, "Yes, and it concerns the school. You mentioned a benefactor. His name is a closely guarded secret?"

The Bishop threw back his head, and laughed.

"He has not told you? I suppose, as he will not be in Wells soon, and as you are his protégé, it will do no harm to tell you. Why, he is *your* benefactor, too! It is no less than Jolyon himself!"

Chapter Fourteen

There was no answer. He knocked, peered in the window, left, returned, blocked out the sunlight with his hands, his eyes on stalks, but there were no signs of anyone living there. Where were the urn and tablecloth? Emma gone? This time, he tried the handle: a quick turn and a yank of frustration.

Over the road, his every move was being watched by a man who could have saved him the bother, with a word or two, but Jethro did not want Edgar to find her, not when she had given him the slip. She deserved saving from him.

Just a few fish were left on Jethro's cart. One – the biggest - was for his tea; the others could go cheaply. The sun, which had given the muddy street a sheen, was gone, and it was nearly dark.

Edgar enquired at a few houses. Jethro saw a woman shake her head, and quickly shut the door; another shrugged, smiled, tried to keep Edgar there with wild speculation.

Wellesley waited patiently in the slush, which was starting to freeze again. The lanes will soon be dark, and tonight's moon is but a paring of a fingernail, and will not light the way, realised Edgar. Jethro abruptly grabbed the cart's handles, and, head down, pushed, the mackerel unsold.

Is it Leonard or Jethro? I cannot remember, thought Edgar, when he saw him, but her brother-in-law will know where she has gone.

Jethro sensed him on his shoulder; it was more a restraining hold than a polite tap. Then the name returned like an eagle to a gloved hand.

"You remember me, Jethro?"

"I do, but you must talk as we walk. I have other business to attend to."

Jethro increased his pace, and Edgar knew why.

"She has left? The house sounds and looks empty. Whatever your need, tell me where she has gone. I must see her."

"'Tis true she has gone." Jethro refused to look at him, and strode more purposefully. The mackerel jumped, as if still alive, when the cart juddered over stones and holes. Underfoot, the slush was almost ice, so quickly had the temperature fallen. Jethro looked up as Edgar drew level. "She baint in Bridport no more."

"But you know where? You must tell me."

"I don't know. Besides, 'tis no business of yours no more. You can't turn up here like a ghost and expect to claim kin. Now, if you don't mind."

But Edgar grabbed his arm, and pulled him away from the cart. They slipped on the ice, nearly lost their balance, clung to each other in a clumsy dance.

"Don't deny me. There are things she needs to know which only I can tell."

Steady again, Edgar let go.

"She married my brother, not you."

"But it was me she loved. Is that why they parted?"

Jethro composed himself, and shook his head.

"Things you don't know, things you no right to. She gone and aint ever coming back to that house. 'Twas her own mind decided."

"She is on her own? I will see your brother."

"He is pained enough. If you rake the embers of his loss, 'twill be his pleasure to make your coffin, and 'twill be mine to watch him nail you in it. And you will suffocate, and claw in vain at the lid, for I swear I will hold you down in it till your screams are but muffled begging."

Jethro was trembling.

"I will find her," swore Edgar. "For the woman I spoke to was not Emma, and I must see her restored to sound mind, or I can never be happy again."

"Remember this: that no lid can ever be prised from my brother's coffins."

With that, he picked up the handles of his cart, and continued his way home.

The next day, after a night at the inn, Edgar found himself again in Bucky Doo. Nothing had changed: Emma's house still had a slight echo. He thought of the milkmaids, their inevitable alarm; they were now others in a gallery of women he had abandoned. Edgar had left no note, as he had not when he had run away from Emma, all those years ago. And they could not look for him in the fields, to see if he needed help, as the snow was still thick. There would be disarray, questions, tears.

Bartholomew. Jethro's strong warning was enough to deter Edgar from going to see him. What was the point? Emma and Bartholomew were no longer man and wife. At least, they did not live together, and whatever had torn them asunder Edgar could only guess.

So, must I leave Bridport, thwarted in my attempt to ease my conscience? he wondered. If I abandon my search for her, I shall always believe she suffers. I need her to forgive me, give me absolution I can believe in and take with me. But she has gone, so I must remember her as I saw her on my return, her mind a maze in which reason is forever lost, her face not that of the girl who tried on Clementine's crown. Then let me return to that field where she danced, and to the lane in which I proposed to her, showed her my stigmata, the lacerations by hawthorn on my hands and face, so that I can again see her as she was.

The walk to Frederick Canonicorum's field was full of pain. Edgar imagined accusations, reminding him of his promises, on the lips of passers-by. His pledges had been ripe cherries, but she had hated spitting out their bitter, hard stones.

Fields had swapped places in the snow. He identified the triangular one, in which the maypole had been put up, and shivered, his feet wet. Whiteness was blinding him. The pole used to be in the middle, and there was the gate through which the dancers had walked, and the May queen ridden. Fiddlers. Tables. Tents. Food. Cider. He saw them all again, had forgotten that he had kissed Flora in secrecy behind a tent, and did not know Clementine had seen him.

For the last time, I am here. One last look. Jethro was right: I am a ghost, and all I could have had has gone, as the snow when spring awakens.

He was not aware of being watched by a man who had been smashing ice in the stone troughs so that his cows could drink. His herdsman was coughing up blood, and was so dizzy that he could not stay upright. In his gloved hands, Farmer Canonicorum wielded an axe, and pulled out thick shards of ice. On his white beard, his breath changed to beads of moisture, and was thin and grey.

"Too old for this," he moaned. "Still, can't see a sick herdsman die in a frozen field."

Frederick's legs, bent like the slats of an oak barrel, still worked, but all was an effort, every stride took its toll.

He had watched the visitor pace out a circle, stagger to the hawthorn, and retrace his steps. The man's hat hid his face. The circle means something, guessed Frederick. His first call was weak, dull, and could not travel in the misty, cold, dense air, so Frederick crunched tentatively towards him.

Edgar saw him, and waited. Frederick was so swathed in coats and scarves that his movements were restricted. Once or twice, he nearly fell over, and Edgar lurched forward, ready to help him up.

"You lost?" asked Frederick, before he made eye contact.

"Yes and no."

They looked at each other from under their drooping hat rims. Frederick knew before Edgar. The eyes, of course. Then it was Edgar's turn. Words were shy, at first, and then sentences stumbled, till Frederick, dropping the axe he had unwittingly held across his chest like a warrior, said, "Is it Alfred?"

Seconds passed before Edgar recognised his former name.

"It is, Frederick. A long time."

Frederick wanted to open his arms to him, but the years, as much as the weather, had frozen them.

"The circle."

Edgar looked over his shoulder, and sighed.

"'Bout right? The tents there," he nodded, "and the pole in the middle of the circle. Least, as I remember."

Frederick rubbed his chin, recreated May Day, and shrugged.

"Hard to tell be all this snow."

Silence and embarrassment averted eyes. Neither man dared refer to the past too quickly. This dithering about the dance would lead them at a leisurely pace, would stop at the right time.

"'Tis Dorset all over, this."

"'Tis certain."

"And the farm?"

"Tolerable."

Frederick began to shiver, visibly. Edgar thought him a bit shrunken.

"You cold?"

Frederick guffawed, and his teeth resumed chattering.

"You coming in? Heard you were back. Wondered whether you'd come."

In Edgar's head, the snow melted. The field was filled with sunlight, people, music. Dancers skipped to the clapping. Youths picked sweethearts daisies.

"Yes, Frederick. I'd like that."

Edgar bent for the axe.

"Not too fast, mind. I'm not as you left me."

"Nor am I the same."

They went at Frederick's pace, Edgar taking his arm. The contact felt good to them both, presented possibilities.

"My wife, Lizzie, been gone ten years," said Frederick before they entered the farmhouse. He didn't want it to be a surprise. "'Tis hard on a farm."

"I'm sorry."

"Here."

Frederick threw him some dry socks, and placed their boots by the fire. Melting snow made pools on the flagstones.

It's the same, noticed Edgar, even the smells: hams smoking in the chimney, dribbling, dripping candles, clothes drying in the inglenook.

"You heard?"

"'Tis certain."

Both knew they must do more than snatch sly glances at each other, and leave out truths. Important words, stored like apples in a box over winter, needed airing.

"Frederick, I'm glad we have met again."

"It's been too long. My door has always been open to you. You know that." Then, after a moment or two: "Broke my heart, you going."

"And the way. 'Twas not what I wanted. You know?"

Frederick nodded, and said, "Yes. 'Tis hard to keep such goings-on quiet in Briddy. My heart be beating hard, now you back."

He pushed bread and cheese in front of him. Butter, too, which Frederick nicked with a knife, and licked, to see if it was off, and his wink said, "Eat."

"You been Bridport all your life?"

"You never leave the place you grow up in. 'Tis always there, and be what makes you who you are."

Edgar chewed the bread and cheese, and Frederick saw the pleasure in his face. The butter made it better. Without offering, Frederick passed him a brandy. His own he took to chase away the cold; the second and third would warm him.

"I came back for a reason."

After a lengthy pause, Frederick said, "There be a reason for everything."

Edgar held up his hands to the fire. In seconds, his fingers tingled as if nettled.

"Emma." Nothing. Frederick was staring at the flames, and had no reprimands in his heart. "I came back to explain, apologise. My life could not be lived properly beout. When I saw her, she was confused, thought we were married with children, and now she has gone I know not where. I came here to this field to remind myself of the day I proposed to her."

"And are you truly sorry you left her? There was another, too."

"I am truly sorry. I went because I could not bear her knowing of the other."

Flora and the daughter he had never known. His mistakes filled the room, reeked of wet clothes, yet Frederick did not rebuke him. This warmth, kindness, he had not expected. And time: Frederick still made it for him.

He looked for signs that Lizzie Canonicorum was still there, in the room, with Frederick: only the bonnet hanging from a hook on the dresser, as if she were elsewhere in the house and might need it when she slipped out to fill a basket with eggs.

In the warmth, and with a man he trusted, Edgar felt safe. It had been a long time. Too long. And if Frederick asked him to stay, do jobs for him on the farm, he would. For no money. Just bread, butter, cheese. And an occasional burn of brandy.

But Emma.

"You married?" blurted out Frederick, as if he had been saving it up, and the pressure to say it had been too great. That was the crux for Frederick. All was won or lost on the answer.

"No."

The shaking of the head lasted twice as long as the utterance. Frederick was relieved, his breathing hoarse, laboured. This news brought them closer, in front of the fire, which was thawing them.

"Don't suit everyone, marriage. Break a man as much as a woman, you get it wrong. Seen plenty right, plenty wrong. 'Tis a meadow or a mire."

Edgar was cautious. All he had done, over the years, was so different from the travails of a farmer that he feared it might distance him from Frederick. He could tell his story only up to his arrival in Wells, but then he became a stranger. His hands wielded a pen, not an axe. Could Frederick cross that vale Edgar's written words put between them? Yet Frederick would wonder. The years needed filling.

"Emma married."

"'Twasn't her fault. Nor the undertaker's, come to that."

"Mine."

Frederick shook his head, and said, "Her father's. Pushed 'em together. She tried, but . . . "

"A coffin-maker?"

"Bartholomew. They say you'd better be dead in one of his. There be men, I hear, who sell bodies to doctors, but they don't come scavenging in Briddy as they knows the lids won't lift. They'd be a-hacking in vain. People pay good money to keep their loved ones dry and in one piece!"

Frederick chuckled. Edgar winced. Winifred. Poor, cold, rotting Winifred. Frederick saw a shiver of horror, and knew he had been too vivid.

"Pushed, you say?"

"Bartholomew be rich. Steady money, dying. Never starve, Bartholomew. Decent enough man, but not a husband. No, not your romantic type. Oh, she took her time, bided it for you, but when you didn't write, she crumbles like the cliffs at Briddy harbour. Gave it a year, and leaves him. 'Twas a scandal. Those there were who speckleated. Said she couldn't stand him smelling of wood and body potions, couldn't bear his hands after 'em touching death all day. Can't blame her. 'Tis a particular trade, coffin-making and burials."

Edgar shuddered, was glad Emma had had the strength to leave.

"And children?"

"No. 'Twas not consummated, and, by law, the marriage baint proper. That be what gave her hope that she could walk away."

Edgar sat forward in his chair. All this, public knowledge? Had all these personal details become a feast for idle gossips in Bucky Doo? Humiliation, disapproving looks and silence from people, who before would have nodded and passed the time of day, were her punishment. How lonely she must have felt! empathised Edgar. And it was her father who had compelled her.

"And so she is not really married?"

"No. Her parents took her back, but no man who knew would touch her after that. 'Twas as if she were a spectre."

After a few moments' reflection, Edgar said, "You know a lot. You speak to her, those days?"

"Tolerable. She was your fiancée, she said, and so we took an interest, believing you would return. Cried her eyes out to us when she tells us about Bartholomew. 'You were my daughter, I would not let you marry him,' I says. 'He be a good and kind man who will look after me,' she says. 'You and him be no match,' I says. But I baint her father, so . . . "

"Bartholomew tried to win her back?"

"Not at all. He believed 'twas Providence took her away from him, and that 'twill keep her safe. His brother, Jethro, gives her money now and again, and keeps her company. A fisherman, he be. A loyal man."

"And does he expect anything in return?"

Frederick looked up, knew what he meant, and frowned.

"A *good* man, Jethro. When her parents died, he visited her. I used to see him there. Then she starts to get sick, sees things, muddles names, sees monsters, and screams for them to be taken away. All been too much for her."

"And you have seen her recently?"

Frederick fidgeted, and asked, "You living near?"

Edgar lied, and reminded him of his single purpose in returning to Bridport.

"House looks empty."

"Things aren't always what they seem."

"It's all too late anyway."

They sat for some time before Frederick said, "You know about your parents?"

"Probly dead."

"Went to Dorchester."

"They alive?"

"Don't know."

Dorchester. It was out of the shame I brought upon them, decided Edgar. They, too, became outcasts, just like Emma.

"Where will you go?" asked Frederick, at length.

"I don't know. If only I could be sure Emma knows I'm sorry, and what happened, I could wake up, and begin to make something of my life again."

"Again? You manage to be something once?"

But Edgar thought Frederick would scoff, find it impossible to believe that he had become an illuminator of manuscripts, at the expense of Emma.

"A sailor, then I worked at Wells Cathedral."

"You baint a vicar?" laughed Frederick. "There be a vicar under my roof?"

"Helped the Bishop. You imagine that? An agnostic helping a Bishop?"

"Your words be a thicket to a country farmer. Pity you didn't open that school."

So Emma has told him, he realised: his lie, her future.

"Yes, I suppose so."

Frederick rose, and nudged the brandy bottle. During the five minutes he was out of the room, Edgar let the heat from the fire consume him. I do not wish to leave here. I have missed Frederick. He is a good man, said Edgar to himself.

When he returned, Frederick stood in front of him, and said, "And your words for Emma?"

"I would give anything to hear her forgive me, but I cannot make her understand even if she were still here in Bridport."

Edgar's eyes jumped from Frederick to the door, through which walked a woman. Frederick stretched out his hand to her, and she took it.

"I once loved you," she said to her Alfred, "and you left me, but I will forgive you – on one condition. And, as Uncle Frederick is my witness, that condition be a test of your sincerity as a grown man."

"Emma?" gasped Edgar. "You been here? Frederick is your uncle?"

"Well, taint a ghost!" cried Frederick. "My niece baint a spirit."

"I be Emma, though 'tis true I been seeing the world in strange ways, betimes, which makes me seem not myself."

Edgar rose to embrace her, but Frederick stopped him with a raised hand.

"What is the condition you impose on your forgiveness of me?"

"That you build the school you once promised me, and that you teach the poor children of Bridport."

Edgar looked at Frederick, then Emma, and realised forgiveness demanded a high price.

"I will. With all my heart, I will."

"Then I will forgive you, Alfred. With all my heart, I will forgive you."

Chapter fifteen

His back to an angry fire, Yeoman said, "So your mind is fixed? Money cannot persuade you? The milkmaids like 'ee, so 'tis a shame. When you didn't return, they *all* trudged through the snow, a-wailing you were probably buried under it. 'Twill leave me in a difficult position again. In time, you would have made a good Farm Manager."

Edgar was weighing Emma's challenge, with all its unexpected strangeness, against Yeoman's old one at the farm, to which he had already risen: in time, I could plough straight lines, catch and gut a pig, but I must not devastate Emma a second time.

"'Tis kind o' 'ee, but I find myself having to keep a promise I made a long time ago, and I should have honoured it then."

"Clementine and Cressida will be disappointed."

"I cannot bear the parting. Let you and I shake hands. In time, our natural friendship will draw us together again."

"Then let it be done quickly. There is no more to be said?"

"Guy. Let him take my place. 'Twas only Billy Eype he hated. Guy knows every rill, every hill; on the horses, he has made the estate his kingdom."

"I will give it some thought."

They shook hands, each forcing himself to go, both knowing they felt better for having met each other again.

Later, when Yeoman told Clementine and Cressida of Edgar's

departure, Clementine was sad that part of her past had gone before she had had time to find out what Edgar remembered. Cressida was full of anguish, and blamed it on finding Winifred hanging like a sculpted saint high up on a church wall.

There was no tearful farewell to the milkmaids. Let them curse me. In time, reflected Edgar, they would have tried to take advantage of me, or tempt me, till I gave in. Then I could not have continued as their master. There can be no authority when women beg favours, and men too easily give in.

Frederick's hug, when Edgar had accepted his offer to live at the farm, had been tight and prolonged. Emma could now return to her own house, knowing that her uncle would protect her. It had been Jethro's suggestion, as he feared that Edgar's presence at the farmhouse would trouble her. Frederick did not accept that Edgar would harm her, but did advise Edgar that if ever he wished to speak to her, it should be at the farmhouse, and Edgar agreed.

His promise to set up a school in Bridport excited but daunted him. He hardly dared speak about it to Frederick, who wanted him to succeed, but did so, to sharpen his own thinking about it.

"A farm be for smelly animals and crops, so 'taint proper to have tiddy ones 'ere. Besides, 'twould wear their legs out, walking to and fro. Most of 'em got no shoes anyway. They'd fall asleep, they'd be so tired. What we – *you* – need to do is find a suitable place up in Briddy itself. Now, you been gone a while, and there a-been a few changes, but I knows every alley, every building, proper or broken. But 'twould take a penny or two to rent. So what you needs is a benefactor, who got a mind for the poor and needy."

"And you know of anyone?" asked Edgar.

"Might do, though Peter be busy twining rope for the navy, and the vicar, who always asks us to pray for the less fortunate, needs his pennies for his new lectern. You might go up to see Yeoman Symondsbury, though he been beout a Farm Manager for a while, and might have other things on his mind."

Edgar's eyes dropped at the mention of Yeoman, as he had not yet told Frederick that he had been working for him. To ask a man whose employ you have just left to be the benefactor of your school might not be a good idea.

"The school will need books, maps, slates and desks. I have promised much. Without money, I can achieve nothing. There is no one in Bridport?"

"No, but you must persevere in finding a room. I know a man who has a school for the children on his estate. He has his own library, and may help in some small way. I shall ask him."

"'Tis kind, Frederick. And will you tell Emma how I progress in all this, from time to time?"

"If she asks, which be likely if the day appears well, I will, or not if it be strange. 'Tis better, Edgar, if you pay her no visit, or send her messages. She is a grown woman, but she must take her time with you. Jethro and me will look after her."

Jethro. And why? She could not be a wife to his brother, so 'tis out of a sense of duty he calls on her. Duty? He has no obligation, reasoned Edgar, angry that Jethro could visit her, and he could not.

"I will, of course, do as you say. Do you think it likely the man of whom you spoke will consider our request?"

"There be a chance. I shall remind him of a favour I once did him, and of his offer to return it, one day. He be a man of his word."

"A friend?" pressed Edgar.

Frederick shaped his answer carefully.

"We once knew each other better than we do now, 'tis certain, but I would push the brandy towards him if he walked through the door."

"There is a school in Dorchester, too, I hear. I will post a notice for a teacher."

Frederick frowned.

"But your promise," he reminded.

"I promised I would set up the school, and I will teach the

children till I appoint a replacement, but my inclination be to resume my work as an illuminator. There is a great demand for the art, not just in churches but noble families who wish to record their histories."

"And these early days be enough to show Emma you are worthy of forgiveness?"

"Bridport needs a school, and I shall do my best, as I know *you* will, to make sure they have one. I shall go now. There are doors to be knocked on. Later, I shall do what you ask on the farm. These hands are not quite a woman's!"

Frederick was caught off guard by Edgar's smile, and took the hand offered.

"No, not a woman's."

On his way into town, Edgar saw a few children playing in the snow. They wore thin clothes, and their gloveless hands clawed and patted it into balls, which they threw. Edgar walked Wellesley slowly, not wanting a fall. Then he was struck on the back of the neck by a snowball, and ice ran down his collar. He turned, and the boys looked away innocently. What, even in winter, these children are full of joy and high spirits? Oh, had I but a spickle of their innocence again! he wished.

"A good shot! 'Twas true but cold and wet. Do you read as well as you throw?"

The boys looked at each other, not understanding, so Edgar asked, "Would you like to go to school? Be in a warm room, and learn how to read and write?"

As they had never seen their parents do either, they did not know what he meant, and their blank expressions convinced Edgar of the urgency of his mission.

He turned right at the clock. One, perhaps two, classrooms? Ten or twenty pupils, to start with? How old would they be? And the classroom would need a stove in winter. Cows could be herded, and did not throw snowballs. Children were joyful, and did not hang themselves.

Bartholomew was supervising the loading of a coffin onto a cart in the street. His two assistants, who wore black frockcoats in need of a stitch or two, and tall, battered, black hats, had laid out a canvas sheet on the cart, to help them lift the coffin out at the churchyard.

"Feels like he hab all his silver nailed in," whispered the taller to the shorter.

"No point licking your lips, as the lid be tight as these trousers. I heard the man's wife tell master that his hound was to go alongside him, as 'tis common, because he paid more attention to it than her."

"Big brute, then."

"Now make sure you lowers it into the correct hole, which be beside the yew, left of the path, and not the one by the oak," Bartholomew reminded them.

"Do it make any odds? They both be big, the graves, and in respect of the coffins, they both bear the dead," said the shorter.

"It makes all the difference in the world, Jeremiah. Imagine 'tis you in one of these 'ere coffins, and you end up in the wrong grave. Why, your wife comes to visit you, but whispers all her tender love to another man, and, worse, when 'tis her time, she be buried snug up to him and not you. How think you then, Jeremiah, when another woman, not as pretty, ugly, even, comes and curses you, and tells you how mean you were to her?"

Jeremiah took Bartholomew's point, but still believed that declarations of eternal love and remembrance, and insults and curses, meant nothing to corpses buried so deep and beyond hearing.

Edgar had lingered at a respectful distance, but now that the cart had pulled away, he moved forward, and caught Bartholomew's eye.

"You come to request a coffin, sir?"

"I do not, but have something I would show you in the hope that you can be of assistance."

"Please come in, then."

The room was sparsely furnished. Emma had once suggested placing a vase of daffodils on his desk, to light up the gloom, but Bartholomew had dismissed her sentiment, declaring, "A mourner don't want blinding. First, you have to grieve in the gloom before you can go out in the sunshine."

"I've caught you at an inconvenient time?" asked Edgar.

Unsure whether Edgar had suffered a recent bereavement, Bartholomew trod carefully, indicating an empty chair, and sitting down himself in an attempt to make the dark room seem less filled with his corpulence.

Before Edgar sat down, he took out a piece of paper and passed it to him, and Bartholomew cast his eyes over it. There then ensued a discussion, after which Edgar tried to steer it towards Emma, but did not refer to her by name. Bartholomew studiously avoided mentioning her, so Edgar became more direct.

"Your wife minds not the nature of your profession? Some might find it rather . . ."

The right epithet eluded him, but not Bartholomew.

"Lugubrious? No, sir, she does not. She has passed away."

"I am sorry to hear that. I hope my insensitivity has not caused you too much pain."

"I have been a widower for many years."

What made Edgar continue his pursuit he knew not, but he asked, "And did you have the unenviable task of having to make your wife's coffin?"

Bartholomew stood up.

"Sir, I must confess that I find your questions too intrusive."

There was no sharpness in his objection; he was the model of diplomacy. But Edgar felt warned to withdraw, and did so.

"Of course. Forgive me. A man who has lost his wife must have privacy. I meant no harm. Shake my hand to signify that you are not too wounded by my thoughtlessness."

Bartholomew's hand, when it was extended, remained only briefly in Edgar's.

When Edgar had gone, Bartholomew sat down, and read again the sheet of paper, but the conversation he had just terminated had distracted him.

"'Tis true to say that Emma be passed away in the sense that she don't live here as my wife, so there be truth and yet none in what I told this man, who showed more than a passing interest. Few know death as well as me. 'Tis a daily companion, and I must not join the endless line of mourners, yet I feel Emma's absence as one, as if she were really buried in the churchyard. I love her with all my heart, so much that I dare not venture into Bucky Doo. All these years make it seem like a death, and my numbness has not gone, and cannot be rubbed away."

He often talked to himself. Other people avoided him, lest their association bring a professional need for him closer, so he found solace in his monologues, in which he made sense of his lonely existence.

In a corner of his back room stood a coffin. Each day, he dusted it, polished the brass plate on which he had engraved an inscription:

BARTHOLOMEW SHERBORNE
BORN 1795
DIED
DEATH WAS HIS FRIEND
BUT EMMA WAS HIS LOVE

And the plot he had purchased was clearly identified in his will as the one next to his father's and mother's, and which basked all day in the sunshine.

"I've come to know 'ee, Death, as an invisible and cruel coward, but I be not frightened of my time coming." The smaller coffin, in the far corner, he had made long after Emma had returned to her parents. "And hers be 'ere if she want it, as Jethro knows, and I fashioned it mindful how time adds fat to us, so 'twill suffice in width and length."

Bartholomew closed the door. Death waited for no one. That very morning, a man had called and asked him to bury his wife, who had gone unexpectedly in the night. "On the Dorchester road, we be. Not got much money, mind. Take her bed instead," the man had pleaded. So Bartholomew had gone to measure her, wondering what to use instead of oak, which cost more, being harder, longer work.

Meanwhile, Edgar resumed his search for premises, and found a warehouse a corn merchant was prepared to make available when not in use, but the roof was too high, and there was no natural light. It was cold and unwelcoming, not the place to inspire pupils. All his other enquiries met with rejection, and he returned to the farm dispirited.

In the next few days, he threw himself into working as Frederick wished. The snow slowly melted, the lanes became gushing streams, and hedgerows found themselves in the middle of long lakes.

Frederick made no mention of Emma, or Edgar's fruitless search. It was as if both men wanted a period when they could consolidate their friendship, and take things slowly.

Days passed, and Edgar took out his pens, and wrote a letter, which he sealed and sent. When he returned, he found Frederick had a visitor. Edgar had discovered a splendid horse feeding in the barn, when he was taking Wellesley to his box.

Frederick heard Edgar enter the house, and called to him. The visitor was sitting by the fire, and stood up when Edgar appeared.

"Ah, you're here. There be someone I wish you to meet. He has come on behalf of his father, a friend of mine, who has caught a bad cold and has taken to his bed." The man stepped forward and offered his hand, which Edgar took mechanically. "The news is good. I sent a letter to Jasper, asking for a little assistance for your school. He places, as I told you, great importance on books, and has sent his son to talk to you about what you need. 'Tis time now for my afternoon nap, which I needs as much as air, these days, so I'll leave you twain alone."

Frederick left the room, and shut the door.

Embarrassed, the man said, "Your father forgot to introduce me. I am Geoffrey Burton-Bradstock."

"I know who you are. I could hardly forget you."

Nervously, Geoffrey asked, "We have already met? Your face is not a total stranger, yet I cannot say where we have been introduced before and in what circumstances. I detect some stiffness in your manner which suggests a previous encounter has offended you."

"Picture a lane, and therein two horses, I on one, and Cressida Symondsbury on the other. I prevent a collision between her horse and mine, and then you arrive and knock me to the floor. You accuse me of ungentlemanly intentions, and embarrass your fiancée."

Geoffrey eventually remembered the occasion, which had meant so little to him. It had been more important to win the race against Cressida than apologise for his brutish behaviour.

"I am afraid I owe you an apology, which you should have received immediately after you explained what had happened. Since then, I have suffered the loss of my fiancée, who has broken our engagement on account of my appalling behaviour. My parents, too, regret what has happened. The Symondsburys have been good neighbours for many years. Our marriage would have been of mutual benefit to our families, and would have secured our happiness. But I hope you will now find me a changed man, and fair in our dealings."

Edgar was about to reveal that he had worked for Yeoman, and already knew of Cressida's decision, but did not. Had not Geoffrey caught her trying to kiss Edgar? Geoffrey knew he had lost her, that she, not Edgar, had forsaken him. Behind them, in the barn,

Winifred's eyes had rolled up into her lids, as if reluctant to watch them.

Geoffrey was truly contrite, and sincere in representing his father in the matter of the school, which Edgar acknowledged.

"You speak with a maturity you then lacked, 'tis certain, and I accept your apology."

Edgar proceeded to explain why he needed help, and Geoffrey listened carefully. The school on the Burton-Bradstock estate was run by a strict master, and Geoffrey called in regularly to see the progress the children were making.

"It is a laudable idea, one I am sure we can support. My father feared you required the purchase of a building, which would be beyond our means, times being what they are, but I am sure that a year's salary of a master, and the purchase of essential materials, could be managed."

Edgar shook his hand warmly. The lack of a building was an obstacle he was loath to mention.

"Then I thank you and your father. This means so much to me."

"And to the children of Bridport, too."

"Of course. The children, above all. But satisfy my curiosity, Geoffrey, before you leave. The speed with which your father dispatched you to us betokens a strong affinity. Know you the fertile ground in which its seed grew so strongly? Frederick has referred to some favour he once did for your father."

"Favour?" laughed Geoffrey. "'Twas no favour, by all accounts."

"Then enlighten me. Your smile teases!"

"'Tis no secret. Frederick saved my father's life."

"But how?"

"Nay, I was only a young child, and fear my telling of it would not do your father justice."

"He is not my father," corrected Edgar.

"I am sorry. You bear a strong resemblance in demeanour and appearance."

"I will ask him, then, to tell, though I wonder he has not recounted it before."

"Modesty forbids him. True goodness vaunts not itself, preferring to whisper when necessary, and to remain silent by choice. I shall await an inventory from you, and present it to my father, who will instruct me further. I came unwittingly as your assailant, but leave, I hope, as your friend."

"'Tis certain, Geoffrey, and the incident is forgotten."

Geoffrey left, happy that he had had the chance to apologise.

Edgar reported to Frederick on his meeting, but did not press him to reveal how he had saved Jasper Burton-Bradstock. How different Cressida would find Geoffrey! Edgar mused. Geoffrey was not at all the headstrong young man she had known. Edgar wondered how she fared, whether she still felt constrained by her father's authority.

She was, at that very moment, throwing her arms around her father's neck, crying, "Thank you, father. It means so much to see you have changed your mind. You have seen it? And mother knows?"

Yeoman was happy to feel the love of his daughter again, yet knew not its immediate cause. Her sullenness had woven a tapestry of complaint and accusation, which she displayed to her parents in whichever room she found them, and no bribery or sweet words could persuade her to roll it up and lock it away for ever.

"Speak plainly."

"You know what! Come, see it. You truly have not seen it yet? The sods are but newly replaced. Sit. You shall be blindfolded." She pressed him into a chair, and tightly tied a scarf around his head. "There! You cannot see?"

"No."

She took his hand, and led him to the churchyard.

"Nearly there, father. Hold by my side. The flagstones be uneven."

The creaking of the gate had given away their destination, yet still he did not know what he was going to see. She undid the scarf, and he rubbed his eyes.

"The day is brighter than I imagined. My eyesight is blurred."

"There," she pointed. "Our shame is banished."

Yeoman looked at the headstone erected by Bartholomew, that very morning.

Cressida read aloud the inscription:

> "HERE LIES WINIFRED DRIMPTON,
> A LOYAL MILKMAID,
> A TREASURED COUSIN.

Edgar would be glad to see her marked out like this. I am proud of you, father."

Yeoman turned to Cressida, and said, "No doubt he would, but your thanks are misplaced, for I have not ordered this. It is the work of another."

Then a man's voice came from behind.

"Master Symondsbury?" asked the shorter of the two who had appeared.

The taller doffed his hat, reminding the other of his manners.

"'Tis certain."

"Then this be for you, sir."

Yeoman took the piece of paper from him and broke the wax seal, and the two men restored their hats to their heads, and left.

"What is it, father?" asked Cressida.

"'Tis passing strange. 'Tis the account for Winifred's headstone."

"Then you jest not? 'Twas not you who ordered it, after all?"

"No, Cressida, 'twas not, and I shall not rest until I have found who makes me the laughing stock of Bridport."

Chapter Sixteen

The early morning sun appeared in Edgar's window, encouraging him to put down his pen. He stretched, alleviating the tension in his aching shoulders, the consequence of sitting over the book in which he had been recording the life of the cathedral. How tedious he had found his work, that morning! His concentration had been as brittle as the grey, spent faggot he had prodded to coax a last warm breath from it. He had found it hard to lock out the images, thoughts, and desires that had interrupted him, of late. And he had taken to weighing the dryness of the Bishop's notes against lines he had himself composed, words that arranged themselves into what he supposed were poems.

In the months following him taking up residence in Josiah's house, he had expected a letter from Jolyon, but none had come. The months had stretched into years, and Jolyon's silence caused Edgar, now and again, to contemplate its meaning.

"Ah well! I am too selfish. Has he not done more than enough for me? Why, his tuition has made me a wealthy man. I have work enough to bind me to this chair till midnight. And 'tis mostly the vanity of grand families which tie the rope's knot, 'tis certain. My life has shrunk to the size of this small room, and I hardly dare leave it for fear I might pronounce my desire."

His thoughts were interrupted by a knock at the door. No one usually disturbed his peace, so he rose.

"Zillah," he stuttered, surprised. "It is not yet time for our study of the kings and queens of England. The sun is yet yawning."

"I know. I come to tell you that the Church school will open on Monday, sooner than I expected, and that I must take up my position there. I am afraid our lessons must end, Mr. Porlock, and I tell you that I have come to value the knowledge you have imparted."

"Value?"

"Yes. I have learned much. It cannot have been easy for you, casting light into the darkness of a woman's head."

She smiled, but Edgar was too numb to appreciate her humour. As tall as him, she had become more beautiful than any angel in a manuscript. Her head eclipsed the sun, but light radiated from behind it, making her seem newly arrived from Heaven.

"Monday," he said flatly. "'Tis soon."

"Yes. I will understand if you do not wish to meet, this afternoon."

"What is *your* will?"

Edgar watched her lips tremble at the prospect of an emotional last lesson, when her voice would crack, and she would weep. All those lines he had written and kept in a drawer of his writing desk were an expression of his fascination, love. And now she would spend her days elsewhere, use all that he had taught her to help others. Yet I am selfish to wish she would not go, he chided himself.

"There are things to which I must attend," she said, at last. "The Bishop wants to go over some matters of pedagogy."

Then he owns both of us, reflected Edgar.

"Of course."

They hesitated. What she had planned to tell him she had never said before. No tutor, save that in a romantic novel, could have taught her how. And he, surprised by her arrival at his room, had not had time to prepare the declaration of love, as her tutor, that he had been at pains to gag.

"Mr. Porlock, I - "

"*Edgar* now, please, Zillah. I am no longer your teacher."

"Edgar, I . . . "

Her eyes filled with tears, and she tried again, but the moment when she would have thrown her arms around his neck, and pulled him to her, had gone.

The door shut behind her, and the sun had now passed by.

Edgar took out his poems, scanned them, and put them back. Will she ever read or hear them? he wondered. He felt betrayed, strangely jealous that she was embarking on something he had once promised to do for Emma. Zillah's commitment to the school shamed him, and if he had confessed his love, that would have been selfish, and have distracted her, when she should have been concentrating, as he had to.

"Then the Bishop has our undivided attention," he laughed. "I must speak to Josiah about my position here."

The arrangement had been simple: a room in exchange for Zillah's tuition, but Josiah had taken more. There had been times when he had felt abandoned by the Bishop. When Josiah's congregation had coughed and spluttered so loudly that his sermon had become inaudible to those lolling in the pews at the back, he had felt that God, too, was unhappy with him. During those dark moments, he comforted himself with the thought that he would soon be uplifted by a conversation with Edgar, who was an excellent listener, always saw good in the world, and put things into perspective.

"Why, sir, I have never seen the Bishop in that light! You open my eyes so wide, sir, that I see way beyond the object of my regard. There is some merit in your assertion that, if I suffer the wrath of the Bishop, then I do so in God's name, and that I need only look out for one dagger alone, whereas he must be alert to many making their way towards his back. Ha, sir! A truth garbed in a jest! Well done, sir! How much better I feel to know he suffers more than me," he had once said, when Edgar had had to put up with yet another account of the Bishop's hostility.

On such occasions, Josiah had invited Edgar to dine with them. Edgar had been careful not to join them too often. He had seen that Mrs. Watchet observed his self-conscious utterances to Zillah, and Zillah's flushed face. Mrs. Watchet's eyes would flit from one to the other of them, and she would leave the room to hide her confusion and embarrassment.

Edgar knew he had to leave, and Josiah must not be subjected to the ignominy of having to ask him. Zillah was about to start earning money, and would be independent, could study at her own leisure, and he himself would be superfluous, so he went to see Josiah as soon as possible.

"But, sir, you assume your place in this house has depended solely on Zillah's needs, but that has not been the case for many a year. You come and go as you please, sir, with our blessing. You must not feel you have to go. Of course, you are not chained here like some creature in its cave. Indeed, Mrs. Watchet has expressed the view that you will, one day, marry someone suitable and go to live in a delightful, rose-covered cottage, and that we must not develop too strong an attachment to you. I said to her, 'Mrs. Watchet, we *are* attached to him, as closely as turnips to chops!' and she said, 'But it isn't natural for a man in his prime to sit in his room all day and night, writing and not enjoying the world.' And I said, 'It's the life he chooses.'"

"But our arrangement, which has given me more advantages than you, has enabled me to save money, and I am wealthy beyond my wildest dreams. Indeed, I have been considering making a donation to the church school myself to supplement Jolyon's generosity. I have enough to buy a house, too."

Josiah's jaw dropped, and his monocle fell, so wide did his eyes open in surprise.

"Jolyon?"

"Yes, the man who has made it possible for Zillah to teach."

"*Jolyon* is the benefactor?"

"Indeed, he is. Did you not know?"

"No, sir, I did not. The Bishop has always maintained that the benefactor did not wish his identity made public. This changes everything, sir. I must go at once to tell Zillah!" When he got to the door, he turned, put a shaking finger to his lip, as if working out a solution to a difficult problem, and asked, "And pray, sir, how do *you* come to know the name of the benefactor, when we are all kept in the dark?"

Edgar detected irritation in this question, and was himself annoyed that he had let slip what the Bishop had long ago told him in confidence.

"I fear I have made a grave error in telling you what I had no right to, even though to conceal the truth is always an open invitation for it to be sought. I have no doubt that Jolyon offered the money for altruistic reasons. Is there really cause to be angry with him? I sense resentment in your tone."

Josiah drew a deep breath, wrestled with the choice he had to make.

"The name of the person first, please. Was it Jolyon himself?"

"No, sir. It was the Bishop, a long time ago."

Josiah hung his head, then shook it slowly, decisively.

"Then this changes everything. I must to Zillah, sir. And my attempt to persuade you to stay you must forget."

When Josiah had gone, Edgar looked around his room, and found it a stranger. By the end of this sombre day, I will be gone, he decided. I shall find a house to rent, until my future is decided.

He found himself a room at an inn, and returned to collect his belongings. He had promised the Bishop that he would deliver a completed volume, which would take its place in the gloomy vault of the archives. That had to be done immediately. An inn was not the most secure of places.

His door was ajar. He was sure he had left it shut. Mrs. Watchet looked up from the chair in which she was sitting, in her lap a sheaf of papers she had taken from his drawer. The poems. She is reading them, stealing my words, my feelings, he guessed. They are meant for another, not her.

"Forgive me, Edgar. Josiah has told me what has passed between you. Must you really go? The place will seem so empty without you."

Edgar closed the door. Her pleading took him by surprise. She made no attempt to put down his poems, or to explain why she had taken them.

"I must go. My poems. You have been in my drawer."

"Yes. I cannot deny it. They are so beautiful. The woman for whom they are meant is lucky to have such an ardent lover. I wish they had been meant for me." She sifted through them to find her favourite. "This one is bold and hopeful. I was uplifted when I read it the first time, and - "

"First time? There have been other occasions when you have come into my room and been through my possessions?"

His voice had the sharp teeth of accusation and condemnation.

"Oh, yes. You did not know? I make no secret of my forays into your sacred den. You have never found your poems in a different order from which you left them? And the lock of my hair is still there where I left it. I wonder you did not find it and match it to this."

She took out the combs from her tightly coiled hair, which, though beginning to change colour by her ears, was still lustrous and thick. When she shook it, it became brown waves splashing onto her cheeks and shoulders.

Carefully, she took the lock of hair from the drawer, held it against the ends of the torrent which had cascaded from the severe bun, and approached him, so that he could examine the match.

"Why have you done this? It makes me feel that all the time I have lived here, you have been someone different from the person I thought you. How long have you been coming here while I have been out?"

Mrs. Watchet slowly ran her hand across the shoulders of his coat hung on the back of his chair. Then she stretched out on his bed, making room for an imaginary person to join her. She patted the pillow, and he knew then that *he* was the reason. All those times he had been with the Bishop, she had crept into his room, on the pretext of having to clean it, to enact a fantasy she knew was forbidden in real life.

"You understand now. Yet I see from your disapproving eyes that you would deny me such moments of intimacy in my loneliness. You cannot know how I have lived in torment from the moment you came here. All those sleepless nights, I have wondered what might happen if I came to you, and ended my misery, broke free from my gaol of shame, but I feared rejection, which I now face, I know."

As she spoke, she became more passionate, and Edgar understood that he was the object of her love. And her confession, like that of a prisoner who has long denied her crime but feels the painful burden of guilt, had come on his imminent departure.

"But Zillah. Knows she of your obsession, this infatuation? I have many times seen in her face a secret she dare not tell. Tell me her earnest face is but the natural whim of a student and not a sign of her knowledge that you . . . "

His unfinished sentence hung in mid-air. He could not bear to say *love*. Mrs. Watchet was older than him, but not enough for her years to deter attraction. How stupid he had been not to see that her reluctance to talk at length at the table was a sign of her liking him, her fear that her voice would illuminate her feelings.

"Love? Is that your next word? Edgar, your head is so buried in books that you have failed to understand Zillah, too. You should know how she loves you but lacks the words. Prepare yourself for the day when she demonstrates it instead, for it will come soon, and when it does, bask in it, as you would in the sunshine when it races over the hills and finds you in a field or lane. Let it hold the moment as still as death. Know what it is like to be possessed by her love, as, one day, it will withdraw from you, and leave you as a husk."

"She has spoken to you?"

Mrs. Watchet shook her head, and smiled.

"She does not have to. How many lessons with you has she missed? None. Has she ever complained? No. And does she tire of telling me what she has learned with Mr. Porlock? Everything you have taught her is a thorn in my flesh, which festers. We both keep the same secret from each other."

"I will go, and then your . . . feelings for me will die till they are no longer a rose but a scattering of brown petals. Where they are now red, they will fade and rot."

"But come the summer, the rose tree blooms again. I can never love another man."

He sat in the chair in which she had been reading his poems. She had read them many times, and longed for a new one, in case she should be its subject, his love. The gold-leafed metaphors would immortalise her. Just one poem, and she would be happy, but she read knowing they were meant for Zillah.

"It pains me to think that I have supplanted Josiah in your affections. He is a good man, whose kindness towards me I can never repay."

She took his hand reassuringly.

"Supplanted? You are mistaken, Edgar, for I have never loved him in that way. It is impossible, too, for him to do so me."

Edgar contemplated the possibility that Josiah might discover Mrs. Watchet's love for him, and believe that he had encouraged it, and abused Josiah's trust. It would call into question her moral judgement, bring shame upon her, end a marriage that had endured so many years, despite the inequality of their love for each other.

"I go now, lest Josiah believe me the architect of this madness."

He carelessly began to pack his pens, ink, and books into the chest he had bought. The poems would be safe in it. There was no telling what she might do to them, now that he had spurned her.

"Let me help," she suggested. "I have prepared myself for this moment. I do not wish your abiding memory of me to be a mewling woman. A man packs not his clothes as neatly as a woman. I have had plenty of practice when Josiah has visited distant parishes on Church matters."

She made to begin, but Edgar cried, "No! There is not much. Will you go now with my thanks for all that you have done for me? 'Tis true I love another, and know the frustration of having its declaration chained by necessity. But I beg you, forget me, though the act feels painful."

She moved towards the door.

"Will you leave your key to the house on the table?"

"Of course."

Hesitating, she said, "From time to time, we may bump into each other, as we did at the cathedral, and 'tis to be hoped you will not pass me by as if we were strangers."

"I would not do that."

"Then thank you. I shall go now, though there is one thing that puzzles me, and it concerns how much you know of this family. It has been my lot to carry a burden heavier even than my forbidden love for you. Know you anything of it? Have you ever suspected its existence?"

"I know not of what you talk, but hasten your disclosure of it. I fear my prolonged presence here invites more surprises than I can bear."

"What think you of Josiah and me?"

"I think you the dutiful wife of a parish vicar, and guardian of your niece, Zillah."

"And that is what the world compelled us to seem, yet nothing is further from the truth. Josiah loves God, his master, Zillah, his niece, and me, his sister."

"You have grown apart, but love stretches."

"No, Edgar. He loves me as his sister because I *am* his sister. Wells had to see us as man and wife, or the Bishop would never have given Josiah the living. Zillah is my daughter."

Edgar gasped, incredulous.

"And no orphan made by tragedy?"

"No. I sinned, and God thought fit not to forgive. My only happiness has been to know that you have been sitting at that table, writing with these pens, sleeping on this bed. My happiness has been my misery."

"And Zillah knows she is your daughter? Her father lives?"

"She believes that her parents are dead. I know not where her father lives or even if he does so. I am past caring. He went away without a word. A man who does that has the greater sin. Can you understand that, Edgar?"

"Yes, I can, more than you will ever know, and it will follow him as his shadow for the rest of his life."

Mrs. Watchet went to her room, and opened the box in which she kept various papers. On top of them, she placed a poem she had taken and hidden inside her dress pocket before Edgar had surprised her.

"On composing this particular poem, he has become the author of his own tragedy, which will make mine seem a mere interlude of misfortune. And now I must to the kitchen, where the turnips need peeling, and the chops await a delicate seasoning according to Josiah's taste."

And at the inn, Edgar held his head in his hands, wondering how he would tell the Bishop that the completed volume he was due to give him had disappeared from the chest in which he thought he had packed it.

Chapter Seventeen

During the Mayor of Bridport's self-inflating speech, which declared the school open and himself the most beneficent civic dignitary the town had ever had, children stood nervously, looking at each other with an expression somewhere between fear and terror. Some had arrived in their best clothes, others in the only rags they possessed, though the difference was hard to discern. All smiled and cheered when the Mayor, in his iridescent apparel, and like a cockerel which has been preening himself for hours, rang the bell, signifying the start of the school day. He opened the door, and the children entered, after an initial jostling and stern words from Edgar. Fifteen, the Mayor counted.

In the corner of the classroom stood a stove glowing orange, and as the children passed it, Geoffrey Burton-Bradstock warned them not to touch it. The money his father had donated had transformed part of the warehouse kindly offered by its owner, a merchant with no merchandise to fill it, and no inclination to find any. Interior walls had been added to form a classroom, and desks and benches were ranged facing Edgar's table at the front. No permanent teacher had yet been appointed, though Geoffrey had informed Edgar, that very morning, that he had received a promising application from a Miss. Eleadora Melplash, whom he had invited to interview.

"Let us hope she is as able as her letter suggests," Edgar had said.

"In the meantime, I will do my best, but I fear I will not have the patience to help these benighted children."

When all the pupils were seated, they fell silent. They were tall and short, some several years younger than others.

"Good morning, everyone, and welcome to your new school. I am Mr. Porlock."

One boy, who had avoided the wet rag his mother had waved at him, suddenly giggled. The name Porlock amused him.

"And pray, boy, what causes such mirth? You laugh for no apparent reason."

The boy screwed up his face, not understanding the question.

Geoffrey had offered to stay for the first hour, and was used to this reaction, having seen it many times in the Burton-Bradstocks' school.

"Your teacher asks you why you laugh. Have you no answer?"

The boy glanced at his fellow pupils, and realised he was alone in his reaction.

"'Twas Porlock. 'Tis a ticklish name, and be like a feather under my armpit."

The others giggled, though Geoffrey's stern look stopped them.

"'Tis not for you to laugh at your teacher. And now be the time for a prayer to start the day. Close your eyes, put your hands together like this, and bow your heads. When I say *Amen*, at the end, you must repeat it together."

Some parents had already taught their children to pray, but most had not, and the pupils could not resist looking to see if others were complying.

"Eyes closed, all of you!" shouted Edgar, his voice making those who had not followed the instruction jump.

"Dear Father, bless this new school, and grant these young children knowledge and wisdom, that they might grow up to follow in thy footsteps. Amen." Geoffrey waited for their response, but none came. "*Amen*," he stressed. One or two opened their eyes to check what the others were doing, and gradually, the mumbled word spread along the benches.

"And now your first lesson: the alphabet, and how to write your name."

This took them to the pupils' first break, when they went into the yard.

"Boys, come this way!" Geoffrey beckoned.

"Girls, go that way!" pointed Edgar.

The boys shyly aimed into the buckets lined up against a wall, and the girls refused to go behind curtains, in another part of the warehouse, preferring to wait till they got home.

"When there are a few more, the class should be divided," pointed out Geoffrey. "Boys and girls have different needs."

"Then let us hope that Miss. Eleadora Melplash comes sooner rather than later! There are many things I have not thought of."

During the morning, two boys slouched self-consciously, followed by their mother, into the classroom. Their mother had not heard the cock crow, she explained, and what with her being up all night with her husband's biliousness, she had slept in and must apologise for their late arrival, though she could not guarantee that it would not happen again, as he suffered from the affliction regularly, and only a drop or two of wine or cider could ease the pain. They had none in, having not a sou to their name till he was earning again, which would not be in the foreseeable future, on account of him being unable to bend in case his disease took a grip of his innards and wrung them out as she did the washing.

"A most unfortunate set of circumstances," observed Geoffrey. "Leave your children with us, and 'tis to be hoped your husband recovers soon."

"Thank 'ee kindly, sir," said the woman, curtseying. "I shall pass on your good wishes, which will help him on his way, though there be no guarantees in this world. No, sir. None whatsoever."

She left, and Edgar could not help smiling at her description of her domestic trials and tribulations.

Geoffrey stayed to the end of the session, which finished in the early afternoon. A few of the children hung about Edgar's desk, but he urged them to go and play in the sunshine.

"Your first day over," remarked Geoffrey. "You have survived?"

"I am as tired as if I'd worked all day in the fields!" complained Edgar. "But the children have made progress. They have all written their name on the slates."

"Let us see if they can do so tomorrow. Children are as up and down as barrows and vales."

"Then they be no different to the rest of us."

"And 'tas been an up Pilsdon Pen day for you?"

"'Tis certain!"

Edgar tried his best to teach them all that he thought important. More children came, the noise level rose, and so he had to be more disciplinarian than he wanted. Those who had initially yielded to his gentle persuasion to learn now became more cautious. Where he had once had time for every pupil, making each feel special, he now stared out of the window, longing to be in the fields with Wellesley, or in his room, writing poems, and illuminating them, so that skills he had sharpened would not be blunted.

Frederick began to miss him on the farm. Sheep needed shearing, rams raddling, ready to be put to the ewes, so that, in the spring, there would be lambs to save and fatten. So he decided to set someone on. The man came from Dorchester, and had, on his own admission, flitted from farm to farm, staying only till his master had had enough of him.

"Something in him, I reckon," said Frederick to Edgar. "Strong and had enough of journeying. Sheared me a sheep, and trimmed a horn curled so bad it was sticking in the ram's cheek. I asks him what he'd do with a teat that's souring the milk, and he says, 'Dry hay till the moon waxes nearly round, and mix a bit of meadow garlic with butter, and smooth it in gently.' I asks him where he gets all that from, as 'tis not known, these parts, and he says 'tas come from an old conjuror who lived beyond the woods at the back of Bockhampton. Heath be full of the white flowers, which fill the air with their glicky scent. 'Try it,' he says, 'and 'twill soothe the cow in seconds.' Conjuror be dead now, but his son has picked up the knowledge."

"Then he be worth his weight in blue vinney, or he have a tongue so honeyed he'd sweeten the most stinging onion!" scoffed Edgar.

"Well, I gives him a go. Starts in the barn tomorrow. You up in the school, mornings, and 'tis sliding here a bit. Come the sun step this side of Golden Cap, I be fit for only a swallow of cider and a dream or two in this 'ere chair."

"A woman comes in a few days. Geoffrey reckons she be the one, way of her writing."

"What think you of that? What will you do?"

"You have me back here a while?"

Frederick sat up in his chair. Too much slinking into it had given him an aching back. What he had to say required a straight spine.

"Always a bed for you here, but you free to go anywhere now. You done what you should have, and now there be nothing holding you back. Then there be Emma, who asks me how goes the school, and I say well 'sfar as I know."

"And what says she to that?"

"Smiles and nods. Just smiles and nods."

"That all?"

"What you expect? 'Tis all done you said you'd do, though things be different with her now. You being here be vinegar as well as strawberries. Longer you tarry, the worse it'll be for her. A second going'll send her all muddled again, just when she's starting to put words together as she used to: all sharp and straight as no nonsense. Don't want her like scrambled eggs no more. So . . . "

Frederick was on Emma's side, Edgar knew. I have done as she asked, Edgar reasoned, and now her forgiveness must be confirmed before I can drop this heavy sack of worry from my back. Maybe I should show her the school, the children, as proof.

But that was not a good idea, thought Frederick.

"And why not? A school is what she wanted," argued Edgar.

"No, what *you* wanted," reminded Frederick. "She sees you in the classroom, she'll be sad that 'tis only half of what your lives together should have added up to. 'Tis so simple a sum, I wonder you can't do it!"

"Then will you bring her here, tomorrow afternoon? I must speak with her."

"'Tis certain."

And Frederick left the room.

The next day, the new man came. His dog, as liquid in its movements as a brook, followed him closely. Frederick set the man to work, warned him to take good care of Wellesley, and not to ride him. Then hay had to be dropped off in the fields for the cows and sheep.

"Take the cart and the bay, but keep to the driest paths. Water still clagging the land, and wheels sink and stick," instructed Frederick. "The new swamps suck hard."

"Saw a fence or two leaning. You want them fixing?"

The man wanted to make a good impression, start afresh, and his dog was panting, eager to control the sheep.

"Yes. And then, while I'm up at Briddy, if you get the time, clean the plough, as 'tis crusted, and the blade be nicked by stubborn stones. We'll need it soon."

"You planting?"

Frederick laughed.

"No, *you* are!"

After school had finished, Edgar went to see Wellesley. He wanted to ride him along the cliff-top, where the wind would deafen him to all other thoughts but what he would say to Emma.

The barn seemed to have been replaced. New hooks held aloft saddles and bits; forks had been retrieved from the straw and propped against the wall behind rope; and flagstones had been scrubbed.

The new man, guessed Edgar, making towards Wellesley.

Then the humming, becoming a song. The new man, rubbing with a rag the blade of the plough he had cleared of hard, caked mud, and washed, was crouching. Edgar saw him, at last, and the man stood up.

"I'm Edgar. That be my horse: Wellesley. You new set on?"

The man nodded.

"Billy Eype, and this be my dog: Yeoman."

Edgar reached to stroke the dog brindled with splats of cow muck from scurrying across the farmyard.

"A good name and solid, though not a dog's," remarked Edgar, wiping his fingers on his trousers.

"A name borrowed in jest and revenge. I once knew a rich man called Yeoman, and I worked for him till he got rid of me and a few milkmaids."

Yeoman allowed Edgar one touch, then growled faintly.

"What he do that for?"

"Just a warning."

"No, the man."

"On account of a story made up by a youth."

"What said the story?"

"That I been a-tupping all the milkmaids like a ram the ewes."

"And 'twasn't the truth?"

"No. Wish it was!"

"That all?"

"All Yeoman Symondsbury accused me of."

"And the dog's name?"

"Treated me like a dog, did Master Symondsbury, so I treats him like one. Jumps to my command, and I feed him scraps."

Edgar chuckled.

"But why did your master believe the youth?"

Billy Eype took a step closer, and lowered his voice, as if he did not want anyone else to hear.

"'Twas commonly thought among the maids that Guy be his bastard son. Women sense these things more than men. 'They even smells the same,' said Fanny. And 'twould be a hypocrite who sacks a man for what he does himself. Aint that right?"

Edgar recalled Flora's declaration that she would never reveal the name of Guy's real father. If the rumour turned out to be true, then Clementine would leave Yeoman. O, the hypocrisy of believing that Winifred's suicide would bring shame on the family name, when Yeoman had himself invited it by fathering a child out of wedlock! By employing Flora, he provides for a son, and buys silence, worked out Edgar.

"'Tis certain. You staying long?"

"Long as Master Frederick'll have me. Been like a horsefly too long. Made mistakes. Some to regret, others to put right."

Edgar understood; this was not the Billy Eype he had pictured, and the others had painted in lurid colours.

"Then you and I, though strangers, have more in common than we think. Heard the gossip. Even took your job for a while, when the farm had weeded up."

Billy's eyes shone, and he ruffled the dog's fur.

"He got rid of you, too? That Guy still there? He the reason you here?"

Edgar shook his head.

"Came here for other reasons."

A silence settled. Billy's next revelation worked its way out slowly. Some words would not do. He had to choose them wisely, not knowing what had happened after he had gone. When they came, Edgar weighed them, had been thinking how he would let him know about Winifred.

"Girl there called Winifred Drimpton. We were going to be married."

"Going to? Things burned out?"

"I made a mistake."

"She was not for you?"

"Yes, she was," Billy corrected earnestly, "but, the other maids . . . I . . ."

"I heard things. Nothing to do with me. I don't judge a man so."

"But I shall go to see her, now I've learned, and try to pick up again, apologise. Got a good job here. Going to save, buy her a ring if she'll wear it."

It was not the time to tell him, but it would be cruel, thought Edgar, to let him return to the farm and find out with a ring in his pocket.

"Stop by when you're done here."

"'Tis certain."

From then till Billy took up his invitation, Edgar rehearsed. Some words sounded brutal, others over-polished. Winifred was swaying before his eyes, had kicked over the chair from a height guaranteed to break her neck. And loneliness was what he had put it down to, but there was more that she had held back from him. Her begging to take her with him had been about giving her a chance to start again somewhere – anywhere. But more: Billy Eype.

Edgar's heart ran ahead of itself. Emma. What if she had done the same, cracked and stretched her neck till her heart had spluttered and stopped? Who would have found her? Not him, certainly. It would have fallen to someone else: her parents, probably. O, Billy, why did you dally with the others? Why?

Billy came. Yeoman whined, at first, when left to sit outside, then slid his head between his paws, and waited.

"You want to see me?" opened Billy.

"Cider?" Edgar noticed the hesitation, a sign that he had been tempted too many times, and had set his mind against it. "There's water."

"No, thanks."

"You sleeping in the barn?"

"'Tis certain."

Not the best place, thought Edgar. A man could hang himself in one.

"I just wanted to let you know that I didn't stay long at the Symondsbury place. Made a start. Cleared up the house!"

Billy hung his head, knew to what Edgar was referring: the negligence, the failure.

Not the time for that; Edgar could have bitten off his tongue.

"Won't happen again. I've got a chance now. A man who spends more time with his dog than a woman soon changes his ways."

"Winifred had a hard time when you all went. Yeoman left her to get on with it. The cows mainly, the rubies, as she called 'em. She got stuck on her own, wanted to leave but had nowhere to go."

"Beaminster," recalled Billy. "So she said."

"Billy, there baint an easy way to tell you, but she's gone."

"Where?"

"Hanged herself. She be buried in the churchyard."

Billy wobbled, clutched a chair, steadied himself.

"What, my Winifred? Gone?"

Edgar nodded.

"But why?"

Not a time to speculate, decided Edgar; not the moment to apportion blame.

"You want that cider now?"

Billy moved to go, his shoulders sloping submissively, as Yeoman's when he wriggled towards him for fuss. Then Billy remembered.

"The ring. I was going to buy her a ring. You know, to show her I was sorry."

190

Edgar looked away, not fit to advise. Billy left.

Children's questions boomed in Edgar's head, and Billy's loss was eventually pushed out. Before Frederick came in to bring bread, cheese, and onions, there was time to reflect upon his own circumstances. Emma was still alive; he had earned his forgiveness. I must hear it from her. Let her see the school, the children, myself at work. Then I will be able to hold my head up, and look the world in the eye again. Life, measured by swelling moons, passes. Let me make no more mistakes. Not one.

"A morsel till dinner?" said Frederick, offering the plate.

Vinegar fumes from the onions tickled his nose, jolted him.

"A morsel but no more, for my appetite, just now, be a mere spickle."

Chapter Eighteen

How will I explain it to the Bishop? wondered Edgar. Mrs. Watchet must have taken the book during one of her secret forays into my room. Anticipating my rejection of her, she had already planned her revenge, is my guess, though she strenuously denies it.

"You think me capable of such malice? I who have loved you in suffering silence, all these years? I would not do such a thing, and it saddens me to think you suspect me."

Edgar saw no theatrical gesture in the dabbing of her eyes with her embroidered handkerchief. She composed herself, and looked at him. Then it must have been stolen, he concluded. That or I have stupidly left it somewhere.

"Has the house been left open while we have all been out? Is it possible that someone might have sneaked inside, and recognised the value of the book?"

He seemed to be addressing himself rather than Mrs. Watchet, but she responded with, "All things are possible, as we have both come to learn recently. Yet in all my time at the rectory, even when we have taken in destitute men and women begging for help, nothing has been stolen. In fact, they usually leave more than they take: their gratitude, and joy that God can help them rebuild their lives. I feed them chops and turnips, but Josiah nourishes them with kind words, challenges them with truths as stinging as nettles, and soothes them with the gospel. I have been thinking. Is it possible that you have left it somewhere? Taken it, in its incompleteness, to show the Bishop, and left it in some place? An inn, for example?"

He racked his brains to think of occasions when he had taken it to the Bishop to acquaint him with its progress. Yes, he had stopped to sit and rest, had let the warmth of the sun lave his face. Then he had shut his eyes, his face turned upwards, as if offering it to God to kiss. But the book, heavy itself in an even heavier, protective box, had never left his side, he was sure. Only in a rare moment of forgetfulness would it have gone missing. He tried to think of the last time he had worked on it, and his head felt empty, as an inkwell needing to be filled, all memories now faint hieroglyphs, handwriting faded in bright sunlight.

"I know not," he said, at last. "My thoughts are dead leaves spiralling in an autumn wind. Forgive me, Mrs. Watchet, for I have been clutching at them in vain, and you have done nothing to deserve my suspicion. I must simply report to the Bishop that the volume on which I have been working has disappeared, and that I can offer no satisfactory explanation. A year's work, countless hours of painstaking illumination. All his notes and instructions remain, but it would be a crushing blow to me to have to begin again, and I do not think my hand would be as steady. My inclination would be to rush, make up for lost time, and such an art must not be so insulted. Besides, beauty lost can never be recaptured."

"Then go immediately to the Bishop, and let him know. Josiah speaks ill of him, but out of personal prejudice, and you may find him more forgiving than you anticipate."

"You speak wisely. I shall go now. The sooner I tell him, the lighter shall my burden be."

The Bishop, when Edgar had told all, stared into the middle distance.

"And you make no mistake? Have not hidden it for safe-keeping in a nook in Josiah's house?"

Without thinking, Edgar replied, "No. I have left and am in

temporary lodgings. Mrs. Watchet assures me that no intruder has entered."

The Bishop raised his eyebrows at the news that Edgar had moved out.

"You took the book to your new residence?"

"Not at all. I was about to leave the rectory when I discovered it missing. I am staying at an inn till my new lodgings are settled on. I would never have taken so an important a work there, though the inn is clean and discourages excessive drinking. The landlord is God-fearing."

"I am pleased to hear it, though less so to receive news of this terrible . . . "

The Bishop weighed several words which might adequately describe Edgar's mistake. Each sounded harsh, yet there could be no denying that the history of the cathedral, never in jeopardy when it had been Jolyon's responsibility, had been put in grave danger. Edgar felt the incompleteness of the sentence a dreadful indictment. The Bishop's facial expression constantly changed: now a grimace, then an accusation, and, finally, a condemnation.

"Your notes and wishes are safe. I shall begin again, though my hand yet trembles too much to do it immediate justice."

The Bishop looked at him; God had advised.

"No, Edgar. It cannot be. My heart is heavy. This feels like a sin that cannot be readily forgotten. There is no further requirement to work for the archive. In time, God will forgive you, though his anger banishes you from the cathedral and its precinct. His will be obeyed. Now go. I must pray, in the hope that He will not punish me for placing too much trust in you."

Edgar left, his numbness preventing him from thinking logically. No book, no home, no job. There was little left for him in Wells. He thought of Zillah in her classroom, her children looking up into her seraphic face. Why, he smiled, I would learn nothing if I were in her lessons! He sat on the bench on which he had found the newspaper reporting the loss of the *Lyonesse*. If you truly love her, you would tell her, he told himself. If what Mrs. Watchet said is true – that Zillah loves me – then I must be brave. Otherwise, Zillah, like the book, might soon be lost to me.

Edgar made his mind up quickly not to return to the rectory. Instead he would wait for her to return at the end of the school day, when he could ask her to walk with him, find a quiet stretch by the water, where gnats hover in the polished light. Josiah would have told her that Edgar was no longer in the Bishop's employ. Edgar expected nothing of her but to spare him time to express his feelings. Since their last meeting, he had felt lost in the space, as vast as the womb of the cathedral, their lessons had once occupied. In them, she had learned to squeeze words together into rhymes, grudging ones, to begin with, that looked and sounded absurd, but which became twins, not identical, though born with a similar sound. Now she must listen to him one more time, then promise herself to him, or compound his unhappiness in Wells.

She seemed tired when he approached her. He called her name from a distance, so that it would appear he had not contrived their meeting. Her emaciated shadow stretched across the green in front of the cathedral.

"Forgive me. I was on my way to eat. No chops and turnips, I'm afraid. Less wholesome food, these days. But I manage. How goes the teaching? You are inspiring them?"

"I am not you," she sighed.

"If you were, you would be miserable."

They walked, side by side. Zillah's eyes found him, then her feet again, as if his look were too bright a light.

"Why so?"

This is not the time, he decided. She is tired. Disappointment muffles her voice. The children, perhaps; a failure to respond to her enthusiasm.

"Zillah, will you meet me on Sunday? I should like to hear about the new school, how you are."

Her smile was weak, suggested suffering.

"Me? I am as well as can be expected."

"*Expected*? There is some obstacle to your happiness?"

"Sunday," she agreed firmly, stopping. "You will come to the house?"

"No," he said, too quickly. "It is best if you do not tell them. Outside the doors of the cathedral. Two o'clock."

"It is a public place."

"It is where I first saw you."

She raised her eyebrows in curiosity.

"You remember?"

"We can go somewhere else."

"The doors, then."

After a moment's hesitation, she continued on her way home.

"Two," he called.

Sunday came. The light was thin and gleaming, the air calm and warm. Against the stone, Edgar felt safe, protected. She came from the side, catching him unawares. Edgar had not expected her black bonnet. Perhaps, she does not want to be recognised, he thought.

"You are early. Your shadow is yet a Bishop's rod from two."

She looked nervously about her. Her face stayed shy in the pit of her black bonnet. Edgar felt a distance between them: more than the years separating them, a heath of mire, and rabbit-holes in which he might injure himself if he tried to come closer to her.

"What do you intend we should do? I had forgotten I had promised to help in the garden, this afternoon."

"You have a few minutes in which to hear me?"

"I do."

"My words require privacy."

"I have a key to the school."

"Then lead the way."

She commented on that morning's sermon: how Josiah had tried with all his heart to lift the spirits of his congregation, and how they had demonstrated their usual indifference.

"They sang as if compelled, and not out of joy of worship. They reminded me of my pupils. He is likely to resign the living. The Bishop lacks understanding, and is unlikely to try and persuade him to stay."

All that she said made her a stranger, and he no more than a mere acquaintance. She took her seat behind her desk at the front, and Edgar was her only pupil.

"We have swapped roles!" he pointed out.

But she did not laugh; not even a brief smile changed her cold mien, once her bonnet had been removed. Edgar thought her cheeks and corners of her mouth a little pinched, as if she were piqued by something. He felt foolish, even ashamed, that he had come to swear his love for someone who seemed so aloof.

"I cannot teach you anything."

She waited. *He* had requested the meeting. What do you have to tell me? said her eyes.

"Zillah, you cannot know what pain I have endured as your teacher. You have grown into a woman so beautiful that it has been sometimes unbearable to look at you. Living under the same roof as you has restrained me, kept me from the outside world. When I have not been writing, I have been moping on my bed, knowing you were in the same house, but powerless to declare my love for you. Now that I am no longer your teacher, and you are no longer a child but a grown woman, I must tell you that I love you, and that, when we have grown closer to each other, I hope you will consent to be my wife."

She wiped tears from her sad eyes. The beauty of which he spoke had abandoned her. I am losing her before she is even mine, he panicked. If ever she had feelings for me, they have evaporated as early morning dew when the sun dries the grass. Emma, Captain

Lydeard, Jolyon, the book, and now Zillah. All gone. And must I close my eyes and sleep, in the hope that when I awake I can feel better? Will I always feel punished?

"I grew to love you, but I cannot marry you," she sniffed. "If circumstances were different . . . "

"Circumstances. Yes, I know. I have no job, no home, but I have more than enough money to provide for us. You can continue to teach, and I will make money from my illumination. There are rich families, churches, who will pay for it handsomely."

Zillah shook her head, bit her lower lip; the pain stops the crying, the involuntary shuddering accompanying the runaway sadness. This she had learned from bitter experience.

"They are not the circumstances I mean. Your words are butterflies, Edgar. You think that they have only to alight on me and I will open my petals to them."

Edgar screwed up his forehead. This was not the conversation he had wanted.

"Butterflies? You think I am inconstant?"

Her pride stiffened her, and her eyes widened accusingly.

"I know so."

His heart began to race. How can she know? Has my history not been so cleverly disguised, after all? he wondered. Will it always dog me?

"Emma? You know about her? Who has told you? I was but a callow youth. You will surely forgive me that! I am a different man now."

It was time for Zillah to be puzzled.

"You talk in riddles, Mr. Porlock. I know of no Emma, nor care I for her, whoever she is, or how you have sinned against her, though if you have hurt her, you have done no more than any other man has done to a woman, at one time of his life or other."

Edgar was sad to hear such cynicism from one so young. And his mistake had now closed the gate through which he had hoped she would pass into his adult life.

"But my inconstancy. You say you are confirmed in the knowledge of it. How so? Ask me any question you like about Emma, and I will be truthful, but do not besmirch my love for you with the accusation of inconstancy. Anything but that!"

"I have no questions. Your past is your own, however you may have spent it, though I glean you have played less than fairly with Emma. She is lucky, as I am, to have escaped you."

He wriggled on the bench, which was lower than her seat. She had the superior position in more ways than one. Yet he remained surprised that she was being so sharp with him, when all he had done was to tell her he loved her. She had not tricked him to tell her about Emma; he had not deceived her.

"Let us not wound each other, Zillah. I will leave, as you have made clear I must, when you have told me in what way I have been disloyal."

She placed her hands flatly on her desk, as if she had made a momentous decision.

"There is evidence."

Angered by her persistence, he stood up, and she leaned back in her chair.

"Then show me it. I should be glad to see it! But I assure you it will be as much a stranger to me as *you* seem. Let me see it, hear it, touch it, smell it, taste it! Only then will I believe it."

The strength of his conviction made an impact, and, for a moment, she doubted the importance of what she had in her possession. Without taking her eyes off his, which demanded her focus, she slipped her hand into her coat pocket. It was there. She knew the handwriting to be his, had seen it many times.

"You taught me to read and write. Poetry, you said, is our language's finest attire."

"And that remains the case. I hope, one day, you will show your pupils how it is so. But come to your evidence. I like not your procrastination. My mood will not bear it."

"Not yet. You must know that I have written poems, some immature, fanciful, when I was younger. I always wanted to show you them, but I was scared you would think them the pathetic creations of an adolescent. But more: that you would read between the lines, and discover them to be a poorly disguised expression of my growing love for you. I was afraid you would end our lessons, that you would be compromised."

At last, she melts, her love no longer frozen in the rectory's icehouse.

"Then, my love, what is all this fire? How can I douse your opposition to me? Speak plainly. I must be told. All the years of denial are as nothing compared to this torture, which tears me apart."

She took out the piece of paper, fingered its tight folds.

"Will you stay seated till I have finished? I am fearful of you in your present state."

Reluctantly, Edgar sat down, and stared at what she held.

"I am sorry. I did not mean to scare you. Continue and end this examination."

She opened out the sheet, ran her eyes over the words again. A thousand times she must have read them. Edgar saw her pain. Then she coughed. She had considered reading it passionately, but feared she would break down. Flatly and disinterestedly would sound odd. Perhaps, *he* could read it, so that she could see him squirm when he recognised the author. Too cruel? she wondered. She had eventually opted to read it as a puzzle, so that her interrogative tone would give him the impression that its meaning eluded her, that she needed an interpretation of its images and inexorable iambic pacing to the resolution in the final rhyming couplet. And he would recognise each quatrain as a stepping-stone towards the most miraculous, holy confession a man or woman can make.

She began. By line two, Edgar's head was bowed. By the end of the sonnet, he was looking at her, but had not the air of defeat.

"And where did you find the poem?"

"You recognise it?"

"Of course. It is mine, or, rather, yours. At least, *for* you. I had hoped, one day, to hand them all to you, to let you know how much I love you."

A shadow of confusion passed over her face: her brow knotted, her eyelids fluttered erratically, as if prior to fainting, and she licked her dry lips.

"There are others?"

"Many more, in my trunk. But answer me how you come to be in possession of that particular one."

"Edgar, I . . . Mr. Porlock, I think you know."

"Unless you yourself took it, which I doubt, then you received it from the hand of a thief, who had a particular reason for stealing it."

The poem shook in her hand. Mrs. Watchet had been so convincing when she had passed it to her.

"And I let you have this, Zillah, knowing your feelings for him," Mrs. Watchet had said. "Of course, you must never tell your uncle about it. I told Mr. Porlock plain and simple: 'You must go. I can never love you. Your poem means nothing to me. You have abused the trust placed in you.'"

Zillah had been heartbroken when Edgar had left the rectory, believing herself to be the single object of his love.

"There has been a mistake," she said, at length, "a terrible mistake."

"Your aunt gave it to you?" Zillah nodded. "Do you want to know the truth?"

"Please," she said, trying to calm herself. "She said you had written it for *her*."

"It will change what you think of her."

"I am ready."

So her teacher taught her a lesson that changed the way she saw the world. She had learned so much about the history of kings and queens and other famous people with Edgar, but never expected him to reveal her own past.

"It changes not my feelings for you," said Edgar.

"My *mother*?" gasped Zillah.

"Yes. Your mother."

Her face became as white as death.

"But my parents are dead. My mother and father *live*?"

"I am sorry, Zillah. Your mother must pay the price for taking my poem. She used it to deceive you, and so it is she who must tell you the rest."

Chapter Nineteen

Emma slowly lifted the cloth, releasing a sweet smell. She prodded the cake gently, testing its sponginess. On her face were faint fingers of flour, made whiter by her cheeks cooked damson by the heat of the range in Frederick's kitchen.

Edgar watched her. Frederick winked to him. In a dish sat a pat of cream, and stewed gooseberries bubbled and popped in a pan.

"'Tis all ready for the coating and cutting," said Emma.

Then it came, the smile, transforming her, lighting up her face as the sun spreads the vale with washed light when the cloud obscuring it passes.

The years have fled from her, this day, noticed Edgar. They matter not, the few wisps of grey hair loosened by her bending at the oven door. There are redcurrants in her cheeks, and blackcurrants in her eyes again.

Frederick could not bear to look at Edgar, dared not admit that this was how it should have been, with Emma hot and fussing, and Edgar slumped in front of the fire, watching its light ripple and throb when the wind blew down the chimney. And, at that moment, when Emma's once scared eyes had banished their demons, Frederick entertained the thought that, even after such a long separation, they might find again the happiness Edgar had promised her.

Edgar went to the table. Emma looked flustered, but he said,

"Can I put the cream on? 'Tis an art to pat a thickness that makes a man happy. And I hope that these gooseberries don't make me squint and my tongue tingle. Not even Frederick's cream can douse the smart of a Dorset sour!" and she was soon smiling again.

"Alfred Morcombelake, you be a man ahead of himself to think this cake or cream will be squashed together for *you*! 'Twas Billy drove the cows to be milked, the maids milked 'em, Nature, in her clever hat, made the cream, Frederick ground the flour, and I baked the cake. Pray, tell me, do, what *you* have done to deserve to choose the thickness of your own taste?"

"You tell him, my dear. He become a lazy one, though, in his favour, he does a bit of chopping and a spickle of mending," teased Frederick.

"If we all have a hand in the making of something before we can partake of it, then Emma and I must leave, as this fire been a-chopped and flamed by you alone, Frederick, and that means only you can take its heat. 'Tis a principle which makes life difficult for us all, sooner or later," argued Edgar.

"'Tis the jest which sours you as much as these gooseberries, Alfred," said Emma, "so I will grant you your layer of cream on two conditions. Firstly, it must not be such a smear that it seeps out of the middle when you cut it."

"I agree. Those bits are best licked off, so that it be cream alone moistens the mouth."

"Such manners! No more than the thickness of my finger, I say."

Edgar took her hand. Frederick looked away to the fire. Emma let Edgar measure her forefinger, and he tutted.

"Your thumb be more generous," said Edgar. "This finger be a twig."

He let go of her hand. Emma felt she had to do something, continue as if they had not touched each other again, so she leaned over the table, and brought the cream towards them. Edgar pushed in his finger.

"'Tas gone off?" he asked, after he had tasted it.

He offered her a fingertip of it, and she hesitated. If she refused it, the cake, the cream, the moment, would sour more than any fruit.

"'Tis passing perfect," she judged. "Now smooth it according to your fussiness. Frederick, you will have the first piece, and I the second. 'Good things come to all who wait,' be a wise saying of my father."

"You are wicked and cruel, 'tis certain!" laughed Edgar. "But I obey. Tell me, though, what be the second condition for my spreading?"

Emma looked at Frederick, who rose, and said, "I'll just amble over to Billy, run over a few things. Need to keep a lookout for odds and ends, as 'twill be market-day on Wednesday."

When he had gone, Edgar looked at Emma, and she said, "You want to smother your cake first? Eat your fill, and lick the cream where 'tas spurted?"

"'Tis tempting, but I be intrigued. Tell me your worst."

She wiped her hands on her apron.

"Frederick has told me you a-off to Dorchester to look for your parents, now the new teacher starts on Monday."

"That's right. Came back here to wake up and start a fresh day again. Been deep asleep. Left loved ones too long. My parents ran in shame, and I need to put things right, if I can. They might even be dead. No one knows. No one heard of them for years. Might just be a couple of headstones stained by berries and birds, but I shall find them if Dorchester be their resting ground. I shall . . . "

But he became overwhelmed.

Emma put her hand on his, lightly.

"Then if it be certain, I must go with you."

"You?"

"Yes, me. I be the only one knows where they be."

"They alive?"

"Daub your cream, Alfred, after all the fuss you kicked up. 'Tis better than sour, though beout sour, the cream don't sweet so much. 'Twon't be a cake worth eating unless."

"You knew *of* them, but never met them. I even lied about where we lived. I remember your anger when you found not me but old men drowsy with poppy fumes."

"Eat your cake, Alfred. 'Twill do you more good than tormenting yourself. Look to the pan, quick! It spills!"

When Frederick returned, after a period long enough to allow them time to talk, he rubbed his hands in anticipation of food. Soon, in the order decided earlier by Emma, they all partook of the cake, their faces illuminated by its sweetness, and contorted by its tartness.

The clock clanged ten. Moths fluttered against the two oil lamps. Billy had gone into Bridport to slake his thirst. Emma rocked peacefully in a chair. Frederick fell to snoring. Suspicious, Edgar wondered whether he was merely feigning sleep to eavesdrop on his conversation with Emma.

"Will you walk home soon? The dark is thick; the moon hides. Are you not scared of the blackness?" asked Edgar.

"Yes, but tonight I will stay. Frederick needs things doing: washing, drying, cleaning. His bones are too clicky-clacky to manage. I have made a start, and will finish in the morning."

After a while, Edgar said, "And you will come with me to Dorchester?"

"I will. 'Tis a pleasant place, though a spickle roguish on market days, when thieves and trampers mingle with farmers and gentlemen and ladies."

"And my parents fare well? Are in good health? I have often wondered."

Frederick jolted himself, allowing Emma to change the subject. "You back with us?"

"I'm off to bed. Will you lock up, dear?"

Edgar watched him rub his eyes, give in to his age, with a long sigh.

"'Tis certain. Now go 'ee to bed, where you can rest proper. Alfred here can keep me company, though I shan't be long. Just till this moth sleeps when I snuff the light, shortly."

When Jethro found Emma not at home on three consecutive visits, he went to the farm to see Frederick.

"Take something?" asked Frederick, holding up a flagon.

With a jerk of his head, he had asked Billy to make himself scarce, when he had seen Jethro, a rare visitor, making his way purposefully up the lane.

Jethro's news could not wait for cider.

"Emma gone somewhere? Three times I've called, and not a sound. She been here?"

"Yes, and she's gone again."

Frederick moved around, gave some objects new places, shoved others into overflowing drawers, to avoid eye contact.

"Where?"

"Dorchester, with Alfred."

Jethro struggled for words as if fighting for breath, and rocked on his heels. Reasons raced through his head, bumped into each other in a mêlée of panic. She will not come back, he concluded. The man who abandoned her had got what he wanted now, had he not? Had smashed her to pieces as if she was an unwanted vase, then stuck her together again, for his own ends.

"'Tis sinful in the eyes of the Lord, what he has done. And she will suffer again at his hands. 'E be a wicked man. By rights, she should have been Bartholomew's wife," protested Jethro.

"She's a grown woman, free to do as she pleases. Besides, you don't know why they've gone, and 'taint none of your business, though there be not a spickle of wickedness in it. You been kind to her. Let her go, Jethro. This moment been a-coming, and I must say it: you don't let her go, you will be as bad as Alfred was. She don't love you, Jethro, leastways how you love her."

Jethro hung his head. All those years, I cared for her, loved her, and now she's gone to Dorchester. Well, 'tis Providence, as 'twas with Bartholomew, he decided.

Frederick watched him leave, thought about calling him back to help him deal with the hurt, but sat down, closed his eyes and ruminated. 'Taint no use anyway. One day, somebody you love be here, and, the next, they're not. And it is worse than any pain inflicted by blade or horse-kick. When Alfred went, I leaned on the gate, and looked down the lane. Years of hoping, and nothing. Then he came, in the snow, but the agony be there still; never goes. So, Jethro, go you home and grieve, for you have lost the woman who could never marry you. No, Jethro, 'taint never to be.

There came a knock at the door. The thought that Jethro had returned to ask more questions roused Frederick.

"Wellesley hobbling. No obvious reason. Checked his shoe, and scraped his hoof. Master Alfred riding him today? Won't get far. Could have done it in the night," said Billy.

"Gone for a day or two. Let Wellesley rest. Feed him well to get his strength up."

Billy noticed the anxiety in Frederick's face. There was more to it than the horse.

"Master, don't 'ee fret so. If you don't mind me saying, your face be all sadness. Be you sick? If so, I can go to Briddy, and fetch Dr. Coryates, who they say hab a potion for most things. There baint an ailment he can't treat. Or if 'tis bile, I can go to Conjuror Dottery. Now, I know there be those who say he sups with the Devil, but some swear by him, and go to him, time after time. 'Tis mere superstition that be driving him and his like out of Dorset. Shall I hasten now, master?"

"Thank 'ee, Billy, but lay a blanket on Wellesley 'stead. 'Tis kind, and I would have had more of a mind for old Dottery than young

Coryates, with his new instruments for poking and a-prodding. Now *there* be the Devil's armoury, if ever I saw it. No, I shall rest as much as Wellesley, as 'tis better than work if nothing else!"

The light was dying, and The King's Arms began to fill.

"Fit for Prince or pauper, Queen or servant, be all the rooms, and so be our food, served whenever you wish, for a sum which don't add up to the portions. Robbing us, you'd be, sir, if you was to eat here, this evening," opined the man to whom Edgar spoke.

"Then we shall take two rooms, if you please. Adjacent to each other, preferably, but, in any case, close, and we shall dine on your ample meals, for which we shall pay an amount reflecting their size. It would not be our wish to rob anyone, and certainly not you," said Edgar.

Emma turned away just in time to hide her amusement. The man looked at his customers, and winked.

"Your two rooms be next to each other, though I baint able to let you have any adjacent ones, on account of this being a respectable inn with a repitation to consider," he said.

"I understand. Here, in advance, is payment, and more, for our food and rooms."

The man quickly recognised Edgar's generosity, and bowed as if in the presence of a Prince or Queen, for whom all his rooms and food were more than fit.

"Let me show you to our best ones, sir. The best in Dorset, I assure you. They comes from all over to stay here: Lords, Ladies, Generals. There baint a worthy who hant rest their head on one of my pillows."

Over dinner, Edgar and Emma spoke little, the journey in the coach having tired them, but Edgar asked, "Is it far from here, where my parents might be? I will not press you any further to tell me how you come to know of their whereabouts. No doubt, I will learn, in due course. This authority you have I accept as part of my having left, and there is much I feel you hold back for me to learn myself. Your willingness to come with me smells not of revenge, whose reek is unmistakable, but of Providence, in which we all must trust. I know some truth awaits me here. The school may be open, and I be forgiven, but there are things I have yet to face."

"The place I take you be an hour's walk from Dorchester to the village of Stinsford, a pretty place away from the noise and bustle of town. 'Tis a spot to be solemn, merry, shy or sociable, a hiding place amongst friends."

"You speak of it as if you have lived there, and know its inhabitants. My parents never hinted at a knowledge of it, or of distant cousins living there."

"Ask no more tonight, Alfred. Yawns rob me of answers, and tomorrow will come soon enough."

The next day was warm, fine, robed in invitation. People rose early, and voices and the rattling of carts drew Edgar and Emma into the street after a breakfast of a considerably more modest size than promised, the evening before.

"You know Dorchester?" asked Emma, leading him down the hill from The King's Arms.

"Hired here once by Yeoman Symondsbury. Farm Manager."

"Can't see you ringing pigs' noses, and keeping milkmaids' cheeks to the cows!" laughed Emma.

Winifred, staff in hand, and cursing rubies, ambled into view and passed through a wall.

"Didn't stay long."

"What stopped you?"

"You," he said frankly. "I had to find you, pay my dues."

Emma went quiet, and took his arm. A cart passed. A sheep's wool was stained with blood, and its gashed throat gaped.

"'Tis passing warm already," called the man with the reins.

"A day for picking fat berries, sir, 'tis certain," agreed Emma.

Green all around them. The church spire behind them. Stinsford in the distance, but out of sight.

From time to time, they stopped and rested.

"We lost?" asked Edgar, wiping his brow.

"It be this way, I think."

"*Think*?"

"'Tis up, down a bit, up, down, and further down. Or be it up a spickle more after the first down? The church be at the bottom of the last down, 'tis certain."

"Know you not your ups from your downs?"

"They be all the same. It depend which way you going. An up be a down on the way back!" she laughed.

"Emma Broadoak, stop thy teasing!"

"Ten more minutes, Alfred."

She went quiet. Edgar began to think about what he would find and say. Emma was light-hearted, as if she were bringing him to a reunion that would put to rest her own as well as his troubled youth.

Then she stopped, removed her arm, and put a hand to her brow to shade her eyes.

"This is where I leave you. There be the cottage, and the smoke which stretches from it speaks of a presence. I will sit on that there log, long fallen, judging by its dryness, and wait for you. Take the visit as it comes; I will not leave you here. The brightness of the sun might push me into the shade of those spreading branches, but call if I be out of sight."

Edgar squeezed her hand.

"This moment has long summoned me, and what it brings I am owed, one way or another."

Emma left him, and to the cottage he walked, his legs willows trembling with doubt.

The palings were newly mended, and flowers were shooting purple and tall against the limed wall. Under the thatch twitching with birds, the window and door were ajar.

'Tis now or never, he decided.

His knuckles were timid, so he knocked again, and the door opened.

The young woman peeked out, holding a small pan. A weapon? wondered Edgar. In the bright light, she shone as if in one of his illuminations.

"I am looking for Hannah and Stephen Morcombelake. I am told they live here. I knew them in Bridport, but know not whether they are still alive. I come to see them again. Will they agree? Ask if you can, but deliver the blow quickly if they be gone."

The young woman glanced over her shoulders, and opened the door a little more. Alfred thought he saw someone in a chair in the far dark corner.

"What be your name? You're no tramper, 'tis certain, and your voice be half Dorset, half gentleman, but 'twon't do 'less you give me your name," insisted the woman.

"I am Alfred Morcombelake, once of Bridport, then of Wells, now returned. Been gone a long time, been told my parents used to live here. 'Tis true? You know what happened to them?"

She stepped out into the sunlight. The prominent plume of white hair was there, though softened by others of its hue. She squinted, wiped back her loose brown hair, thought best to hear more before she told him.

"What colour eyes hab your mother and father?"

"Look into mine, and you will see father's. They be the same colour as the sea in Lyme Bay when there be no clouds. And mother's were green as these leaves."

"And you say they are your parents? Are you sure? There are many with such colour eyes."

"I be sure. And more: father loved a scraping of lavender honey on his bread and butter, and mother was last to sleep and first to rise. Taller than him by that pan on his head, she was, though he measured up to her in other ways."

The woman hesitated, then said, "Alfred, I had a feeling, this morning, when the blackbird sitting on the gate chaunted notes as high as Heaven that things bill be different before the bushes bustle, and butterflies play in the hollyhocks. And 'tis so. If you be their son, then I be your little sister, though not so little, on account of me being as tall as you."

Into the bright light shuffled the person in the corner of the house. She wobbled the stick in her hand, witnessing a resurrection.

"Lorna, girl, you be wrong there. You baint his sister. This be my Alfred, and though the telling of the story be best done in the shade with a jug of elderflower cordial and a slice of bread and blue vinney, 'tis best you know he be your father. Now go put the pan back while a mother cries and hugs a son she thought she'd never see again."

Chapter Twenty

The horse was fidgeting; too many strangers' hands were examining him. His admirers complimented him: strong bugger, a Trojan, powerful beast. Cheaper horses were bought quickly, but Merlin, said to have come up from Tintagel, and so named because of the magical feats he was reputed to have performed, could not attract a buyer. His owner, a man who had originally brought him back from France, and had briefly and ironically named him Boney because of his great size, needed money to settle on the land with a wife equally, if not more so, expensive to keep. To drop Merlin's price was unthinkable, now that the good lady had made clear the manner in which she would like to be kept.

And so it was that Edgar found himself the fortunate owner of a horse he would name Wellesley, after his illustrious, military namesake, in recognition of all the attributes other prospective buyers had identified. The sum demanded was not a problem, and Edgar's quiet murmurs of praise stilled the horse on which he had set his heart, once he had finished all he had to do in Wells.

"I have a feeling you would have been cheap at twice the price!" flattered Edgar, when they had left the horse-fair.

Wellesley hung his head, as if understanding that modesty was required.

It had been a long time since Edgar had ridden. The ground seemed a long way down, but Wellesley sensed that, in time, they would be well matched, so was patient and predictable, and was well fed as a reward.

Edgar gave notice at the inn that he would shortly quit his room for ever, though the landlord urged him not to have so decisive a view of the world.

"*Ever* be a time neither you nor I will reach, and only Providence will say whether you return and disturb the other guests biv your snoring! 'Tas been thunder beout lightning ever since you found our beds softer than clouds!"

"You are wiser than you look, which I say in equal jest and not insult. I intend to return to Dorset, and in haste, lest Providence snatch me before I mend the things I must. So, thank you and your good wife for your kindness, which be greater than the sum I have paid you. Is she about, your good lady?"

"She's gone to her bed, which must be drenched, on account of the tears she hab shed for your sorrowful parting. 'There bon't be the like of such a kind and gentle and learned man under these beams no more, there bon't,' she said, in so many bits and pieces that it was hard to string 'em all together, so sad she was. 'Tis womenfolk: all a-sad 'stead of a-joicing that they been blessed with just knowing a soul such as 'ee."

"Wiser still, and wiser," responded Edgar, shaking the landlord's hand, and bringing to a close that episode of his life, for fear that it should move closer to the *ever* he had wished to avoid, at all costs.

Edgar felt sad that he could not return to the rectory to bid goodbye to Josiah, who had shown him such friendship. Then he had an idea: I must write when I have the time, by which he will either know all about Mrs. Watchet's feelings and her lying to Zillah, or remain in blissful ignorance.

But how to communicate to Zillah, whose world he had turned upside down with his revelation of her true parentage? She, to whom he had proposed, had been the agent of his revenge on Mrs. Watchet. Too much disaster surrounds me here for Zillah to forgive me. What love can flourish after such a secret is carelessly shattered by selfishness? he pondered. My life languishes. 'Tis like some conjuror's foul and drowsing medicine has placed me in a nightmare from which I must awake. And even if Mrs. Watchet admits her deception, that spring of love, which should gush from a young woman, has been dammed by my thoughtlessness.

He left instructions for the safeguarding of his substantial funds in the savings bank, so now he could leave Somerset and return to Dorset, where he would labour, to show his contrition. His reason was clear: so many mistakes I have made in my life that I must make no more. I must end Emma's, and my parents', ignorance of what happened to me. I was wrong to go, more guilty not to let them know I live, whatever their feelings for me now. Then I must start again, wake up and begin anew.

But he needed one last look upon her face, one last word, reassurance that Mrs. Watchet had told her she had lied about the poem. He would have written Zillah another, given her all of his poems, as a testimony of his love; after all, they were hers, not meant to fade to yellow and disintegrate as a long-dead butterfly's wings kept years in a box. He had to know that she accepted his version of events. It would be unbearable for him to part from her, their lips never having pressed each other, the scent of her body never lingering on his bedsheets.

He waited for her, at the end of the day, but she did not follow her usual route. He only just caught sight of her. Not wishing to alarm her, he called her name, but she continued, head slightly bent, as if avoiding the public gaze. Edgar was sure he had called loudly enough to be heard. Again her name rang out, and she stopped, and turned slowly enough to suggest she knew who owned the voice, that she wanted to avoid a conversation.

"Do not be afraid. I mean no mischief but to say goodbye. Spare me a moment, please. Let us part with you knowing you are my true love, and that your mother has lied to you."

Her face looked haunted. In her eyes were such pain and suffering. He was angry with himself, had not witnessed Emma's face, all misshapen and sore, when she realised there would be no wedding; and Zillah's mouth dropped loose, as if the utterance of one syllable were too much.

"Does it matter any more?" she said quietly. "I know the truth, but all has been spoiled, and I dare not think too much about it, or I shall throw myself in the water, and my floating image shall be a reminder to all that I have been badly treated."

"Speak not of dying, Zillah!" cried Edgar, moving to embrace her, but she recoiled.

"No, Edgar. I love you, but that is not enough. Speak to me no further. I am lost, and my strength has gone. I no longer wish to live at the rectory, and my uncle suffers as I do. In time, we will all mend. I, at least, know what it is like to love hopelessly."

"Here, take this box containing all the poems I have written for you. Have them, darling, and know that no one can love you as I do."

She hesitated, tempted, but shook her head.

"How can I take them? They would wreck me. Go now, Edgar. Make not this parting the moment which pushes me into the water."

Zillah burst into tears, and hurried away.

Edgar listened to her cries.

"*I* should be the one to drown," he said. He took a deep breath. "Let these poems stay in this box, their coffin. I have made a fool of myself. My years too many to win so young a woman, I face a lonely and uncertain future. Still, 'tis a curse I must embrace, for the water, even in pulsing summer, is cold on the hand, and must not take me. In time, she will acknowledge 'twas she I loved."

Edgar became oblivious to passers-by. They were merely puppets, and he was tired of their show, their indifference to his desire to play a role, too. Had his mind been clearer, and his eyes more focused, he would have seen Josiah walking briskly towards the cathedral. Josiah's intention was to surprise the Bishop with his unannounced arrival, and to address him on matters that had come to his attention. It was most unusual for a vicar to challenge a Bishop, but Josiah felt compelled to. If Edgar had followed him to the Bishop's palace – "Pah!" Josiah had once huffed. "Palaces are for kings and queens! A calling to God is a humbling, not an aggrandising, experience!" – and waited for his reappearance, he would have noticed that Josiah now walked with not just alacrity but a spring in his step, as if he had received excellent news, and was hastening to share it with a loved one.

And had Edgar eavesdropped on the conversation Josiah had with Mrs. Watchet, he would have been surprised to hear such unexpected news. Indeed, Mrs. Watchet, urged to take a seat before Josiah commenced his speech, was shocked.

"And you have resigned your living? Why?" she asked, incredulous.

"Because I can no longer continue to live a lie which has troubled me increasingly as I have got older and become aware of the Bishop's antipathy towards me. I confessed that we were brother and sister, and that the lie had become so burdensome that it had come between my congregation and me. I saw in each face the incipient detection of my – *our* – falsehood. I told him: so important had it become to maintain the pretence, that our declared marriage had felt real."

"After all these years?" she sighed. "Our lives have crumbled, Josiah. What shall we do? Where shall we go?"

"I have money saved. It is not a lot. Now that Zillah intends to rent a room or two elsewhere, we have only ourselves to think of."

"And the Bishop tried not to persuade you to change your mind? He had not the heart to forgive after your confession?"

"No, dear. He welcomed my news. I have saved him a job. He even said he had identified a young curate who could take my place.

We have to be out within a week. 'Charles is a popular fellow,' the Bishop said. 'He's done well in a parish near Bath. A good education, and a wife in the offing.' The Bishop's words wounded me, I can tell you, but he has not escaped unscathed."

Mrs. Watchet watched her brother's eyes light up.

"Unscathed? You have not disgraced yourself in an act of petty revenge? Oh, Josiah, I thought you above that!"

Her disapproving tone made him laugh demonically.

"Disgrace? Nothing beyond that which clothes our joint deception. Indeed, the opposite, for it is I who have exposed his hypocrisy, his double standards! I – we – have paid a terrible price, and so will he."

"But how? You speak in riddles, Josiah."

"All in good time, my dear. All in good time. And if you are not too exhausted by what must seem my incoherent rantings, I hope you will, with all the skill and vigour upon which your body can call, prepare some chops and turnips, after which the world will seem an infinitely better place. We are liberated, my dear. Well and truly liberated!"

Mrs. Watchet began to prepare the meal, while Josiah went to his study. He ran his fingertips over the spines of his books, some of which he had not touched in years.

"I shall get a good price for some of these, among the scholars of Wells and Bath, but some, with which I will not part, are priceless, especially this one, the agent of the Bishop's downfall. Till that time, I shall guard it with my life!" he said, stroking the book's cover. "And 'tis a forfeit, a parting gift from Edgar, though he knows it not."

Astride Wellesley, Edgar left Wells. The letter he had written to Jolyon, *dear* Jolyon, whom he greatly missed, had gone on the mail coach, that very morning. Not everything that had happened had found its way into the letter, but the key fact had: that he had ceased working for the Bishop – he had not mentioned the disappearance of the book – and that he was returning to Dorset. Edgar promised Jolyon that he would resume his illumination of manuscripts just as soon as he was settled again.

From time to time, he saw Zillah in his mind, her face torn apart, and so urged Wellesley on a little, to put a greater distance between Wells and himself. In the landscape, he found much to distract him: hawthorn with constellations of white blossom, buzzards gliding high in the sky, and labourers offering him cider when he passed within shouting and waving distance.

Soon he began to feel he could concentrate on his journey. He learned not to rely on the directions of any man who began by scratching his chin, saying, "Now Dorset, last time I heard, be that way yonder," and pointing back whence Edgar had come. But one man, a seasoned tramper used to straying from vale to vale, gave him some invaluable advice: "If 'ee rise early, which bill be the case if you been a-shivering in a field, all night, you see where the sun peep out above its blanket, and that be the east. Watch where it climbs, and where it lies down, at the end of the day, be the west. As long as 'ee knows that, 'ee can find most places with a bit of begging."

The man held out his hand, having noted the good quality of Edgar's clothes.

"You speak wisely," said Edgar, passing him two coins.

"You get to Glastonbury be your next town."

"And how far be it?"

"You bill see the hill, though on a misty day, the church a-sitting atop it be shrouded, a mile or two before you rest your limbs, and 'tis a landmark all know. And from the top, when mist and murk have drifted out of sight, 'tis said for fifty miles all in a circle volk may see. And such a sight helps strangers find their way."

Edgar handed him another coin.

"And wiser still, good friend. There I'll wend my way forthwith, as hunger and thirst have sapped my strength."

"Then, friend, go 'ee at an even step. Be never in a rush, as 'tis well known, these parts, that places back away in measure to your pace."

"The wisest!" laughed Edgar, placing one final coin the way of the tramper. "Tell me, sir, where you acquired such knowledge."

"Now that bill cost 'ee twice what you already gi'n me!"

The tramper resumed his journey, chuckling to himself.

In Glastonbury, Edgar dined well at an inn, and stayed to hear the fiddles. The cider emboldened him, and, when the tables and chairs had been pushed aside, he joined in the dancing. In Wells, he had not come across such revels, and not since stomping in the barns and yards of Bridport had he whirled and felt the waists of women.

"And what be your name?" asked one who had slipped her own – Pearl – into his ear when she had pressed herself closely.

"Alfred," he replied, realising that revealing his original name to Pearl was of no consequence.

"'Tis a royal name," she laughed.

He blamed too much cider for forgetting his adopted name.

"Though Edgar be what they call me," he quickly added.

"A royal be better than Edgar," she teased. "You walking me home? 'Tis a street or two, and the moon and stars be frightened by the ghosts."

She giggled. The cider had gripped her, made her abandon her judgement, and as much as he wanted to remind himself of the softness and compliance of a strange woman's body, he released her.

"Ghosts there be everywhere. I be passing through, and 'tis likely neither of us will see the other as we would in daylight and in a sober state. The pot be strong, its fumes of potent apples headier than the poppy's hold."

"You talk in riddles, your majesty."

"The draught has addled you. Goodnight, Pearl. You be aptly named, and 'tis another who must prise you from your shell."

She moved away, resentful that he had refused her encouragement.

In bed, the reek of dirty sheets on which he had tossed money returned to his nostrils. The whores of Wells had all smelt the same to him, their odour attracting and disgusting him, feeding his addiction, till he, with superhuman effort, had conquered it with a potion a conjuror, living outside the boundary, had concocted for him. For days, he had hallucinated and writhed in sickness, till he was cured.

"'Twon't fail," the conjuror had reassured. "'Tis the whortleberry which mingles with the bitterberry. 'Tas worked in the regiments for years."

And so it had proven, when Edgar had put himself in the way of a lusty woman, and had resumed his illumination. The potion had worked.

Remembering that Bridport faced France and Spain, and the advice of the tramper, Edgar made his way, at a leisurely pace, stopping to feed and water Wellesley in fields and villages. Soon the mounds and rills of Dorset became recognisable. The landscape will soon give up glimpses of the sea, I am sure, said Edgar to himself. I am nearly home.

Wellesley plodded. Edgar felt hungry. There were no houses in sight. Berries had made his stomach sore. In a field, Wellesley grazed, and Edgar drank from a brook. At the foot of trees, orange toadstools clustered. They are poisonous, he reminded himself, and can kill a man. Then he saw mushrooms, which he pinched, plucked and held against the water. They yielded willingly to his bite after he had smelt their earthy sweetness.

Not since childhood had he seen a moonball. Like the moon, it had pitted, white skin, and it sat at the foot of a hedge. He remembered holding one in his hand, feeling its skin. Would it float, he had wondered, if I throw it? But, though light as thistledown, it had fallen and split a little.

Edgar picked and popped it, the one by the hedge, gently ripped it. Still hungry, he bit off a small piece. It tasted unusual, not as bitter as he imagined it would, so tore a strip, and fed it, bite by bite, into his mouth. It quickly satisfied his lingering hunger, so he tied Wellesley up, and found a ditch well sheltered from the breeze's push.

It was getting dark, and the moon, nearly full, began to move, leaving a scar of white light as he moved his head. He felt the world turning. When the stars appeared, they, too, danced, till the sky was scored with white light.

"Help me!" he called.

He found the ground, and shut his eyes. The moonball, he remembered. 'Tis its magic that grips me. When he opened his eyes, he touched the moon, and dragged his finger through the stars. He wrote a name, embellished the first letter with imagined gold. *Emma* stretched across the sky, and stayed there till his lurching stopped, and sleep held the moonball's effect at bay.

Chapter Twenty-One

Blinded by unexpected words as well as the sun, Lorna fled inside the cottage. As they embraced, Edgar and his mother could hear her quick tread on the creaking stairs, then the bang of her bedroom door.

Edgar was fuller, Hannah thought, taller than she remembered, though perhaps slightly shorter than Lorna, who had her mother's build: square-shouldered and slender, not easy to hug with all her jutting joints.

"You never told her."

Edgar's voice was muffled in his mother's padded shoulder.

"Come inside," she said. "You want to fetch Emma first?"

Edgar blinked. *So, she knew I was coming, and Emma had planned it with her. It seems Lorna's not the only one to find things out today. I should have spotted it: Emma found this place too easily. Then why did Mother not tell Lorna before we arrived? But 'tis none of* her *making; 'tis mine, and therefore must I face up to the telling of it.*

Inside again, Hannah poured him a cup of elderflower cordial, and placed her hand on his shoulder as she leaned across him to put the cup in front of him.

"She waits by a tree over the grassy knoll, yonder."

Hannah hobbled to the foot of the stairs, and called, "Some elder down here. Dry your eyes, and fetch Aunt Emma, who be biting her nails, no doubt, back of top hill."

There was no reply, but Lorna came down, glanced at Edgar, and went out.

"By a felled tree," called Edgar, "or within a shout!"

"She'll find her."

"*Aunt* Emma?"

"We never knew about her till she came looking for you. She was a stranger to us, took us by surprise. By that time, we'd had Flora a-hammering on our door, hunting you. Your father took it bad. Had his head in his hands for weeks. All he'd say was, 'Good God, Hannah. Has it all come to this?'"

"And *both* women came? They ever meet? The very thought kills me."

"'Twas me who told Emma."

"And?"

"Became like a daughter to us. We felt responsible for her. She took to coming round, every day, case you came back. Moped till it got me down, she did. ''E aint coming back, dear,' I said. 'Not now there be Flora, too, and 'er biv a child a-coming.'"

Edgar sighed. All that time, Emma had clung to his memory, with the help of his parents. She had never let him go despite everything.

"How you come to have Lorna?"

"The shame of it brought her. Flora was only a young slip. Her parents weren't happy, see. Neighbours, folk, talk. Fingers wagging and vicious gossip be too much for any family in a place like Briddy. Well, your father and I puts to her mother we bring the child up here. She agrees, says Flora's not to know the truth. Couldn't stay where we were. Here, no one recognises us. Only the Lord knows folk, these parts, 'cepting the Hardys, the Mistertons, the Palfreymans, and Conjuror Sayer, over the heath, yonder."

"And Emma still stuck? She came? Wrote?"

"On and off. Her father pushed her into marrying, but 'twas a mistake. Did for her father. Took to his bed, and never got out of it till he was carried out by Bartholomew Sherborne, the husband she could never love. Got *something* out of it, he did: the price of a coffin and funeral."

"And her mother?"

"Stayed to see her husband gone, then went herself, without even a goodbye."

"And Flora's mother gave Lorna to you?" he asked, at length.

"'Twas best. Lorna been our daughter till today, when you comes, so now she be our grand-daughter. 'Tis certain, by blood. She'll get used to it, though it throws her now. Folk do, see, Alfred. You get used to things as they are, not what you want 'em to be. Same biv Emma, who be here now, by the look of it."

Emma's left arm was round Lorna's waist, and Lorna's head was resting on Emma's shoulder. Despite their difference in height, Emma managed to pull her closer, comfortingly.

Edgar looked to his mother to begin. It was she who had to open up the past. She had had all those years to choose her words and rehearse them. Yet there must also come a time for me to add to them, he thought. Mine might sound as thin as gossamer silvered by sincerity, but say them I must.

Hannah began to Lorna.

"All these years, I've brought you up. What could I do, dear, when Alfred, here, your father, a-vanished and didn't even knowing you were a-coming into the world? And your real mother, thrown out onto the street by her parents, had no choice, see, but to make her own way in the world – without you. What were we to do, dear? See you, our son's little girl, die in the cold workhouse? 'Twasn't Alfred who mattered any more but you. And Emma here, left biv a broken promise of marriage, has been your aunt. We girls been here, but you, Alfred, been Heaven knows where. Emma wrote to tell me you was back and wanted to come, and as I still be your mother, I be listening. You got anything to say?"

Edgar felt all those years separating him from his mother. How stupid I have been to think I can turn up as if nothing has happened! he realised. I cannot tell them about my past, with or without a gloss. Wells was another world, another time, a new name.

"I left, as many young men do. You know about, and have been hurt by, my wrongs. They have affected us all. I came today not knowing what would happen. I discover I have a fine, beautiful daughter, whom I know not, who probably despises me, resents my calling her *daughter*. I have apologised to Emma, and we are friends again." He looked at her for a contradiction, and there was none. "I ask for forgiveness, expecting the worst, for the hurt I have caused you, understanding that it will be difficult for you. Your hearts may find me a stranger."

"A mother rarely finds her son a stranger; she is always a mother. As for Lorna, it is unreasonable to demand anything of her, at the moment, though she may think otherwise."

"Mother – for I can still call you only that after what you have told me – I am grateful to you for loving and caring for me, as father did, too. But you, sir, who present yourself as a pale imitation of him, can claim nothing of me. You are here, and will leave, no doubt, as before."

Lorna escaped Emma's arm, and returned to her bedroom, as noisily as the last time.

"Don't know which side she gets that from!" laughed Hannah.

"She's done nothing you wouldn't expect after hearing all that," reassured Emma. "Shall I go up to her?"

"Leave her be. 'Tis true what you say, but she be a girl who loves a platform, and 'tis best she spend some time alone. There be nettles as well as roses in the garden, and both be painful if you grabs 'em all wrong. Alfred, do something useful and pour Emma a drink. I'll open the windows, let in a blow of air. A bit stuffy in here, what with all these words a-wafting about like smoke from a blocked chimdey. Go chop some wood, Alfred. There be soup for later, and it'll need bubbling to join the wild garlic and tatties."

Edgar poured some elderflower, and asked, "Axe?"

"Lorna chops. Try the top of the garden where the other gate leads into the copse."

Emma sipped, and looked up at the sound of the floorboards creaking.

"He just wanted to know if you were all right, mend things," she said.

"Pity he didn't come sooner. His father went afore his time. Will you take Alfred to Stinsford churchyard, show him where the grave be? In the second field, through the gate, far left corner. Remember? Stephen was shy in life, and be still so in death."

"I'll ask Alfred, but not yet. Let him heal with you and Lorna first."

"You two staying? Flora don't know where we be, and I don't want her come looking. That's why we be here, on the heath, behind the knoll."

Emma thought that, one day, Lorna will feel the yearning for something different, will not want the owls' screeching to be her lullabye but the whispered promises – some ambitious, inevitably – of a husband.

The thud, thud, thud of the axe trying to split the wood distracted them. Edgar remembered the importance of rhythm, of swing instead of brute force. From her window, Lorna watched him, her father. But he didn't know about my mother carrying me; he had gone before then, she reminded herself. She could not rid herself of this thought, too: he is handsome. Aunt Emma would not have brought him here, among the bees and sweet sting of garlic drifting from the woods, to do me harm. She is a good woman. I trust her.

Edgar rolled up his sleeves, and his arms glistened in the heat. Lorna felt odd now there was a man there. Only Jacob Misterton dropped by, on Sundays, with Mary, to take them to church at Stinsford, but he never came in, only removed his hat, and told Hannah they were ready to go. Now this new man had come and claimed her as his daughter, and wielded her axe. A stranger, yet one of them now. And her dead father could not be hurt by his return. Edgar had lost a father, and she had gained one.

She stepped away from the window so that he would not see her looking furtively at him. Under his right arm, he carried the wood, and, with his left hand, he lifted up a wild rose, wrapped round a crude arch she had made, and smelt it. He has sensitivity, at least, she noticed. A worthless man would walk past without a second look. Edgar stopped and turned slowly. On the heath beyond the paling, a pony was licking the last of the dew. Edgar went over to the boundary. He's taking in the heath, *my* heath, and is drawn to it. He will not go as quickly as I thought. If he strolls onto it, disturbs an adder, hears the owls splitting the night before the great silence deafens him, he will not go, whatever the calling. And if he feels the warmth of the fire he has chopped for, tastes Mother's soothing soup, he will not think beyond the gate. And let him sit in the settle and watch Mother toasting bread till it be ready for a spreading, and he will never eat elsewhere.

Emma went to fetch her. The soup was thick and steaming. The bread was broken into boulders. Emma brought the smell of garlic into the bedroom.

"The soup is ready. Come. He is a good man," said Emma. "Let him see what he has missed."

"'Tis passing strange."

"'Tis certain. I have forgiven him, and, in time, you will feel differently. But, for now, let not the soup spoil, for there are extra chives in it, if my nose be not beguiled."

"I will come, though the moment robs me of my appetite. Will he speak to me?"

Emma laughed.

"No! He will turn his back on 'ee as if you were a witch with warts a-scattered all over your face!"

Lorna huffed and turned away.

"You tease me, and I am not a child!" she protested.

"You are not, indeed, so come and let us eat. 'Taint a solstice feast, 'tis certain, but taint a wake with bits a-spoiling in dishes on account of folk a-wailing."

"Will he sit facing me?"

"If you want."

"No, I should die if he do!" cried Lorna.

"Then we shall sit him *next* to you."

"No, I pray 'ee, aunt, no. I could not bear it."

"Then sit in the garden biv your dish, for none of us shall bring it to this room."

"'Taint fair."

Emma took her hand. Lorna could not resist the pull without it ending in farce, so complied.

"There. You don't want him thinking you be a grumpety cat, do you?"

Downstairs, Edgar was sitting at the head of the table. The sun had rolled over the house, and the room was darker now. Lorna looked to her mother for guidance.

"You sit there, girl," Hannah pointed. "Emma, you be there, facing Alfred, and I be here, next to the pot, so's I can keep an eye on it."

Lorna's eyes darted this way and that to avoid direct contact with Edgar, who himself was still nervous.

"You work?" he asked her.

"Kitchens, over at the manor."

The steam from the soup became a veil between them, but did not stop words. Edgar looked at his mother.

"Palfreymans' estate," she amplified. "It be a job, though today be her day off."

Conveniently, thought Edgar. Didn't want to miss me, no doubt.

The soup burnt his lips, and his spoon clattered on the side of the bowl where he dropped it.

"The soup," he explained.

"'Tis passing hot," said Hannah. "Mind you don't burn yourself."

Emma bit her tongue to suppress a laugh, and, without thinking, Lorna said, "Blow on it be what we does round 'ere."

"Stephen liked it piping hot," reminded Hannah.

Well, he's not here any more, Edgar wanted to say. Instead, he said to Lorna, "You read and write?"

"As well as anyone, these parts," she bridled.

"She got books," added Hannah, proudly. "In her room."

"Your father be an illuminator," Emma informed Lorna.

Lorna looked at Hannah, who shrugged.

"'Taint something I knows," admitted Lorna.

"Wait here," said Edgar.

The soup required leaving longer. From his bag, he fetched a poem, one of his early ones to Zillah. It captured his growing feelings for her, and had inspired him to form extravagantly his capital letters. He was proud of their design, and liked the combination of colours: blue, gold, and red. It was a good example to illustrate his profession.

Lorna took it, but instead of looking at the design of the letters, she read the poem to herself. She liked to read aloud, but was too embarrassed to do so, on this occasion.

"'Tas affected her," remarked Emma. "Her colour rises. Her cheeks are ripe apples."

"Read it, then, girl, so we knows the stir of it," ordered Hannah.

"What think you of the formation of the letters? They are labours of love, and pay well," said Edgar.

Outraged that he sold such beautiful words, Lorna said, "You sell

231

these? 'Tis a sin that such poems be taken to market, as if they were a sheep or a chicken!"

"I meant that people pay good money for my illumination, not my poems. Bishops, Lords, gentlemen, mainly," explained Edgar. "This one be not for sale."

Then this was meant for a sweetheart, deduced Lorna. My father be a poet! Who was the woman for whom this was writ? 'Tis surely Aunt Emma, she speculated. She looked at Emma, who asked, "May I see?"

Edgar hesitated.

"'Tis a youthful fancy," he said, reaching to retrieve it.

But Emma snatched it away, and read it.

"'Tis passing sweet," she remarked. "She be a lucky one for who this be meant for, and the curls and tails please the eye as much as the words."

She gave it back to him, and he folded it again and put it back in his bag.

"No use me a-looking," said Hannah. "Words be all smeared to me, these days, though I do like to hear Lorna read a page or two. She do the characters all sweet, one minute, and then like thunder, the next, when 'tis a man who be speaking."

"I should like to hear you," encouraged Edgar. "Have you a special passage for me?"

"No!" cried Lorna, and then, a little more softly, said, "'Tis too early. I never read at this time. Usually, my hands be red now from hot water, up at the manor."

"Then later, perhaps. If you like, I could teach you how to illuminate manuscripts. 'Tis an art which serves beauty."

She wanted to accept his invitation immediately, had been amazed by the perfection of the curls and images wrought from the alphabet. But she shied away from such intimacy. It was too early, though she had admired his poem, which demonstrated his capacity for loving.

"'Tis true they be like paintings, but I fear I have no skill that way."

"I, too, felt it was beyond me. Perhaps, you might wear the idea like an invisible hat till you feel brave enough."

"'Tis kind," she said.

Emma looked at Hannah, and smiled, and Hannah said, "Come, finish the soup. 'Tis wondrous, the first slurping, but, saved for a later, it be sharp on the tongue when the garlic has turned angry."

After the meal, Hannah avoided asking questions, preferring to savour the moment as much as the soup, and Emma and Lorna went into the garden.

"What think you of your daughter?" asked Hannah.

"She still be yours, by her bite. Perhaps, you give her too readily."

"Not so, Alfred. I have waited for this moment since Flora's mother handed her to me. Every day, I have longed to return her to you, which is as it should be. None of us really belongs to anyone else. You ask your father, when Emma takes you to Stinsford. 'Tas been a secret I've kept from her, 'tis true, but I prayed for you to come back. 'Tis Providence, Alfred."

Outside, Emma closed her eyes, and sniffed the roses. Lorna knelt and wound a loose, dangling stem around her rustic arch.

Edgar was troubled, and could leave it no longer. What he had to do was part of the mending, of the sorting out of things. Firstly, he told his mother, who laughed.

"'Tis passing strange, and don't suit," she said. "You'd best call those two in and tell 'em. And don't you get all huffety if they laughs, too."

He would heed his mother's warning. The garden was the best place to speak, being warm and full of butterflies flapping at flowers.

"I have something to tell you," began Edgar.

They turned, said nothing. Emma held a red rose in her fingers like a glass of wine, and Lorna protected her eyes with a cupped hand.

"You both know me as Alfred Morcombelake, but when I left, I adopted a new name, suggested by a ship's captain, which I have used ever since. Emma, I am sorry I have not confided in you yet, but I want you to know the truth: I am Edgar Isambard Porlock."

Emma released the flower.

"'Tis a name you wouldn't call a rose, but what be in a name? Am I not the same person if I call myself Lucy or Elizabeth?" she asked.

"You do not seem shocked."

"I am not. I have known your new name for some time. Yet you do not correct me when I call you Alfred. It does not bother you?"

"No," replied Edgar. "But how did you come to know about my other name?"

"That is for another day, Alfred. Just as you chose this moment to tell us your other name, so I will know the right time to tell you how I know it already. Till that hour, stroll with Lorna and me in the garden. The sun is pleasant, but soon it will droop, and the shadows will chase us inside. Look, Alfred, at the poppies and broom, for they are the brightest in Nature's palette, today, and illuminate the heath."

Emma took his arm, and led him to the paling. Lorna stayed where she was, and looked on.

He wiped his tears with his free arm.

"I'm sorry," he said. "I truly am."

"I have already forgiven you. But waste not the moment. Look upon the heath, Alfred, and see its beauty."

He squeezed her hand resting lightly on his forearm.

Only Hannah's voice broke the spell.

"Emma, you taking him to Stinsford, see Stephen's grave? Don't 'ee forget!"

Emma looked for an answer in Alfred's face, and he nodded.

"Yes," she answered.

"Then go now as 'tis a proper walk, and the bats swoop early, these days."

Lorna went inside.

Emma suddenly stopped, and said, "I think I shall call you Edgar."

"No. I am Alfred. Alfred Morcombelake, again."

'Taint certain, she thought, and they continued their walk to Stinsford.

The lichen on the grey stone of the church caught the sun, and turned into bright daisies. The lane was quiet except for birds. Emma led him through the gate, and along the path, till they reached a second graveyard.

"'Tis peaceful," remarked Alfred.

"'Tis a graveyard! At night, the quiet be rent by owls."

"And ghosts."

"'Tis certain."

Emma laughed. Then they reached Stephen Morcombelake's headstone, which was light grey patterned by bird and berry droppings. The grime of time had taken a hold, and no flowers illuminated the plot.

"This be father," said Alfred.

Emma said nothing, was standing a step behind him, so that she felt the warmth of the sun on her head, and did not intrude.

The gate behind them banged. An elderly woman, head down, took quick, little steps towards the church doors.

"'Tis a woman hastening to prayer," said Emma.

Alfred looked at the inscription. Name and dates, place of birth.

"Born Wootton Fitzpaine? All this time, I've thought him a Briddy man. Maybe he went there for the work. He never said. I wonder why. Secrets go to the grave with a man if they aren't written down."

He thought of the cathedral at Wells. If the Bishop had not asked

Jolyon and I to record its history, then there would be a thousand guesses, a million lies, he mused.

The stone *was* his father. If there had been no inscription on it, Alfred would have picked it out. Not too big, not too small. Neither wide nor narrow. Upright, not stooping. In a corner but not hidden. And the inscription fitted him: prosaic. No witty observation of him, no tribute to his love for his family.

"Reliable," Alfred muttered.

Emma stepped forward, having not quite heard.

"'Twas cholera did for him."

"Reliable don't deserve cholera."

"Nothing, *nobody*, deserve cholera."

"'Tis certain."

Alfred wanted to say something to the headstone. Stephen's voice was still in his head. He could still recall his father's smell in the house. Work and reliability clung to Stephen's clothes, and no mood or other person could wash them out.

"He was a good man," observed Emma.

"Then why did Mother not chisel it into this stone?" he asked. "This be worthless. In a hundred years, his descendents will know nothing of him from this."

"Your mother is not a poet. She is a widow."

Alfred turned.

"Come," he invited, offering his arm. "Let us disturb him no longer. Mother's words hide more than they reveal."

Approaching the knoll, Emma said, "We will stay the night, for *all* our sakes."

"There be enough room?"

"Your mother will make room. Say nothing about the headstone. Words chosen to last eternity are carefully weighed and not easily changed."

"You speak wisely. And there be Lorna, whom I must win. She must not hear me harsh."

"You are learning. It takes more than an afternoon to catch up on so many years and then some."

"Wiser still, dear."

Dear. He had said it, let it slip off his tongue, and silence them both.

Lorna had swept the floor, washed the dishes, made her mother comfortable in her chair. The thought of returning to the kitchen at Palfreyman Manor irritated her like a nettle rash, but she soothed it with thoughts of rhythm and rhyme. Those words, that poem. I, too, may have that sorcery within me to catch a love, she thought. I should let him show me his art. 'Tis in my blood, too, I'll wager.

"I have prepared the bedrooms. You take mine, and I will sleep with mother. Fa - "

"'Tis natural. Say it. It be the truth, which you must grasp," reassured Emma.

"He can sleep in the other one, which be cold, on account of it being next to the stairs, though I shall light fires in all three. The days be warm, but the nights be chilly."

Hannah then stirred and, hearing voices, said, "You back, Alfred? You seen it?"

Alfred replied, "Yes, Mother."

"Emma show you?"

"She did. 'Tis the prettiest of churches."

"'Tis certain."

"'Tis full of puddled fiddlers on Sundays," added Lorna.

"Aint no harm in a drop. That church be cold, all year round," said Hannah. "Bring that chair up, Alfred. There be something I want to tell you. 'Taint rightly for the ears of a young woman, Lorna, but best you stay and hear. My goodness! All on one day, too!"

"You talk in riddles, Mother," said Lorna.

"'Tis always the tapping of the feet first that lead to the dancing, girl."

Alfred drew up a chair. The walk had given him a thirst, and the sooner Hannah had spoken, the sooner he could quench it.

"One day, I shall be buried in Stinsford, Alfred. 'Tis my solemn wish that be written in my papers in that box over yonder. You got that, girl?" Lorna nodded. "Now, none of your sweet-talking. These things are best lifted out and aired so there be no surprises, though that aint strictly true. Alfred, you tell me you've been Edgar Porlock, after you've worn the name of Alfred Morcombelake. Now, who be you, truly? Speak plain and loud, for my ears be dim."

"I wear the name *you* gave me, Mother. I be Alfred Morcombelake. I no longer wish to be Edgar."

"No, Alfred. You be mistaken, though taint none of your fault. You be Alfred *Canonicorum*, but how you come to be so be one for tomorrow."

Chapter Twenty-Two

The next day, Hannah said nothing. The story be for another time, he remembered her saying, so I must wait. When the words are ready, she will tell me how what I have often felt came to be.

So he spent mornings chopping wood, and stacking it tidily in the ramshackle outbuilding. There it would dry out, ready for winter.

At mid-day, at the table, the women, except Lorna, who was usually at the manor, would watch him, waiting to judge his mood, for him to decide the topic of conversation.

He would only come in, at the end of the day, when the bats began to dive, and trees became stark silhouettes against the blue and pink sky. When Lorna was late from work, he lit a lantern, and walked to meet her. The first time she had seen the swinging light, she had wondered who it was, but, in bed, that night, had been happy he had shown concern for her safety.

No one asked how long he and Emma would stay. He showed a sign that he wanted to connect with the outside world again when, after supper, one day, he laid out a pen, ink, and a piece of paper on the kitchen table. Lorna, who sat at one end, was darning an apron she had snagged on a hook, at work. She held it close to the lamp; Cook would expect a neat repair.

"You enough room biv me here?" she asked. "I can shift."

In the settle by the fire, Emma had closed her eyes. The silence of the evening had allowed her to retreat into cosy relaxation. Opposite her sat Hannah, asleep, too, mouth open, head lolling.

"No, stay."

Occasionally, Lorna looked up at him. He was too far away for her to see what he was writing, but she knew he was coaxing words from his pen, biting his lower lip to help him.

"'Tis a poem?"

"No, a letter."

Emma listened self-consciously, her breathing shallow.

"I did not mean to pry."

"It be to Jolyon, who taught me the art of illumination. I must let him know how I am. I should have done it before now. I shall send him Frederick's address."

Frederick, his father, with a history Alfred had yet to hear.

"Not *this* address?"

After a pause, Alfred added, "And this."

Lorna glanced at him, from time to time, though pretended to concentrate on her sewing. He wrote quickly, with much, she guessed, to say. After signing the letter, he sat upright, and sighed.

"You write in a hurry," she remarked, "as if you might forget things."

"'Taint an illumination."

Then he took a sheet, and began another letter, careful to place the box in which he kept his pens and ink in front of it, obscuring Lorna's view.

"A poem?" she asked, when she could bear the tension no longer. "A pretty one, like the other?"

Emma held her breath. They had lowered their voices to a murmur so they would not wake the sleeping women.

"No, not a poem."

Lorna tied a knot in the cotton. The apron was mended. It should more than do for Cook.

It was now or never, Lorna decided.

"Will you teach me how to illuminate?" she asked. "'Twon't wait much longer."

He looked up from the letter he wanted to send with Jolyon's.

"Yes," he said. "I will."

His pleasure that she had wanted to be taught by him was moderated by a need to write with a sensitivity matching his message. He needed to concentrate.

"When?"

"Tomorrow night, though 'twould be better on Saturday or Sunday, when there be daylight, and you are not so tired after a long day at the manor."

"Saturday, then. But, in the meantime, may I borrow a pen and paper to practise my handwriting, which sprouts in all directions like a clump of heath grass?"

"'Tis certain."

He passed her what she wanted, and she placed her sewing box in front of the paper, imitating Alfred's secrecy. It was not lost on him, and he smiled.

"No looking!" she told him.

Emma almost broke her pose, happy that they were talking to each other less awkwardly, at last.

"And now I must concentrate, as must you."

For the next fifteen minutes, they wrote, Lorna crossing out words, and replacing them with others she considered more effective, Alfred careful to capture the right tone. And they finished simultaneously.

"Will you read to me your composition?" asked Alfred.

"If you read yours afterwards."

"I cannot."

"Then yours must be a private letter."

Emma opened an eye a little at this.

"It be to a man whose money helped to establish the school in

Bridport. It is an enquiry about how the new teacher fares, and would not interest you in the slightest. Now, will you read?"

Lorna folded her paper, and said, "I will, but only after sleep has improved the sound of it."

"Always a good idea, though I shall listen through the wall at your marching to the rhythm of your poem."

"How do you know 'tis a poem?"

"You are my daughter," he said quietly.

Emma closed her eyes again.

In the distance, male voices could be heard, and the singing came gradually closer, till the raucous choir's presence at the paling could not be ignored.

Lorna opened the door. Lanterns lit smiling faces. A fiddle struck up a tune.

"'Tis only I and the orchestra come to play 'ee a tune," called Thomas Hardy. "'Tas been practice at Stinsford, and 'twas commonly decided that we should visit our neighbours to let 'em hear how well we do. 'Taint so late that we a-woken Mrs. Morcombelake, I hope."

"No," called Lorna, "but only one song, to blow away your strong fumes of cider."

"Why, Timmy Porcorum here has not touched a drop since Stinsford bells, and Dick Denhay picks his notes as if he'd never even sniffed an apple!" jokingly protested Thomas.

"You know these men?" asked Alfred of Lorna.

"'Tis our good neighbour, Mr. Hardy, and his friends, who cheer our winter evenings betimes with their merry tunes, and oft has he tried to drag us to his cottage to dance smooth his flagstones."

"Just one, Miss. Lorna, then we shall leave you in peace, for I see you have a gentleman visitor. Will you have a merry or a sad?" called Thomas. "A sad we do just as well as a merry, though if a sad you choose, we must wash it away with a merry afterwards, as the sad been known to leave not an eye dry."

"'Tis true, Miss. Lorna," added Peter Swyre. "Our sad been known to make one partickler bride throw her vows back at her new husband, so a merry be better."

"What about our autumn merry? 'Tis famous, these parts, for lifting the spirits," suggested Thomas, "and 'tis one which don't hab difficult notes."

"'Twould be passing merry, and then enough, as the air feel a spickle hoary, and my cloak be indoors."

Dick Denhay counted in the fiddle, and the men began the merry. Soon, the three or four other followers began to sing.

Alfred clapped his hands, and when the merry subsided into a phased cessation, dug into his pocket, and handed over a few coins.

"For the merry, sir, which was all the merrier for being unexpected," said Alfred.

"'Tis passing generous, though be pleased to keep your money, as the merry be a gift to all the heathfolk," explained Thomas.

"Then be sure to give it to the vicar, who will make good use of it."

Alfred felt the men examine him. They did not recognise him, and Thomas said, "Well, goodnight, Miss. Lorna. My compliments to your mother. Tell her there be a pot or two of honey soon, which Jemima will collect and bring. Goodnight, Mr. . . . "

Thomas waited for Alfred to introduce himself, but Lorna leapt in with, "Morcombelake. This be my father."

Thomas looked at Alfred, then turned to his troupe, and said, "Back to our cottage, men, where there be a bit of supper a-waiting if we don't make too much of a racket, and upset Jemima."

Out of earshot, Thomas turned to Peter, and muttered, "Father? Then our merry has a-raised him from the grave, for I swear her father be long dead and buried. Ah well! 'Tas been a strange night, 'tis certain. They say that the last cottage, over the hill, have a conjuror now, and that he have a special potion, which they say gives you knowledge of things."

"'Twon't be better than cider!" said Timothy, and the others laughed.

When Lorna and Alfred returned indoors, Hannah was at the foot of the stairs.

"Mr. Hardy says Jemima will bring you honey soon," said Lorna, "when it be collected."

"You used to like that, Alfred," she said, yawning. "Honey on bread."

"Still do."

Emma awoke.

"I will go up now," said Lorna. "I am tired. I have cleaned the kitchen at the manor till there be not a spickle of dirt anywhere."

Lorna picked up her composition, and went to bed.

Emma prodded the faggot in the grate, and Alfred took that as a sign she was not yet tired.

"The men had been drinking?" she began. "They disturbed my dream."

"'Tis certain, but the tune be jolly."

Alfred put his pens and ink in his box, and folded the second letter, which he had left on the table when he had gone outside to hear the singers.

Emma returned to the settle, and Alfred took his mother's still warm seat.

"You know that Lorna will want to find her, once she knows," said Emma. "'Twill be impossible to stop her."

Alfred screwed up his face, inviting explanation.

Emma sighed.

"The letter to Flora. Are you really going to send it?"

Alfred then understood. The singers, the instruments, the merry. He had left the letter on the table, and Emma had read it.

"You had no right."

Though a protest, his words lacked true condemnation.

"Right? You speak of rights? Your description of Lorna will torture

Flora. What mother would not want to see such a daughter again? Sleep on it, Alfred. If you send it, you may do more harm than good."

Emma looked over to him. She had pins and needles in her legs, from having them tucked beneath her. Alfred felt her lips rest on his forehead, then watched her go to bed.

He read again his letter to Flora. The truth. Was not the way he told it how he would be judged? Flora's letter must go, as much as the one to Jolyon. How careless I have been! he mused. In the space of five minutes at the paling, I have let Emma know that I know where Flora lives.

In the morning, he walked to Dorchester to post Jolyon's letter. Flora's letter he had torn up. In time, I will speak to her, face to face, which be the way to do it. A letter be a coward's way.

Emma stayed at the cottage, did Lorna's chores. Hannah let her. It took till the sun was overhead to get her limbs moving. Emma fried bacon for her, two eggs in the fat, but she merely picked at it.

"Where's Alfred?" she asked, looking up from the plate. "'E gone again?"

"Dorchester, to post some letters."

Hannah set to the food, building up to the bacon, now that she knew he was coming back.

"Those eggs be Bathsheba's?"

"Hers or Tessie's."

"Bathsheba's. 'Tis certain."

When he returned, Alfred gave his mother a pair of gloves.

"For church, when the hoar burns," he explained.

Emma busied herself, would not look at him so that she would not appear to be expecting a present, yet the possibility of a similar act of kindness put her on edge, and she fumbled objects, moved them pointlessly, so that he would think she had not noticed the gloves.

"My hands too fat for a lady's gloves," Hannah said, when she had put them on.

"Nonsense, Mother. They be just right."

Hannah then showed them to Emma.

"You'll be the talk of the pews!" said Emma. "Kids' leather, too, like creamy skin."

"And this be for you, Emma, for when the nights start to pinch."

Alfred gave her a box, which she opened with trembling hands. It had been tied with a red ribbon. Emma put the box on the table, and carefully unfolded the red shawl.

"Here," said Alfred, taking it from her, and draping it round her shoulders. "Now don't that feel warm?"

Emma stroked it as if it was a new-born lamb.

"Must have cost," she said.

Alfred smiled.

"Got to keep warm. The wind fair lifts up the thatch, these parts, I imagine."

"'Tis certain!" confirmed Hannah.

Emma began to take it from her shoulders, but Alfred stopped her, and said, "Keep it on, a spickle. Get to know it."

Impulsively, she reached up and kissed him on his cheek. Hannah sat looking at her gloved hands, and said, "Don't know about the pews, but I shan't get these off, my fingers so fat and red with pain."

Alfred went to lie down, leaving the women to talk.

When Lorna returned, she noticed Emma was wearing her shawl. Emma would not meet her eyes, was not sure if Alfred had bought his daughter a present, too.

Lorna took off her bonnet and cloak. The pot over the fire was steaming. There was lamb in the air, if she was not mistaken, and onions, turnips, garlic. Hannah ripped her a fistful of bread, and spread butter on it. Lorna ate hungrily, without speaking. There were days like that, up at the manor, when she would not stop, would be driven till she dropped.

"Smells good," she said, at length, when the bread and butter had revived her. "The bread be wondrous."

Alfred fetched a box from his room, and offered it to her, without explanation. She looked up at him, and nodded.

"For me?" she gasped.

"For Saturday."

Lorna stood up, and hesitated. Alfred opened his arms, and she edged into them. Shuddering, she began to cry. The box was still between them, a hard barrier.

"I cannot wait for Saturday," she said, composing herself.

"Pens," he said, turning to his mother and Emma.

Lorna ran upstairs, needing the privacy of her own room.

Emma had gone to stir the stew, not wishing to intrude on their intimacy.

"Go see her," said Hannah. "Alfred and me'll watch the pot."

When they were alone, Hannah in her chair, Alfred in Emma's spot on the settle, Hannah said, "What I said about you being a Canonicorum, the other day."

"Why didn't you tell me? I might have gone to my grave not knowing."

There was no anger in his voice, but Hannah wriggled to make herself more comfortable; the question, though expected, was an accusation.

"We met on May day. Frederick's father owned the field where the maypole be. That year, I was Queen, in all my finery. Folk's eyes were on me. His, too. 'Twas too hot to dance. He walked with me, fetched me a cool drink. He was a year or two older, and I thought him the handsomest man there. At the end of that week, he asked me to marry him, and I said I would."

"But what happened? He did not love you?"

She laughed ironically, and shook her head.

"Words, Alfred. Mere words that shine and then are tarnished by selfishness."

She got up to put plates on the table; there was not much more to say, he guessed.

Words, he reflected. We illuminate them, but sometimes they are not what they describe, no matter how colourfully we paint them.

"He deserted you?"

She shook her head.

"No, I left him."

"But he was going to marry you."

"Me and Lizzie Dottery."

"I see."

"'Twasn't love, not like with Stephen. I'd never met anyone from Wootton Fitzpaine. It sounded so far away, like where some Lord or Lady lived. Within a month, he'd asked me to marry him. I said no, after Frederick, but he did things proper: asked my parents, bought me a ring. When you came along, I tried to convince myself that you were Stephen's, but I knew the truth. The hair, the eyes."

"And you kept that, all those years?"

"Why not? Stephen been a good father to you, and husband to me. No point. And these matters be like the garden, where things grow where they will. Trees in the copse be there all a-mingled. 'Tis Providence, Alfred."

"But me. What about *me*?"

The heat from the fire was almost too much, on top of what he saw as an injustice.

"Me never gets a spickle in this house!" she snapped. "You be Frederick's, 'tis certain, just as Lorna be yours. Things you just get on biv, Alfred. Things you can't do a thing about."

Lorna's bedroom opened. Voices could be heard. She and Emma were about to come down.

Alfred leaned forward, urgently.

"And what did Frederick say when you told him?"

"Nothing."

"Nothing?"

"Nothing. I never told him"
"Why not?"
"Because he loved Lizzie Dottery."

Chapter Twenty-Three

During Alfred's absence, Geoffrey Burton-Bradstock had welcomed Miss. Eleadora Melplash, the school's new teacher, and introduced her to Bridport and the pupils, who had expressed doubt that a woman could increase their knowledge, and had taken a day or two to understand that *she* was in charge, and not them. When she had finally established her authority, she began to take an interest in them as individuals, asking after their brothers and sisters, and mothers and fathers. This surprised them, and angered some parents, who took the view that she was prying into none of her business.

Attendance improved amongst the regulars, and others registered when they heard that she was kind and caring, unlike that strict Mr. Porlock, who insisted they keep as silent as monks when they were writing. Children began to arrive early, to increase the time they spent with her. Even fathers turned up to see her, for her beauty had quickly acquired fame. Indeed, Geoffrey himself began to find flimsy reasons for turning up unannounced.

"Really, Mr. Burton-Bradstock, I am in need of nothing. You have made my introduction to Bridport as pleasant as it could possibly be," she said, when he arrived, at the end of one day, with his mother's parasol.

"The sun has been so fierce today, though we be in autumn's youth, that I thought you would need this. You live far from here?"

He would have me in his bed, or as his wife, I suspect, but I am yet a stranger. The children are my priority. I must disappoint him.

"You are most kind, but I have, as you can see, been indoors, all day, and I shall benefit from a little exposure to the sun," she replied, not mentioning that she was renting a room in a house on the road to Symondsbury.

"Then as the day is fine, and my father requires nothing further of me, I hope you will allow me to stroll with you, a little of the way."

She could think of no reasonable objection, so agreed.

"Then just a *little* way, Mr. Burton-Bradstock. It would not do for us to be seen by any of my pupils."

"Why not? We are merely strolling in the sunshine."

She shook her head.

"I am their teacher. They would ask questions, and my answers would be subjected to closer scrutiny than would be comfortable. You must appreciate my position. I am an unmarried woman. There would be speculation. I would find myself required to explain my conduct. To the clock only, and even then I shall hide behind this parasol so that my face cannot be seen."

She took from him the silk parasol, on which had been painted exotic flowers.

"It is a pity to deprive Bridport of such a pretty face."

So I am right, she thought. He does like me, but he is my employer, and should not try to take such liberties.

"Mr. Burton-Bradstock, there is one thing I must make clear: I do not welcome such gallant compliments. Whatever your motive in paying them, I assure you that they make no impression on me. Indeed, they do much to harm my good opinion of you. I think I no longer wish to walk with you."

She thrust the parasol towards him, but he did not grab it.

"Keep it. Fair skin will burn easily today. You misinterpret my praise, which is genuine. I am without female company, these days, and admire beauty wherever it glisters or is coy. For example, the hills and sea are a constant source of inspiration to me. But I regret the impulsive speech I made, and ask your forgiveness. I will be a model of restraint, in future."

"I cannot keep what belongs to your mother, even for a day."

"Why not? It is merely a parasol."

She sighed.

"It is not the parasol itself, but my borrowing it. You would have to return to collect it. As a teacher and employer, our relationship must be clearly defined. I can only consider you as just that: my employer. You pay my wages."

He saw in her that independence of spirit he had found such a challenge in Cressida. Their engagement, he had long since known, had been premature. He vowed he would not repeat his mistake. Eleadora would not be rushed. Her resistance to him was no coquetry but genuine wariness. As he took his leave, the parasol again in his hand, he bade her good evening.

"And I will be content in that knowledge. I admire your dedication to your children. That is what the founder hoped for. When he returns, he will discover, as I have, that I have made an excellent appointment."

Geoffrey nodded briefly, and left the building. Outside, the warmth embraced him. *If only she were less beautiful!* he wished. *I suffer the curse of my sex, but I shall not make the same mistake again. These matters are best left to Providence, whose authority is absolute. No arrangement of honey-glazed words will sweeten her.*

When he had gone, Miss. Melplash tidied her room. The great bolts of sunlight, which had wilted then baked the children, persuaded her that it was time to go home. Home: a small bedroom in a widow's townhouse. Mrs. Seatown provided her with breakfast and an evening meal, and chose to eat with her. This had been initially welcome, but Mrs. Seatown, who had no children of her own, and whose husband had fallen off a ladder and killed himself, had decided to adopt her, and offered advice closely resembling instruction. The town clock said that there was still an hour of liberty, so Eleadora strolled through Bucky Doo and down South Street.

She felt people watching her, marking her as a stranger, but others, mostly children she taught, called to her, ran indoors to drag their weary mothers onto the step to see her. Soon she had a following. The tranquility of late afternoon, for which she had hoped, evaporated, and her enjoyment soured.

Back at her lodgings sooner than she wanted, she sat in her chair and reflected upon the visit of Geoffrey Burton-Bradstock. In the gloom of her room looking onto the road to Symondsbury, she wondered whether she had acted too hastily. Even his too direct manner is preferable to the isolation I must endure till I am established and can afford a house of my own, she concluded.

Her thoughts were interrupted when Mrs. Seatown knocked on her door, and called that dinner was ready, but that she must hurry, as mackerel goes cold quickly. Mackerel – again; whole, so that she had to ease the oily flesh off its bones with the dexterity of a ship's surgeon.

But when Eleadora reached the dining room, Mrs. Seatown was grinning widely. Eleadora wondered what aspect of her appearance could incite such a reaction, but she need not have been concerned, as Mrs. Seatown nodded to the sliced beef on the table. See what I have treated you to, said the grin.

"Now, didn't want you thinking that all I serve is mackerel, and I admit we have had it too often. Here be some of the best slices of beef in Dorset. One of Farmer Canonicorum's herd, according to Balson, the butcher. And there be tatties, all a-swimming in butter, and livened up biv a pinch of salt. You like carrots? There be a few of them, too. And just when you be thinking that you be full, there be honey and cake to follow. Now, what do you say to all that, then?"

Eleadora's eyes welled up unexpectedly.

"Why, marvellous."

"'Tis wondrous,' we say round 'ere. '*Tis* wondrous.'"

"'*Tis* very wondrous, then.'"

"No, girl. We say, ''Tis *passing* wondrous.'"

"'Tis *passing* wondrous."

"Perfect. Now, you sit down, but, as always, only if you've washed your hands, which be a Godly tradition in this house ever since Boney lost the war, or thereabouts. My husband had the cleanest hands in Bridport."

Smiling, Eleadora showed her hands, a ritual she had come to tolerate, and sat down.

"Girl, you been 'ere long enough for me to know that you aint full happy. A girl turning up in a strange town to start a new life aint natural. So," Mrs. Seatown said, serving the tatties onto Eleadora's plate, "you tell me what all this is about, in between mouthfuls, because out is better than in if 'tis ruining your good looks."

Eleadora began with basic information: where she used to live, what she used to do. Mrs. Seatown was a skilled listener, and did not try to steer her to people or events responsible for her sadness. Soon, however, Eleadora ran out of domestic trivia, and began the tale of her trials, such as privacy and dignity permitted. Even when she shed a tear or two, after the last slice of beef had gone, Mrs. Seatown passed no comment, but merely reached across the table and patted her hand.

"You'll be in need of something sweet after all that," she said, clearing the plates and knives and forks from the table.

When she returned, the first signs of a smile appeared on Eleadora's face.

"Thank you, Mrs. Seatown. I feel much better now. Please don't worry about me. I shall get used to Bridport and the children soon enough."

Mrs. Seatown did not, at first, respond but concentrated on cutting the cake without making too many crumbs. The honey had been warming and thinning in the sunshine, and was easy to spread.

Eleadora closed her eyes, and bit into the slice, and the sweetness soothed her.

"Passing delicious."

However, such was her pleasure in the taste that she failed to notice that a chord in her landlady had been struck by her tale. Mrs. Seatown's eyes stared into her past. In Eleadora, she could recognise some of her own history.

"We've all wanted a fresh start, dear. There be a part of us all that we feel will heal if we go somewhere else and balm it with new faces and voices, but taint so, girl. For the ghosts follow us, and we aint quick enough to lose 'em. So we just 'as to put up with 'em, till they stop bothering us. Days when they torment us, days when they leave us alone. Just remember: folk we be alive with today are the ghosts of the future. Just remember that, girl, and all their clankings and pestering, and a-waking you up in the night, will become sheep a-baaing, and birds a-whistling."

Eleadora watched her clear the rest of the table, never saw her dab her eyes.

Geoffrey Burton-Bradstock: one for clanking or a-baaing? she asked herself. She felt his recent lack of visits a sign that he had been discouraged by her harsh treatment, but, in fact, he had pressing work to do on his father's estate.

One day, he paid a visit to Frederick's farmhouse, where he knew Edgar, as he thought him named, resided, to see if he knew when to expect him back.

"Edgar?" Frederick asked. "You mean Alfred?"

Quickly, Geoffrey said, "Yes, Alfred. A slip of the tongue. There are matters relating to the new teacher we must discuss."

"I aint rightly sure where he be, though he went Dorchester way. 'Tis over a matter which will take as long or short a time as it will."

"Then I would be grateful if you could pass on the message from me that I should be pleased to see him as soon as possible, on his return."

"Why, you may do it yourself, sir, as that looks like him now, a-coming down the lane biv Emma, if my eyes don't deceive me."

Frederick went to the window to verify his suspicion, and Geoffrey followed him.

"So it is. Then I shall stay and impart my news in person, if you allow."

"Granted, sir. 'Tis wondrous they be back, as day hab seemed night bivout 'em."

Emma withdrew from the men, after exchanging warm greetings. Alfred had invited her back to the farm. Your house will be cold, will need airing, he had thought of, to persuade her. Only the fact that he had enjoyed her company again, that she seemed as if she had nearly put behind her the spectre of the past, remained unspoken.

Frederick left Geoffrey alone, went to fetch a duck that had been hanging in the barn since he had wrung its neck.

"I did not know when you would be back," explained Geoffrey. "I came to tell you that Miss. Eleadora Melplash, the new teacher, has made an excellent start. She has asked after the school's founder several times."

"Then I shall visit her as soon as I can. My excursion to Dorchester, being of a personal nature, was unavoidable. Miss. Melplash is popular?"

"'Tis certain. Knowledgeable, independent of mind."

Alfred guessed what that meant; Geoffrey's eyes had widened significantly.

"The children must learn, and she will be judged on that alone."

You would not say that if you had seen her, thought Geoffrey. Her beauty far outweighs her knowledge.

After a glass of port, Geoffrey said, "I must call you Alfred?"

Frederick, guessed Alfred.

"'Tis my proper name. Edgar Porlock be who I was in Wells, but I be back in Briddy now."

His laugh was strained, unconvincing. Geoffrey raised an eyebrow: he did not understand but would not press the matter. Instead, he changed the subject.

"Will you come tomorrow, after lessons? I do not know if you wish to play a prominent role in the school. There is much I must attend to on our estate, and she must have someone to whom she can apply for help if she needs it."

The promise. How could he tell Geoffrey that he had wronged Emma, that the school was a symbol of his contrition, his attempt at reparation?

"You and your father have done more than enough. I shall not desert Miss. Melplash. I shall introduce her to Emma. Miss. Melplash lives close to the school? Is short of female company?"

Geoffrey jerked his shoulders, as if they had been lifted by a puppeteer.

"She has made it quite clear that she requires no help in establishing herself. I offered, but she refused me."

"She is all thorns?"

"The children love her. Her face is an angel's, and lights up their lives. I must warn you that you will avert your gaze when you first see her!"

Alfred noticed a change in Geoffrey's voice. Why, you have fallen in love with her, he deduced, and she does not reciprocate.

"Then I shall beware. She has made an impression on you."

Geoffrey swallowed the last of his drink.

"She has a beauty so rare that time must not chafe it. Oh, if I could paint her portrait, I should beg her to sit, that I might immortalise her! But, alas, my control of a pencil and brush falls well short of that required."

"But we do not all see the same thing, though we look together upon an object. We call this wine red, but have no way of knowing 'tis the colour we *both* see."

Geoffrey stood up.

"The time be too slouching for such philosophical conundrums. Tomorrow, then, when I wager you will be smitten. 'Taint natural nor earthly, and 'tis to be hoped that the children's demands do not dim her lustre."

The next day, mist muffled the vales and hills, leaving them gasping for breath. Emma had made up her mind to go home when the sun broke through. Her house needed airing, Alfred, space.

After she had left, Alfred threw himself into tasks, poked his nose into the barn, drew glares from Billy Eype. Wellesley galloped strongly, as if he had been saving up his longest strides, having not wanted to waste them on Billy Eype, who had recently used his whip too harshly, and had been thrown off.

The day became hard to fill. Before she had left, Emma had said to him, "You will tell him you are his son?"

He could not think clearly. What would change? he wondered. The knowledge might breed resentment of Hannah's secrecy, might place him between two parents whose life together had been as short as stubble. Better to wait for his instinct to guide him, for the right moment. Frederick, it occurred to him, might take it badly. "All those years," he might sigh. "All those years."

Alfred smartened himself for his visit to see Miss. Melplash. The school was as much for Emma as Bridport, and I have kept my promise, but must I play its keeper for ever? he asked himself. My pens lie idle. I do not practise. The channel in my forefinger is not so pronounced. There are no ink stains on my hands. No one asks me when I will finish the work for which they have paid handsomely, in advance. This visit is a duty, but I must soon resume my own work. Lorna will be my apprentice. She is her father's daughter.

Geoffrey met him in Bucky Doo, and they went to the school.

The children ran onto the street and aimlessly into spaces, having been confined too long behind their desks.

"They are like frisky lambs," remarked Alfred.

"They are free again."

Alfred followed him inside. Miss. Melplash was sitting at her desk, staring at rows of empty desks. The day is over, the diminishing whooping of children reminded her.

Geoffrey knocked.

"Come in!" she called, expecting their visit.

Geoffrey went first, and said, "I have brought Mr. Morcombelake to see you."

She rose. Another demand on her blunted mind and tired body, and she smiled weakly.

Geoffrey was conscious that his company had not been wanted, the last time he had spoken to her, so nodded, almost bowing, and withdrew. He glanced at Alfred, whose face had reddened. Such beauty arrests, noted Geoffrey. I told him what she was like, and the effect is immediate.

Miss. Melplash, too, was blushing. She placed her fingertips on her desk, to steady herself. The odour of children's unwashed bodies lingered, so she went to open a window, to give her time to think what to say.

"Miss. Melplash, you are making a huge difference to the lives of your pupils, I hear from Mr. Burton-Bradstock."

"Oh, I don't know about *huge*."

"Before, they had no one. Now they have you."

She turned to him.

"There is something I must ask you."

"And I, you."

At that moment, the tension eased at the mutual need to acknowledge each other.

"Why did Mr. Burton-Bradstock call you Mr. Morcombelake, when you are Edgar Porlock, a poet, master illuminator of manuscripts, a former house guest of my Uncle Josiah, in Wells?"

Alfred smiled.

"A good question. And now mine. Why did Geoffrey say that you were Eleadora Melplash, when you are Zillah, the pupil who kept a roof over my head till you became a teacher in Wells, and I was dismissed by the Bishop?"

"In time, there will be answers," said Zillah, enfolded by his embrace.

Through the window, Geoffrey watched, till the chance of discovery moved him out of sight.

"'Tis passing quick for them to kiss. The ways of women are as unfathomable as the sea!" he muttered, hastening away.

Chapter Twenty-Four

With a flourish, Tremayne Maurward draped his cloak around his shoulders, more out of haste than for effect upon an audience. There was no bright moon to help him find his stirrup; he groped his way up his horse like a blind man. The primordial blackness disorientated him. He murmured, once in the saddle, and the horse moved. The urgency of the moment spurred his thoughts. They will notice me gone before long, and, therefore, I must lose no time. The night shrouds me; they cannot track me.

Soon, he heard someone whisper his name, and he stopped his horse, dismounted, and asked quietly, "You are sure? There is yet time to change your mind."

"Yes, I am sure. And you?"

"I am here, as arranged, though midnight is a place I like not. These vapours deaden sound, and awful thoughts steal upon me like an outlaw, making my hand rest near my dagger."

"Talk not of such things. 'Tis our enterprise alone which makes it hover there. Will you lift me? We must be gone. If we tarry, we risk discovery, and are not safe till we reach Lyme, the first stop on our journey."

Tremayne lifted her up. Sitting behind her, with his arms around her, so that if she fell asleep, she would not fall, he tightened the reins.

Knowing the country lane well, the horse slowly made its way to the Lyme Road, where the gossamer moonlight fell and reflected off the sea, enabling the travellers to proceed safely.

Tremayne concentrated on keeping Fanny in the saddle. Occasionally, he felt her give way to sleep, slip and slump against his shoulder. His arms, strong as mooring rope, began to ache, but he held fast, knowing Lyme was close, down a long hill, waiting for them. He had been before, knew its steep main street stepped out of the sea, and climbed to a vantage point, high above the town.

Lyme was asleep: no lights, no movement; only the grumbling and hissing of the sea could be heard.

Tremayne guided the horse through an inn's entrance. The lack of motion, when they had stopped, woke cold, confused Fanny.

"They expect us," he reassured. "A few moments, dear, and we will be in a warm bed. In the morning, you must eat breakfast as a wife, remember. Wear the old ring you brought for this purpose. This discomfort be but for one night, as tomorrow we travel to Sidmouth, where arrangements have been made for our wedding proper. Then 'tis done, as we want. Devon be more welcoming than Dorset, in this matter."

Exhausted, Fanny felt vulnerable, wiped her eyes.

"Knock up the innkeeper, dearest, for I shall never manage Devon without a soft pillow."

When he answered Tremayne's call, the innkeeper said nothing, and led them to their room. He passed them his candle, and returned to his tiny lodge by the courtyard, knowing his step in the dark, and clutching the coins he had just been given.

It was almost mid-day when they descended to eat. Refreshed, Fanny opened the curtains. Below in the street, women with baskets, and horses and carts, moved slowly but purposefully up and down the hill. The sun was out but had not yet fully lit the buildings on both sides. Fanny felt an irresistible urge to go out into the fresh air, but the memory of her clandestine escape, the night before, robbed her of the joy she should have felt at the prospect of marriage.

Tremayne saw her sadness, and, at a low ebb himself, held her hand, and said, "The day will be fine. Let us eat. We will feel better. A thousand times have we talked about the obstacles we faced in Symondsbury. Our differences, however, be our strength. You have no second thoughts?"

She smiled weakly, and shook her head.

"I would this could be done a different way, but it cannot."

Though hungry, they ate with little heart. The serving girl, jolly and plump, observing few of the house rules, told them it was a Lyme day, 'twas certain, and that the sun, which didn't always show its face, at this time of year, was in the harbour, on the beach, in the wider bay, in little courtyards, through which she had skipped, for she was passing glad to be alive on such a morning. It peeked into fishing boats, and into the undercliff, no doubt, where she had never gone, on account of it being known to snap shut and swallow visitors.

Tremayne and Fanny shared the coach with a tall man, who looked like a parson, but was, in fact, a tailor travelling to Sidmouth to take the measurements of a gentleman needing new vestments for a funeral he was expecting to attend. Next to him sat a woman, humming quietly. And squeezed in was a thin woman with a young child.

"You are returning to Sidmouth?" asked the man of Tremayne and Fanny.

"We are taking a rest there," answered Tremayne.

The tall man looked at him, then Fanny, as if comparing them. The slight inclining of his head to the left suggested he suspected they had some other reason for going there. It was not exactly a regard of disapprobation, but there was a hint of superciliousness in it that irked Fanny.

"And you, sir?" she asked. "You are from Sidmouth?"

He shook his head so emphatically that the humming lady ceased humming and looked alarmed, feared that his head might be jolted from his neck.

"Oh, no," he said. "Sidmouth is an inferior place. For a start, it is in Devon. Though a mere stride away, Lyme is much more genteel, don't you think? No, I am a tailor, bound there to measure a gentleman for an anticipated, solemn occasion." He examined Tremayne's attire, and risked a condescension. "Might I suggest you come to me for your next suit, sir? I would be pleased to provide one more compatible with your height and skin tone."

"I never go to tailors, sir," said Tremayne. "They usually come to me."

"Tradesmen should always come to rich clients," added Fanny. "We would have them thinking they are better than us if it were the other way round."

The woman took up her humming again.

The child spoke, and was answered in French.

The tailor, put in his place, smiled disjointedly, and stared out of the window, till he shut his eyes, and began to snore.

The hotel, shutters pulled up, giving the impression of being asleep, faced the sea, and basked in fine weather. Fanny had sent there a letter of reservation, having heard a friend of her parents sing the hotel's praises. Tremayne had not yet mastered all his letters, though was improving under Fanny's demanding but effective tutelage.

Outside the grand, white hotel, a man with a beard greeted his French wife and Celestina, his daughter. The lady took her humming into the town, and the tailor donned his top hat, retrieved his client's address from his pocket, and began his search for it. Tremayne and Fanny stepped into the bright light.

"We shall need to buy a trunk before we go in. In it, we must keep our wedding attire, which we have yet to find, for tomorrow. You have the name of the church? It is legal to marry in this parish?"

"Dear Fanny, 'twas you who wrote the letter, and I passed to you his reply, which came to me to avoid discovery by your parents. 'Tis you who read and write better than me, so 'tis to be hoped you read it right!"

Fanny scowled. The arrangements for their imminent wedding had suddenly no colour or precision, were yoked to her, holding her back when she should have been striding forwards towards a life with Tremayne.

She delved into her bag, pulled out the confirmation of their reservation of a room, but could not find the letter from the vicar.

"Oh, why could you not have kept it yourself, taken it back when I had finished reading it? My mind is frozen. I cannot remember the church, the vicar's name, or the time we are to be wed. What are we to do? I begin to wish - "

Tremayne took her wrists, and said, "Harbour not such doom-laden thoughts. Though I remember not the name of the vicar, the church be called St. Swithin's. 'Twill be easy enough to enquire after. Dry those eyes. We must not attract questions. And from the church, we shall find a quiet country inn, where we may sit by the hearth and drink to our good fortune."

Fanny suddenly felt lonely, despite the pretty scene he had painted. There would be just the two of them, her family absent, ignorant of the act of which they would have disapproved.

"This is not how I thought it would feel," she sobbed.

Tremayne pulled her to him, felt her stiffness.

"You are tired. Let us rest, then eat. Think only this, dear: we have nowhere to live, and shall find lodgings more easily as man and wife. Remember: you must put on your ring; it must seem that we are already wed. Come. We have travelled this far, and must not falter."

She began to control her sobbing, then suddenly held her hand up to her mouth, and gave a cry of alarm.

"Oh, no!"

"What, more distressing thoughts? Cast them aside before they destroy you, *us*."

"I wish I could, but I cannot."

"Why? You must banish them."

"The letter. If it is not in my bag, then . . . "

Tremayne then deduced its whereabouts.

"What's done is past. Let us hope that you have taken care to hide it, or else perish the thought! They may this very moment be on their way to stop us. There is no choice but to hasten to St. Swithin's, and beg the vicar to bring forward the ceremony."

Fanny saw the panic in his widened eyes.

"But we have a room here. They expect us. Will the vicar really marry us here today? What if he is indisposed? I like not all this, and I am as miserable as can be."

"I, too, feel this keenly, but we must act swiftly. Come, to the church. The bells must be silent, lest it bring others thither."

Fanny felt hungry. Exasperated, Tremayne looked up to the sky. They could eat later. There was a more pressing matter: to find the church of St. Swithin.

"Zum zay it be up there, over yonder," an old man told them. "Though I don't rightly know myself. They be all the same to me, and I aint been in one since I were a tiddy un." Then a woman, flustered to be asked the same question, indicated five other directions they might try. "Be it a grey box of a building with a broken-off spine?" she asked. It seemed that no one knew of its whereabouts, or even if it existed.

If the coach be still there, and we haven't found the church soon, I've a mind to go back, thought Fanny.

"We must not give up so soon," said Tremayne. "We know it exists. We will look fools if we go back."

Just then, as if his determination was being rewarded, he saw a man in a cassock, gliding, it appeared, towards them. Tremayne felt sure this man would know.

"St. Swithin's?" repeated the vicar. "You will find it up the hill and down. May I enquire about your reason for going thither?"

Tremayne looked at Fanny, who shrugged.

"We are bound there to ask the vicar if he will bring forward our wedding by a day," he said. "You know him?"

The vicar looked at each, in turn, and said, "Then your search is at an end. I am the Reverend Dawlish, and I think this should be discussed at the vicarage rather than in the glare of the public. Your name, sir?"

"I am Tremayne Maurward, and this is my fiancée, Fanny Colmer, both of Dorset."

"Dorset, you say. Did you write to me? Someone from there did, I remember, but your name is a stranger, as is the reason for your marrying so far from home. A day early, you say? We must first check my records, but I am not sure about changing dates; it only causes confusion. It is best if we speak privately. I must cogitate upon your request. It is most unusual."

The vicar led the way, and the two elopers followed quietly, despondently.

Alfred Morcombelake saddled Wellesley. In the silence of the night, he wrestled with a dilemma. Should he keep Flora and Lorna apart, as they had stayed, for so many years, or should he tell Flora that he had found and met their daughter, and knew where she lived? Had not his return to Dorset been about just that: telling the truth? He would tell Flora that he intended to become a father in more than name, that he was going to pass on all his skills as an illuminator of manuscripts, so that Lorna could belong to a tradition going back to the Middle Ages. But he had to protect her privacy. He would not reveal where she lived.

Only he did not tell Emma of his visit to Flora, which, he resolved, would be his last to Symondsbury Manor. Emma would disapprove, he knew. It would not take long for him to tell Flora that her daughter was safe and well, had a name and a bright future.

Outside the farmhouse, the milkmaids stood, arms folded, talking animatedly. One or two were pointing in different directions, while others were watching Wellesley carry Alfred up to the manor. Alfred did not look at their faces, did not want to be recognised, suffered unexpectedly with shame at what he now felt to be a betrayal of their trust in him. The smell of them, the way they cleaned the house, fed him, cheered him with their coarseness – all were pleasant memories. But not Winifred, the cousin he had invented, shooing cows, swinging by her stretched neck, buried not far away. Yes, Billy Eype, I shall interrogate you soon, and find out who lies in this matter.

A maid he had not seen before greeted him. The master and his lady were not seeing anyone, she said.

"Miss. Flora be the one I wish to talk to," he informed her.

The maid eyed him up and down, assessing him. What did a well dressed man like him, distinguished by a white scar of hair, want with a common servant no better than herself? he saw her thinking.

She went inside, the door not completely closed but sufficiently to deter him from following. When she came, Flora looked pale, her hair hastily pinned up instead of being tidily combed. Her eyes bulged like a frightened deer's, and reminded him of Emma's, the evening he returned from Somerset.

Flora waited, surprise robbing her of words.

"I have come to tell you something."

"Say it, then. The house is in mourning, and I will be wanted soon."

Her voice was weary rather than hostile.

"Our – " He was going to say child, but Lorna was not that. "Our daughter. I have seen her."

Flora opened her mouth, questions jostling to escape.

"You talk in riddles. Speak plainly. There is trouble beneath these rafters, and I must attend elsewhere."

"I have found her. She is well."

Flora looked over her shoulder, felt pulled back inside, but wanted to hear more.

"She is well yet has been dead to me, all these years. You have dug her up from an airless grave to haunt me? Why, Alfred? Have you not done enough to me? You left your parents as well as me. You, too, may have been dead, for all we knew."

Flora was trying to keep her voice down, and did not understand why he must add to her heartache. Must she always suffer? Did he think she passed a day without reliving that awful moment when her mother handed over the baby to Hannah and Stephen?

"Stephen is dead."

He could not bring himself to call him father. That could wait for another day.

"I am troubled, and you will kill me with all your talk of a girl I have not been a mother to. Go, Alfred. I am needed inside. There is fear in the house, and this doubles it for me."

"Her name? You do not ask her name?"

"'Twon't be the name *I* gave her. No."

Flora did not want to know the new name. It would give a visage to the memory, bring her closer.

"Then I will guard her name, but what ails the house of Symondsbury? Death stalks its corridors? If so, my timing misses the mark."

Flora bit her lip. Should she tell him? He had no right to know. It affected Yeoman and Clementine as much as her. It was a private matter.

"Ask not. I must go."

Flora closed the door behind her.

The maids: why had his replacement not put them to work? Whatever agitated them was the cause of Flora's distress, too. He would enquire there, even if he risked their insults for leaving them.

He turned to untie Wellesley from a nearby post. I have tried, he reflected. At least, she knows her daughter lives, and, in time, may take some comfort in that knowledge.

As he made his way to the farmhouse, he rehearsed his answers for their questions. The truth. That is all it requires: the truth, no matter how cold, how bitter its taste.

Then he heard his name.

"Edgar, come hither!"

His name, once worn and now shed, sounded strange, and the notes were from another time, from Frederick's field, on May Day. She wore a crown, let Emma wear it for a kiss.

He moved towards her, her copper hair now greying, her face a mirror of Flora's. Lack of sleep and tears had robbed her of her beauty. Whatever had happened had savaged her radiance.

"You have returned to the farm?" Clementine asked. "You want work again?"

It was not the right time to tell her he was no longer Edgar. Was withholding his change of name a kind of lie? he wondered.

"I have come to see Flora."

"Flora. Poor Flora! As wretched as me, and most wronged of us all!"

"Whatever is amiss you need not disclose to me if it causes such pain."

"It matters not. I am in need of a friend. You were once a good one to us both."

"Where be Yeoman?"

"Gone," she croaked.

"Whither?"

"To find Cressida and Guy, who have fled we know not where. Oh, that she had not treated Geoffrey so! They would still be together. I found a letter to Guy left in her room. It seems they have eloped to be married. Yeoman has gone to stop them."

The impetuosity of young people, thought Alfred.

"It is the hallmark of their age. You disapprove of their marriage?"

Clementine nodded, dabbed her eyes, took a deep breath, and said, "Disapproval be too thin a word. Yeoman must stop the marriage before it is too late, and some great, scandalous, moral wrong be committed."

"You talk in riddles, Clementine. I am no wiser."

"They *cannot* marry. It seems I have lived as the only one not to have heard the rumour as old as Cressida, who be, in unexpected truth, Guy's sister."

"Sister?" gasped Alfred. "How so?"

She trembled.

"Yeoman's conscience has kept Flora and her son with a roof over their heads, though not a single sign of their error have I seen, and no further lapse has Yeoman made with her. But his confession, forced by Guy's and Cressida's avowed intent to marry, is enough to destroy me."

"Know you where they have gone?"

"To Sidmouth, apparently. The vicar who wrote to Guy lives there."

All around hung brooding hills. To find a love in all these sweeping vales, where an embrace might be considered a proposal to marry, is nigh impossible. 'Tis enough to put a noose round the neck of the best of the milkmaids, thought Alfred.

"Then I am truly sorry."

"Trouble 'ee not, Edgar. Rejoice that no such secret haunts you as this one does me. And Flora, poor Flora, victim as much as I, suffers equally. Go hence, and be glad you left and severed all connection, and treasure when our lives were a meadow of buttercups, and a dance with long ribbons."

She returned to the house.

"What have we done?" he cried in anguish. "Oh, what have we all gone and done?"

Chapter Twenty-Five

It had been years since Yeoman had travelled so far on horseback. The saddle had made him sore, and he was glad of a good night's rest at an inn, on the way to Sidmouth. In his bag was the letter leading him to where he hoped to prevent the disastrous wedding of his son and daughter. He did not doubt that their marriage could be annulled, but wished to prevent their physical union, which would cause them untold misery on their discovery of the truth. Had Cressida given herself to Guy already? he wondered. If so, his own and Flora's silence had unwittingly permitted her.

Sidmouth was indifferent to his desperation. St. Swithin's church? Never heard of it. Be that in Lyme or Axminster? 'Taint round these parts. No one could help. This is my punishment, he concluded: an endless, frantic search.

His luck changed when, after walking through every street in town, he sat down to rest, and closed his eyes. The sun, a comfort, warmed his face. The light was then momentarily interrupted, and he opened his eyes to see a woman, younger than Cressida, passing, a bunch of flowers in her hand. She started when Yeoman flinched at her brief blocking of the light.

"I did not mean to startle you," she said. "I am merely on my way to the churchyard."

"Think nothing of it. I am no tramper but am resting my weary limbs on account of the long journey I have undertaken. Do not be afraid. Churchyard, you say? There is one nearby? 'Tis a church in Sidmouth I seek. St. Swithin's be shy, and must be skulking in some hidden dell. You have heard of it?"

"Indeed, I have, and 'tis thither I go to lay these flowers on the grave of my sister, who was taken before she ever kissed a man or wove a ribbon round the maypole, on Solstice day. One day, I will dance for her."

"Then I beg your forgiveness for delaying your solemn act of remembrance."

"Time pushes me not, for she has been gone two years, and though I miss her, she will go nowhere. I am as constant as she, but the hour of my visit matters not."

"'Tis far, the church?"

"A spickle up and down, and skulks not but sits there to greet travellers arriving from the north, and to wave them goodbye when their time here is done."

"I may walk with you?"

"You may."

The girl described Sidmouth for Yeoman, to pass the time, and soon the church came into view.

"Your sister has a name?" asked Yeoman.

"She does. A pretty: Rachel."

"And you?"

"I am Ruth Abbas, last of that name. And you?"

"I am Yeoman Symondsbury, from Bridport, come to find my son and daughter."

"Bridport is a fine place?"

"Sun and showers, though more sun."

"Then thither shall I go, as here there is nothing 'cept aching loneliness. Sometimes I think I'd rather die than stay here, cooped up like a chicken."

"Say not that," said Yeoman. "Come to Bridport, but know loneliness has a bed everywhere. We are arrived, and I thank you. I must find the vicar so take my leave, in the hope that Bridport will gain whom Sidmouth has wronged."

Ruth walked round the back of the churchyard. There was no rectory nearby. The church door was open. Sunlight had warmed the pew on which Yeoman sat, and his mind returned to Guy and Cressida.

"Strike me down, Lord, here and now, so that, at least, I know you hear me!" he cried. "Punish me as you will."

He held his head in his hands, oblivious of the verger, who had entered to turn to Psalms for the vicar.

"Oh, I did not think to have a visitor," he said, seeing Yeoman.

"Are you the vicar?"

"No, but he follows. If 'tis a spiritual matter, I shall return another time."

"Private rather than spiritual."

The vicar arrived.

"You wish to pray?" he asked. "Though 'tis the hour I keep for myself, you may join me if you wish. My time with God is precious, but my parish is important, too."

The verger left. The vicar could find Psalms for himself.

"I will speak with Ruth," the verger whispered, passing the vicar. "She seemed sadder than usual, yesterday."

Yeoman began by showing the vicar the letter Cressida had carelessly left behind.

"I shall come straight to the point, not wishing to divert you from your devotion. Is this your hand?"

The vicar cast his eyes over it, and nodded.

"It is."

"And may I ask whither they went when they left here? I must find them as soon as possible. 'Tis important."

The vicar felt Yeoman's distress.

"You know them?"

Yeoman hesitated, and said, "I do. Are they long gone?"

"'Twas their intention to stay at the inn, a mile down the road."

Yeoman ran out of the church, and called, "Commence your prayers, and wait at their *Amen*, for I shall return here within the hour, and bring the couple with me, and acquaint you with the damnable news."

The vicar ignored *damnable*, and called, "A moment! They - "

But Yeoman was gone. The marriage had to be undone, the sooner, the better.

He broke into a run, walked, ran again, panted, wheezed, coughed, all the way to the inn, a cottage draped in wisteria, its long bunches of lilac grapes fringing the windows.

His face was red, his chest rose and fell like a blacksmith's bellows, and his hands trembled in anticipation of finding Guy and Cressida. He had not rehearsed his words. They would come in the right order, he knew, because of the gravity of the message.

The door required a barge of his shoulder before it would open. A warm draught from the hearth added to his discomfort. In front of him stood a man, in his raised hand a glass of wine. It looked to Yeoman as if he was toasting the woman sitting in front of him, her hands crossed demurely on her lap, on her face a sweet smile, an acknowledgement of the man's good wishes for her health and future happiness. The sentiments had pleased her; the man's sincerity was unquestionable.

Yeoman surveyed the scene: in the middle of the table separating the man from the woman was a decanter; on the floor, a parasol; at the window, two urchins' faces, which disappeared when Yeoman scowled at them.

Cressida recognised him first, and Guy turned when he saw the unforgettable look of guilt on her face.

"Father!" she cried.

Guy's tongue was paralysed. Feeling foolish, he put down his glass, and looked to Cressida to respond to Yeoman's arrival.

Panting, faint, Yeoman sat down in Guy's chair. Guy offered his glass, but Yeoman shook his head. It was a moment's rest he needed, not wine.

"This is a sorry scene," he said, at length, "as much of my making, if not more so, than yours."

Just then, the landlord appeared.

"Will you take your victuals now?" he asked.

"Later," answered Cressida. "My father is unexpectedly arrived, and we must talk."

"Just as you wish, but 'twon't keep hot beout drying out," he pointed out, returning to the kitchen.

"Fear has robbed me of appetite," said Yeoman.

"You have come to fetch us back?" asked Guy, after a long silence. "We are not tiddy uns any more."

"No, 'tis true, but the act of disappearing without telling us be that of unruly children."

"How did you know where we were?" asked Cressida, saddened by the distress she had caused her father.

"The letter."

Guy looked accusingly at Cressida, and shook his head. Carelessness, he thought. A woman's carelessness.

"That letter was private," he snapped.

"But Symondsbury Manor be mine, and I do as I please in it!" Yeoman shouted, slamming his hand on the table.

"Father, let not our thoughtlessness anger you so," said Cressida, moving to Yeoman, and holding his head to her, to soothe him.

"Thoughtlessness?" questioned Guy. "We have been thoughtless? 'Twas planned with much consideration by both of us."

"And 'twas a mistake, which took us far less time to realise," admitted Cressida.

Guy turned his back on them.

Yeoman said, "We had no idea, your mother and I, never saw a sign of what was between you. 'Twas a secret kept close."

"You and mother would not have approved."

Cressida released her father, took a step back.

"'Tis certain."

Guy snorted, and said, "Because I am a labourer, son of a poor servant. We are kept apart, you and I, by birthright. But I tell you, Yeoman Symondsbury, that though you have paid my wages, you do not own me."

Yeoman ignored him, and addressed Cressida: "You have gone behind my back, and 'tis a sorry way to treat me. You had a good man in Geoffrey. He loved you, and you discarded him. Think how that sat with us."

Cressida compared her current situation with her engagement to Geoffrey Burton-Bradstock, and replied, "He was arrogant, Father. You did not know him as I did. I could not marry him just to save your embarrassment in front of his parents."

"He was young. That is what an engagement is: time to grow together, to mature. You would have changed him, and he you, for you can be as sharp as a Weymouth wind."

Guy began to feel excluded from what he believed was becoming a family argument.

"Sir, I ask you to leave us now. This is a moment for us alone, not one to be interrupted. Can there be no adventure, at our age? We are confined to the estate, and rarely meet anyone else. And now 'tis all spoiled. Go, sir, and let us return at our own speed, if you will still have us, for we must hold our heads high. Our defeat we have already turned to our advantage, for we have listened to our hearts, and they have whispered wise counsel, which, like a tyrant wind, must wreck us as the sea a ship on granite teeth before it can soothe us like a conjuror's balm."

The landlord reappeared, a decision made.

"If I may make so bold as to say that this be a quiet inn where wayfarers may rest and eat and drink. My wife and I be common folk, unused to betters like yourselves, which I gleans from your apparel, and from your airs, which be more suited to a manor or even a castle, by the sounds of it. This thatch may be lowly, but it be all mine, and one which I rule over, so to speak, even though you aint eaten your victuals. Raised voices don't fit 'ere. Never have, never will. Good manners don't cost a penny."

The landlord spoke with such dignity that, ashamed that his arrival had disturbed the inn's tranquillity, Yeoman was moved to make the sincerest of apologies.

"Forgive me, good innkeeper, for the disturbance it must seem I have begun. It ends now under this thatch, which has had to hear more than it should. Allow me, sir, to settle the bill generously, as recompense for your inconvenience. In another time, another place, other circumstances, you would find us more agreeable."

The landlord counted the sum Yeoman handed over, nodded in acknowledgement, and said, "I shall bid you goodbye. Please mind the step on your way out, as it be a spickle too high for the door, or the door be a tiddy bit long for it. Anyroads, make sure the door be closed. You wouldn't believe what blows in betimes."

On the way back to the church, they did not speak. Each walked as if he or she did not know the other two, and wondered what the future held.

At the church, Yeoman stopped. There was no sign of Ruth Abbas or the verger. The vicar must be still at prayer, guessed Yeoman. To disturb devotion was the last thing Yeoman wanted, but it was necessary to put Guy and Cressida asunder.

"'Twas the vicar said you were bound for the inn. 'Tis he who must declare your marriage unlawful, eradicate any trace of it from the parish records. My only hope be that the fire of desire has not compounded all our woes," said Yeoman.

Cressida said, "You talk in riddles, father. Marriage? We are not wed, and our names baint recorded in this parish's records, nor ever will be, on account of our thinking again."

"'Tas been a rushed and sorry dash based on thoughtless impulse," added Guy. "We are of one mind: 'tas been a big mistake."

A perplexed Yeoman scratched his head.

"Not married? Say again you are not married, and they will be the sweetest words."

Guy bridled.

"Am I so hated that 'twould be the death of you to see us married? You riding like the wind to rip us apart signifies a dislike of me as great as Golden Cap."

Wishing to dampen the growing conflict between the two men, Cressida said, "When you burst into the inn, our smiles were to mark our decision to be mere friends, nothing more. Both of us have been foolish, and shall return wiser."

Yeoman saw the vicar emerge from the church and make his way towards them.

"So you have found each other, at last!" he said.

"Yes," said Yeoman, "and I know now that you never joined them in holy matrimony. I have acted hastily."

"Yes. I was going to tell you of their change of heart, but you rushed off before I was able. The cause of your haste be yours and not mine to know, so I bid you good-day."

When the vicar had gone, Yeoman had one further issue to address, one no combination of words could make less difficult. There was still the matter of their being half-brother and half-sister. How to tell them? Keeping Cressida ignorant for all those years, while looking after his son and Flora, had allowed Guy and Cressida to meet and mistake each other for lovers. My fear is that they have had physical union already. I know what is possible, having myself succumbed to temptation in my younger days, he admitted.

"I can go no further without telling you something I had hoped to conceal and have interred with me," he began. "Prepare yourselves, for your worlds will be different henceforth. Cressida, you may hate me, deny I am your father, but, at least, you will understand why I have pursued you with such determination. What I have done is unforgivable, and I know not whether I have a wife when I return, such is my sin."

Guy's blood ran cold. This man, who had hunted them down, had always behaved oddly towards him. Yeoman had never barked at him as he had others. Yeoman's smiles had always been cut short, as if he had suddenly remembered how they might provoke an enquiry about their cause.

"Let me leave you both in peace. I shall walk ahead, as this pertains not to me," said Guy.

"Stay!" said Yeoman. "This *does* concern you. I wish it did not, that your mother had never come to milk in the parlour."

"My mother was a milkmaid? She never told me."

"'Twas but brief, our first acquaintance being a fault of mine and none of hers."

"Father, you talk in riddles again. Be plain. Mother awaits me. She has suffered enough," said Cressida.

"A fault?" said Guy, anxious to learn the truth.

"Guy, I have watched you grow into a fine young man, but have not had the freedom to acknowledge you as my son. Silence was the promise extracted from me by your mother, with whom I shared a moment of madness. Just as a kind of loneliness drove you and Cressida together, so it was with your mother and me. Let no one believe that marriage is a magic spell that wanes not like the moon. It does, brews separation of hearts, and no conjuror's potion can heal the rift, only time, whose passing slows the more you wish it to hasten."

Cressida took a step backwards, and looked at Guy.

"He is my brother?" she asked.

"'Tis certain."

"And you be my father?" asked Guy.

"'Tis certain, and I hope with all my heart your affection for each other has been but kisses. Please tell me 'tis so."

Guy could not speak. The look of horror on his face petrified Yeoman.

"'Tis certain," said Cressida.

"Then I am glad."

"Poor Mother knows?"

"She does, and Heaven knows how I shall find her. I fear I have lost her."

"Then a daughter, too," added Cressida.

"And the son you never claimed," said Guy.

"What? Everything? I have lost all? Then I deserve it. All our sorrows I would tie round my neck, and let their weight sink me to the bottom of the sea."

Guy and Cressida walked away, leaving Yeoman alone.

"Come, new-found sister," said Guy to Cressida, taking her arm to support her.

"Things are altered," she said, "altered for ever."

Chapter Twenty-Six

Frederick's life had no regular rhythm, and often he would ask Billy or Alfred what day it was. Only Sunday mornings were distinctive, when the clamour of the church bells would cut through the thin air. Then Frederick would take a chair outside, remember what Lizzie had meant to him. There had been a time when he could hear her voice clearly in his head, smell her when she was all perfumed in flour, but now she sounded remote, different. He talked to her, convinced himself she was listening:

"Lizzie, dear, when you went, I was sure you'd be back. Every creak and squeak in the house was you here again, I thought. But you aint coming, I know, and 'tis so lonely here I wish I was with you. 'Twon't be long, and we will be together again, for ever."

Even lambing did not interest him. When Billy brought him the first lamb of the spring that Alfred decided to visit Conjuror Dottery, Frederick stroked its nose, and leaned back into his chair. Billy said nothing, noted it as yet another example of Frederick's withdrawal from life on the farm.

Alfred was not always there to make decisions for him, so Billy had to, and was careful to tell Frederick what he had done, and, later, Alfred, when Alfred returned from visits to Stinsford to see his mother and Lorna. Soon, Billy felt he was *Farmer* Eype, and not just the manager, and this made up for his false start at Symondsbury Farm, where he had been dismissed, on the tale Guy had made up about him.

Alfred spent as much time as possible with Frederick, but there was never a right moment to tell him he was his son. It was the truth. What it would do to an old man, who barely had the strength to stand, he could only guess. Frederick's heart was tired, his hips locked and painful. How would he tell Lizzie, whom he was ready to join, that he was a father, when God had not blessed her with a child? Alfred recalled Emma's haunted eyes, and did not want to see Frederick's bulge, too.

Choices are the offspring of Truth, and are named Risk and Hurt, reflected Alfred.

"A penny for them," said Billy, catching Alfred leaning on the fence, and thinking about the illuminated letter Lorna had sent him. It was her voice, her gentle mocking, more than the letter's appearance, that bewitched him. *Dear Father*, she had begun. *Aunt Emma* figured prominently. *Mother* – Lorna could not bring herself to call Hannah anything else – talked about him a lot. All Lorna's news, recounted with such candour, made him feel he belonged to a wonderful family.

"Just thoughts about what may be, Billy. You have them?"

Billy lowered his eyes.

"About what *might* have been, mostly."

"You're still young."

"Getting older."

After a long silence, Alfred said, "When Frederick goes, stay on, will you?"

"Why?"

Alfred whispered, "For Winifred."

Before Billy turned in for the night, Alfred asked, "Conjuror Dottery. You know where he lives?" Billy nodded, looked up. "You been before?"

"Yes."

"And does it help?"

"'Tis certain."

"How?"

"Helps you see things. Gives you knowledge. He saved me. *Saved* me."

Alfred patted him on the shoulder, and left him alone to dry his eyes, cope with the memory.

The next day, Billy told him how to get to Conjuror Dottery's house.

"Head for Pilsdon from the bottom of the hill, down from the clock. Cling to that road, and float gently up to a signpost saying Beaminster ahead. Turn right, and you be at Dottery itself, two or three houses shunning each other biv no other place to go. Neighbours yet strangers," explained Billy.

"And how shall I know the conjuror's?"

"'Tis the furthest down the hill, on the right. Set back a spickle, it don't want to be seen, on account of the conjuror, who be outcast and one of only a few left in Dorset. The Church hab frowned on 'em, these long years."

"How shall I recognise him?"

Billy gave a short laugh.

"He has long hair down to here."

Billy made a cut with the flat of his hand to the middle of his upper arm.

"He has powers?"

"The knowledge."

Alfred set off, his question ready.

"Be him the weathervane I need, then I shall care nothing for gossip's poison but judge him on what instincts we have all but lost," Alfred muttered.

After twenty minutes, he saw a signpost for Dottery. On the way up to it, he had become nervous, wondered what Emma would say if she knew. This had to remain a secret. Billy would not tell. Loyalty would buy a future on the farm, money, security.

Chickens wandered into the lane. A black and white collie appeared at the gate of the first house, growled, barked, howled.

The second house was hidden behind a high hedge. Only the roof was visible, its thatch bedraggled, suggesting abandonment.

Conjuror Dottery's must be the next, deduced Alfred. Much I hope he will tell me, and in the right direction point me. In his potion I will trust.

The conjuror's house was wide, and had no upstairs. The grass was long and clumpy, worn only from the door to the lane. Apples and plums were like open sores on the floor. Elderberries, dark constellations, hung heavily where they were smothering the hawthorn. Green and black rashes had spread across the limewash. Objects were at odd angles: a door on the outbuilding had one hinge broken; a window-frame leaned to the right; a bent wall had been buttressed.

Alfred's knock was a dull thud. The curtains were closed. Somehow the whole property had the air of being empty. Have I made a wasted journey? wondered Alfred. Have I lived all these years to take the words of a maligned stranger as gospel?

Again he knocked and thought he heard a noise within. A cat purred, a curtain moved. The rattle of a key being put into the lock made Alfred jump, step back, in anticipation of a grotesque, old man. Long hair, Billy said he had. Alfred prepared himself.

The door opened. There stood a woman in a long black dress. Her red, swinging ringlets hung on her shoulders. On her face and the backs of her hands were dense swarms of freckles. Cressida, he thought. She reminds me of Cressida, and is not much older. She smiled an invitation to speak.

"I have come to see Conjuror Dottery," Alfred said.

"Do 'e expect 'ee?"

Her voice was warm and creamy.

"No, but I have come to consult him on a matter of some importance to me."

She stood aside, and Alfred entered.

"'E won't be long. Gone to the traps. Lanes be twitching with rabbits."

The room was not what he was expecting. A fire was lit, the flagstones shone in its light, and a dresser was neatly adorned with plates. On the table was a white cloth, and two candlesticks gave it the appearance of an altar.

Alfred took the chair offered.

"I have never been to a conjuror before," he said apologetically.

The conjuror's wife moved into view.

"'Tis nothing to fear. At least, less so than a surgeon's knife or the plague," she said, smiling.

"I have suffered at the hands of neither."

"Then think of your visit as one to a friend. You would like a drink? There is nettle tea, elderflower wine, or cider."

"'Tis kind, but nothing, thank you."

He was thirsty but could not conquer his wariness, his expectation of an odd experience. This welcome was warm.

"My husband does not have so many visitors, these days. Only a few come, from time to time. You heard of him? You are in genuine need? Some folk come to see if he is a freak, a monster, a wizard."

"There be always superstition and doubt. When someone is different, there is always suspicion."

"'Tis the Church who rant the most. We lives tucked away up here because we can't live down there in Bridport. Burnt at the stake be what they wanted. Called us when we were there, drove us out by pointing and whispering. Used to go to church, but the vicar turned us away. 'No holy prayer will cleanse your soul of the evil your devil-worship spawns,' he told us. 'Well,' I said, ''Taint the devil we worship,' but he just says we are not allowed in God's house, neither will we be buried in the churchyard."

Alfred was filled with sympathy for them. Looking round the room, he saw no sign of denial of God's authority.

"'Tis Nature poisoned by ignorance and prejudice."

"'Tis certain," she concluded.

The door opened. His back to it, Alfred felt vulnerable. The conjuror's wife smiled at her husband, and Alfred stood up.

"Good morning. I be Alfred Morcombelake."

The smell of wet grass and fur followed the conjuror as he dropped his full sack in the corner of the room. Rabbits, guessed Alfred. And the conjuror let them fall as if they were tatties.

Billy was right. Down to the middle of his upper arm was the conjuror's hair. Was the beard new? He moved slowly to offer his hand to Alfred.

"Edmund," he said.

His face promised a smile to come on acceptance of his hand. Alfred felt Edmund's hand slowly tighten when he encouraged it with a squeeze of his own. Then the smile: open, genuine, blue eyes, darker than his own. Now on Alfred's hands: rabbit fur, dead rabbit reek.

"I have come to ask for your help."

"What sort?"

"They say you can tell what will be."

Edmund grinned.

"And who told you that?"

Hazel went to the cupboard, leaving the men to talk.

"Billy Eype said you saved him."

"'Tis kind, but I am no saviour. The Lord alone saves."

"You are a soothsayer?"

Edmund wiped his hands on his trousers. The blood on them was the pig's. The rabbits were less messy, till the skinning. He thought carefully about his answer.

"A conjuror, as was my father, and his father before him. I be one in a long line. Might stop with me, 'less we have a child."

He glanced over his shoulder. Hazel, her back to them, momentarily stopped sorting through bottles and pots, then continued.

Alfred was embarrassed, looked away, did not want to come closer to what her silence and his glance were saying.

"You want to start soon?" called Hazel.

"Depends." Edmund turned to Alfred. "A woman?"

"How do you know?"

"'Tis usual."

"Emma."

"Tell me," invited Edmund.

So Alfred began, summarised his journey, and asked the question.

"You are prepared for the answer?"

"Yes. I am older than you and used to the ways of the world, the way dreams are shattered."

"Tell me what she was wearing when you first proposed to her."

A field at Canonicorm Farm; a long white dress; a crown of flowers woven into her long hair; a blush the sun had brushed gently onto her cheeks. All he could remember he described, till Edmund nodded, had enough to work with.

Edmund turned to Hazel.

"Prepare yourself," he said to her, and she went through the only other door in the room.

Edmund lit dried herbs, passed his nose through the smoke, inhaled.

"'Tis strong and good," he said. "Two seconds only."

"What is it?"

"Dried dangleweed. Grows at the foot of chestnut trees when 'tas been wet and warm."

Two seconds later, the smoke began to make Alfred feel peaceful, that Edmund could save him.

The elixir came next.

"Drink," instructed Edmund. "'Twill unlock you, but you are

safe. Trust me." Alfred hesitated. "Watch," said Edmund, and he himself drank, and Alfred did likewise.

Soon the table rippled. Edmund opened the sack in the corner, and the rabbits leapt out slowly, hundreds of them, till they covered the floor.

"Argh!" cried Alfred. "Keep them away from me! They will eat me alive!"

Edmund spoke soundlessly to him. Save me! mouthed Alfred. Between them, the glass wall was impenetrable, and the rabbits began to scratch at Alfred's legs, to hiss. He screamed in silence.

The candles went out, and in the darker light rabbits squealed, crawled onto his lap, his shoulders, head. I will die, thought Alfred, frozen as I am. 'Twon't be long before I am gone. He resisted no more, was resigned to death.

Then nothing. Quiet. A return to the conjuror, who was looking at him with bleary eyes. In the corner, the rabbits were once more in the sack. Hazel was not there.

"I am alive?"

"'Tis certain."

"The rabbits!"

"Guilt," said Edmund. "But now you are unlocked."

"Unlocked?"

"Your coming here baint necessarily believing. We all need unlocking."

"But my question. How shall I know the answer to it?"

"Hazel," said Edmund. "You will know shortly."

Conjuror Dottery yawned, looked out of the window, and said, "An hour we have been gone."

The candles were lit again. Hazel returned in a white nightdress, and on her head sat a crown of holly. The conjuror picked up his fiddle off the dresser. Hazel pointed her toes as she took measured strides around the table. The conjuror played well, and Hazel moved fluidly as she rose and dipped to the tune. Her song was plaintive, and she wove it round Alfred:

> "You told me you loved me
> yet left me to cry;
> for years you were lost,
> and I wanted to die.
>
> And now you are back,
> say you love me anew.
> But how do I know
> that to me you'll be true?
>
> Convince me, my darling,
> that you will stay mine,
> and won't leave me again
> with no hope, and to pine.
>
> Around the tall maypole
> I did dance for your heart;
> convince me, my love,
> you and I will not part.
>
> Forgiveness is yours
> already, you know.
> You ask for my hand,
> say I yes? Say I no?

The last note faded, and Hazel stood before him, breathless.
    The conjuror put down his fiddle.
    "Convince me, Alfred," said Hazel.
    "How can I? Know me by my actions alone," replied Alfred.
    "Know that I shall not be convinced before death comes."

"I will die?"

"So many years cannot be forgotten; promised vows were not kept at their birth. They follow you to their conclusion before I am convinced."

"Yet you will be convinced, in the end? Say 'tis so, and that death does not steal me."

"It comes to us all."

"'Tis certain," added the conjuror.

Hazel took a step backwards, and Alfred reached out to her.

"Farewell, Alfred. Till the embers of those years are cold and grey, my answer is withheld. Know that I love you, that I shall always love you."

She left the room, and Alfred turned to the conjuror.

"There are things which must happen?"

"'Tis certain."

"Death comes untimely. Is it Emma?"

"Is it not enough to know she will love you for ever?"

Alfred rose and took out money from his pocket.

"Is this enough?" he asked.

Without counting it, the conjuror nodded.

Alfred walked up the hill, and turned left out of Dottery.

Death, and I know not whose. I am not saved, Billy, as you were. Not saved. And I must wait, wait for death to call, tell its worse and snatch me.

The landscape tilted, righted itself.

Not worn off, the elixir, he thought, though 'tis feebler.

Back at the farm, a letter lay on the table. Frederick said, "Somebody written to you."

Alfred did not recognise the handwriting. When he had read it, he sat down. Oh, Hazel, he cried within, why did you not warn me it would come so soon? *This* soon?

Frederick said, "Says *Edgar Porlock*."

"Never knew you could read." Alfred's hand began to shake. "I must leave for a few days."

"'Tis bad news. Your face be the morning's ashes."

"The pen of Providence, of whose deadly words I was forewarned, summons me."

"You speak in riddles, Alfred."

"Jolyon is dying, and to him I must hurry. Tell Emma I shall return." Frederick looked into his eyes. "'Tis certain, this time."

Chapter Twenty-Seven

The landscape did not interest him. Through the window, he saw merely places, not villages with living creatures, trees, and people. Usually, he linked them into local narratives, gave them names, loves, triumphs, and tragedies. Now they were lifeless. Inside the coach, he made it clear he did not wish to converse. He closed his eyes, and, occasionally, read, but the words were obstacles over which he stumbled, his mind on Jolyon, who was in bed, suffering his last hours in a gloomy room. That is, if he had not already died.

Porlock was as Alfred remembered it, yet not. The cottage on the Nether Stowey road looked the same, but others had been built, he could swear. In the graveyard, there should have been two more headstones: for Edgar Isambard, taken by a greedy disease, and the Captain, among the smashed beams of the *Lyonesse*, at the bottom of the sea. Both should have been buried in Porlock.

Alfred had not written to Mrs. Lydeard, warning her of his intention to visit. There had been no time to waste, and when she saw he had come, she smiled weakly, as if putting on a brave face to a bout of biliousness.

"I knew you would come. I found your letter. There were two addresses, so I sent a letter to each. He has not much longer. Come through," she said.

Inside, no candles or lamps were lit. It was as if the house had gone into mourning already, in anticipation of Jolyon's death. With the door shut, the hall felt like a crypt.

"Is there no hope?"

"None. The doctor said it was only a matter of time. Jolyon has refused laudanum. He is much changed: his face is thin, his cheekbones stick through his skin. He - "

She burst into tears, and Alfred comforted her.

"'Tis the Lord's will, though cruel."

"Come," she said between sniffs. "He is in the room on the right. I will warn him."

She left the door ajar, allowing Alfred to hear mumbled words.

Mrs. Lydeard returned, and nodded to Alfred. Jolyon was lying flat, still. How small you look! thought Alfred, standing by the bed. Age and illness have conspired against you. The life had all but fled from Jolyon's eyes, and his breathing was erratic and shallow. When he turned his eyes to Alfred, they were nearly all white, the iris colourless.

"Edgar," croaked Jolyon.

"I have come to see you."

There was no point trying to explain he was again Alfred Morcombelake.

"I am a sorry sight. I have minutes, seconds." He turned to Mrs. Lydeard, and said, "My desk." The skeletal hand he urgently raised waved at it lest she mistake his intention. "The scroll in the drawer. Quickly!"

He tried to raise his voice to make her hurry, but it cracked.

Mrs. Lydeard brought the scroll to him. In one movement, he snatched it and tossed it across the bed to Alfred, who began to unfurl it.

"Try not to distress yourself," suggested Mrs. Lydeard quietly, knowing anything firmer would have provoked a strong reaction likely to kill him.

"Leave it," Jolyon said to Alfred, ignoring the advice. "You must do something for me. Come closer."

Alfred saw that Jolyon's lips were dry, cracked, and his eyes sunken, vague. Close up, however, the eyes fixed him in desperation.

"'Tis close enough?" asked Alfred, not wanting to inhale Jolyon's foul breath.

"Josiah Watchet," whispered Jolyon.

"What of him?" asked Alfred.

"Tell him that I forgive him."

Alfred nodded, expecting a revelation of what Jolyon was forgiving. In all the time Alfred had lived with the Watchets at the rectory, he had wondered why Josiah had never asked about Jolyon. Indeed, when his name had been mentioned, Josiah had changed the subject, shown no desire to talk about him.

"Of course. Is there anything else I should say to him? I did not know you were closely acquainted with him."

Jolyon struggled to form words, and his head fell to his left, his mouth formed an oval, and his eyes stared at the wall.

Alfred listened for breathing, turned to Mrs. Lydeard, and said, "He is gone."

Mrs. Lydeard came forward, rested her head on his chest, and clutched his hand, which resembled a claw.

"Goodbye, dearest Jolyon," she said. "Go with the angels."

She moved him onto his back, closed his eyes, and placed two coins from her pocket onto his eyelids.

"Shall you say a prayer?" asked Alfred.

"No," she said.

She tucked Jolyon's arms under the cover, which she pulled up to his chin, as if trying to keep him warm as long as possible.

"Let us go now," said Alfred.

"'Twill do till later. You will stay?"

"Of course. There is the funeral."

"'Tis kind, but stay at the inn. This is no place for you tonight. My hands will not cook, my tongue will be tied. Come tomorrow, Edgar, but forget not the scroll."

She passed it to him.

"You know its message?"

"I do. I wrote it as he said it, and he signed it. 'Tis all a spider's wandering but recognisable, for all that."

"I will return in the morning." At the door, he turned and said, "He taught me what I am now teaching my daughter. None will ever match his illumination. I owe him everything."

When Alfred had left, Mrs. Lydeard said, "'Tis an age since the Captain died, and now I am alone again. 'Twill be *my* turn next."

The funeral took place, and Alfred had reason enough to mourn with the deepest gratitude, as well as sadness: Jolyon had left him all his wealth, in a bank in Wells.

"And you are well provided for?" checked Alfred, once more. "You could expect something. I already have money enough."

Mrs. Lydeard said, "My husband was a successful Captain of a merchant ship. I do not want for a thing except his company, of which I had too little."

"You have friends here? There is room on the farm in Bridport. Frederick be your age, give or take a spickle in your favour. I offer not out of obligation but desire to repay you. 'Twas the kindness as much as the advice to go to Wells which gave me a clear direction in life."

"Friends? The raucous choir of the salty wind be always here in Porlock. I would miss the bent horizon, and imagining that my husband was just beyond it, out of sight, but coming home to me. And you, Edgar Isambard, my honorary son, are mine, too. 'Tis kind, but I shall be buried here with Jolyon. The vicar knows, the money has been paid. He will write to you if you be at the two addresses you sent to Jolyon, though I shall not expect you to make such a long journey. Let me go as I wish – alone. 'Tis the way we should all go. Now kiss me one last time."

Alfred left her, and his thoughts turned to home: I do not want Emma to think I am not coming back.

By Taunton, the expectation of soon being in familiar surroundings buoyed him, and the landscape acquired life again. In his bag was the scroll, confirming that he had inherited all of Jolyon's money. Then came an idea: I have more than enough to build a better school in Bridport. That would be a fitting tribute to Jolyon. I will speak to Geoffrey, ask his opinion. The current space is inadequate, and it lacks an exterior appearance betokening knowledge. Emma will see a proper school built, and 'twill be more spacious for Zillah, who looks pinched between her desk and the wall.

His idea occupied his thoughts till he reached Bridport. Billy was the first to see him, and stopped in his tracks, unable to resume his duties. Something important was on his mind, and Alfred sensed something was wrong.

"'Tis the look of a mourner you give me," remarked Alfred.

"The master. Miss. Emma be with him now. Couldn't send, not knowing where you were."

A fact given the tone of a reprimand. Alfred made straight for the farmhouse.

"Frederick? Emma?" he called. "I'm back."

Emma came, her face as anxious as Billy's.

"He's been asking for you," she said. "Took a turn. Dr. Coryates has given him a linctus, and says Frederick's heart has worn out, and 'twon't be long before it stops."

Alfred went straight through to Frederick's bedroom, trying to make sense of dashing across counties to witness death calling. How many more old men must I see a-waiting to be taken? But 'tis Providence, which don't space the snatching evenly. Come all at once, come spickle by spickle, 'tis our common lot.

"I be back, Frederick. You not so well?"

Frederick tried to sit up but, exhausted, fell back onto his pillow. "I am cursed," he said weakly.

"I'd never have gone if I'd known."

"No one ever knows the moment, just the prospect, which aint a Dorset January to me no more, at my age. Lizzie be a-waiting for me."

Alfred rested his hand on Frederick's forearm. Under the loose, puckered skin, there was still muscle.

"Then let her wait a spickle more."

Frederick smiled at the futility of Alfred's optimism.

"Listen well, Alfred, as there be something I have to tell you. Many has been the time, in fields and fairs, when I have been tempted to speak of it, but no more. 'Tis now or never."

"Rest. Do not upset yourself. Whatever it is has waited all these years."

With a grimace and a struggle, Frederick pushed himself into a sitting position.

"You know I've always taken an interest in you, never treated you like the others when you came to work on the farm." Alfred nodded, acknowledging his own awareness of Frederick's favouritism. "Well, there be a reason." Mother said she never told you, Alfred remembered. Told me because it was the time for all her secrets to breathe some fresh air, whatever the consequences. But she was clear that Frederick never knew. Alfred's silence invited him to continue. "Before Lizzie, there was your mother. But then there came Lizzie, my wife. Your mother found out, and left me, but 'twas the timing of it all, you see. The *timing*."

Frederick's breathing deteriorated. He had laid too many words on the confessional path, so Alfred decided to help him, realising that few more were left.

"Speak plain, and then I shall tell you something."

Emma entered soundlessly, stood back, fearing for Frederick but not wanting to intrude on their confessions.

"You, Alfred, bear not the name I would have chosen for you. You are the son I always wanted but could not acknowledge. Your mother married Stephen Morcombelake so quickly. More a gentleman than me, he was, but you are mine, I have no doubt. I have always worn this beard to paint a difference, to tighten tongues."

"I know, father. I have known without the telling."

Emma stepped forward.

"Enough. 'Tis said, and there let it rest," she said.

Frederick grimaced and clutched his chest. Emma and Alfred went to him, but their gesture was futile. The pain overwhelmed him, and his eyes became lifeless.

"He is gone," said Alfred.

Emma listened for a heartbeat, kissed Frederick's forehead when she moved from her bent position.

"'Tis certain."

"Then I am an angel of death."

"Why so?"

"First Jolyon, and now my father. Take care, Emma, lest a similar fate befall you."

"Talk not such nonsense. He died with the truth on his lips, and saved you the task."

Alfred put coins on Frederick's eyelids when he had pulled him from his upright position by his legs.

"Blue and white marble already," remarked Emma.

"A good man."

"'Tis certain. You will tell Billy?"

"I will, though the answer to the question he will ask I know not."

"In the top drawer the will be."

"Frederick told you?"

"I put it there."

"You wrote it?"

"Your father signed it. I said it, and he nodded. Dare you look?"

"Tell me."

"The farm, the house, his deposit in Dorchester. You are rich, Alfred. Father to son, as is tradition."

"Richer than you can know, Emma, for Jolyon, too, has left me everything, and I have an idea. What say you of me building a new school for Bridport?"

"Wondrous, but first let us lay Frederick to rest. To discuss his bequest before the burial is disrespectful. You must read his last will and testament. 'Tis all writ."

"I agree. Will you stay here while I tell Billy? Then I must go to order a coffin. In Bridport will Frederick be buried, and come the next solstice, a prayer will be said in the field."

Billy stopped cutting the pig, listened without looking up. Blood on my hands, he thought, be what I add up to. Just blood. And where does Frederick's passing leave me? 'Twill be up to master Alfred now, and he aint sure whether I stays or goes, judging by his glances betimes.

"He was a good man," Billy said.

"'Tis certain." Knowing what Billy, in his stillness, must be wondering, Alfred added, "I want you to stay, run the farm. I am no farmer. There will be more money for you. The farmhouse be yours to live in."

Billy could not shake on it, his hands so bloodied. There was nothing else to think about, no other ambition to fulfil.

"You will go again?"

He had not meant anything by *again*. It was just a figure of speech to him. Alfred's comings and goings were not even rumours to him.

"I will build a new school, pay for it, but I won't stay in my father's house now he's gone. He'd be in every room, every chair."

Billy looked up. Father? Had to be. Why else would a man like Alfred come and go, have the run of the place? Now Billy's wariness of Frederick's confidence in Alfred had an explanation.

"I'll stay, then, but let master be buried a while afore I moves into the house. Won't tread on his toes, then," said Billy, picking up his knife again.

The pig was cleanly cut, its entrails in a bucket. Once butchered, it was bound for Bridport.

"You'll come to his funeral?"

"'Tis certain."

Billy began to behead the pig, ending the conversation, and Alfred left him to contemplate his new position on the farm.

Hannah. What was Frederick to her but her son's father? A letter would not do. He would go to see her, take Emma, check how Lorna was progressing, be her father in the flesh again.

Bartholomew had sawdust in his hair and on his clothes.

"I will come and measure him. You want him here or there?" he asked. "Some like a vigil. Folk will want to see him for the last time."

There was not Bartholomew's usual patience with a bereaved customer. His words were clipped, sharp. Both men knew they needed each other, that Emma connected but divided them.

"My father will stay in the house. You will arrange the funeral?"

Father? Bartholomew thought. Emma a cousin? 'Tis passing strange. I must see Jethro, tell him of the death.

"I will. The day be set by the vicar, and I will let you know."

Emma will be there, Bartholomew realised, and so I will stay away from the carrying. My men will manage on their own.

"The money?"

"Later. You want oak, 'tis more, there being more worth and strength in it. The wood is harder than most and lasts longer."

Does it matter, the wood, when 'twill rot at eternity's march anyway? Alfred wondered.

"Oak, then."

"He will be available to measure, this afternoon?"

"He will be there."

He has no other commitments, sneered Alfred to himself. *This choice of language, meant to soften the unbearable reality of death, is as comic as it is respectful*, he observed.

Emma stayed away from the measuring, had seen how Frederick had been shrinking. Then there was Bartholomew; she could not be near him now.

"Will he require room for personal possessions?" asked Bartholomew.

Alfred looked around the room. Where Frederick was going, there would be no need for earthly comforts.

In the four days it took to make the coffin and dig the grave, Alfred and Emma went to see Hannah and Lorna.

"I will not come," said Hannah, removing dead flowers from a pot. She picked up the petals that had fallen on the floor, groaned at the bending of her stiff back, the aching of her legs.

"I thought not."

When her mother was out of hearing, Lorna asked, "May I come? Is he not my grandfather?"

"Come, then. In the meantime, I have a commission for you. I will pay you well."

"What is the nature of it?"

"Later, when we are alone. Trust me."

"I trust you," said Lorna.

Emma heard the low voices, and went to talk to Hannah.

On the day of the funeral, Barthomew's men arrived, and Billy and Alfred helped them to lift the coffin onto the wagon, and followed in their own cart. Alfred, Emma and Lorna sat in the back, and Billy took the reins.

As they made their way into town, people threw flowers at the coffin, had eaten Frederick's meat at one time or another.

"His lamb be the best in Dorset," remarked one man to another.

"The farm will go to the dogs now he's gone," opined the other.

In church, the pews filled up with corn merchants, butchers, day-labourers, and anyone else who knew him. The vicar painted a glorious picture of him. Emma, all in black, wept, and Alfred put his arm around her. Several rows back, Jethro watched this affection, did not look at the coffin at the altar.

'Tis time, he decided. Long has it been coming, and now 'tis here, let it not pass me, for we are all defined by such moments.

Chapter Twenty-Eight

Geoffrey had attended Frederick's funeral on behalf of his parents, who were themselves suffering from ailments they had endured for a number of years. They had sent their sincere apologies and condolences, and were saddened to hear of Frederick's passing. Alfred had seen no need to tell the Burton-Bradstocks that he was his son, and assured them he fully understood them putting their delicate health first.

After Geoffrey had first introduced Eleadora Melplash to Alfred, and had seen them, through the window, unexpectedly embrace, he had been tormented by his feelings for her. Women to whom he had been introduced since the end of his engagement to Cressida had lacked the intellectual promise of Eleadora and the spirit of Cressida. The beauty of some had lured him, but their conversation had been dull. There is nothing more likely to put a man off marriage, he had opined to his father, than a woman who is more interested in her mirror than him. His father had humphed, and muttered that Geoffrey had much to learn about women.

Geoffrey wanted to know how Eleadora and Alfred had come to know each other, but could not bring himself to reveal that he had been peeping at them through the window. However, his chance to know more came when Alfred had ridden to tell him of his intention to build a new school.

"You are most welcome, though the rarity of your visit, I hope, betokens not further bad news."

"Far from it."

Geoffrey listened, and said Alfred was most kind to commit to repay Mr. Burton-Bradstock every penny he had lent to modify the warehouse and employ Eleadora.

"And you intend retaining the services of Miss. Melplash?"

"I certainly do, unless you know of a good reason why I ought to dispense with them."

Geoffrey hesitated enough to puzzle Alfred.

"No. She is well liked, and the children are learning how to read and write, and about England's history. What finer recommendation can she have? There is, however, a matter on which I hope you can shed light. You will forgive me my bluntness, which I hope you will not interpret as rudeness, but were you already acquainted with Miss. Melplash, prior to her appointment?"

Alfred smiled.

"I was, though I had no inkling that she was going to apply for the position." He realised that he ought not to reveal her previous name; it would cause much embarrassment, and make her position untenable. "I lodged at her abode, at the kind invitation of her uncle, and not by design. She worked, as you know, in a school at Wells."

"Then her connection with you is purely historical?"

Alfred then guessed Geoffrey's motives for asking.

"Indeed, it is. Do you see it as an obstacle in any way?"

"No, not at all. The matter is cleared up and closed."

"Right, then let us return to the primary reason for my visit. I came to ask you to assist me in appointing a master builder, and to oversee the construction of a new school. I realise, of course, that you have considerable work here on your father's estate, and would understand if you declined, but I have come to know you as a man on whom I can rely completely. Now, what say you?"

The prospect of consulting Eleadora over the design of the new school was so inviting that he gave his answer immediately: "I am busy here, and my father has no longer the energy he once had, but I would like to accept your offer. 'Tis most kind, and 'twill give me a stronger purpose in life."

The two men shook hands, Alfred relieved, Geoffrey excited by the prospect of seeing Eleadora more often, and demonstrating his affection for her.

"I will speak with Miss. Melplash as soon as possible. After I have acquainted her with my plan, I shall hand over to you all responsibility for its progress, and thereafter must you involve her in organisational matters pertaining to it. Shortly, I am going away for a few days to make arrangements for the money required for our venture to be withdrawn. I ask you to begin your search for a master builder and a suitable plot of land. The school should not be too far away from the centre of Bridport. We must not give the children an easy excuse for staying away!"

Alfred told Eleadora of his plan, at the end of a day gloomy enough to make the classroom look miserable, and to dampen her spirits. She listened to him, and he could not fail to notice she lacked enthusiasm for the idea.

"The children deserve the very best," she said, "but I am afraid I can no longer provide it."

Alfred was stunned, had not expected her pessimism.

"There is some particular reason? If you lack anything, tell me, and you shall have it," reassured Alfred.

"What I lack is not easily obtained. I am lonely in Bridport. I spend all my spare time in a sad room, exhausted. The children drain me."

"They love you!"

"My life is not what I wish it to be. You cannot know what it is like to come to a strange place. I have no friends here, and there is little chance of meeting a suitable companion. Bridport has welcomed me, but I lack fulfilment here in so many ways that I feel like . . . "

Alfred was suddenly distracted by thoughts of Winifred, and he remembered how she had begged him to take her with him, and how he had refused. This time, he would not let the supplicant down.

"Come and stay on the farm. There the space and hills will make you feel better. Leave your room, this very day."

"What will people say? That I am your creature?"

"People always make assumptions. 'Tis natural, but you are free to go wherever you wish. We have a long association. I am still your friend, even though circumstances compelled me to leave Wells and return here."

"I cannot live under the same roof as you, after what passed between us. Can you not see that my reputation - "

"I shall be away, for a few days, in Wells. Josiah lives there still? You have his address?"

She nodded.

"Why now, after all this time? Have you not got back what he took? Punish him not."

"Punishment? I know myself too well the pain of it. I wish to see him on another matter. You will give the farmhouse some thought?"

The day had been such a trial that she agreed to. He would send Emma to see her, to coax her into going there. There must be no more deaths at the end of a rope.

Alfred left for Wells, Geoffrey began his search for a builder in Dorchester, and Emma went to see Eleadora at the school.

"Baint no good a-knocking as 'tas been closed all day. She never came, this morning. No message, nor nothing," said one mother.

"She sent no word that she was ill?"

"Rumour be that she has left, or is dead, or kidnapped. My boy been a-wailing all day!"

"'Tis passing strange," said Emma.

The next day, Emma tried again, to no avail. What has happened? she wondered.

"No use," said a voice from behind. "She be gone," said Eleadora's landlady. "Never heard her, mind. The stairs always creak, so she must have tip-toed. Ah well! 'Tis her choice. A girl got a right to go wherever she pleases. Heart be broken, be my judgement. Which case, 'twon't ever be mended. Not known one to mend yet."

This will be a blow to Alfred when he returns, thought Emma, on her way home.

Wells looked familiar yet strange. Buildings had grown, shrunk; colours had faded, deepened; and some features had disappeared. Yet even Alfred's long absence could not change the cathedral's solidity, mass, domination of the grassy space in front of it. He held tightly the volume whose theft, Eleadora had revealed, was by Josiah, and had resulted in his own dismissal. It was time for the book to be returned to the Bishop. Someone else must now complete it, in another hand. Men like him were few, and he wondered who his successor was, and if the Bishop had ended his own obsession: the recording of his time in office, his self-regarding history.

When Eleadora had returned it to Alfred, he had gasped, wondered if she herself had taken it. When it came, the explanation had absolved her mother and herself, but identified Josiah as the thief.

"And he told you why he took it? It was some attempt to discredit me?" Alfred had asked. "Or, perhaps, it was mere curiosity?"

Eleadora had shaken her head.

"He would not divulge his reason. I discovered him poring over it, one evening. He was feverishly racing through the lines with his finger. Not even the moth frantically flapping its wings against the oil lamp distracted him. 'Is this Edgar's?' I asked. Caught out – he knew I recognised it – he admitted he had taken it. I held out my hand for it. He closed the book and clutched it to him. 'Pass it to me,' I said. 'It was Edgar's to complete for the Bishop. Edgar was dismissed on account of your taking it. Let me have it.'"

"Why did you not give it straight back to the Bishop? Why keep it yourself? Was it some bizarre premonition that I and it would be reunited, one day?" Alfred had asked.

"No, not at all."

"Then please explain."

"It was to give you your moment, to confront the Bishop with the truth: that you had not been negligent. It would have robbed you of that satisfaction."

Now that moment was near, he did not want revenge but to set the record straight.

The Bishop agreed to see him immediately, eyed the book Alfred held as if it were an offering at the altar.

"You have it after all?"

"I am returning it. Ask not who took it or how I came across it again. It is enough that it is back in your possession, and to know that you treated me harshly."

The Bishop accepted it with shaking hands.

"Thank you," he said, swallowing hard.

He put it on his table, and turned to the last page of writing.

"It has come to no harm," reassured Alfred.

"My life and the cathedral's are enshrined in this and previous volumes. I can live again."

"You did not appoint another illuminator to continue it?"

"As you know, the art of illumination takes several years to master. Men like you are rare. Would you continue it as before? I am truly sorry for my haste."

"No. My life has taken me in a different direction. I am building a school in Bridport."

"A worthy venture. You no longer practise your art?"

"No. It locked me in my room for too many years. The theft of the book freed me. It is now, for me, too solitary an occupation."

"Yes, as is mine. Jolyon, too, lived like a hermit. You and he were well paid, mind."

"Sometimes such a sacrifice is too great. You will find someone to continue the history."

"I doubt there will be another such as you."

"Then let us part knowing we are not enemies. "

The Bishop had what he wanted, and Edgar was exonerated.

Jolyon's message for Josiah was next. Alfred weighed the worth of his deliveries: a book and forgiveness. Would Josiah embrace the hand of peace?

The address Eleadora had given Alfred he could not, at first, find. On leaving the rectory, Josiah had contemplated living in another town or city, but his sister had persuaded him not to. To do so would have seemed like running away, and the Bishop would have achieved what he had wanted.

"Do you think that your parishioners will spare the new vicar their yawns and indifference? Of course, they won't," his sister had said. "Let us take a different house in Wells. We have money enough. You could give lessons. There is an income to be got from experience, surely. If Zillah can teach, then so can you."

"All in good time, dear," he had replied. "But you are right: a house in Wells we ought to take, to show the Bishop he cannot drive us out completely."

Alfred knocked on a door of one in a long line of squashed terraced houses. The prospect of meeting Mrs. Watchet again did not deter him. The task Jolyon had entrusted to him must be carried out. It was, in fact, Mrs. Watchet who answered the door.

"I have come to see Josiah," said Alfred, anxious to make clear his reappearance had nothing to do with her.

"He had been hoping that, one day, you would return," she said, inviting him in.

Josiah was reading by an empty grate. His monocle was fixed in place, and when he heard the door open, he looked up, saw his visitor, put down his book, and stood to shake hands.

"Why, it is Edgar Porlock, Mrs. Watchet, come to see us. You are most welcome, sir, and though the hour is early, there exists the heavenly promise of chops, tatties, and turnips a-plenty! The prospect appeals, sir? After all this time and circumstantial turbulence, the vista is too tempting to resist, sir? What say you?"

"I say, sir, that the fare sounds as appetising as ever, though I must admit, at the outset of my visit, that I have come at the behest of Jolyon Dursley, who has extracted from me the promise that I would let you know that he forgives you. They were the most prominent among his final words. I myself heard them, and they were said with as much sincerity as a man breathing his last can muster."

The monocle fell from its home, and Josiah slumped into his chair, as he reeled at Jolyon's attempt at reconciliation.

Mrs. Watchet went to her brother, and placed a hand on his shoulder.

"Forgives me, dear. Jolyon forgives me," said Josiah, incredulous.

"Then accept his gesture for what it is," urged Mrs. Watchet.

Alfred felt he should now leave, but wanted to know what Josiah had done to merit such an absolution. Feeling uncomfortable yet wanting to be satisfied, Alfred took a step backwards to remind them that he was still present.

"Come, sir. Will you stay and dine with us, later? What say you linger a while in our humble abode, and relate the story of your travels since you left us? That should pass the time in a sufficiently entertaining way till chops, tatties and turnips are served," suggested Josiah.

Alfred did not wish to stay in Mrs. Watchet's presence for so long, and kindly declined the offer.

"This is a personal time," began Alfred. "You will, no doubt, wish to reflect upon Jolyon's words, and a stranger's presence will be unsettling."

"Stranger, sir? *Stranger*, you say? Pah! Pah, sir! There is the rest of my life to consider his words. I have waited for them for many years, so an hour or two more will not harm. Besides, what began the journey to his forgiveness I would like to share with you, but if you must go, then go now, for I hate long goodbyes. They are all push and pull and full of promises upholstered with hypocrisy!"

Alfred fidgeted, took a little while to consider Josiah's invitation lest he appear too keen to become acquainted with that particular part of their history.

Eventually, Alfred said, "Tell me, then, sir, if you want to, but I must decline dinner. I have to return to Bridport, to meet a man who will help me build a new school."

"Very well. I understand, so will begin by apologising for taking the volume on which you were working. I had not intended to keep it but to check that my years of service to the Church were recorded in it. My suspicions were confirmed. I could not find my name, but instead was that of my intended successor. The Bishop was so ashamed of me that he had expunged me from the diocese's archive!

Imagine my anger at that discovery! By that time, I realised that my faith, which had become a mere skeleton, was not strong enough to win the argument with the Bishop, so I took the book to deprive him of the pleasure of denying me my tiny place in Wells' history. I had thought to destroy the book, do you know?"

"What stopped you?"

"You, sir. All your effort, your art – for it is a beautiful object – would have been wasted."

"I am grateful to you. The absence of your name from the Bishop's notes was not obvious to me. I concentrate on the accuracy of the spelling, the strength of the sentence construction, and the artistry of the illumination. I recorded and illuminated only what the Bishop put before me, and did not question its substance. But Jolyon?"

"Ah! Jolyon."

Mrs. Watchet interrupted with, "Are you sure, Josiah? What use is digging up the past?"

"Let it be exhumed just this once, and then nailed into its coffin for the rest of eternity."

"If you are sure, Josiah, then go ahead. Good may, after all, come from its resurrection."

"You have a brother yourself, Edgar?" Alfred shook his head. Not that I know of, he privately admitted. "Then you cannot know the intense rivalry that can exist. Brothers compete for their parents' affection and approval. It is Nature. But our father loved Jolyon and I equally, and divided his estate between us without advantage to either one of us."

"Then you are Jolyon's brother? Is it really so? Why, Jolyon's last will and testament confirms that his personal wealth will pass to me! This I cannot now allow. You have more right to it than me. Your circumstances here are . . . not what they were. Jolyon's money will make you and Mrs. Watchet comfortable for the rest of your lives. Mrs. Lydeard is well provided for by the Captain. I shall not take a penny belonging to you. My father, too, died recently, and what he left me is more than enough to build a small school."

"I also will not touch Jolyon's money, not out of hatred for him, but out of respect for his wishes. You see, I took something far more precious than money from him. I robbed him of dear Nancy, the woman he loved, stole her on the day of their wedding. She loved me, you see, more than him, yet dare not tell him. I looked upon it as saving her, at the time. There. It also caused a rift between Demelza and I. Indeed, a chasm. What do you think of me now, sir? Eh? *Eh*? But I shall not steal his money. No, sir. I sinned, and turned to God for forgiveness, and, for years, I thought he had forgiven me, till the Bishop, the worst appointment God ever made, drove me out."

Josiah's speech was full of self-pity. Mrs. Watchet feared that his heart would give way, and she asked him to stay calm. He put his head in his hands, and cried, "Oh, the shame, sir! The ignominy of it all!"

"You married her, sir?" asked Alfred.

"He is distressed! Please, no more, Edgar!" implored Mrs. Watchet.

"Married her, sir? *Married* her? I did, sir, and we were happy, till God took her from me, as punishment, I believe. So I turned to the Church, secured the living on the back of a lie, and vowed I would do penance in my pulpit, seven days a week. For a time, it eased my conscience, but I still resented God for taking my wife. Who knows? Perhaps, that is the reason my congregation turned against me, were unsure of my faith. So you see, sir, I am a sinner. I have lost my brother, my wife, my congregation, and my beloved niece."

"But you have me, dear," comforted Mrs. Watchet. "You will always have me."

"But the name Dursley is not Watchet," observed Alfred.

"True, sir. After he was left at the altar, Jolyon felt he could not share the surname of the man who had deceived him. Why he chose the name Dursley is a mystery he took to the grave with him."

Mrs. Watchet shook her head.

"I thought you would not have wanted to know, Josiah, but the Bishop himself once told me. Zillah was only a young girl. I had been on an errand to the cathedral; I was ever your go-between. The Bishop, of course, did not know you were related to Jolyon. 'Ah! Here is Jolyon Dursley now,' he once said, 'come to show me his manuscript. Strange name, Dursley. Chose it after he illuminated an account of the collapse of the steeple, during bell-ringing, of the parish church of St. James, in 1699.' Jolyon told him that, like the steeple, his life had collapsed around him as his own wedding bells were ringing, and, therefore, Dursley was a name he would wear till his dying day."

Just then, there was a knock at the door, and seeing that his hosts were too emotional to go and open it, Alfred went. When he returned, a minute or two later, to the room in which Josiah was at pains to compose himself, he said, "And someone else is here to see you in your dark hour."

"Zillah!" cried Mrs. Watchet.

"I have come home, mother. Forgive me," said Zillah, rushing into her mother's arms.

Alfred quietly left the scene of the reunion, and made his way to the savings bank. From there he immediately set off for Bridport. The children needed a new teacher now. Without one, there was no point building a new school. To go away is easy, he knew. To return is always much harder.

Chapter Twenty-Nine

The classroom felt eerie to Alfred and Geoffrey. There was no clamour for the teacher's attention, just the spirits of the children who had reduced Eleadora to a mere whisper. There remained a few signs of their last lesson: desks not straightened into rows, one or two personal but inconsequential items left on Eleadora's desk, a note to remind herself to speak to James' mother about his behaviour.

"'Tis a sad place," remarked Alfred. "Empty, as if the children had fled with her."

"And she has returned to her home in Wells?" checked Geoffrey.

"She has, and there she will stay." And then, seeing the misery of Geoffrey's loss in his face, Alfred added, "A beauty as rare as that, so perfect in its lines and colours, was never destined for mere mortals such as us. We must both forget her, and find a replacement for her."

Geoffrey understood and sighed.

"Yes, you are right. 'Twas not to be, and we must seek another teacher, one who is, perhaps, more advanced in years, more likely to stay and impart their knowledge."

"There is a spickle of truth in what you say, that experience is knowledge's twin, but wisdom is a will o' the wisp. 'Tis something I have often thought within my grasp, only to find it has slipped through my fingers like water from the Frome. But I have come to be a more practical man, and believe that we have, in fact, a temporary solution not too far away."

"Indeed? Then tell it. We are making progress. I think I have found a builder of the highest quality and reliability. He has excellent references, and his work is much admired in Dorchester and nearby villages. We should hire him before he embarks on another restoration."

The urgency in Geoffrey's tone heartened Alfred, who said, "The answer is so obvious I wonder I did not think of it before."

"Then to the point! You take a Sunday stroll on the matter instead of a brisk walk."

There came a knock on the door, which opened before either man could reach it.

"Ah, Emma. On time," said Alfred, grinning.

"I hope you have spoken to Geoffrey of my idea," she said.

"He has not, Emma, or should I now call you *Miss. Broadoak*? If you are the proposed solution to our problem, then I am glad. I know this school means as much to you as it does to us."

"Yes, though I must add that my help will be confined to teaching reading, writing, and the wonders of Nature. I shall do all that I can, but I know that a trained teacher would be able to do so much more."

"I am sure you will shed light into their darkness," said Alfred. "You agree, Geoffrey, with her temporary appointment?"

"I do, indeed. There could be no better!"

Emma blushed, recognised that such high praise was born out of relief that the school could open again.

"Then I shall put a notice in the window. Lessons will resume in the morning," she said.

"And have you found a suitable place to build a new one?" Alfred asked Geoffrey.

"I have, and will show it to you. Miss. Broadoak, I am sure, wants to make herself at home – or should I say school? – now that she is in charge."

Emma was glad to be left alone. At last, she thought, I am doing something worthwhile – for Alfred. He trusts me, and I, him, and, for a short while, I can make a difference to the lives of the children.

The site Geoffrey showed Alfred did not appear to belong to anyone but the parish, and even the Mayor knew nothing about its true ownership.

"Take it. 'Tas been there, all overgrown and neglected, as long as I can remember. 'Twill be just what Bridport needs, and I hopes I shall live long enough to preside over the opening of it, just as I did the present one, which be temporary but good. By the way, I hears Miss. Melplash have upped and gone, all unannounced. Not really a Bridport woman, be my opinion, though as pretty as a Dorset sunset."

So Alfred returned to the farm in such good spirits that he decided to take Wellesley for a gallop. He squeezed on his riding boots, and made for the stable, where Billy was whispering soothingly to Wellesley, in a low voice.

"'E all right?" asked Alfred.

"Legs a-going," answered Billy. "Not quite right at all."

Alfred rubbed Wellesley's nose, irritating him.

"Will he eat?"

"Nose bag be still full."

"Sick, 'e be, by the looks of him. Even a horse as strong as him gets laid low."

"'Tis certain, but touch. It be more than a fever."

Alfred felt the heat, wiped the horse's sweat from his hand onto his trousers. Wellesley wobbled, and the men stood back, to avoid being crushed. They watched his legs buckle, saw the desperate appeal in his eyes.

"Been like this long?" asked Alfred.

"Last hour. Rode him, as usual, this morning. Took him to the shore and back. Been hedging since."

Billy showed him the bloody scratches, and Alfred thought of robins, how it is said one was pricked by a thorn on Christ's crown.

Wellesley gasped for breath, and his legs twitched.

"Steady, old soldier," said Alfred. "Easy."

Billy shook his head, hope gone.

"You going to do it? Put him out of his misery?"

"Already? How can a horse this strong die so suddenly?"

The two men knelt over him, as if at prayer, worshipping him.

"Only seen this once before. Poison, 'twas. Looks the same."

"How?" Billy shrugged, went to the nearby bucket, sniffed it, and threw it down. "Why?"

"'Tis the water."

"Who could have done it?"

Another shrug, a long exhalation of breath.

"He's *your* horse, but I'll do it if you want."

Billy didn't wait for an answer but went over to the wall against which his gun rested, butt upwards, its barrel burrowing into the straw.

The whites of Wellesley's bulging eyes were full of fear and desperation.

"*You* do it," said Alfred. "*I* can't." Alfred rested his head on Wellesley's neck, as if it were a pillow. "God bless you, my trusty horse."

The shot rang out, and the surprise of Billy's speed made Alfred clench his eyes, and grab Wellesley. Alfred could still feel and hear laboured breathing.

"Why didn't you wait till I was out of the way? You know the best shot is to the head," snapped Alfred. "Wellesley be a strong bugger. One in the head would have done it."

"Had to shoot. He came from nowhere. His finger was squeezing the trigger."

Billy walked past Alfred and Wellesley, turned the man over with his foot, and kicked the gun away.

Alfred turned, saw the intruder's body on the floor. *So Billy has not shot Wellesley, after all,* he realised.

"Who is it?" asked Alfred.

"You were right. One shot in the head be all it takes. One more second, and 'twould have been *your* brains a-spilling all over the floor. He must have crept in. I saw him aim at you, so bam! If I'd missed, you'd be dead."

"'Tis Jethro Sherborne, come to kill me, after all this time. And now he'll need one of his brother's coffins, 'tis certain. 'Twas not the end to the day I was expecting, and let us hope that we be believed by the magistrate. Put Jethro and his gun back where they were, as it must appear as it really was."

When he was told of his brother's death, Bartholomew dropped into his chair, and gripped its arms to steady himself.

"'Twas the farm manager," said the policeman. "Seem Jethro was about to shoot Mr. Morcombelake, and the manager gets his shot in first. Fact is, this be your brother's gun, found side of him."

Bartholomew took it, ran his eyes over it, and rested it across his lap.

"'Taint his. 'Tis mine. He borrowed it to shoot a few pigeons."

"We'll bring him to you. Bullet be to the head, so taint a pretty sight. Long and short of it be, your brother went to take the life of another man, and ended up dead himself. Seems a man has a right to prevent that. No charge will be brought against Billy Eype."

Once alone again, all Bartholomew could think about was Emma, that she might be feeling guilty that Jethro had died because of her association with Alfred. Bartholomew went into his back room, removed the sheet from one of his coffins. He himself towered over it, tried to fit Jethro into it, explaining, and almost apologising, to Emma for all that had happened.

"Should squeeze in. He be the same size as you, dear, and now you must have another made. Jethro needs this one. And I must inscribe, according to the law, the name Leonard Shaftesbury, the one on his birth certificate, on the brass plate. Shaftesbury was Jethro's mother's maiden name. She died unexpectedly, father said, on her way to the workhouse, and then he and mother moved here with the infant Leonard, whom they adopted from the parish. Called him Jethro Sherborne, so's people would think he was one of the family. Leonard Shaftesbury been locked up in a secret till the day he goes a-snooping in mother's drawer, and finds the certificate. *Name of mother: Lucy Shaftesbury. Name of father: unknown*, it said. No one mentioned to me I had an aunt Lucy, who was mother's sister. In time, Leonard came to call Jethro his imaginary twin brother. Never thought it'd come to this, though. All those years at sea, a-speaking to the wind, made him a sad soul. Things be clearer at sea than on land. 'Tis Providence, and if the vicar of Bridport baint willing to bury him in the churchyard, then I shall pay one of the boatmen to take him out a mile or so, far enough from the shore so's he don't get washed up. He's my cousin, the only brother I shall ever have, and he should be sent to the Lord in a proper manner."

As expected, the vicar objected to a Christian burial.

"You and I, Bartholomew, know death more than most. We deal with it, truss it up in boxes and scripture, so I feel bad about reminding you that the churchyard be consecrated ground, and therefore I can't bury him in it."

"He was a God-fearing man. Does the Lord not forgive such a one?"

"Jethro went to kill a man. Whichever way you look at it, 'tis the worst sin of all."

"Then your God is cruel."

The vicar shook his head emphatically, would not be persuaded to change his mind.

"We all make our own bed and must lie on it."

Back at the farm, Billy said to Alfred, "You want him butchered?"

Alfred replied, "I'll bury him in the solstice field. Can't bear to think of him being eaten."

"You want a hand to dig?"

"No. 'Tis *my* job, though it be a giant of a hole. You can empty the buckets of soil instead."

Alfred began by pacing out the plot, allowing generous margins. Unsure about putting Wellesley on his back or side, he added ever more width and length; he did not want him to be uncomfortable. The first sods were lifted. Alfred had already made up his mind not to mark the grave; it would remind him that Wellesley was gone, when he wanted to imagine him still galloping in the field, whinnying ecstatically at the freedom he had.

Alfred dug to a depth that required Billy to haul soil out of the grave in buckets. The progress was slow, even though one was being filled while the other was being emptied. The men did not speak unless to clarify what each should do. As the grave became deeper, Alfred feared a wall might collapse and bury him. When he was surrounded by high walls, he called enough, and Billy pulled him out with a rope, as if drawing water from a well. All that remained to do was to get Wellesley from the stable to the grave.

"Want him in one piece," said Billy. "We're going to have to tie him to another horse, and drag him. Hay cart too high for us. Take some messing around with a cradle and winch, which we don't have. I'll drag him. You don't have to look."

Alfred saw the sense of it, and nodded.

"I'll fill in, though."

Billy fetched Wellesley. It took two horses, not heavy ones, and the tussocks and the knolls made it hard. Taking it slowly, Billy guided the horses along the shortest route, but still Wellesley shuddered, bounced, as he met obstacles.

"No other way," Billy told him. "If there was, I'd do it."

Alfred was waiting.

"Just going to have to let him slide in," said Billy. "We can use the horses. There'll be an almighty thud, and it won't look good, but there's no other way."

Alfred let Billy do it, and looked away. Billy closed his eyes when he saw Wellesley's legs contorted. The landing had been brutal.

"Now the earth," he said.

One each side of the grave, the men returned the soil. Both threw without looking down. There was some left, and Billy suggested stamping on what was in the grave so they could return more, as much as possible.

As he made his way back to the farmhouse, Alfred said, "Return the sods proper, later. Don't want no sign of it left."

Emma was waiting for him. He was glad to feel her beating heart against him, her warm, gentle breath on his chest.

"'Tis done?" she asked.

"Yes," he replied. "Billy is making over."

She had taken the news of Jethro's death better than Alfred feared she would. Her door had never been closed to Jethro, but she had found him becoming more demanding, less friendly, possessive, even, and so had cut short his visits with flimsy excuses.

"He would have killed me," Alfred had told her.

"And you could have died for me," she had replied. "All because I love you again."

That is what gave her the strength to comfort Alfred now, in the moments after the burial of his beloved horse.

Meanwhile, the idea that had been forming in Geoffrey's mind acquired such clarity that he mounted his horse and rode to Symondsbury Manor. The last time he had been there was when he had last set eyes on Cressida, but he did not feel at all nervous. Indeed, she might feel flattered that he had thought of her.

He asked initially for Yeoman, as a matter of courtesy, and could see that his once prospective father-in-law's face had been ravaged by some traumatic experience. The freshness of his visitor's smile made Yeoman ashamed of his own dishevelled appearance.

"Geoffrey? After all this time? This is a pleasant surprise. Come in. You will find us an unhappy household, and 'twill take us some time to restore our good humour. Nevertheless, you are welcome, and it does me good to be reminded of a time when we Symondsburys were at peace with ourselves," said Yeoman, leading him through to a room in which Geoffrey used to whisper endearments, pay compliments, to Cressida.

"I will not pry into the cause of your present unhappiness, but am, too, reminded of sweet moments under your roof. I trust your wife will forgive my unexpected visit."

"She is indisposed, and her ailment confines her to her room. There she is likely to stay till its cause passes. There be no need for concern on your part. Please, be seated. I shall have a maid bring us some refreshments."

"Flora works here still?"

Yeoman was momentarily thrown, but quickly recovered enough composure to say, "She has recently left to take up a position on a big estate, near Dorchester."

"After all these years?" gasped Geoffrey. "I had thought her part of the house."

"These things are never certain. Now, tell me that your parents are well. I had hoped, as you recall, that we would become related."

His indirect reference to the broken engagement allowed Geoffrey to introduce his purpose in coming.

"It was with great sadness and regret that I accepted Cressida's rejection of me, but she was right. I did not deserve her," began Geoffrey. "My faults were too conspicuous to ignore, but I have changed."

"And you come to see her? Then you have my permission. This family needs some good news."

Geoffrey was embarrassed by this encouragement, and felt that he ought to make it clear that he wished to see her on another matter.

"Alas, I must disappoint you by saying that I am here to seek her help and not her hand."

"Well, that is a start, one I thought I'd never see. I shall fetch her, personally."

During Yeoman's absence, Geoffrey began to feel nervous, wondered whether she would misinterpret his request. When she came, she stopped abruptly in the doorway.

"Father, you did not say it was Geoffrey who had come to see me. You did it on purpose!" she cried, turning to escape.

Yeoman, however, blocked her exit.

"Please, Cressida, give him a moment of your time. You prejudge him if you think he comes to claim you again. Hear him, I beg you."

Geoffrey stood up.

"It has been a long time, Cressida," he said.

His face was familiar, yet different: fuller, less quick to match expression with feeling.

"What brings you?" she asked. "Father, will you leave us?"

"Geoffrey wants me to stay to hear in what way you can help him."

"*Help* him? How?"

"I am helping a man to build a school in Bridport. You already know him. He was the farm manager here. One day, I struck him, believing him to be an outlaw about to steal more than your purse. You remember?"

Geoffrey was tactful enough not to mention his discovery of her in an embrace with Edgar, in the barn, in the presence of Winifred.

"I do."

"Since then, he and I have acquired a common purpose, but the first teacher left unexpectedly. We have a temporary replacement - Emma Broadoak - who is untrained but passionate about helping the children. Think how awful it would be if they were not to have their thirst for knowledge slaked, having already tasted its sweetness."

"But what has all that got to do with me?" asked Cressida, perplexed.

"Emma needs an assistant. The children are inquisitive but lively. Another pair of eyes, someone with the spirit to match theirs, would help enormously. What say you, Cressida? I thought of you immediately. Let not what happened between us stop you saying yes. I will be too occupied with the building of the new school to interfere with your work. You would be well paid."

"But I have hardly any experience with children," said Cressida.

"Children are just small human beings," Yeoman reminded her.

"Will you give it a go, Cressida?" pleaded Geoffrey. "Emma is willing but not young any more. She does it to help."

"I will think about it," said Cressida.

"Will you give me your answer tomorrow?"

"I will."

The door opened unexpectedly, and there stood Clementine, wan but a hint of a smile on her face.

"Geoffrey, you have come back to us," she said.

Geoffrey looked at Cressida, and said, "How could I stay away?"

Chapter Thirty

"The farm be all yours to look after, Billy. I'll write, let you know when to come," said Alfred.

Up on the cart, Emma was waiting patiently, her trunk full. She had sold many of her possessions: furniture, ornaments that meant nothing to her, clothes she felt had had their day. Alfred had taken little, too, so that they would both fit into the cottage without too much of a squeeze, and not put Hannah and Lorna out too much.

Billy laughed, and said, "I'll do my best, though I baint one for reading, on account of me always jumbling up the letters. 'Tis like they play hide and seek with me."

"Then you should enroll at the school, and let Miss. Symondsbury teach you," joked Alfred. "Taken to it like a chicken to grain, she has. No need for Emma now."

"Forgive me, Master, but I and the Symondsburys don't match at all, if you remembers."

"I do, and 'twas a jest on my part. I'll get word to you when 'tis time. I would not leave you out, not after all you've done for father and me."

"'Tis kind. Miss. Emma been waiting long enough. Time to go," said Billy, offering his hand.

Alfred took it, and looked into Billy's eyes. Here is a man I can now trust, Alfred said to himself. And Billy is right: Emma been waiting long enough – in more ways than one.

Billy did not wave goodbye. There were holes in hedges to fill, milkmaids to hire. Canonicorum Farm would be Eype Farm soon, in spirit and practice, if not in name and ownership.

"One last look?" Alfred asked Emma, as they passed her house. Bucky Doo was busy; it was market day.

Emma breathed deeply. The house did not look like hers now. Then she realised that it was just bricks and slates. What her life had been in it – the memories, the love, the deaths, the devastation of loss – she still had, would never be able to give away, shake off. Already the house looked different.

Bucky Doo was cluttered with chickens in cages, and people were gathering as if expecting some major event. They, like the birds, had been cooped up, and were keen to talk and be out of their house, doing something.

"There are no children," remarked Emma.

"They are all in Miss. Symondsbury's classroom!"

"She is good with them, far better than me."

"A natural?"

"'Tis certain."

Soon, the road to Dorchester became clearer. The two strong and biddable horses had been Frederick's.

"No point looking for another Wellesley," he had said to Billy.

"'Tis certain," Billy had replied.

Alfred looked at the ring on Emma's left hand, and had often wondered about it. Had it been the one Bartholomew had given her? Yet their marriage had been such that she would hardly have continued to wear it.

"'Tis my mother's wedding ring. She gave it to me just before she died, but I shall wear yours instead when we are married."

She squeezed his forearm, and he smiled, then took her hand, kissed it, and said, "I love you with all my heart, Emma Broadoak."

"And I love you, too, dearest Alfred."

They stopped in Dorchester to buy some food to take to the

cottage. Emma did not want the dead pig, selected by Alfred, next to her trunk. Her choice was turnips, flour, and a tonic for his mother. There was no blood on them.

"And I shall buy a book for Lorna if you stay with the cart, dear. The shop be not far. We need to take the road to Stinsford, so 'twill be quicker on foot."

Inside the shop, an old man, reminding him very much of Josiah, looked up from his desk.

"Ah! A learned man, if ever I saw one. A Latin was it? A biblical? I have acquired recently, sir, a number of scientific essays, complete with sketches. Was it one of those you might be after?"

"None of them, sir, though they might all be of some interest to me on a future occasion. No, sir, I ask whether you have any books or poems for my daughter, who is of an age when she might be impressed by their romantic nature."

The man scratched his head, ran his eyes along his shelves, and said, "Poems? Of a romantic style? No, sir, I do not believe I have. Dorset has never been beknowned for its poems nor stories. The county cries out for a wizard with words, sir, though I don't believe we shall ever see such a one."

"And why is that, sir?"

"Fog, sir. The fog be a curse, these parts. Dorset fog puts a pen off, sir."

"I see. Then I must bid you good-day."

Alfred called in The King's Arms, and passed some coins to the landlord as settlement of the debt he had once incurred.

"I don't rightly recalls you, but your honesty becomes you," remarked the landlord. "We gets all sorts in here, and never had no one who returned to pay his dues. Thank 'ee, and 'tas restored my faith in human nature, which seem, these days, to take more than give."

Emma began to feel anxious; Alfred had been gone longer than expected. When he returned, he noticed her pallor, and said, "You are much changed. What has happened?"

"'Tis nothing but a woman, who has seen better times, come up to me and ask for charity. I took from my purse a small coin, and bent to her to give it. She had the look of someone who has lived comfortably in a former life, and has had to embrace sudden poverty."

"The world is full of such people, these parts. They cling to existence by their fingertips. Did she say what led to her current plight?" asked Alfred, struck by the impact the encounter had had on Emma.

"She said her name was Flora, that she had been a servant on the Symondsbury estate. I knew her face immediately, and she mine, and my heart sank at her lines of woe."

"Whither went she? I must find her."

Pointing towards the church, Emma said, "That way. 'Twas your delay which has taken her out of sight."

"Stay."

Alfred ran towards the church, shot up side-streets, physically stopped people to ask whether they had seen such a woman. They sent him in all directions, and soon he was out of breath. She has disappeared, he concluded, and now my chance to help her has gone.

"Come, rest, Alfred. You will harm yourself, dashing so. Let us on to your mother's, where we be expected."

"Did Flora say anything else?" panted Alfred.

"No, but *I* did."

"Repeat it, then, dear."

"I shouted, 'Stinsford! There shall you be given relief and comfort!'"

"She said nothing?"

"I could not swear that she heard me, for the meeting of our eyes, and the feel of the coin in her palm, seemed to hasten her departure. Dorchester has her somewhere in its net of alleys, and only in time will we know if she will come. In the meantime, your mother and Lorna are waiting. Let us not delay our new life. 'Tis its beginning, and your daughter must learn of your proposal, which I believe will take her from the kitchens of Palfreyman Manor."

"You are right, dear. Let not my mistake even now chase us to mother's front door. But I cannot see Flora die of hunger while her daughter thrives."

Emma hugged him.

"It is because of her plight and not who she be?"

"'Tis certain."

"Come, then. I love that cottage. Chop your mother some wood, as befits a son. Tomorrow, we will go to Stinsford to make arrangements."

That first night together, as a new family created by desire, discovery, and circumstances, was marked out by what was not said but done. Little acts of kindness brought smiles: Alfred helped his mother out of her rocking chair and to the table; Emma stood at Lorna's elbow, tasted the soup for her, and sliced the onions which had been hanging to dry in the outbuilding; and Lorna brushed Emma's hair after the meal.

Alfred left the women when all the crumbs had been scraped off the table. The bats had been visible from his seat, and outside he watched them, these black, flapping creatures, appear and disappear into silhouettes of trees and hedges. An owl's cry slashed the air. Alfred leaned on the gate at which he and Lorna had listened to Thomas Hardy's orchestra. What more fitting performance could they give now than play for Alfred, Emma, and their guests! And if all cannot comfortably fit into Stinsford church, they must stand in the aisle and by the door, for none, he resolved, should miss what had been too long coming. The only significant person who would not be there would be Stephen, the father who had brought him up, but Stephen was in the churchyard, within earshot of the fiddles and vows.

Inside again, Alfred took Lorna aside and said to her, "The letter you sent me shows you are ready, if you have a mind. You could stay here, travel when you have done the illumination, put money in a savings bank, as I did."

'Father, you talk in riddles," said Lorna.

"The Bishop of Wells has asked me to continue the illumination of the cathedral's archive. 'Tis work which feeds the soul, and pays well. I will recommend you, and he will hire you. We all have to make our way in the world, and 'tis a worthier occupation than washing dishes in the Palfreymans' kitchen."

"There is much companionship among the servants. They are the only friends I have. You forget that adders, horses, and owls be our neighbours, and unless you be one of Mr. Hardy's fiddlers at a dance Tolpuddle way, or you get hot a-twirling in Jemima's hearth, soup be your only friend, and to-ing and fro-ing 'twixt table and fire be your only merriment, which you'll find out soon enough. And 'tis certain my aim be to make my own way in the world."

"But a kitchen . . . "

"'Tis kind of you to think of me for the Bishop's archive, but old Mr. Palfreyman been so taken biv the illumination I showed him that he's asked me to do a little history of his family. His wife's been gone two harvests, and Miss. Florence and Master Robert will, one day, inherit the estate. 'Things be best written rather than said face to face,' he told me."

Alfred smiled and said, "He pays well? He don't take advantage?"

Lorna whispered, and Alfred took her hands, and said, "A young woman can live handsomely on that, keep her hands soft, and have some to spare. But the Bishop's work would drape you in gowns of silk and the finest gems."

Lorna smoothed down her dress, and teased him with, "You say a girl needs finery to turn heads?"

"No, dear, for all the stars and moon on the clearest night cannot outshine your beauty. I love you, my Lorna, and I will make up for the lost years."

"Your poetry be dazzling. I have poems, too, and I have written one, though it must keep till the day of your wedding."

Overcome, Alfred wiped his eyes on his sleeve, and said, "You will stay in the kitchens?"

"Why cannot I serve Mr. Palfreyman *and* the Bishop?"

"Why not, indeed?"

With that, he went to bed, and Emma said to him, "Your mother don't mind, what with us not yet wed?"

"Not sure she got her thoughts on it, what with her sleeping so much. Lorna says she's taken to staring at her, as if she was trying to place her from somewhere."

"'Tis old age, which be waiting to take us all by the hand, and lead some of us to confusion, and some to limping, though either aint much of a friend."

The day of the wedding, Alfred stirred first, heard Emma's steady breathing. Carefully, he slipped out of bed, put on his trousers, and tip-toed to the window. It was misty, but the sun was beginning to push through, promising a fine day.

"You getting up already?" Emma muttered.

"'Won't always be first up, after today," replied Alfred.

"You're not the first. Lorna went down, earlier."

The fire had already taken, and Lorna was at the table, snipping the stems of the flowers for her bridesmaid's posy. She had left them in the garden till that very morning, to keep them fresh, and the dew was still on the petals. She showed them to her father, and he smelt them after sleepily kissing her.

"You doing one of them for Emma?"

"Wait and see."

Then down came Emma, yawning, unable to drift back to sleep, knowing that a different and special day had begun.

"Pretty," she said.

"Let mother sleep in," said Alfred.

"All our clothes are ready," said Emma. "And the cart? 'Tis trimmed with ribbons and garlands and bells?"

"No mud on the wheels, if that's what you mean. Horses been done, too."

"I'll put some eggs in the pan. The wedding must take its turn."

So the morning passed, and each pretended it was just a normal day, but returned to some detail of the arrangements, some insecurity.

When she got up, Hannah asked, "What time be the wedding?"

Lorna smiled, was glad that Hannah was going to have a good day, when simple things did not need explaining.

"And we will walk down the aisle *together*," Emma reminded Alfred.

"Don't the man wait for the woman at the front?" queried Alfred.

"In our case, he don't."

Alfred knew what she meant, realised it was not a jest in bad taste.

"Both done enough waiting," blurted out Hannah, in case Lorna had not understood.

Some locals had gathered to see them married, and when the church was full, they waited in the churchyard.

Near the front pew stood Geoffrey Burton-Bradstock, at his side Cressida Symondsbury.

"We would have been married by now," ventured Geoffrey.

"We still can be married," Cressida replied.

Geoffrey turned to see her smiling at him, but then, on the balcony, Thomas Hardy and his orchestra began to play. The first few notes sounded more like a collective tuning of instruments, but, as each musician found his rhythm, the music acquired a distinctive and recognisable identity.

Billy Eype had made an effort to dress smartly, though each item of his clothing appeared at odds with its neighbour. He had looked at himself in the mirror, that morning, and had thought himself presentable, though as he was walking out of The King's Arms, where he had stayed the night, he had heard a servant girl snigger.

"Take no notice," another had said to him. "She is young and foolish, as we all have been, and means no harm."

Billy had felt for a coin, and had asked, "What be your name?"

"Flora," she had replied.

"Well, then, Flora, this be for your wisdom and kindness."

Old Mr. Palfreyman had been unable to attend, and had assured Lorna that it was only a big toe inflamed by gout that prevented him from shaking her father's hand. Palfreyman Manor was represented instead by Cook and Lorna's fellow kitchen helpers, who dabbed at their eyes throughout the ceremony, stopping only to speculate, in a whisper, on which of them would be next at that particular altar.

Yeoman and Clementine were not in church. Cressida told Alfred that her mother was improving, and that neither parent wished to cast a shadow over the wedding.

"But mother sends you this," said Cressida.

"Why, 'tis the May Queen's crown!" cried Emma. "She let me try it on, if I remember right."

"She said you should have been the Queen anyway, that you would know what she meant."

"Tell her 'tis kind, that I shall look after it, and that it be a sign of our lasting friendship."

"And tell your father I wish him well," said Alfred. "And Guy?"

"He has gone to Yeovil, to study how to sow seed, the newfangled way. 'Tis for a short while only, and when he returns, 'twill be to shake up the farm."

The vicar, who delivered his words with particular emphasis on the consonants, but failed to adequately sharpen his vowels to disguise his upbringing in Sherborne, asked, "And may I expect you, next Sunday, when my sermon will take as its theme sin and redemption? I find there is nothing like them to grip a congregation."

Not wishing to be gripped by anything, especially by two such particular ideas, Emma replied, "'Tis passing kind, but we'll come for the Harvest service, and bring some flowers for the altar."

Alfred pressed the vicar's fee into his hand, suppressing further exhortation to come to church, and steered Emma away.

The crowd cheered as Alfred, Emma, Lorna and Hannah returned to the cart. Thomas Hardy counted his fiddlers into a merry tune to set them off. Emma looked down at his wife, Jemima, holding her young son's hand.

"And what be he called?" asked Emma.

"Tom," replied Jemima, "and twelve months hence, he will bow his fiddle as well as he reads and writes, which be more than tolerable for his age."

"Come to the cottage, Tom, and see Alfred. You will be welcome, I'm sure, because he likes to illuminate words with his special pens, as does Lorna."

Jemima thought, and 'tis my belief that, one day, Tom will make words shine so brightly that readers will be passing dazzled, and they will shield their eyes, till the glare of them wanes enow for the story to take them on its journey.

Tom looked up at Emma, and said, "I like your name. 'Tis wondrous."

"That be so sweet, Tom, and thank you. Now 'tis Providence that, one day, you will marry one with such a name."

"There now, Tom – Emma!" said Jemima, though then thought: such a name means nothing if she be not good enow for him.

Back at the cottage, they ate ham and bread, and drank elderberry wine and cider. The cake was sweet and creamy, and when they had had enough, Lorna said, "I have written a poem, which I hopes you will listen to. 'Tis in memory of Stephen, my first father, who be in Stinsford churchyard, and though it seems strange to you, it must be read. Every poem has a time, and this poem's is now."

Hannah had fallen asleep in her rocking chair, so Lorna read it softly.

> "When I, so old and sleepy-eyed,
> recall this day, a groom, a bride,
> my posy held with swelling pride,
> I'll miss the man who loved me, died.
>
> And in a corner lies he still.
> Though looks he down on stream and rill,
> I will remember him until
> Like him an earthy grave I fill."

"'Twas well said, my dear," said Alfred, who feared, when her voice began to waver in the last two lines, that Lorna would break down.

"He would have liked that," said Hannah, eyes still shut.

"You awake, mother?" asked Alfred.

Emma went inside, to give them time alone. Somehow this day seemed about more than a promise broken and mended; more about life as it is felt and not lived. Emma felt at home, though the cottage was new to her, and Alfred felt a husband, though he had only been one for just a few hours.

It began to get cooler, so Lorna helped her mother inside, and placed her chair by the fire. Emma went out to Alfred, who was leaning on the paling. A horse was nibbling grass. The sense that evening was close became stronger. The air went quiet, and in the sky floated a moonball.

Emma wrapped Alfred's arm around her shoulder.

"'Tis chilly now, dear husband," she said. "Warm me."

"This be our home now, dear."

She could feel in his sagging shoulders a touch of sadness, so said, "And we will embrace it. 'Tis *our* time now."

He drew her to him, tightly. On her head, she wore Clementine's crown. This is why I could not take you with me, Winifred, dear, said Alfred to himself. This is what I was anxious to do. Forgive me. Can you now understand?

"Yes, I know," replied Alfred.

"Then let it go, whatever it be that makes your eyes bulge so."

His forehead nudged the crown. He thought of Frederick Canonicorum's field, and how, next Solstice day, under a cerulean sky, he would build a maypole in the garden, to remind himself how it all began. And Lorna could bring her friends, and they could weave coloured ribbons, just as Emma and Clementine had done, the day all their lives had become plaited for ever.

ALSO AVAILABLE BY VANCE WOOD

The Exile of Nicholas Misterton

A search for forgiveness and maturity

When Farmer Stockwood dismisses Nicholas Misterton for dallying with Victoria, his daughter, Nicholas begins his return from an exile imposed by his father, for a wrong that could not be forgiven. On this journey, he discovers that his wife, Ruth, whom he left, is thought to have jumped off the cliff at West Bay, leaving a daughter he believes might be his. However, his search for her, and a desire for a new start with his family in Higher Bockhampton, are frustrated by problems of his own making. Forgiveness seems a forlorn hope – until Conjuror Sayer lends a mystical hand.

CONJUROR

AVAILABLE BY VANCE WOOD IN 2016

BOOK THREE OF THE
MARSHWOOD VALE TRILOGY

The Best Intentions of Toller Burstock

A man's fraught quest for a better life.

When Toller Burstock is rejected by Hepsy Valence, he leaves home, in one of the worst snowstorms Dorset has ever seen, to make something more of his life. In Dorchester, he meets Mattie Venn, who has been jilted at the altar, and gives her the key to his cottage in Pilsdon, a kind gesture with far-reaching consequences. His attempts to forge a career that might make him more attractive to Hepsy founder, so he decides to return to working on the land, and is taken on by Miranda Misterton. Their love blossoms, but when Hugo Lockington, a lawyer, is compelled to reveal secrets about the past, Hepsy, Mattie, Toller and Miranda see the present in a totally different light. His revelations bring sadness and happiness in equal measure.

CONJUROR